Assassin of Gor

Assassin of Gor

John Norman

AN [e-reads] BOOK
New York, NY

Copyright © 1970 by John Norman
An E-Reads Edition
www.e-reads.com
ISBN 0-7592-0091-2

The Gor books available from E-Reads:

Table of Contents

Chapter   Page

One

Kuurus

Kuurus, of the Caste of Assassins, crouched on the crest of the small hill, leaning with both hands on the shaft of his spear, looking down into the shallow valley, waiting. He would not yet be welcome.

In the distance he could see the white walls, and some of the towers, of the city of Ko-ro-ba, which was being rebuilt. It is an old word in Gorean, Ko-ro-ba, meaning a village market, though few considered its archaic meaning. Kuurus looked on the city. It had once been destroyed by Priest-Kings, but now it was being rebuilt. Kuurus was not much interested in such matters. His was the Caste of Assassins. He had been called to this place. In the early part of the eighth Gorean hour the distant white walls took the sun and blazed like light in the green hills. The Towers of the Morning, thought Kuurus, the Towers of the Morning.

The Assassin shifted a bit and turned his attention again to the valley, where the men below were almost ready.

The logs had been prepared and carefully placed. There were hundreds of them, trimmed and squared, mostly of Ka-la-na wood, from the sweet-smelling wine trees of Gor. They crossed one another in the intricate traditional patterns, spaces between to permit the rush of air, forming a carefully structured, tiered, truncated pyramid.

Kuurus observed, curious, as the last log was placed by two men in the red of Warriors.

Then free women, veiled and in Robes of Concealment, each carrying a jar or canister, approached the structure. Even from where Kuurus waited he could smell the perfumed oils, the unguents and spices, which the women, climbing and moving about the pyramid

1

slowly, as though on stairs, sprinkled about or poured over the wood.

Beyond the wood, toward the city, Kuurus could see the procession. He was surprised for, judging from the colors of the garments of those who marched, it contained men of many castes, perhaps all castes of the city, only that he did not see among them the white of the Caste of Initiates. That puzzled Kuurus, for normally men of the Initiates are prominent in such events.

These men of Ko-ro-ba, he knew, when their city had been destroyed by Priest-Kings, had been scattered to the ends of Gor but, when permitted by Priest-Kings, they had returned to their city to rebuild it, each bearing a stone to add to its walls. It was said, in the time of troubles, that the Home Stone had not been lost, and it had not. And even Kuurus, of the Caste of Assassins, knew that a city cannot die while its Home Stone survives. Kuurus, who would think little of men on the whole, yet could not despise such men as these, these of Ko-ro-ba.

The procession did not chant, nor sing, for this was not a time for such things, nor did it carry boughs of Ka-la-na, nor were the sounds of the sista or tambor heard in the sunlight that morning. At such a time as this Goreans do not sing nor speak. They are silent, for at such a time words mean nothing, and would demean or insult; in such a time there can be for Goreans only silence, memory and fire.

The procession was led by four Warriors, who supported on their shoulders a framework of crossed spears, lashed together, on which, wrapped in the scarlet leather of a tarnsman, lay the body.

Kuurus watched, unmoved, as the four Warriors carried their scarlet burden to the height of the huge, sweet-smelling, oil-impregnated pyre.

Averting their eyes the Warriors threw back the scarlet leather that the body might lie free on the spears, open to the wind and sun.

He was a large man, Kuurus noted, in the leather of a Warrior. The hair, he remarked, was unusual.

The procession and those who had been earlier at the pyre now stood back from it, some fifty yards or so, for the oil-impregnated wood will take the torch quickly and fiercely. There were three who stood near the pyre; one wore the brown robes of the Administrator of a City, the humblest robes in the city, and was hooded; another wore the blue of the Caste of Scribes, a small man, almost tiny, bent now with pain and grief; the last was a very large man, broad of back and shoulder, bearded and with long blond hair, a Warrior; yet even the Warrior seemed in that moment shaken.

Kuurus saw the torch lit and then, with a cry of pain, thrown by the Warrior onto the small mountain of oiled wood. The wood leaped suddenly alive with a blaze that was almost a burst of fire and the three men staggered backward, their forearms thrown across their eyes.

Kuurus bent down and picked up a stalk of grass and chewed on it, watching. The reflection of the fire, even in the sunlight, could be seen on his face. His forehead began to sweat. He blinked his eyes against the heat.

The men and women of Ko-ro-ba stood circled about the pyre, neither moving nor speaking, for better than two Ahn. After about half an Ahn the pyre, still fearful with heat and light, had collapsed with a roar, forming a great, fiercely burning mound of oil-soaked wood. At last, when the wood burned only here and there, and what had been the pyre was mostly ashes and glowing wood, the men of a dozen castes, each carrying a jar of chilled wine, moved about, pouring the wine over the fire, quenching it. Other men sought in the ashes for what might be found of the Warrior. Some bones and some whitish ash they gathered in white linen and placed in an urn of red and yellow glass. Kuurus knew that such an urn would be decorated, probably, since the man had been a Warrior, with scenes of the hunt and war. The urn was given to him who wore the robes of the Administrator of the City, who took it and slowly, on foot, withdrew toward Ko-ro-ba, followed by the large blond Warrior and the small Scribe. The ashes, Kuurus judged, since the body had been wrapped in the scarlet leather of a tarnsman, would be scattered from tarnback, perhaps over distant Thassa, the sea.

Kuurus stood up and stretched. He picked up his short sword in its scabbard, his helmet and his shield. These he slung over his left shoulder. Then he picked up his spear, and stood there, against the sky, on the crest of the hill, in the black tunic.

Those who had come to the pyre had now withdrawn slowly toward the city. Only one man remained near the smoking wood. He wore a black robe with a stripe of white down the front and back. Kuurus knew that it would be this man, who wore the black, but not the full black, of the Assassin, who would deal with him. Kuurus smiled bitterly to himself. He laughed at the stripe of white. Their tunic, said Kuurus to himself, is as black as mine.

When the man near the smoking wood turned to face him, Kuurus descended the hill. He was now welcome. Kuurus smiled to himself.

The man did not greet him, nor did Kuurus lift his hand to the man, palm inward, saying "Tal."

The man was a strange man, thought Kuurus. His head was totally devoid of hair, even to the lack of eyebrows. Perhaps he is some sort of Initiate, thought Kuurus.

Without speaking the man took twenty pieces of gold, tarn disks of Ar, of double weight, and gave them to Kuurus, who placed them in the pockets of his belt. The Assassins, unlike most castes, do not carry pouches.

Kuurus looked curiously down at the remains of the pyre. Only a bit of wood now, here and there, missed by the chilled wine, clung to flame; some of the logs, however, still smoked, and others held as though within themselves the redness of the fire they remembered; but most were simply charred, now dead, stained with the oil, wet from the wine.

"Justice must be done," said the man.

Kuurus said nothing, but only looked at the man. Often, though not always, they spoke of justice. It pleases them to speak of justice, he said to himself. And of right. It eases them and gives them peace. There is no such thing as justice, said Kuurus, to himself. There is only gold and steel.

"Whom am I to kill?" asked Kuurus.

"I do not know," said the man.

Kuurus looked at him angrily. Yet he had in the pockets of his belt twenty gold tarn disks, and of double weight. There must be more.

"All we know is this," said the man, handing him a greenish patch.

Kuurus studied the patch. "It is a faction patch," said he. "It speaks to me of the tarn races of Ar."

"It is true," said the man.

The faction patches are worn in Ar by those who favor a given faction in the racing. There are several such factions, who control the racing and compete among themselves, the greens, the reds, the golds, the yellows, the silvers.

"I shall go to Ar," said Kuurus.

"If you are successful," said the man, "return and you will receive a hundred such pieces of gold."

Kuurus looked at him. "If it is not true," he said, "you will die."

"It is true," said the man.

"Who is it," asked Kuurus, "that was slain? Who is it that I am to avenge?"

"A Warrior," said the man.

"His name?" asked Kuurus.

"Tarl Cabot," said the man.

Two

Kuurus, of the Caste of Assassins, entered the great gate of Ar.

Guardsmen did not detain him, for he wore on his forehead the mark of the black dagger.

Not for many years had the black tunic of the Assassins been seen within the walls of Ar, not since the siege of that city in 10,110 from its founding, in the days of Marlenus, who had been Ubar; of Pa-Kur, who had been Master of the Assassins; and of the Koroban Warrior, in the songs called Tarl of Bristol.

For years the black of the Assassins had been outlawed in the city. Pa-Kur, who had been Master of the Assassins, had led a league of tributary cities to attack Imperial Ar in the time when its Home Stone had been stolen and its Ubar forced to flee. The city had fallen and Pa-Kur, though of low caste, had aspired to inherit the imperial mantle of Marlenus, had dared to lift his eyes to the throne of Empire and place about his neck the golden medallion of a Ubar, a thing forbidden to such as he in the myths of the Counter-Earth. Pa-Kur's horde had been defeated by an alliance of free cities, led by Ko-ro-ba and Thentis, under the command of Matthew Cabot of Ko-ro-ba, the father of Tarl of Bristol, and Kazrak of Port Kar, sword brother of the same Warrior. Tarl of Bristol himself on the windy height of Ar's Cylinder of Justice had defeated Pa-Kur, Master of the Assassins. From that time the black of the Assassins had not been seen in the streets of Glorious Ar.

Yet none would stand in the way of Kuurus for he wore on his forehead, small and fine, the sign of the black dagger.

When he of the Caste of Assassins has been paid his gold and has received his charge he affixes on his forehead that sign, that he

6

may enter whatever city he pleases, that none may interfere with his work.

There are few men who have done great wrong or who have powerful, rich enemies who do not tremble upon learning that one has been brought to their city who wears the dagger.

Kuurus stepped between the great gates and looked about himself.

A woman carrying a market basket moved to one side, watching him, that she might not touch him, holding a child to her.

A peasant moved away that the shadow of the Assassin might not fall across his own.

Kuurus pointed to a fruit on a flat-topped wagon with wooden wheels, drawn by a small four-legged, horned tharlarion.

The peddler pressed the fruit into his hands and hurried on, not meeting his eyes.

Her back against the bricks of a tower near the gate, a slender, slim-ankled slave girl stood, watching him. Her eyes were frightened. Kuurus was apparently the first of the Caste of Assassins she had seen. Her hair was dark, and fell to the small of her back; her eyes were dark; she wore the briefly skirted, sleeveless slave livery common in the northern cities of Gor; the livery was yellow and split to the cord that served her as belt; about her throat she wore a matching collar, yellow enameled over steel.

Biting into the fruit, the juice running at the side of his mouth, Kuurus studied the girl. It seemed she would turn to leave but his eyes held her where she stood. He spit some seeds to the dust of the street within the gate. When he had finished he threw the core of the fruit to her feet and she looked down at it with horror. When she looked up, frightened, she felt his hand on her left arm.

He turned her about and thrust her down a side street, making her walk in front of him.

At a paga tavern, one near the great gate, cheap and crowded, dingy and smelling, a place frequented by strangers and small Merchants, the Assassin took the girl by the arm and thrust her within. Those in the tavern looked up from the low tables. There were three Musicians against one wall. They stopped playing. The slave girls in Pleasure Silk turned and stood stock still, the paga flasks cradled over their right forearms. Not even the bells locked to their left ankles made a sound.

Not a paga bowl was lifted nor a hand moved. The men looked at the Assassin, who regarded them, one by one. Men turned white under that gaze. Some fled from the tables, lest, unknown to themselves, it be they for whom this man wore the mark of the black dagger.

The Assassin turned to the man in a black apron, a fat, grimy man, who wore a soiled tunic of white and gold, stained with sweat and spilled paga.

"Collar," said the Assassin.

The man took a key from a line of hooks on the wall behind him.

"Seven," he said, throwing the Assassin the key.

The Assassin caught the key and taking the girl by the arm led her to a dark wall, in a low-ceilinged corner of the sloping room. She moved woodenly, as though numb. Her eyes seemed frightened.

There were one or two other girls there, kneeling, who drew back, with a sound of chain.

He thrust the dark-haired girl to her knees by the seventh collar and snapped it about her neck, turning the key, locking it. It gave her about a two-foot length of chain, fastened to a slave ring bolted into the stone. Then he looked down on her. Her eyes were lifted to his, frightened. The yellow of her livery seemed dark in the shadows. From where she knelt she could see the low-hanging tharlarion oil lamps of the main portion of the paga tavern, the men, the girls in silk who, in a moment, belled, would move among them, replenishing the paga. In the center of the tables, under a hanging lamp, there was a square area, recessed, filled with sand, in which men might fight or girls dance. Beyond the area of the sand and the many tables there was a high wall, some twenty feet or so high, in which there were four levels, each containing seven small curtained alcoves, the entrances to which were circular, with a diameter of about twenty-four inches. Seven narrow ladders, each about eight inches in width, fixed into the wall, gave access to these alcoves.

She saw Kuurus go to the tables and sit cross-legged behind one, a table against the wall on her left, that there might be no tables behind him, but only the wall.

The men who had been at that table, or near it, silently rose and left the area.

Kuurus had placed his spear against the wall behind him, and he had taken from his left shoulder his shield, his helmet and the sheathed short sword, which blade he had placed at his right hand on the low table.

At a gesture from the proprietor, the grimy man in the tunic of white and gold, one of the serving slaves, with a flash of her ankle bells, hurried to the Assassin and set before him a bowl, which she trembling filled from the flask held over her right forearm. Then, with a furtive glance at the girl chained at the side of the room, the serving slave hurried away.

Kuurus took the paga bowl in both hands and put his head down, looking into it.

Then, somberly, he lifted it to his lips and drank.

Putting the bowl down he wiped his mouth on his forearm and looked at the Musicians. "Play," he said.

The three Musicians bent to their instruments, and, in a moment, there were again the sounds of a paga tavern, the sounds of talk, of barbaric music, of pouring paga, the clink of bowls, the rustle of bells on the ankles of slave girls.

Scarcely a quarter of an Ahn had passed and the men who drank in that room had forgotten, as is the way of men, that a dark one sat with them in that room, one who wore the black tunic of the Caste of Assassins, who silently drank with them. It was enough for them that he who sat with them did not this time wear for them the mark of the black dagger on his forehead, that it was not they whom he sought.

Kuurus drank, watching them, his face showing no emotion.

Suddenly a small figure burst through the door of the tavern, stumbling and rolling down the stairs, crying out. It bounded to its feet, like a small, hunched animal, with a large head and wild brown hair. One eye was larger than the other. It could stand, even if it straightened, no higher than a man's waist. "Do not hurt Hup!" it cried. "Do not hurt Hup!"

"It is Hup the Fool," said someone.

The little thing, misshapen with its large head, scrambled limping and leaping like a broken-legged urt to the counter behind which stood the man in the grimy tunic, who was wiping out a paga bowl. "Hide Hup!" cried the thing. "Hide Hup! Please hide Hup!"

"Be off with you, Hup the Fool!" cried the man slapping at him with the back of his hand.

"No!" screamed Hup. "They want to kill Hup!"

"There is no place for beggars in Glorious Ar," growled one of the men at the tables.

Hup's rag might once have been of the Caste of Potters, but it was difficult to tell. His hands looked as though they might have been broken. Clearly one leg was shorter than the other. Hup wrung his tiny, misshapen hands, looking about. He tried foolishly to hide behind a group of men but they threw him to the center of the pit of sand in the tavern. He tried, like a frantic animal, to crawl under one of the low tables but he only spilled the paga and the men pulled him out from under the table and belabored his back with blows of their fists. He kept whimpering and screaming, and running one place or the other. Then, in spite of the angry shout of the proprietor, he scrambled over the counter, taking refuge behind it.

The men in the tavern, with the exception of Kuurus, laughed.

Then, a moment later, four men, armed, brawny men, with a streamer of blue and yellow silk sewn diagonally into their garments, burst through the door and entered the room.

"Where is Hup the Fool?" cried their leader, a large fellow with missing teeth and a scar over his right eye.

The men began to hunt about the room, angrily.

"Where is Hup the Fool?" demanded the leader of the four men of the proprietor.

"I shall have to look around for him," said the proprietor, winking at the fellow with missing teeth, who grinned. "No," said the proprietor, apparently looking about with great care behind the counter, "Hup the Fool does not seem to be here."

"It looks like we must search elsewhere," said the leader of the four men, attempting to sound disappointed.

"It appears so," said the proprietor. Then, after a cruel pause, the proprietor suddenly cried out. "No! Wait! Here is something!" And, reaching down to his feet behind the counter, picked up the small animal mass that was Hup the Fool, which shrieked with fear, and hurled it into the arms of the man with missing teeth, who laughed.

"Why," cried the man with missing teeth, "it is he! It is Hup the Fool!"

"Mercy, Masters!" cried Hup, squealing, struggling in the grasp of his captor.

The other three men, hired swords, perhaps once of the Caste of Warriors, laughed at the frantic efforts of the tiny, sniveling wad of flesh to free itself.

Many in the crowd laughed at the small fool's discomfort.

Hup was indeed an ugly thing, for he was small, and yet thick, almost bulbous, and under the dirty tunic, perhaps that of the potters, there bulged the hump of some grotesque growth. One of his legs was shorter than the other; his head was too large for his body, and swollen to the left; one eye was larger than the other. His tiny feet thrashed about, kicking at the man who held him.

"Are you truly going to kill him?" asked one of the patrons at the low table.

"This time he dies," said the man who held Hup. "He has dared to speak the name of Portus and beg a coin from him."

Goreans do not generally favor begging, and some regard it as an insult that there should be such, an insult to them and their city. When charity is in order, as when a man cannot work or a woman is alone, usually such is arranged through the caste organization, but sometimes through the clan, which is not specifically caste oriented but depends on ties of blood through the fifth degree. If one, of course, finds oneself in effect without caste or clan, as was perhaps the case with the small fool named Hup, and one cannot work, one's life is likely to be miserable and not of great length. Moreover, Goreans are extremely sensitive about names, and who may speak them. Indeed, some, particularly those of low caste, even have use names, concealing their true names, lest they be discovered by enemies and used to conjure spells against them. Similarly, slaves, on the whole, do not address free men by their names. Kuurus surmised that Portus, doubtless a man of importance, had been troubled by the little fool Hup on more than one occasion, and had now decided to do away with him.

The man who held the sniveling Hup held him with one hand and struck him with the other, and then threw him to one of his three fellows, who similarly abused him. The crowd in the tavern reacted with amusement as the small, animal-like body was buffeted and thrown about, sometimes flung against the wall or on the tables. At last, bleeding and scarcely able to whine, Hup curled himself into a small, trembling ball, his head between his legs, his hands holding his ankles. The four men, then having him between them in the pit of sand, kicked him again and again.

Then the large man with missing teeth seized Hup's hair and pulled up the head, to expose the throat, holding in his right hand a small, thick, curved blade, the hook knife of Ar, used sheathed in the sport of that name, but the knife was not now sheathed.

The eyes of tiny Hup were screwed shut, his body shivering like that of an urt clenched in the teeth of a sleen.

"Keep him on the sand!" warned the proprietor of the tavern.

He with the missing teeth laughed and looked about the crowd, his eyes bright, seeing that they waited with eagerness for his stroke.

But his laugh died in his throat as he looked into the eyes of Kuurus, he of the Caste of Assassins.

Kuurus, with his left hand, pushed to one side his bowl of paga.

Hup opened his eyes, startled at not yet having felt the deep, cruel movement of the steel.

He too looked into the eyes of Kuurus, who sat in the darkness, the wall behind him, cross-legged, looking at him, no emotion on his face.

"You are a beggar?" asked Kuurus.

"Yes, Master," said Hup.

"Was the begging good today?" asked Kuurus.

Hup looked at him in fear. "Yes, Master," he said, "yes!"

"Then you have money," said Kuurus, and stood up behind the table, slinging the sheath of the short sword about his shoulder.

Hup wildly thrust a small, stubby, knobby hand into his pouch and hurled a coin, a copper tarn disk, to Kuurus, who caught it and placed it in one of the pockets of his belt.

"Do not interfere," snarled the man who held the hook knife.

"There are four of us," said another, putting his hand on his sword.

"I have taken money," said Kuurus.

The men in the tavern, and the girls, began to move away from the tables.

"We are Warriors," said another.

Then a coin of gold struck the table before the Assassin, ringing on the wood.

All eyes turned to face a paunchy man, in a robe of blue and yellow silk. "I am Portus," he said. "Do not interfere, Assassin."

Kuurus picked up the coin and fingered it, and then he looked at Portus. "I have already taken money," he said.

Portus gasped.

The four Warriors rose to their feet. Five blades leaped from the sheath with but one sound. Hup, whining, crawled away from the sand on his hands and knees.

The first Warrior lunged toward the Assassin but in the darkness of the side of the room, in the dim light of the tharlarion lamps, it was difficult to tell what happened. No one heard the striking of sword steel, but all saw the turning body of the man with the missing teeth falling sprawled over the low table. Then the dark shape of the Assassin seemed to move like a swift shadow in the room, and each of the three Warriors leaped toward him, but seemed to fail to find him, and another man, without even the flash of sword steel, dropped to his knees and fell forward in the pit of sand; the other two men struck as well, but their blades did not even meet that of the Assassin, who did not seem to deign to cross steel with them; the third man, soundlessly, turned away from the blade of the Assassin, seeming surprised, took two steps and fell; the fourth man lunged but failed to meet the shadow that seemed to move to one side, and now, before the fourth man had fallen, the shadow had resheathed its blade. Now the Assassin picked up the coin of gold and looked at the startled and sweating Portus. Then the Assassin threw the coin to the feet of Hup the Fool. "A gift to Hup the Fool," said the Assassin, "from Portus, who is kind." Hup seized up the coin of gold and scrambled from the room, like an urt running through the open gate of a trap.

Kuurus returned to his table, and sat down cross-legged as before. Once more the short sword lay at his right hand on the table. He lifted his paga bowl and drank.

Kuurus had not finished the bowl of paga when he sensed a man approaching. The right hand of Kuurus now lay on the hilt of the short sword.

The man was Portus, heavy, paunchy, in blue and yellow silk. He approached gingerly, his hands open, held from his body, ingratiatingly, smiling.

He sat down, wheezing, across from Kuurus, and placed his hands deliberately on his knees.

Kuurus said nothing but observed him.

The man smiled, but Kuurus did not smile.

"Welcome, Killer," said the man, addressing the Assassin by what, for that caste, is a title of respect.

Kuurus did not move.

"I see you wear on your forehead," said the man, "the dagger."

Kuurus examined him, the paunchy flesh beneath the blue and yellow silken robe. He noted the hang of the garment on the man's right arm.

The short sword moved from the sheath.

"I must protect myself," said the man, smiling, as the blade of Kuurus lifted itself through the sleeve, parting the silk, revealing the sheath strapped to his forearm.

Not taking his eyes from the man, Kuurus cut the straps on the sheath from the man's forearm, and with a small movement of his blade, threw the sheath and its dagger some feet to the side.

"I am of the opinion," said the man, "that it is a good thing we have those in the black tunic back amongst us."

Kuurus nodded, accepting the judgment.

"Bring paga!" called the paunchy man imperiously, impatiently, to one of the girls, who hastened to obey him. Then he turned again to Kuurus, and smiled ingratiatingly. "It has been hard in Ar," said the man, "since the deposition of Kazrak of Port Kar as Administrator of the City, and since the murder of Om, the High Initiate of the City."

Kuurus had heard of these things. Kazrak, who had been Administrator of the City for several years, had finally been deposed, largely due to the agitations of certain factions among the Initiates and Merchants, who had had their various grievances against the Administrator. Kazrak had offended the Caste of Initiates primarily by levying taxes on their vast holdings throughout the city and upon occasion upholding the rulings of the administrative courts over the courts of the Initiates. The Initiates, in their interpretations of sacrifices and in their preachments, primarily to the low castes, had led many of the city to fear that Kazrak might not long enjoy the favor of the Priest-Kings. After the murder of Om, who had been on tolerable terms with the Administrator, the new High Initiate, Complicius Serenus, in studying the omens of the white bosk slain at the Harvest Feast had, to his apparent horror, discovered that they had stood against Kazrak. Other Initiates wished to examine these omens, being read in the state of the bosk's liver, but Complicius Serenus, as though in terror, had cast the liver into the fire, presumably that such dark portents might be immediately destroyed. He had then collapsed weeping on the pillar of sacrifice, for it was well known that he had been a beloved friend of the Administrator. It was from this time that Kazrak might clearly have been said, particularly among the lower castes, to have lost the confidence of the city. He was further in danger by virtue of his controlling measures restricting certain monopolies important to certain factions among the Merchants, in particular those having to do with the manufacture of bricks, and the distribution of salt and tharlarion oil. He had further imposed restrictions on the games and contests of Ar, such that the loss of life had become infrequent, even among competing slaves. It was argued that the citizens of Ar could scarcely remain strong and fearless unless accustomed to the sight of blood, of danger and death. And since Kazrak was originally, perhaps surprisingly, of Port Kar, a city not on particularly good terms with Ar, or any other Gorean city, there was the hint of sedition in such matters. Moreover, Kazrak had been one of the leaders of the forces that had preserved Ar in the time of its troubles with Pa-Kur, master of the Assassins; as the tale was now told in the streets, the men of Ar themselves, alone, had overthrown the invader; Kazrak seemed a living reminder that Glorious Ar had once needed the aid of other cities, and men other than her own.

Whereas it is only the men of high caste who elect members to the Council of the City, the gold of merchants and the will of the general populace is seldom disregarded in their choices. Accordingly, Kazrak of Port Kar, for years Administrator of Ar, was by vote deposed and banished from the city, being publicly denied salt, bread and fire, as had been Marlenus, long years before him, once Ubar of Ar. Kazrak, with loyal followers, and the beautiful Sana of Thentis, his consort, had left the city months before. Their whereabouts were unknown, but it was thought they had hoped to found a colony on one of the islands of Thassa, farther north than even Cos and Tyros. The new Administrator of Ar was a man named Minus Tentius Hinrabius, an unimportant man except for being of the Hinrabian family, prominent among the Builders, having the major holdings in the vast, walled Hinrabian kilns, where much of Ar's brick is produced.

"It is hard in Ar," said the paunchy man, Portus, "since Kazrak has gone."

Kuurus said nothing.

"There seems little law now," said Portus. "When one goes out at night, even on the high bridges, one must have men with one. It is not well to walk among the cylinders after dark without torches and steel."

"Do the Warriors no longer guard the streets?" asked Kuurus.

"Some," said Portus. "But not enough. Many are engaged in the border disputes as far distant as the Cartius. Moreover, the caravans of Merchants are now given large and free guard."

"Surely there are many Warriors in the city," said Kuurus.

"Yes," said Portus, "but they do little—they are well paid, more than twice what was done before, but they spend the mornings in practices with arms, and the afternoons and evenings in the taverns, the gaming rooms and baths of the city."

"There are swords for hire?" asked Kuurus.

"Yes," said Portus, "and the rich Merchants, and the great houses, those on the Street of Coins, and on the Street of Brands, hire their own men." He smiled. "Further," said he, "Merchants arm and train squads of such men and rent them, for high wages, to the citizens of given streets and cylinders."

Kuurus lifted his paga bowl and drank.

"What has this to do with me?" he asked.

"For whom do you wear on your forehead the mark of the black dagger?" queried Portus discreetly.

Kuurus said nothing.

"Perhaps I could tell you where to find him," proposed Portus.

"I will find him," said Kuurus.

"Of course," said Portus. "Of course." The heavy man, sitting cross-legged, opposite the Assassin, began to sweat, fiddled with the damp blue and yellow silk covering his knee, and then with a nervous hand lifted a shaking bowl of paga to his lips, spilling some down the side of his face. "I meant no harm," he said.

"You are alive," said Kuurus.

"May I ask, Killer," asked Portus, "if you come to make the first killing—or the second?"

"The second," said Kuurus.

"Ah!" said Portus.

"I hunt," said Kuurus.

"Of course," said Portus.

"I come to avenge," said Kuurus.

Portus smiled. "That is what I meant," he said, "that it is good those in the black tunic are once again amongst us, that justice can be done, order restored, right upheld."

Kuurus looked at him, the eyes not smiling. "There is only gold and steel," said he.

"Of course," hastily agreed Portus. "That is very true."

"Why did you come to speak with me?"

"I would hire a sword such as yours," said Portus.

"I hunt," said Kuurus.

"Ar is a vast city," said Portus. "Perhaps it will take you time to find he whom you seek."

Kuurus' eyes flickered.

Portus leaned forward. "And meanwhile," he said, "you might earn considerable sums. I have work for such men as you. And much of the time you would be free, to hunt as you wished. Matters might well work out to our mutual advantage."

"Who are you?" asked Kuurus.

"I am that Portus," said he, "who is Master of the House of Portus."

Kuurus had heard of the House of Portus, one of the largest of the slave houses in the Street of Brands. He had known, of course, from the gown of blue and yellow silk that the man was a slaver.

"What is it you fear?" asked Kuurus.

"There is a house greater than mine, or any on the Street of Brands," said he.

"You fear this house?" asked Kuurus.

"Those of this house stand near the Administrator, and the High Initiate," said Portus.

"What do you mean?" asked Kuurus.

"The gold of this house is heavy in the councils of the city."

"The Administrator and the High Initiate," asked Kuurus, "owe their thrones to the gold of this house?"

Portus laughed bitterly. "Without the gold of this house, how could the Administrator and the High Initiate have sponsored the races and the games that won them the favor of the lower castes?"

"But the lower castes do not elect the Administrator or the High Initiate," said Kuurus. "The Administrator is appointed by the High Council of the City and the High Initiate by the High Council of the Initiates of the City."

"These councils," said Portus scornfully, "know well the way the lower castes yelp in the tiers." He snorted. "And there are many in the High Councils of the City who, if forced to decide between the steel of the hook knife and the feel of gold in their pouch, will choose gold to steel." Portus winked at Kuurus. "There is only gold and steel," he said.

Kuurus did not smile.

Portus hastily pushed his paga bowl up to his mouth, and swilled again, his eyes wary of the Assassin across from him.

"Where does this house obtain riches such that they may so easily outbid all other factions in Ar?"

"It is a rich house," said Portus, looking about himself. "It is a rich house."

"That rich?" asked Kuurus.

"I do not know where the gold comes from—all of it—" said Portus. "My own house could not begin to sponsor the games of even two days—we would be bankrupt."

"Of what interest is this house to you?" asked Kuurus.

"It wants to be the single slave house of Ar," whispered Portus.

Kuurus smiled.

"My house," said Portus, "is twenty generations old. We have bred, captured, trained, exchanged and sold slaves for half a millennium. The house of Portus is known on all Gor." Portus looked down. "Already six houses on the Street of Brands have been purchased or closed."

"There has never been a monopoly on slaves in Ar," said Kuurus.

"That is the wish, however, of the house of which I speak," said Portus. "Does it not offend you? Are you not outraged? Even in terms of merchandise and prices cannot you see what it would mean? Even now the lesser houses find it difficult to acquire premium slaves, and when we obtain them, we are undersold. Few go to the lesser houses to buy slaves this year in Ar."

"How can this house of which you speak," asked Kuurus, "undersell so consistently? Is it that the number of slaves is so great that the profit taken on each is less?"

"I have thought long on it," said Portus, "and that cannot be all of it. I know this business well, the costs of information, organization, planning, acquisition, transportation and security, the care and feeding and training of the animals, the guards, the costs of the auctions, the taxes on sales, the deliveries to distant cities—and the staff of the house I speak of is large, skilled and highly paid—and their facilities are unparalleled in the City, both in size and appointments. They have interior baths which could rival the pools even of the Capacian Baths." Portus nodded in puzzlement. "No," said Portus, "they must have sources of gold other than the income on their merchandise." Portus pushed one finger around in a puddle of splashed paga on the low table. "I thought for a time," he said, "that they intended to sell at a radical loss until the other slave houses were forced to close, and then to recoup their losses with profit by setting their own prices—but then when I considered again the gold which sponsored the games and races honoring the men who were to become Administrator and High Initiate, I decided it could not be. I am convinced the house of which I speak has major sources of gold other than the income on their merchandise."

Kuurus did not speak.

"There is another strange thing about that house I do not understand," said Portus.

"What?" asked Kuurus.

"The number of barbarian women they place on the block," said Portus.

"There have always been barbarian women on Gor," said Kuurus, dismissing the remark of Portus.

"Not in such numbers," grumbled Portus. He looked at Kuurus. "Have you any idea of the expense of acquiring a barbarian woman from beyond the cities—the distances involved? Normally they can be brought in only one at a time, on tarnback. A caravan of common slave wagons would take a year to go beyond the cities and return."

"A hundred tarnsmen, well organized," said Kuurus, "could strike barbarian villages, bind a hundred wenches, and return in twenty days."

"True," said Portus, "but commonly such raids take place on cylinders in given cities—the distances beyond the cities are great, and the prices paid for mere barbarian girls are less."

Kuurus shrugged.

"Moreover," said Portus, "these are not common barbarian wenches."

Kuurus looked up.

"Few of them have even a smattering of Gorean," he said. "And they act strangely. They beg and weep and whine. One would think they had never seen a slave collar or slave chains before. They are beautiful, but they are stupid. The only thing they understand is the whip." Portus looked down, disgusted. "Men even go to see them sold, out of curiosity, for they either stand there, numb, not moving, or scream and fight, or cry out in their barbarian tongues." Portus looked up. "But the lash teaches them what is expected of them on the block, and they then present themselves well—and some bring fair prices—in spite of being barbarian."

"I gather," said Kuurus, "that you wish to hire my sword, that you may in some degree protect yourself from the men and the plans of the house of which you have spoken."

"It is true," said Portus. "When gold will not do, only steel can meet steel."

"You say that this house of which you speak is the largest and richest, the most powerful, on the Street of Brands?"

"Yes," said Portus.

"What is the name of this house?" asked Kuurus.

"The House of Cernus," said Portus.

"I shall permit my sword to be hired," said Kuurus.

"Good!" cried Portus, his hands on the table, his eyes gleaming. "Good!"

"By the House of Cernus," said the Assassin.

The eyes of Portus were wide, and his body trembled. He rose unsteadily to his feet, and staggered backwards, shaking his head, turned, and stumbled over one of the low tables, and fled from the room.

His drink finished Kuurus rose and went to the darkened corner of the room, where the wall sloped down. He looked into the eyes of the girl in the yellow slave livery, who knelt there. Then he turned the key in the lock of collar seven and released her. Thrusting her to her feet and forcing her to walk before him, he went to the counter, behind which stood the man in the grimy tunic of white and gold. Kuurus threw the key to him. "Use Twenty-seven," said the man, handing Kuurus a bit of silk, Pleasure Silk, wrapped about a set of slave chains.

Kuurus threw the silk and chain over his shoulder and motioned the girl to move ahead of him and, numbly, she did so, crossing the room, going between the tables, and stopping before the narrow ladder at the right side of the high wall, in which were found the ledges with their alcoves. Not speaking, but woodenly, she climbed the ladder and crawled onto the shelf near the tiny alcove marked with the Gorean equivalent of twenty-seven and entered, followed by Kuurus, who drew the curtains behind them.

The alcove, with its enclosing, curved walls, was only about four feet high and five feet wide. It was lit by one small lamp set in a niche in the wall. It was lined with red silk, and floored with love furs and cushions, the furs being better than some six to eight inches deep.

In the alcove the demeanor of the girl changed and she suddenly rolled onto her back and lifted one knee. She looked at him saucily.

"I have never been in one of these places before," she said.

Kuurus tossed the silk and the chain to one side of the alcove and grinned at her.

"I now understand," she said, "why it is that free women never enter paga taverns."

"But you are only a slave girl," said Kuurus.

"True," she said forlornly, turning her head to one side. Kuurus removed her slave livery.

The girl sat up, her eyes bright, holding her ankles with her hands.

"So this is what these places are like," she said, looking about her.

"Do you like them?" asked Kuurus.

"Well," she said, demurely, looking down, "they make a girl feel—rather—well—"

"Precisely," agreed Kuurus. "I see that I shall have to bring you here often."

"That might be pleasant," said she, "Master."

He fingered the collar on her throat, yellow enameled over steel. It bore the legend: I am the property of the House of Cernus.

"I would like," he said, "to remove the collar."

"Unfortunately," said she, "the key reposes in the House of Cernus."

"It is a dangerous thing you are doing, Elizabeth," said Kuurus.

"You had best call me Vella," said she, "for that is the name I am known by in the House of Cernus."

He gathered her in his arms, and she kissed him. "I have missed you," said she, "Tarl Cabot."

"And I have missed you, too," I said.

I kissed her.

"We must speak of our work," I mumbled, "our plans and purposes, and how we may achieve them."

"The business of Priest-Kings and such," said she, "is surely less important than our present activities."

I mumbled something, but she would hear nothing of it, and suddenly feeling her in my arms I laughed and held her to me, and she laughed, and whispered, "I love you, Tarl Cabot," and I said to her, "Kuurus, Kuurus—of the Caste of Assassins," and she said, "Yes, Kuurus—and poor Vella of the House of Cernus—picked up on the street and brought to this place, given no choice but to serve the pleasure of a man who is not even her master—cruel Kuurus!"

We fell to kissing and touching and loving, and after some time she whispered, eyes bright, "Ah, Kuurus, you well know how to use a wench."

"Be quiet," Kuurus told her, "Slave Girl."

"Yes, Master," she said.

I reached over and put the bit of Pleasure Silk under her, that it might be wrinkled and bear the stains of her sweat.

"Clever, Master," said she, smiling.

"Be silent, Slave Girl," I warned her, and she heeded my injunction, for she then, for better than an Ahn, served in a silence that was exquisite, broken only by our breathing, her small moans and cries.

Three

The Game

When I deemed it wise to depart from Vella, I knotted her yellow slave livery about her neck and cried out, "Begone, Slave!" and then slapped my hands together at which juncture she let forth a howl as though she had been struck, and then, blubbering hysterically and crying out, she scrambled from the alcove, hastily and awkwardly, half falling, descended the narrow ladder and fled weeping from the paga tavern, much to the delight and amusement of the customers below.

A few moments later I emerged, descended the ladder and went to the proprietor of the shop, throwing the bit of soiled Pleasure Silk and the slave chains to the counter. I looked at him and he did not ask for pay, but looked away, and so I left the tavern and entered the street.

It was still light and in the early evening.

I was not much afraid of being recognized. I had dyed my hair black. I had not been in Ar in several years. I wore the habiliments of the Caste of Assassins.

I looked about myself.

I have always been impressed with Ar, for it is the largest, the most populous and the most luxurious city of all known Gor. Its walls, its countless cylinders, its spires and towers, its lights, its beacons, the high bridges, the lamps, the lanterns of the bridges, are unbelievably exciting and fantastic, particularly as seen from the more lofty bridges or the roofs of the higher cylinders. But perhaps they are the most marvelous when seen at night from tarnback. I remembered the night, so many years ago, when I had first streaked over the walls of Ar, on the Planting Feast, and had made the strike of a tarnsman for the Home Stone of Gor's greatest city, Glorious Ar. As I could I put these thoughts from my mind, but I could not fully escape them, for among them was the memory of a girl, she, Talena, the daughter of the Ubar of Ubars, Marlenus, who so many years before had been the Free Companion of a simple Warrior of Ko-ro-ba, he who had been torn from her at the will of Priest-Kings and returned to distant Earth, there to wait until he was needed again for another turn of play in the harsh games of Gor. When the city of Ko-ro-ba had been destroyed by Priest-Kings and its people scattered, no two to stand together, the girl had disappeared. The Warrior of Ko-ro-ba had never found her. He did not know whether she was alive or dead.

For those who passed in the street some might have been startled had they noted, standing in the shadows, one who wore the black of the Assassins, who wept.

"Game! Game!" I heard, and quickly shook my head, driving away the memories of Ar, and of the girl once known, always loved.

The word actually cried was "Kaissa," which is Gorean for "Game." It is a general term, but when used without qualification, it stands for only one game. The man who called out wore a robe of checkered red and yellow squares, and the game board, of similar squares, with ten ranks and ten files, giving a hundred squares, hung over his back; slung over his left shoulder, as a warrior wears a sword, was a leather bag containing the pieces, twenty to a side, red and yellow, representing Spearmen, Tarnsmen, the Riders of the High Tharlarion, and so on. The object of the game is the capture of the opponent's Home Stone. Capturings of individual pieces and continuations take place much as in chess. The affinities of this game with chess are, I am confident, more than incidental. I recalled that men from many periods and cultures of Earth had been brought, from time to time, to Gor, our Counter-Earth. With them they would have brought their customs, their skills, their habits, their games, which, in time, would presumably have undergone considerable modification. I have suspected that chess, with its fascinating history and development, as played on Earth, may actually have derived from a common ancestor with the Gorean game, both of them perhaps tracing their lineage to some long-forgotten game, perhaps the draughts of Egypt or some primitive board game of India. It might be mentioned that the game, as I shall speak of it, for in Gorean it has no other designation, is extremely popular on Gor, and even children find among their playthings the pieces of the game; there are numerous clubs and competitions among various castes and cylinders; careful records of important games are kept and studied; lists of competitions and tournaments and their winners are filed in the Cylinder of Documents; there is even in most Gorean libraries a section containing an incredible number of scrolls pertaining to the techniques, tactics and strategy of the game. Almost all civilized Goreans, of whatever caste, play. It is not unusual to find even children of twelve or fourteen years who play with a depth and sophistication, a subtlety and a brilliance, that might be the envy of the chess masters of Earth.

But this man now approaching was not an amateur, nor an enthusiast. He was a man who would be respected by all the castes in Ar; he was a man who would be recognized, most likely, not only by every urchin wild in the streets of the city but by the Ubar as well; he was a Player, a professional, one who earned his living through the game.

The Players are not a caste, nor a clan, but they tend to be a group apart, living their own lives. They are made up of men from various castes who often have little in common but the game, but that is more than enough. They are men who commonly have an extraordinary aptitude for the game but beyond this men who have become drunk on it, men lost in the subtle, abstract liquors of variation, pattern and victory, men who live for the game, who want it and need it as other men might want gold, or others power and women, or others the rolled, narcotic strings of toxic kanda.

There are competitions of Players, with purses provided by amateur organizations, and sometimes by the city itself, and these purses are, upon occasion, enough to enrich a man, but most Players earn a miserable living by hawking their wares, a contest with a master, in the street. The odds are usually one to forty, one copper tarn disk against a forty-piece, sometimes against an eighty-piece, and sometimes the amateur who would play the master insists on further limitations, such as the option to three consecutive moves at a point in the game of his choice, or that the master must remove from the board, before the game begins, his two Tarnsmen, or his Riders of the High Tharlarion. Further, in order to gain Players, the master, if wise, occasionally loses a game, which is expensive at the normal odds; and the game must be lost subtly, that the amateur must believe he has won. I had once known a Warrior in Ko-ro-ba, a dull, watery-eyed fellow, who

25

boasted of having beaten Quintus of Tor in a paga tavern in Thentis. Those who play the game for money have a hard lot, for the market is a buyer's market, and commonly men will play with them only on terms much to their satisfaction. I myself, when Centius of Cos was in Ko-ro-ba, might have played him on the bridge near the Cylinder of Warriors for only a pair of copper tarn disks. It seemed sad to me, that I, who knew so little of the game, could have so cheaply purchased the privilege of sitting across the board from such a master. It seemed to me that men should pay a tarn disk of gold just to be permitted to watch such a master play, but such were not the economic realities of the game.

In spite of having the respect, even to some degree the adulation, of almost all Goreans, the Players lived poorly. On the Street of Coins they found it difficult even to arrange loans. They were not popular with innkeepers, who would not shelter them unless paid in advance. Many were the nights a master would be found rolled in robes in a paga tavern, where, for a bit of tarsk meat and a pot of paga, and an evening's free play with customers, he would be permitted to sleep. Many of the Players dreamed of the day they might be nominated for intercity competitions at the Fairs of the Sardar, for a victor in the Sardar Fairs earns enough to keep himself, and well, for years, which he then would devote to the deeper study of the game. There is also some money for the masters in the annotation of games, printed on large boards near the Central Cylinder, in the preparation or editing of scrolls on the game, and in the providing of instruction for those who would improve their skills. On the whole, however, the Players live extremely poorly. Further, there is a harsh competition among themselves, for positions in certain streets and on certain bridges. The most favorable locations for play are, of course, the higher bridges in the vicinity of the richer cylinders, the most expensive paga taverns, and so on. These positions, or territories, are allotted by the outcome of games among the Players themselves. In Ar, the high bridge near the Central Cylinder, housing the palace of the Ubar and the meeting place of the city's High Council, was held, and had been for four years, by the young and brilliant, fiery Scormus of Ar.

"Game!" I heard, an answering cry, and a fat fellow, of the Caste of Vintners, puffing and bright eyed, wearing a white tunic with a representation in green cloth of leaves about the collar and down the sleeves of the garment, stepped forth from a doorway.

Without speaking the Player sat down cross-legged at one side of the street, and placed the board in front of him. Opposite him sat the Vintner.

"Set the pieces," said the Player.

I was surprised, and looked more closely, as the Vintner took the wallet filled with game pieces from the man's shoulder and began, with his stubby fingers, to quickly arrange the pieces.

The Player was a rather old man, extremely unusual on Gor, where the stabilization serums were developed centuries ago by the Caste of Physicians in Ko-ro-ba and Ar, and transmitted to the Physicians of other cities at several of the Sardar Fairs. Age, on Gor, interestingly, was regarded, and still is, by the Castes of Physicians as a disease, not an inevitable natural phenomenon. The fact that it seemed to be a universal disease did not dissuade the caste from considering how it might be combated. Accordingly the research of centuries was turned to this end. Many other diseases, which presumably flourished centuries ago on Gor, tended to be neglected, as less dangerous and less universal than that of aging. A result tended to be that those susceptible to many diseases died and those less susceptible lived on, propagating their kind. One supposes something similar may have happened with the plagues of the Middle Ages on Earth. At any rate, disease is now almost unknown among the Gorean cities, with the exception of the dreaded Dar-Kosis disease, or the Holy Disease, research on which is generally frowned upon by the Caste of Initiates, who insist the disease is a visitation of the displeasure of Priest-Kings on its recipients. The fact that the disease tends to strike those who have maintained the observances recommended by the Caste of Initiates, and who regularly attend their numerous ceremonies, as well as those who do not, is seldom explained, though, when pressed, the Initiates speak of possible secret failures to maintain the observances or the inscrutable will of Priest-Kings. I also think the Gorean success in combating aging may be partly due to the severe limitations, in many matters, on the technology of the human beings on the planet. Priest-Kings have no wish that men become powerful enough on Gor to challenge them for the supremacy of the planet. They believe, perhaps correctly, that man is a shrewish animal which, if it had the power, would be likely to fear Priest-Kings and attempt to exterminate them. Be that as it may, the Priest-Kings have limited man severely on this planet in many respects, notably in weaponry, communication and transportation. On the other hand, the brilliance which men might have turned into destructive channels was then diverted, almost of necessity, to other fields, most notably medicine, though considerable achievements have been accomplished in the production of translation devices, illumination and architecture. The Stabilization Serums, which are regarded as the right of all human beings, be they civilized or barbarian, friend or enemy, are administered in a series of injections, and the effect is, incredibly, an eventual, gradual transformation of certain genetic structures, resulting in indefinite cell replacement without pattern deterioration. These genetic alterations, moreover, are commonly capable of being transmitted. For example, though I received the series of injections when first I came to Gor many years ago I had been told by Physicians that they might, in my case, have been unnecessary, for I was the child of parents who, though of Earth, had been of Gor, and had received the serums. But different human beings respond differently to the Stabilization Serums, and the Serums are more effective with some than with others. With some the effect lasts indefinitely, with others it wears off after but a few hundred years, with some the effect does not occur at all, with others, tragically, the effect is not to stabilize the pattern but to hasten its degeneration. The odds, however, are in the favor of the recipient, and there are few Goreans who, if it seems they need the Serums, do not avail themselves of them. The Player, as I have mentioned, was rather old, not extremely old but rather old. His face was pale and lined, and his hair was white. He was smooth shaven.

The most startling thing to me about the man was not that he was older than one commonly sees in the streets of a Gorean city, but rather that he was clearly blind. The eyes were not pleasant to look upon, for they seemed empty of iris and pupil, and were simply ovoid glazes of massed scar tissue, ridged and irregular. Even the sockets of the eyes were ringed with white tissue. I knew then how the man had been blinded. A hot iron had been pressed into each of his eyes, probably long ago. In the center of his forehead, there was a large brand, the capital initial of the Gorean word for slave, in block script. But I knew that he was not a slave, for it is not permitted that Players be slave.

That a slave should play is regarded as an insult to free men, and an insult to the game. Further, no free man would care to be beaten by a slave. I gathered, from the blinding and the mark on his forehead, that the man had once offended a slaver, a man of power in the city.

"The pieces are set," said the Vintner, his fingers trembling.

"Your terms?" asked the Player.

"I move first," said the Vintner.

This, of course, was an advantage, permitting the Vintner to choose his own opening, an opening he may have studied for a lifetime. Moreover, having the first move, he might more speedily develop his pieces, bringing them into the central areas of the board where they might control crucial squares, the crossroads of the board. And further, having the first move, he would probably be able to carry the initiative of the aggressor several moves into the game, perhaps to the conclusion. Players, when playing among themselves, with men of equal strength, frequently play for a draw when they do not have the first move.

"Very well," said the Player.

"Further," said the Vintner, "I declare for the three-move option at my time of choice, and you must play without the Ubar and Ubara, or the First Tarnsman."

By this time there were four or five other individuals gathered about, besides myself, to observe the play. There was a Builder, two Saddle Makers, a Baker, and a Tarn Keeper, a fellow who wore on his shoulder a green patch, indicating he favored the Greens. Indeed, since there were no races this day in Ar, and he wore the patch, he perhaps worked in the tarncots of the Greens. None of this crowd seemed much to object to my presence there, though, to be sure, none would stand near me. In the prospect of a game, Goreans tend to forget the distances, amenities and trepidations of more sober moments. And through this small crowd, when it heard the terms of the Vintner, there coursed a mutter of irritation.

"Very well," said the Player, looking out over the board placidly, seeing nothing.

"And the odds I choose," said the Vintner, "are one to eighty."

At this a real growl of anger coursed through the onlookers.

"One to eighty," said the Vintner, firmly, triumphantly.

"Very well," said the Player.

"Ubar's Tarnsman to Physician Seven," said the Vintner.

"The Centian Opening," said one of the Saddle Makers. The Baker looked over his shoulder and called down the street to some men gathered there. "The Centian!"

The men ambled over to watch. I supposed they were interested in seeing what the Player's response would be to yellow's fourteenth move, a move on which authorities disagreed sharply, some favoring Ubar's Initiate to Scribe Three, and others the withdrawal of Ubara's Spearman to cover the vulnerable Ubar Two.

To my surprise, the Player chose the withdrawal of Ubara's Spearman to cover Ubar Two, which seemed to me rather defensive, and surely cost him the possibility of a dangerous but promising counterattack, which would eventually, if all went well, culminate with his second tarnsman at his opponent's Initiate Two. When this move was made I saw two or three of the observers look at one another in disgust, and wink, and then turn about and walk away. The Vintner, however, did not seem to notice, but made the standard aggressive response, pressing his attack forward by moving Second Spearman to Initiate Five. The face of the Player seemed placid. I myself was keenly disappointed. It seemed reasonably clear to me, at that point, that the Player had made a presumably weaker move in order to prejudice the game against himself, a move which could be defended, however, on the grounds that certain authorities favored it. I myself, in Ko-ro-ba, had seen Centius of Cos playing his own opening more than a dozen times and he had never drawn back the Ubara's Spearman at that point. When I saw the excitement of the Vintner and the calm, stoic placidity of the Player I felt sad, for I recognized, as did several of the others, that this game, expensive though it might be, was to be the Vintner's. The Vintner, you must understand, was not a bad player. He was actually quite skilled, and would have played well among even gifted Goreans, to whom the game is almost second nature, but he was not of Player caliber, by far.

I continued to watch, but not happily. At one or two points I noted the Player had made subtly ineffective moves, apparently sound but yet leaving weaknesses which could be, even four or five moves in the future, exploited rather decisively. Late in the game, the Player seemed to rally, and the Vintner began to sweat, and rubbed his fingers together, and held his head in his hands, studying the board as though he would bore through it with his gaze.

No one watching was much impressed, incidentally, that the Player was blind and yet remembering each move and the complexities of the board. Goreans often play without the board and pieces, though generally they prefer them because then less effort need be expended on the purely mnemonic matters of keeping the pattern in mind, move to move. I myself had seen chess masters on Earth play twenty boards simultaneously and blindfolded. Yet I, of Earth origin, while recognizing that what I was witnessing was actually not as astonishing as it might seem, was nonetheless impressed. The Vintner, of course, seemed to give no heed to anything but the game.

At one point, when the Vintner seemed hard pressed, I, and several of the others, noted that his hand strayed to the board, moving his Second Spearman to Builder Four from Physician Four, thus placing him on an open column.

One of the Saddle Makers cried out in anger. "Watch out there! He moved Second Spearman to Builder Four!"

"I did not," cried the Vintner—almost a shriek.

The Player looked puzzled.

All eyes turned to the Player and he put his head down for a moment, apparently reconstructing the game from memory, through all of its better than forty moves to that point, and then he smiled. "His Second Spearman," he said, "should be at Builder Four."

"You see!" cried the Vintner, gleefully.

Angrily the Saddle Maker turned away and strode down the street.

No one else said anything further. From time to time others would come to watch, but, as it became clear what was occurring, they would leave. At most times there were, however, some seven or eight individuals, including myself, who were watching.

Finally it grew late in the end game and it would be but a matter of four or five moves and the Player's Home Stone must be lost. The Vintner had taken his three-move option late in the game to build up an incredibly devastating attack. The Player was now in such a predicament that I doubted that Centius of Cos, or Quintus of Tor, or even the city's champion, Scormus of Ar, could have done much. I, and others in the crowd, were angry.

I spoke. The Player, of course, could only hear my voice. "A tarn disk of gold and of double weight," said I, "to red, should red win."

The crowd gasped. The Vintner acted as though struck. The Player lifted his sightless eyes toward my face.

I took from my belt a tarn disk of double weight, and of gold, and gave it to the Player, who took it in his fingers and felt its weight, and then he put it between his teeth and bit it. He handed it back to me. "It is truly gold," he said. "Do not mock me."

"A double tarn," said I, "to red, should red win."

Such an amount I knew would not be likely to be earned in a year by a Player.

The Player turned his head toward me, lifting the scarred remains of his eyes, as though he might see. Every nerve in that old face seemed strained, as though trying to understand what might lie there beyond him in the darkness that was his world, save for the memory of the movement of pieces on a checkered board. He put out his hand over the board, and I grasped it, firmly. I held his hand for a moment and he held mine, and I felt his grip, and smiled, for I knew then, blinded and branded, weak and old, he was yet a man. He released my hand and sat back, cross-legged, his back straight as that of a Ubar, a smile playing across the corners of his mouth. The sightless eyes seemed to gleam.

"Second Tarnsman," said he, "to Ubar's Builder Nine."

A cry of astonishment coursed through the crowd. Even the Vintner cried out.

He must be insane, I said to myself. Such a move was utterly unrelated to the game. It was random, meaningless. He was subject to one of the most devastating attacks that could be mounted in the game. His Home Stone, in four moves, would fall. He must defend, for his very life!

With a trembling hand, the Vintner shoved his Second Spearman to the left, capturing the Player's First Spearman, which had not been defended.

I inwardly groaned.

"Ubar's Rider of the High Tharlarion," said the Player, "to Ubar's Physician Eight."

I closed my eyes. It was another meaningless move. The crowd looked on, staggered, puzzled, speechless. Was this man not a Player?

Relentlessly the Vintner forced through again with his Second Spearman, this time capturing the Player's Ubara's Rider of the High Tharlarion.

"Ubar's Scribe to Ubara's Scribe Six," said the Player.

Under other conditions I would have left at this point, but as I held the gold piece in question I knew that I would have to remain until the end, which, as some consolation, would be but shortly now.

Even the Vintner seemed disturbed. "Do you wish to reconsider your last move?" he asked, offering a rare concession among players of the game, and one I had never expected the Vintner, from what I had seen of him, to offer. I decided he was perhaps not such a bad fellow, though perhaps winning meant more to him than it should.

"Ubar's Scribe to Ubara's Scribe Six," repeated the Player.

Mechanically the Vintner made the move on the board for the Player.

"My First Tarnsman," said the Vintner, "captures Ubara's Scribe."

The capture of the Player's Home Stone would take place on the next move.

"Do you wish to reconsider your move?" asked the Player, looking across the board, not seeing, but smiling. There seemed something grand about him in that moment, as though it were a gesture of magnanimity worthy of a victorious Ubar.

The Vintner looked at him puzzled. "No," he said. "I do not."

The Player shrugged.

"I capture your Home Stone on the next move," said the Vintner.

"You have no next move," said the Player.

The crowd gasped and they and I, and the Vintner, studied the board.

"Aii!" I cried, though the outburst was scarcely in keeping with the somber black I wore, and an instant later the Tarn Keeper and the Saddle Maker cried out, and began to stamp their feet in the dust, and pound their fists against their left shoulders. Then others watching cried out in glee. I myself removed my sword from its sheath and with it struck my shield. Then the Vintner began to howl with pleasure and slap his knees so pleased he was at the wonder of it, though he himself was the victim. "Magnificent!" he cried weeping, taking the Player by the shoulders and shaking him.

And then the Vintner himself, as proud as though it had been his own, announced the Player's next move. "Scribe takes Home Stone."

The crowd and I cried out with delight, marveling on it, the now-apparent simplicity of it, the attack which had been not so much mounted as revealed by the apparently meaningless moves, intended only to clear the board for the vital attack, coming from the improbable Ubara's Scribe, one of the least powerful pieces on the board, yet, when used in combination with, say, a Tarnsman and a Rider of the High Tharlarion, as devastating as the Ubar itself. None of us, including the Vintner, had so much as suspected the attack. The Vintner pressed the copper tarn disk, which the Player had won from him, into the Player's hands, and the Player placed this coin in his pouch. I then pressed into the hands of the Player the tarn disk of gold, of double weight, and the man held it clenched in his hands, and smiled and rose to his feet. The Vintner was picking up the pieces and putting them back in the leather game bag, which he then slung about the man's shoulder. He then handed him the board, which the Player hung over his other shoulder. "Thank you for playing," said the Vintner. The Player put out his hand and touched the Vintner's face, remembering it. "Thank you for playing," said the Player.

"I wish you well," said the Vintner.

"I wish you well," said the Player.

The Vintner then turned and left. As he did so I heard some of the bystanders, the Saddle Maker and the fellow who was the Tarn Keeper, he who wore the patch of the Greens, discussing the game. "It was really quite simple," the Saddle Maker was explaining, "even obvious."

I smiled and I noted that the Player, too, smiled.

"You are a Merchant?" asked the Player.

"No," I said.

"How is it then," asked he, "that you have such riches?"

"It means nothing," I said. "Can I help you to your home?"

"You are surely of High Caste," said the Player, "to have such gold."

"May I take you to your home?" I asked.

34

The Tarn Keeper, breaking away from the Saddle Maker, came over to us. He was a short man, with close-cropped brown hair, a squarish face. I noted the patch of the Greens on his shoulder. He smiled at me. "You did well," said he, "Killer," and with a grin turned and left.

I turned again to the Player, but he was now standing there in the street, seeming somehow alone, though I stood at his side.

"You are of the Assassins?" he asked.

"Yes," I said, "it is my caste."

He pressed the piece of gold into my hand and turned away, stumbling from me, reaching out with his right hand to guide himself along the wall.

"Wait!" I cried. "You have won this! Take it!" I ran to him.

"No!" he cried, striking out wildly with a hand, trying to force me away. I stepped back. He stood there, panting, not seeing me, his body bent over, angry. "It is black gold," he said. "It is black gold." He then turned away, and began to grope his way from the place of the game.

I stood there in the street and watched him go, in my hand holding the piece of gold which I had meant to be his.

Four

Cernus

"Place your first sword before me," I said, "that I may kill him."

Cernus of Ar, of the House of Cernus, studied me, his large face impassive, his eyes revealing nothing, like gray stones. His large hands rested over the arms of the curved curule chair in which he sat, which was mounted on a platform of stone, about a foot high and twelve feet square. In the base of the platform there were mounted six slave rings.

Cernus of Ar wore a coarse black robe, woven probably from the wool of the bounding, two-legged Hurt, a domesticated marsupial raised in large numbers in the environs of several of Gor's northern cities. The Hurt, raised on large, fenced ranches, herded by domesticated sleen and sheared by chained slaves, replaces its wool four times a year. The House of Cernus, I had heard, had interests in several of the Hurt Ranches near the city. The black of the garment of Cernus was broken only by three stripes of silk sewn lengthwise on his left sleeve, two stripes of blue enclosing one of yellow.

When I had spoken several of the men-at-arms of Cernus had shifted uneasily. Some had grasped their weapons.

"I am the first sword in the House of Cernus," said Cernus.

The room in which I stood was the Hall of the House of Cernus. It was a large room, some seventy feet square and with a ceiling of some fifty feet in height. Set in the wall to my left, as in the base of the stone platform, were slave rings, a dozen or so. The room was innocent of the energy bulbs of the Caste of Builders. In the walls were torch racks, but there were now no torches. The room was lit, and grayly, by sunlight now filtering in through several narrow, barred windows set very high in the thick stone of the walls. It reminded me, in its way, of a room in a prison and such, in its way, it was, for it was a room in the House of Cernus, greatest of the slave houses of Ar.

Cernus wore about his neck, on a golden chain, a medallion which bore the crest of the House of Cernus, a tarn with slave chains grasped in its talons. Behind Cernus, on the wall, there hung a large tapestry, richly done in red and gold, which bore the same sign.

"I have come," I said, "to rent my sword to the House of Cernus."

"We have been expecting you," said Cernus.

I revealed no sign of surprise.

"It is understood by me," said Cernus, evidently relaying certain reports which had reached him, "that Portus, of the House of Portus, sought to hire your sword in vain."

"It is true," I said.

Cernus smiled. "Otherwise," he said, "you surely would not have come here—for in this house we are innocent."

This was an allusion to the mark which I wore upon my forehead.

I had spent the night following the game in an inn, had washed away the mark and this morning, early, when I had arisen, had placed it again on my forehead. After a bit of cold bosk, some water and a handful of peas, I had come to the House of Cernus.

It was not yet the seventh Gorean hour but already the slaver was up, conducting his affairs, when I had been ushered into his presence. At his right hand there was a Scribe, an angular, sullen man with deep eyes, with tablets and stylus. It was Caprus of Ar, Chief Accountant to the House of Cernus. He lived in the house and seldom went abroad in the streets. It was with this man that Vella had been placed, her registration, papers and purchase having been arranged. In the House of Cernus, after the sheet, bracelets, leash and collar had been removed, agents of the House of Cernus had checked her fingerprints against those on the papers. She had then been examined thoroughly by the Physicians of the House of Cernus. Then, found acceptable, she had knelt while agents of the House signed the receipt of her delivery and endorsed her papers, retaining one set, giving one set to the seller's agent, for forwarding to the Cylinder of Documents. Then she had submitted herself to the House of Cernus, kneeling before one of its agents, lowering her head, extending her arms, wrists crossed. She had then been collared and turned over to Caprus, to be combed and cleaned, for the smell of the pens was on her, given two sets of slave livery and instructed in her duties. Caprus was said to be a friend of Priest-Kings. There had been no difficulty, it seemed, in placing Vella in the House of Cernus. Yet I feared for her safety. It was a dangerous game.

"May I ask," inquired Cernus, "for whom you wear on your forehead the mark of the black dagger?"

I would speak of these things, to some extent, with Cernus, for it was important, though perilous, that he should understand what purported to be my mission. It was now time that certain things should be revealed, that they might leak into the streets of Ar.

"I come to avenge," I said, "Tarl Cabot, he of Ko-ro-ba."

There were cries of astonishment from the men-at-arms. I smiled to myself. I had little doubt but that in an Ahn the story would be in all the paga taverns of Ar, on all the bridges and in all the cylinders.

"In this city," said Cernus, "Tarl Cabot, he of Ko-ro-ba, is known as Tarl of Bristol."

"Yes," I said.

"I have heard sing of him," said Cernus. I observed the slaver closely. He seemed troubled, shocked.

Two of his men rushed from the room. I heard them shouting in the corridors of the house.

"I regret to hear it," said Cernus, at last. Then he looked at me. "There will be few in Ar," he said, "who would not wish you well in your dark work."

"Who could kill Tarl of Bristol?" cried out a man-at-arms, not even thinking that Cernus had not acknowledged his right to speak.

"A knife on the high bridge," said I, "in the vicinity of the Cylinder of Warriors—at the Twentieth Ahn—in the darkness and the shadows of the lamps."

The men-at-arms looked at one another. "It could only have been so," said one.

I myself felt bitterly about a poorly lit bridge in the vicinity of the Cylinder of Warriors—and about a certain hour on a certain day—for it was on that bridge that a young man, of the Warriors, had walked perhaps not more than a quarter of an Ahn before I myself would have passed that way. His crime, if he had had one, was that his build was rather like mine, and his hair, in the shadows, the half-darkness of the lamps and the three moons of Gor, might have seemed to one who watched like mine. The Older Tarl, the Koroban master of arms, and myself had found the body, and near it, the patch of green caught in a crack in the grillwork of one of the lamps on the bridge, where perhaps it had been torn from the shoulder of a running, stumbling man. The Older Tarl had turned the body in his hands, and we had looked on it, and both of us had regarded one another. "This knife," said the Older Tarl, "was to have been yours."

"Do you know him?" I asked.

"No," he had said, "other than the fact that he was a warrior from the allied city of Thentis, a poor Warrior."

We noted that his pouch had not been cut. The killer had wanted only the life.

The Older Tarl, taking the knife by the hand guard, withdrew it. It was a throwing knife, of a sort used in Ar, much smaller than the southern quiva, and tapered on only one side. It was a knife designed for killing. Mixed with the blood and fluids of the body there was a smear of white at the end of the steel, the softened residue of a glaze of kanda paste, now melted by body heat, which had coated the tip of the blade. On the hilt of the dagger, curling about it, was the legend "I have sought him. I have found him." It was a killing knife.

"The Caste of Assassins?" I had asked.

"Unlikely," had said the Older Tarl, "for Assassins are commonly too proud for poison."

Then, not speaking, the Older Tarl had slung the body over his shoulders. I took the patch from the grillwork. We took the body, fortunately meeting no one at that late hour, to the nearby compartments of my father, Matthew Cabot, Administrator of the City. The Older Tarl, my father and I long discussed the matter. We were confident that this attempt on my life, for that it seemed to be, had something to do with the Sardar, and the Priest-Kings, and the Others, not Priest-Kings, who desired this world of Priest-Kings and men, and, surreptitiously and cruelly, were fighting to obtain it, though as yet, perhaps fearing the power of Priest-Kings or not fully understanding how severely it had been reduced in the Nest War of more than a year ago, they had not dared to attack openly. Accordingly, biding our time, we let it be thought in the city that Tarl Cabot had been slain. Now, in the Hall of the House of Cernus, my thoughts became bitter. I had indeed come to avenge. But I did not even know his name. He had been a tarnsman of Thentis. He had come to the allied city of Ko-ro-ba, and had there found his death, for no reason that was clear to me other than the fact that he had had the misfortune to resemble me.

"Why," asked Cernus, breaking into my reverie, "did not Warriors of Ko-ro-ba come to Ar, to search out the killer?"

"It was not an act of war," said I. "Further," I pointed out, "now that Kazrak of Port Kar is no longer Administrator of Ar it seemed unlikely that Ar would welcome Koroban Warriors within her walls."

"It is true," said one of the men-at-arms.

"Do you know the name of the man whom you seek?" asked Cernus.

"I have only this," I said, drawing forth from my belt the wrinkled patch of green cloth.

"It is a faction patch," said Cernus. "There are thousands of such in Ar."

"It is all I have," I said.

"This house itself," said Cernus, "is allied with the faction of the Greens, as certain other houses, and various of the establishments of the city, are associated with other factions."

"I know," I said, "that the House of Cernus is allied with the Greens."

"I now see," said Cernus, "that there is more reason than I suspected in your desire to rent your sword in this house."

"Yes," said I, "for all I know, the man I seek may be of this house."

"It is unlikely though," said Cernus, "for those who favor the Greens are numbered in the thousands and come from all the castes of Gor. The Administrator of Ar himself, and the High Initiate, are partisans of the green."

I shrugged.

"But you are welcome in this house," said Cernus. "As you presumably know these are difficult times in Ar, and a good sword is a good investment, and steel in these days is upon occasion more valuable than gold."

I nodded.

"I will upon occasion," said Cernus, "have commissions for you." He looked down on me. "But for the time," he said, "it is valuable for me simply for it to be known that your sword is in this house."

"I await your commands," I said.

"You will be shown to your quarters," said Cernus, gesturing to a nearby man-at-arms.

I turned to follow the man-at-arms.

"Incidentally," said he, "Killer."

I turned to face him.

"It is known to me that in the tavern of Spindius, you slew four Warriors of the House of Portus."

I said nothing.

"Four pieces of gold," said Cernus, "double tarns, will be sent to your rooms."

I nodded my head.

"Also," said Cernus, "it is understood by me that you picked up one of my girls on the street."

I tensed slightly, my hand dropping to the hilt of the short sword.

"What was her number?" Cernus was asking Caprus, who stood near him.

"74673," said the Scribe. I had anticipated that there would be some mention of Vella, for it was unlikely that Cernus would be unaware of my contact with her. Indeed, I had instructed her, when she had returned late to the House of Cernus, to bewail and protest what had theoretically happened to her in no uncertain terms. Accordingly, I was not surprised that the Scribe had her number ready for Cernus. Moreover, he probably knew it anyway, as she had been assigned to his staff, primarily to run errands in the city, for Caprus, it was said, seldom cared to leave the House of Cernus. I wished to be able to work closely with Vella in the House of Cernus. I was gambling on the unpleasant sense of humor not uncommonly found among slavers.

"Do you object?" I asked.

Cernus smiled. "Our Physicians ascertained," said he, "that she is only a Red Silk Girl."

"I scarcely supposed," said I, "that you would permit a White Silk Girl to go alone on the streets of Ar."

Cernus chuckled. "Indeed not," he said. "The risk is too much, sometimes as much as ten gold pieces." Then he leaned back. "74673," he said.

"The girl!" cried out the Scribe.

From a side entrance to the hall, where she had been kept, Elizabeth Cardwell, Vella, was thrust into the room. She was dressed as she had been when first I saw her near the great gate of Ar, barefoot, the yellow slave livery, the unbound dark hair, the yellow collar. She ran rapidly to a place before the stone platform, before the curule chair of Cernus, where she fell to her knees in the position of pleasure slave, head bowed. I was amused, for she had run as a slave girl is sometimes taught to run, with rapid short steps, her legs almost straight, her feet scarcely leaving the ground, back straight, head turned to the left, arms at her sides, palms out at a forty-five degree angle, more of a dancer's motion than a true run. Elizabeth, I knew, would hate that. I remembered her on the Plains of Turia, in the Land of the Wagon Peoples. There were few girls with her wind and stamina, her strength and vitality, few who could run at the stirrup of a Warrior as well as she. How offensive she must find some slave keeper's notion of the pretty hurrying of a slave girl.

"Lift your head, Girl," said Cernus.

She did so, and I gathered it was the first time she had actually looked on the face of the master of the House of Cernus. Her face was pale.

"How long have you been with us?" asked Cernus.

"Nine days, Master," said she.

"Do you like it here?" asked Cernus.

"Oh yes," she said, "Master."

"Do you know the penalty for lying?" asked Cernus. Elizabeth, trembling, lowered her head to the floor and crossed her wrists under her, kneeling, as it is said, to the whip. One of Cernus' men-at-arms looked at him, to see if he wished him to secure her to one of the slave rings in the base of the platform for punishment.

Cernus, with a finger, indicated negativity.

"Lift your head, Little Slave," said Cernus.

Elizabeth did so.

"Remove your clothing," said Cernus.

Without a word Elizabeth did so, standing and pulling the loop at her left shoulder.

"You are very pretty, Little Slave," said Cernus.

"Thank you, Master," said the girl.

"What is your name?" he asked.

"74673," she responded.

"No," said Cernus, "what name would you like to be called by?"

"Vella," said she, "if it pleases Master."

"It is a pretty name," he said.

She dropped her head.

"I see," said Cernus, "that you wear the brand of the four bosk horns."

"Yes," she said.

"Kassar," he said, "isn't it?"

"No, Master," said she, "Tuchuk."

"But where is the ring?" he asked. Tuchuk women, both slave and free, have fixed in their noses a tiny ring of gold, small and fine, not unlike the wedding rings of Earth. The ponderous bosk, on which the Wagon Peoples live, among which are numbered the Kassars and the Tuchuks, also wear such rings, but there, of course, the ring is much larger and heavier.

"My last master," said she, "Clark of the House of Clark in Thentis, removed it."

"He is a fool," said Cernus. "Such a ring is marvelous. It bespeaks the barbarian, the promise of pleasures so wild and fierce a man of the cities could scarcely conceive of them."

Elizabeth said nothing.

"I had a Tuchuk girl once," said Cernus, "a wild girl of the wagons, of whom I was fond, but when she tried to kill me, I strangled her in the chain of the House of Cernus." He fingered the chain and medallion about his neck.

"I am not truly Tuchuk," said Elizabeth. "I am only a girl from the islands north of Cos, taken by pirates of Port Kar, sold to a tarnsman, carried to and sold again in the city of Turia, and hence for twenty boskhides traded to the Tuchuks, where I was ringed and branded."

"How came you to Thentis?" asked Cernus.

"Kassars raided Tuchuk wagons," she said. "I was abducted, later sold to Turians." She spoke numbly. "I was later sold in Tor," she said, "far to the north of Turia. A year later, by slave wagon, I reached the fair of Se'Var near the Sardar, where I was sold to the House of Clark, from which house I and many others were fortunate enough to be purchased by the House of Cernus, in Glorious Ar."

Cernus leaned back again, seemingly satisfied.

"But without the ring," said he, "no one will believe the brand of the four bosk horns." He smiled. "You will be regarded, my dear, as inauthentic."

"I am sorry," said Elizabeth, her head down.

"I will have a smith replace the ring," he said.

"As master wishes," she said.

"It will not hurt much the second time," said Cernus.

Elizabeth said nothing.

Cernus turned to Caprus, who stood near him. "Is she trained?" he asked.

"No," said Caprus. "She is Red Silk but she knows almost nothing."

"Slave," said Cernus.

"Yes, Master," said Elizabeth.

"Stand straight and place your hands behind your head, head back."

She did so.

"Turn slowly," ordered Cernus.

When Elizabeth had done so once, she remained standing before him, as he had commanded.

Cernus turned to Caprus. "Was she touched by the leather?" he inquired.

"The Physician Flaminius conducted the test," reported Caprus. "She was superb."

"Excellent," said Cernus. "You may lower your arms," he said to the girl.

She did so, and stood there, standing before him, her head down.

"Let her be fully trained," said Cernus to Caprus.

"Fully?" asked Caprus.

"Yes," said Cernus, "fully."

Elizabeth looked at him, startled.

I had not counted on this, nor had Elizabeth. On the other hand, there seemed to be little that could be done about it. The training, exhaustive and detailed, I knew would take months. On the other hand it would be done presumably in the House of Cernus. Further, such training, though spread over a period of months, normally consumes only about five of the Gorean hours daily, that the girls have time to rest, to absorb their lessons, to recreate themselves in the pools and gardens of the house. During this time, since Elizabeth was nominally of the staff of Caprus, we could surely find time to be about our work, for which purpose we had arranged to enter the House of Cernus.

"Are you not grateful?" inquired Cernus, puzzled.

Elizabeth dropped to her knees, head down. "I am unworthy of so great an honor, Master," said she.

Then Cernus pointed to me, indicating that the girl should turn.

Elizabeth did so, and suddenly, superbly, she threw her arm before her mouth and cried out, as though just seeing me for the first time, and remembering me with horror. She was marvelous.

"It is he!" she cried, shuddering.

"Who?" inquired Cernus, innocently.

I then began to suspect that my gamble, based on the often unpleasant sense of humor common among slavers, might begin to bear fruit.

Elizabeth had her head down to the stone floor. "Please, Master!" she wept. "It is he, the Assassin, who forced me in the streets to accompany him to the tavern of Spindius! Protect me, Master! Please, Master! Protect me, Master!"

"Is this the slave," asked Cernus sternly, "whom you forced to accompany you to the tavern of Spindius?"

"I think she is the one," I admitted.

"Hateful beast!" wept Elizabeth.

"You are only a poor little slave," said Cernus. "Was he cruel to you?"

"Yes," she cried, her eyes gleaming, "Yes!"

Elizabeth, I had to admit, was a really remarkable actress. She was an extremely intelligent and talented girl, as well as beautiful. I hoped she would not be too successful in her exhibition or I might end up bubbling in a vat of boiling tharlarion oil.

"Would you like me to punish him, for you?" asked Cernus, kindly.

Elizabeth threw him a look of incredible gratitude, her eyes wide with tears, her mouth trembling. "Yes!" she wept. "Please, oh Master! Punish him! Punish him!"

"Very well," said Cernus, "I will punish him by sending to his quarters an untrained slave girl."

"Master?" she asked.

Cernus turned to Caprus. "When she is not in training, 74673 will keep the quarters of the Assassin."

Caprus noted this with his stylus on his tablet.

"No!" howled Elizabeth. "Please Master! No! No!"

"Perhaps," said Cernus, "if your training proceeds rapidly and favorably you may, after some months, find other quarters."

Elizabeth collapsed weeping before the stone platform.

"Let that be an incentive to be diligent, Little Slave," said Cernus.

I threw back my head and laughed, and Cernus threw back his head and laughed, pounding on the arms of the curule chair, and the men-at-arms, too, roared with laughter. Then I turned and followed a man-at-arms, who would lead me to my quarters.

Five

In the House of Cernus

Kneeling back on her heels in my quarters, in the traditional fashion of Gorean women, Elizabeth laughed merrily and slapped her knees, so pleased was she.

I, too, was pleased.

"How smoothly it has all gone!" she laughed. "And poor Vella, who must keep the quarters of the Assassin! Poor, poor Vella!"

"Do not laugh so loudly," I cautioned her, smiling, while moving about the room.

I had closed the door, which was of wood and heavy, and barred it with the double beam. When not barred it might be opened from the outside, if the latch string were thrust through the latch hole. Otherwise one would have to cut through the wood. I reminded myself to remember and put the latch string through when I left the room. The disadvantage of such a door, naturally, is that when no one is in the room and the latch string is out, anyone might enter, and either search the room or wait within. Valuables, in such a room, are kept in a heavy, iron-banded chest which is bolted to the wall and kept locked. Most doors giving entry into a compartment, or set of compartments, on Gor do, however, have locks, generally hand-crafted, highly ornate locks, usually set in the center of the door and controlling a long bolt.

Most of these locks, interestingly, though hand-crafted, are of the pin-tumbler variety, in which the locking is secured by a set of heavy pins extending into the lock plug; when the key is inserted the pins, of various lengths, are lifted to the surface of the lock plug, freeing it, so that when the key turns the plug may rotate, thereby moving the bolt. There are a number of other forms of lock also found upon occasion, a common variety being the disk lock in which moving disks, rather than pins, are used.

The small, heavy lock on a girl's slave collar, incidentally, may be of several varieties, but almost all are cylinder locks, either of the pin or disk variety. In a girl's collar lock there would be either six pins or six disks, one each, it is said, for each letter in the Gorean word for female slave, Kajira; the male slave, or Kajirus, seldom has a locked collar; normally a band of iron is simply hammered about his neck; often he works in chains, usually with other male slaves; in some cities, including Ar, an unchained male slave is almost never seen; there are, incidentally, far fewer male slaves than female slaves; a captured female is almost invariably collared; a captured male is almost invariably put to the sword; further, the object of slave raids, carefully scouted, organized and conducted expeditions, is almost always the acquisition of females; commonly one cylinder is struck, its bridges sealed off, its compartments broken into and ransacked for gold and beauty; the men of the compartment are slain and the women stripped; those women who do not please the slavers are slain; those that do have the goods of the compartment tied about their necks and are herded to the roof, with whip and slave goad, either to be bound across tarn saddles or thrust bound into wicker slave baskets, covered and tied shut, carried beneath the great birds in flight; sometimes, after only a quarter of an Ahn, before adequate reinforcements can be summoned, the slavers depart with their booty, leaving behind a flaming cylinder; slavers can strike any city but they are particularly a scourge to those cities which have not trained the tarn, but depend on the ponderous tharlarion.

On Gor, though most locks are of metal, wooden locks are not altogether unknown. In the most common variety there are two sets of matching pins, one fixed on a wooden spatula-like key and the other set, movable, falls into the bolt, securing it. With the key placed under the bolt, and pressed upward, the movable pins are lifted over the bolt, permitting its movement. This form of lock, however, as one might suspect, provides a poor sort of security, for the pins may be lifted individually by tiny sticks wedged in the holes until the bolt is free.

Another form of lock, providing perhaps even less security, is the notched beam lock which may be opened by a heavy sickle-like key which is inserted through a hole in the door, fitted into the notch, and then rotated to the left or right, depending on whether the door is being locked or opened. These keys are quite heavy and are carried over the shoulder, and can, if necessary, even function as weapons.

Padlocks, it might be mentioned, are common on Gor. Also, combination locks are not unknown, but they are infrequently found. The most common combination lock consists of a set of lettered rings which conceal a bolt. When the letters are properly aligned the bolt may be withdrawn.

Some locks, on the compartments of rich persons, or on the storehouses of merchants, the treasuries of cities, and so on, are knife locks or poison locks; the knife lock, when tampered with, releases a blade, or several of them, with great force, sometimes from behind the individual at the lock. On the other hand, knife locks are seldom effective against an individual who knows what to look for. Much more dangerous is the poison lock, because the opening through which the tiny pins, usually coated with a paste formed from kanda root, can emerge can be extremely small, almost invisible to the eye, easy to overlook in the crevices and grillwork of the commonly heavy, ornate Gorean lock. Another form of lock difficult to guard against is the pit lock, because of the natural crevices in Gorean tiling commonly found in corridors of cylinders; when tampered with a trap falls away beneath the individual, dropping him to a pit below, usually containing knives fixed in stone, but upon occasion osts, or half-starved sleen or water tharlarion; sometimes, however, the pit may be simply a smooth-sided capture pit, so that the individual may later be interrogated and tortured at length.

Lastly it might be mentioned that it is a capital offense for a locksmith, normally a member of the Metal Workers, to make an unauthorized copy of a key, either to keep for himself or for another.

The door to my compartment, however, in the House of Cernus, did not have a lock. The two beams, of course, could effectively secure it, but they could only be used when someone was inside. The fact that my compartment did not have a lock was, I assumed, no accident.

I decided it would not be wise to insist that a lock be placed on the door. Such a demand might seem importunate or to evince a concern for secrecy not in place in a house where I, supposedly, had taken gold for the use of my steel. Such a demand might have incited suspicion that I was not what I seemed. Further I was confident that the lock would be placed, for Cernus would insist, by one of his own smiths, and thus that the nature of the lock would be known to him and that a duplicate of its key, in spite of the injunction against such, would doubtless be his.

I was not altogether without an expedient, however, as, upon examination, I discovered that the door had, as well as the latch string hole, another small hole bored below the latch bar, doubtless put there by someone who had used the room before myself.

"This permits," I said to Elizabeth, indicating the small hole below the latch bar, "the complex knot."

"What is that?" she asked.

"Observe," I said to her.

I sprang to my feet and looked about the room. There were several chests in the room, including the iron-banded one with its heavy lock. There were also some cabinets against one wall, filled with plate and cups, some bottles of paga and Ka-la-na.

"What are you looking for?" she asked.

"String," I said, "or cord, anything."

We began to rummage through some of the chests and, almost immediately, Elizabeth discovered some five pairs of sandal thongs.

"Will these do?" she asked.

"Excellent," I said, taking a pair from her.

She knelt and watched me as I took one of the thongs and sat cross-legged by the door, and split it carefully over the edge of my sword. I now had, in effect, a piece of boskhide cord. I then looped the cord over the latch bar and then put both ends of the cord through the small hole, so they dangled on the outside of the door. I then swung the door inward.

"Suppose," I said, "I now tied a relatively fair-sized knot with these two ends of the cord."

Elizabeth looked at the cords for a moment. "Then," she said, "you would have tied the latch bar down, so it could not be lifted with the latch string."

I smiled. Elizabeth was quick, always quick. In tying such a knot, with the cord looped on the inside about the latch bar, and the knot too large to slip through the hole, I would have fastened the bar down.

"But someone could untie the knot," she pointed out, "and enter."

"Of course," I said, looking at her.

She looked at me for a moment, puzzled. Then suddenly her face broke into a smile and she clapped her hands. "Yes!" she laughed. "Marvelous!" Elizabeth was one of the quickest girls I had ever known. She, of Earth, had never heard of this trick, and yet, from the barest of hints, she had understood what could be done.

"Observe," I said. I then took the two dangling cords and began to tie what must have seemed to her an incredible knot. "Actually," I informed her, as I continued to weave the cords together in an ever larger and more complex fashion, "this is only a fifty-seven turn knot. It is, however, my own invention, though I never thought I'd need it. This trick was taught to me by Andreas of Tor, years ago, of the Caste of Singers, for doors in the city of Tor are commonly of this variety. His own knot was a sixty-two turn knot, his father's was seventy-one; one of his brothers used a hundred-and-four turn knot, which, as I recall, Andreas thought a bit pretentious."

"It is always the same knot though," said Elizabeth.

"Yes," I said, "each man has his own knot, as distinctive as a signature, and each knot is his own secret. Only he can tie it, and, more importantly, only he knows the reverse turns by which that knot, provided it has been untouched, is untied."

"Anyone then," said Elizabeth, "could untie the knot."

"Surely," I said. "The problem is to reconstruct the knot after it has been untied."

"The owner of the compartment," said Elizabeth, "returning to the compartment and untying the knot can tell immediately whether or not it is his own knot."

"Correct," I said.

"And thus he knows," said Elizabeth, "whether or not the compartment has been entered in his absence."

"Yes," I said. "Sometimes," I added, "someone enters the compartment and has a confederate on the outside attempt to duplicate the knot, that the man inside may surprise the occupant on his return, but commonly this stratagem is unsuccessful, because of the difficulties of duplicating the knot."

Elizabeth then watched in silence while I, trying to recall the intricacies of my signature knot, worked the boskhide cords.

At last, with a sigh, I leaned back, finished.

"It is a regular Gordian Knot," she said.

"The Gordian Knot," I said, "was quite possibly just such a knot."

"Alexander," she remarked, smiling, "cut it with his sword."

"And in so doing," I laughed, "informed the entire world that the room, or whatever it was, had been entered."

I then untied the knot, slipped the cords through the hole below the latch bar, swung the door shut and set the two beams in place, securing it.

I turned to Elizabeth. "I will teach you the knot," I said.

"Good," said Elizabeth, undaunted by the complex prospect. Then she looked up at me. "I should have my own knot, too," she said.

"Surely," I said, apprehensively, "we can use the same knot." It is, after all, not much fun to learn a signature knot.

"If I am going to learn your knot," she said, "there is no reason why you cannot learn mine."

"Elizabeth," said I.

"Vella," she corrected me.

"Vella," said I, "in spite of all you have been through on this world you yet retain certain of the taints of the Earth woman."

"Well," she said, "it seems to me only fair." Then she smiled mischievously. "My knot will be quite as complex as yours," she said.

"I do not doubt it," I said, dismally.

"It will be quite enjoyable to invent a knot," she said, "but it must be feminine, and it must reflect my personality."

I groaned.

She put her arms about my neck and lifted her eyes to mine. "Perhaps," she said, "after Vella has been fully trained Master will find Vella more pleasing."

"Perhaps," I admitted.

She kissed me lightly on the nose.

"You cannot even dance," I informed her.

Suddenly she stepped back, threw back her head, thrust one leg to the side, and lifted her arms. Then, eyes closed, not moving, except the heel of the right foot, which beat the rhythm, she began to hum a Tuchuk slave song; on the second measure, her hands came to her hips and she opened her eyes, looking at me; on the third measure, her body began to move and, to the melody, she began to sway toward me; when I reached for her she swept back, and danced, her hands at the side of her head, fingers snapping with the melody.

Then she stopped.

"It's all I know," she informed me.

I cried out in rage.

She came to me and put her arms again about my neck. "Poor Master," said she, "Vella cannot even dance."

"Nonetheless," I said, "I see that Vella has possibilities."

"Master is kind," she said. She kissed me again, lightly on the nose. "Master cannot have everything," she said.

"That is a sentiment," I said, "which few Gorean masters will accept."

She laughed. "It could be far worse," she said. "At least I am a Red Silk girl."

At this I swept her from her feet and carried her to the broad stone couch in the room, where I placed her on the piles of furs that bedecked it.

"I have heard," she said, smiling up at me, "that it is only a Free Companion who is accorded the dignities of the couch."

"True," I cried, bundling her in the furs and throwing the entire roll to the floor at the end of the couch, beneath the slave ring. With a flourish I unrolled the furs, spilling Elizabeth out, who shrieked and began to crawl away, but my hand caught at the loop on the left shoulder of her garment and she turned suddenly, trying to sit up, her feet tangled in the garment and I kicked it away and took her in my arms.

"If you like me," she asked, "will you buy me?"

"Perhaps," I said, "I do not know."

"I think," she said, "that I would like you for my master."

"Oh," I said.

"So I will try to please you," she said, "that you will buy me."

"You are not now in the purple booth," I said.

She laughed. The allusion was to certain practices having to do with the merchandising of Red Silk Girls, in private sales for individual and important clients of the House. At certain times of the year several such booths are set up within the courtyard of a slaver's house; in each, unclothed, chained by the left ankle to a ring, on furs, is a choice Red Silk Girl; prospective buyers, usually accompanied by a member of the Caste of Physicians, in the presence of the slaver's agent, examine various girls; when particular interest is indicated in one, the Physician and the slaver's agent withdraw; when, after this, the girl is not purchased, or at least seriously bid upon, she is beaten severely or, perhaps worse, is touched for a full Ehn by the slave goad; if, after two or three such opportunities, the girl is not sold, she is given further training; if after this she is still not sold she is usually returned to the iron pens whence, with other girls, considered to be of inferior value, she will be sold at a reduced price in one of the smaller markets, perhaps even in a minor city. Most girls, it might be mentioned, even extremely choice specimens, are never in the booths; generally the slaver has a chance at a higher price when there are many buyers bidding against one another in the heat of an auction.

"Very well, Red Silk Girl," said I, "perform."

"Yes, Master," said she, obediently.

And, as the hour progressed, perform she did, and superbly so, and I knew that had I been a prospective buyer I would have bid high indeed for the skilled, sensuous little wench in my arms, so striving with all her quickness and beauty to please me. Sometimes I was forced to remind myself that she was Miss Elizabeth Cardwell of Earth, and not, as she lost herself uncontrollably in our pleasures, hands clutching at the slave ring, a Gorean slave girl, bred for the pleasures of a master.

* * * *

Some months before, Elizabeth and I, the egg of Priest-Kings in the saddlepack of my tarn, had returned to the north from the Plains of Turia, the Land of the Wagon Peoples. In the vicinity of the Sardar Mountains I had brought the tarn down on the quiet, flat, gray-metal, disklike surface, some forty feet in diameter, of the ship, some two miles above the surface of Gor. The ship did not move, but remained as stationary in the sun and the whipping wind as though it were fixed on some invisible post or platform. Clouds like drifting fogs, radiant with the golden sunlight, passed about it. In the distance far below, and to the right, I could see, through the cloud cover, the black, snow-capped crags of the Sardar.

On the surface of the ship, tall and thin, like the blade of a golden knife, his forelegs lifted delicately before his body, his golden anten-

54

nae blown in the wind, there stood, with the incredible fixity and alertness of his kind, a Priest-King.

I leaped from the back of the tarn and stood on the ship, in the radiant cloud-filtered sunlight.

The Priest-King took a step toward me on its four supporting posterior appendages, and stopped, as though it dared not move more.

I stood still, not speaking.

We looked on one another.

I saw that gigantic head, like a globe of gold, surmounted with wind-blown antennae, glistening with delicate sensory hair. If Miss Cardwell had been frightened, alone astride the tarn, bound for her safety to the saddle, she did not cry out nor speak, but was silent.

My heart was pounding, but I would not move. My breath was deep, my heart filled with joy.

The cleaning hooks behind the third joints of the Priest-King's forelegs lifted and emerged delicately, and extended toward me.

I looked on that great golden head and its two large, circular, disklike eyes, compound, and the light seemed to flicker among the multilensed surfaces. Across the left eye disk there was an irregular whitish seam.

At last I spoke. "Do not stand long in the sun," said I, "Misk."

Bracing himself against the wind, the antennae struggling to retain their focus on me, he took one delicate step toward me across the metal surface of the disk. Then he stood there, in his some eighteen feet of golden height, balancing on his four posterior, four-jointed supporting appendages, the two anterior, four-jointed grasping appendages, each with its four, delicate, tiny prehensile hooks, held lightly, alertly before his body in the characteristic stance of Priest-Kings. About the tube that joined his head to his thorax, on a slender chain, hung the small, round compact translator.

"Do not stand so long in the sun," I said to him.

"Did you find the egg?" asked Misk. The great laterally opening and closing jaws, of course, had not moved. There was rather only a set of odors, secreted from his signal glands, picked up by the translator and transduced into mechanically reproduced Gorean words, each spoken separately, none with emotion.

"Yes, Misk," I said, "I have found the egg. It is safe. It is in the saddlepack of my tarn."

For an instant it seemed as though the great creature could not stand, as though he might fall; then, as though by an act of will, moving inch by inch through his body, he straightened himself.

I said nothing.

Delicately, slowly, the gigantic creature approached me, seeming to move only the four supporting appendages, until it stood near me. I lifted my hands over my head, and he, delicately, in the fog splendid with the sun, the smooth texture of his golden body gleaming, gently lowered his body and head, and with the tips of his antennae, covered with their sensitive, glistening golden hair, touched the palms of my hands.

There were tears in my eyes.

The antennae trembled against my hands. The great golden blade, his body itself, for a moment trembled. Again the cleaning hooks behind the third joint of each of the forelegs emerged, delicately, incipiently extended to me. The great compound eyes, on which Priest-Kings so seldom depended, were radiant; in that moment they glowed like diamonds burning in wine.

"Thank you," said Misk.

* * * *

Elizabeth and I had remained with Misk in the Nest of Priest-Kings, that incredible complex beneath the Sardar, for some weeks.

He had been overjoyed at the receipt of the egg and it had immediately been given over to eager attendants that it might be incubated and hatched. I doubt that the Physicians and Scientists of the Nest had ever exercised more diligence and care in such matters than they lavished on that one egg, and perhaps rightfully so, for it represented the continuation of their kind.

"What of Ko-ro-ba, and of Talena?" I had questioned Misk, even on the ship, before we returned to the Nest beneath the Sardar.

I must know of my city and its fortunes, and of she who had been my free companion, these many years lost.

Elizabeth was silent as I asked of these things.

"As you might have surmised," said Misk, "your city is being rebuilt. Those of Ko-ro-ba have come from the corners of Gor, each singing, each bearing a stone to add to the walls. For many months, while you labored in our service in the Land of the Wagon Peoples, thousands upon thousands of those of Ko-ro-ba have returned to the city. Builders and others, all who were free, have worked upon the walls and towers. Ko-ro-ba rises again."

I knew that only those who were free would be permitted to make a city. Doubtless there were many slaves in Ko-ro-ba but they would be allowed only to serve those who raised the walls and towers. Not one stone could be placed in either wall or tower by a man or woman who was not free. The only city I know of on Gor which was built by the labor of slaves, beneath the lash of masters, is Port Kar, which lies in the delta of the Vosk.

"And Talena?" I demanded.

Misk's antennae dropped slightly.

"What of her!" I cried.

"She was not among those who returned to the city," came from Misk's translator.

I looked at him.

"I am sorry," said Misk.

I dropped my head. It had been some eight years or better that I had not seen her.

"Is she slave?" I asked. "Has she been slain?"

"It is not known," said Misk. "Nothing of her is known."

My head fell.

"I am sorry," came from Misk's translator.

I turned.

Elizabeth, I noted, had stepped from us as we had spoken. Misk had soon brought the ship to the Sardar.

Elizabeth had been rapt with wonder at the Nest, but after some days, even in the presence of its grandeur, I knew she desired again to be on the surface, in the free air, in the sunlight.

I myself had much to speak of with Misk and with other friends of the Nest, notably Kusk, the Priest-King, and Al-Ka and Ba-Ta, who were humans, and fondly remembered. I noted that the girls who had been once their slaves, captured enemies, now wore no longer their collars of gold, but instead stood at their sides as Free Companions. Indeed, few of the Nest's humans were any longer slaves, save certain of the men and women who had betrayed us in the Nest War, certain men and women who had been reduced to such bondage because of transgressions, and certain others who had entered the Sardar to seek and acquire the riches of Priest-Kings.

A Priest-King named Serus, whom I had not known in the Nest War, but who had been of the cohorts of Sarm, had developed an interesting device for slave control, which I might mention. It consists of four circular metal bands, with facing flat plates, which fasten about the two wrists and two ankles of the slave. He is permitted complete freedom of movement by these bands, which are rather like bracelets and anklets. Wearing these, of course, a collar or brand is not necessary. But, from a central, guarded panel, and from individual transmitters, those of their owners, a signal may be transmitted which causes the two bracelets and the two anklets to immediately snap together at the flat plates, thus, even at a distance, binding the slave. There are individual signals and a master signal, permitting an individual slave to be immediately secured, no matter where he is in the Nest, or every slave in the Nest. "Had Sarm this device at his disposal," said Serus to me, "the Nest War would have turned out differently." I agreed. Since Elizabeth and I were strangers in the Nest Serus had wanted us fit with the devices as a precaution, but, of course, Misk would hear nothing of it.

Also, in the Nest, I met the male, who had no name, no more than the Mother has a name among the Priest-King kind. They are regarded as being above names, much as men do not think to give a name to the universe as a whole. He seemed a splendid individual, but very serious and very quiet.

"It will be fine," I said to Misk, "that there be a Father of the Nest, as well as eventually a Mother."

Misk looked at me. "There is never a Father of the Nest," said he.

I questioned Misk on this, but he seemed evasive, and I gather he did not wish to speak further to me on the matter, so, as he wished, I did not speak more of it.

Interestingly, Elizabeth learned to read Gorean in the Nest, and in less than an hour. Learning that she could not read the language, Kusk volunteered to teach it to her. Elizabeth had agreed but was startled when placed on a long table, actually of a size for a Priest-King, and found her head enclosed between two curved, intricate devices, rather like two halves of a bowl. Her head was fastened in an exact position by metal clamps. Further, that she not become terrified and attempt to struggle or leave the table, she was secured to it by several broad metal bands, plus ankle, leg, wrist and arm clips.

"We found, after the Nest War," Kusk informed me, "that many of our ex-slaves could not read, which is not surprising since they had been bred in the Nest and it had not been generally thought important that they have that skill. But, when they became free, many wished to learn. Accordingly we developed this device, not too difficult with the single, rather simple brain of the human, which so orders the brain that it can recognize letters, in various forms, and words. The neural dispositions which allow the human to read are of course the result of certain patterns of synaptic alignments, which are here produced without the time-consuming process of habit formation."

"In educating a Priest-King," I said, "wires were used—eight—one to each brain."

"We now dispense with wires," said Kusk, "even in the case of a Priest-King. They were used largely as a matter of tradition, but the humans of the Nest suggested refinements in the technique, leaving them to us to develop, of course." Kusk peered down at me with his antennae. "Humans, it seems," said he, "are seldom satisfied."

"Let me up," said Elizabeth. "Please."

Kusk twiddled a knob, and Elizabeth said "Please," once more and then it seemed she could hardly keep her eyes open, and then she closed her eyes and was asleep.

Kusk and I discussed various matters then for about an Ahn, primarily having to do with the extent to which the surveillance and control devices of the Nest had been restored since the Nest War, the increasing role of humans in the Nest, and the difficulties of working out a set of social arrangements mutually acceptable to species so disparate.

There was a tiny click and a small odor signal was emitted from the apparatus closed about Elizabeth's head. Kusk perked up his antennae and stalked over to the apparatus, switching it off. He moved back the two curved pieces, and I freed the girl of the bands and clips.

She opened her eyes.

"How do you feel?" I asked.

"I fell asleep," she said, sitting up and rubbing her eyes, swinging her legs over the side of the table. "I'm sorry. I couldn't help myself."

"That is all right," I assured her.

"I'm awake now," she said. "When can we start?"

"We are finished," said Kusk, the words coming, even-spaced, from his translator.

In his prehensile hooks, those on the right foreleg, he carried a sheet of plastic, on which was the Gorean alphabet, and some paragraphs in Gorean, in various scripts, some printed, some cursive.

"Read it," said Kusk.

"But it's Gorean," said Elizabeth. "I can't read Gorean." She looked at the page, puzzled.

"What is that sign?" I asked, pointing to one.

A look of surprise came over her face, then almost of fear. "It is Al-Ka," she said, "the first letter of the Gorean alphabet."

"Read this sentence," I suggested.

"I can't read," she said.

"Sound it out," I said.

"But I can't read," she said.

"Try," I said.

Slowly, numbly, she began to make sounds, saying what came into her head. "The-first-born-of the Mother-was Sarm..." She looked at me. "But they are only noises."

"What do they mean?" I asked.

Suddenly she cried out, gasping. "The first born of the Mother was Sarm!" she cried.

"She is a very bright human," said Kusk. "Sometimes it takes a quarter of an Ahn before the initial adjustments take place, basically the recognition that the sounds they spontaneously associate with the marks are actually the words of their language. In a short time she will easily read the marks as words, and not as mere patterns associated with arbitrary sounds. Her skills will grow. With some days of practice she will read Gorean as well as most Goreans; beyond this it is merely a question of interest and aptitude."

"When I look at it," said Elizabeth, excitedly, holding the sheet of plastic, "I just know what the sounds are—I just know!"

"Of course," said Kusk, "but it grows near the Ahn of the fourth feeding. I, for one, could use a bit of fungus and water."

We left Elizabeth in the room and went to eat. She seemed too excited to accompany us and kept reading the plastic sheet over and over. That evening, having missed the fourth feeding, she returned late to the quarters I was sharing with Misk, a number of plastic scrolls in her arms which she had managed to borrow from various humans in the Nest. I had saved her a bit of fungus which she chewed on while sitting in the corner raptly unrolling a scroll. It was all I could do to keep her from reading the scroll out loud. Even so, she would interrupt us frequently by saying, "Listen to this!" and read some passage which seemed particularly telling.

"There is controversy among Priest-Kings," Kusk remarked, "as to whether or not humans should be taught to read."

"I can see why," said I.

But, as the days wore on, I, as well as Elizabeth, wished to leave the Nest.

In the last days, I spoke often with Misk of the difficulties connected with obtaining the last egg of Priest-Kings, in particular informing him that others had wished the egg as well, and had nearly acquired it, others who had had the technology to visit Earth, to seize and utilize humans for their purposes, as once had Priest-Kings.

"Yes," said Misk. "We are at war."

I leaned back.

"But it has been so for twenty thousand years," said Misk.

"And in that time you have not managed to bring the war to a successful conclusion?" I asked.

"Priest-Kings," said Misk, "unlike humans, are not an aggressive organism. It is enough for us to have the security of our own territory. Moreover, those whom you call the Others no longer have their own world. It died with their sun. They live in a set of Master Ships, each almost an artificial planet in itself. As long as these ships remain outside the fifth ring, that of the planet Earthmen call Jupiter, the Goreans Hersius, after a legendary hero of Ar, we do not fight."

I nodded. Earth and Gor, I knew, shared the third ring.

"Would it not be safer if these Others were driven from the system?" I asked.

"We have driven them from the system eleven times," said Misk, "but each time they return."

"I see," I said.

"They will not close with us," said Misk.

"Will you attempt to drive them away again?" I asked.

"I doubt it," said Misk. "Such expeditions are extremely time-consuming and dangerous, and extremely difficult to carry through. Their ships have sensing devices perhaps the match of our own; they scatter; they have weapons, primitive perhaps, but yet effective at ranges of a hundred thousand pasangs."

I said nothing.

"For some thousands of years they have, except for continual probes, usually tests to prove the sex of their Dominants, remained beyond the fifth ring. Now, it seems they become more bold."

"The Others," I said, "surely could conquer Earth."

"We have not permitted it," said Misk.

I nodded. "I suspected as much," I said.

"It is within the fifth ring," pointed out Misk.

I looked at him in surprise.

His antennae curled in amusement. "Besides," said Misk, "we are not unfond of humans."

I laughed.

"Further," said Misk, "the Others are themselves a not uninteresting species, and we have permitted certain of them, prisoners taken from disabled probe ships, to live on this world, much as we have humans."

I was startled.

"They do not live in the same areas, on the whole, that humans do," said Misk. "Moreover, we insist that they respect the weapon and technology laws of Priest-Kings, as a condition for their permitted survival."

"You limit their technology levels just as you do those of humans?" I asked.

"Certainly," said Misk.

"But the Others of the ships," I said, "they remain dangerous."

"Extremely so," admitted Misk. Then his antennae curled. "Humans and the Others have much in common," said Misk. "Both depend much on vision; they can breathe the same atmospheres; they have similar circulatory systems; both are vertebrates; both have not unlike prehensile appendages; further," and here Misk's antennae curled, "both are aggressive, competitive, selfish, cunning, greedy and cruel."

"Thank you," said I, "Misk."

Misk's abdomen shook and his antennae curled with delight. "You are welcome, Tarl Cabot," said he.

"And not all Priest-Kings," said I, "happen to be Misks, you know."

"I do, however," said Misk, "count the human, for all his faults, superior to those whom you call the Others."

"Why is that?" I asked.

"He commonly has an inhibition against killing," said Misk, "and moreover he has, infrequently it may be, the capacities for loyalty and community and love."

"Surely the Others have these things, too," I said.

"There is little evidence of that," said Misk, "though they do have Ship Loyalty, for their artificial mode of existence requires responsibility and discipline. We have noted that among the Others who have been settled on Gor there has been, once out of the ship, a degeneration of interrelated roles, resulting in anarchy until the institution of authority resting on superior strength and fear." Misk looked down at me. "Even in the ships," he said, "killing is not discouraged except under conditions of battle or when the functioning of the vessel might be impaired."

"Perhaps," I said, "over the years it has become a way of controlling the population in a limited environment."

"Doubtless," said Misk, "but the interesting thing to Priest-Kings is that the Others, rational and advanced creatures presumably, have elected this primitive fashion of controlling their population."

"I wonder why," I said.

"They have chosen this way," said Misk.

I looked down, lost in thought. "Perhaps," I said, "they feel it encourages martial skills, courage and such."

"It is rather," said Misk, "that they enjoy killing."

Neither Misk nor I spoke for some time.

"I gather," I said, "that the Others are far more numerous than Priest-Kings."

"A thousand times more so, at least," said Misk. "Yet, for twenty thousand years we have stood them off, because of superior power."

"But," I said, "this power is severely curtailed following the Nest War."

"True," said Misk, "but we are rebuilding it. I think there is little immediate and gross danger, provided the enemy does not learn our current state of weakness." His antennae moved slowly, as though they were hands, reflecting thought. "There is some indication, however," he said, "that they suspect our difficulties."

"What are these?" I asked.

"The probes become increasingly frequent," said Misk. "Moreover, in line with their schemes, certain humans have been brought to this world."

"They acted boldly in the matter of attempting to interfere with the acquisition of the last egg of Priest-Kings," I pointed out.

"But largely through agents," said Misk.

"That is true," I admitted.

"Some information on the Nest War is surely available to them," said Misk, "carried by humans who were permitted to leave the Nest following the War." His antennae curled slightly. "But doubtless those whom you call the Others, being suspicious, much as your kind, suspect that this information is false, designed to lead them into a trap. It is fortunate for us that the Others are as sophisticated as they are. Were they simple barbarians, Gor and Earth would now be theirs."

"Perhaps they have seized some of these humans," I said, "and interrogated them, finding out if they tell the truth or not, by means of drugs or tortures."

"Even a drug or torture," pointed out Misk, "will only reveal what the individual believes to be the truth, not necessarily what the truth is. And, we suppose, the Others would suspect that only humans whose brains had been disposed to believe certain things, in virtue of our science, would be permitted to fall into their hands, once again as a move intended to draw them into a trap."

I shook my head.

"It is ironic," said Misk. "We could not now resist a general attack, nor protect Earth, but the Others will not believe it."

"Such," I said, "is the good fortune of Priest-Kings."

"And humans," said Misk.

"Agreed," I said.

"But the Others," said Misk, "are not inactive." He looked down at me. "Movements of probe ships appear to have been coordinated from the surface. It is possible the Others of the ships have made contact with those permitted to live on the planet, under our laws. Moreover, within the last five years, for the first time, the Others have made diplomatic contacts with humans." Misk's antennae suddenly focused intently on me. "It is apparently their intention," said he, "to acquire influence in cities, to win humans to their side, to equip and lead them in war on Priest-Kings."

I was startled.

"Why should they not use humans to fight their battles?" asked Misk. "The human, which exists in reasonably large numbers on Gor, is intelligent, can be taught much, and tends to be a warlike creature."

"But they would only use humans," I said.

"Certainly," said Misk. "Eventually humans would be used only as slaves and feed."

"Feed?" I asked.

"The Others," said Misk, "unlike Priest-Kings, are carnivorous."

"But humans are rational creatures," I said.

"On the ships," said Misk, "humans, and certain other organic creatures, are raised for meat."

I said nothing.

"The Others," said Misk, "see humans, and most other creatures, either as feed or tools."

"They must be stopped," I said.

"If they manage, in time, to turn a sufficient number of men against us and to arm them even primitively, our world is lost."

"How far advanced are they in their project?" I inquired.

"As nearly as we can determine, through our agents, not far."

"Have you discovered the contact points," I asked, "from which they hope to extend their influence in the cities?"

"Only one seems clear," said Misk. "And we do not wish to destroy it immediately. Such would indicate that we are aware of their plan. Further, innocent rational creatures might be destroyed. Further, if we destroy it, and it is a portion of a network, we will have lost valuable information on the degree of their dispersement and penetration."

"You need a spy, Misk."

"I knew," said Misk, "I should not have spoken of this matter with you."

"What is the contact point you have discovered?" I inquired.

"Return to Ko-ro-ba," said Misk. "In that city live and be happy. Take the she with you. Let others concern themselves with the dark business of war."

"Will you not even let me decide the matter for myself?" I asked.

"We ask nothing of you, Tarl Cabot," said Misk. And then Misk set his antennae on my shoulders, gently. "There will be danger for you even in Ko-ro-ba," said he, "for the Others doubtless know of your role in acquiring the egg of Priest-Kings. They may suspect that you still labor, or might again labor, in the service of Priest-Kings, and would wish to slay you. Return to your city, Tarl Cabot, be happy, as you can, but guard yourself."

"While the Others threaten," I said, "how can any man rest easy?"

"I have spoken too much to you," said Misk. "I am sorry."

I turned about and, to my surprise, saw that Elizabeth had entered the compartment. How long she had been listening, I did not know.

"Hello," I said, smiling.

Elizabeth did not smile. She seemed afraid. "What will we do?" she asked.

"About what?" I asked, innocently.

"She has been there long," said Misk. "Was it wrong for me to speak before her?"

I looked at Elizabeth. "No," I said, "it was not wrong."

"Thank you, Tarl," said the girl.

"You said that one point of contact seemed clear?" I said to Misk.

"Yes," said Misk, "only one."

"What is it?" I asked.

Misk looked from Elizabeth to myself. Then the words came forth from the translator, spaced evenly, without expression. "The House of Cernus in Ar," said Misk.

"It is one of the great slave houses," I said, "generations old."

Misk's antennae briefly acknowledged this. "We have an agent in that house," said Misk, "a Scribe, the chief accountant, whose name is Caprus."

"Surely he can find out what you want to know," I said.

"No," said Misk, "as Scribe and Accountant his movements are restricted."

"Then," I said, "you will need another in the House."

"Return to Ko-ro-ba, Tarl Cabot," said Misk.

"I have a stake in these games," I said.

Misk looked down, the great compound eyes luminous. "You have done too much," he said.

"No man," said I, "has done enough until the Others have been met and stopped."

Suddenly Misk's antennae touched my shoulders and trembled there.

"I will go, too," said Elizabeth.

I spun about. "You will not," I said. "I am taking you to Ko-ro-ba, and there you will stay!"

"I will not!" she cried.

I stared at her, scarcely believing my ears.

"I will not!" she cried again.

"I am taking you to Ko-ro-ba," I said, "and there you will stay! That is all there is to it!"

"No," she said, "that is not all there is to it!"

"You are not going to Ar," I told her angrily. "Do not speak more of it."

"I am of Earth," she said. "Earth owes its freedom to Priest-Kings. I, for one, am grateful. Moreover, I am free and I can do precisely what I want, and I will!"

"Be quiet!" I snapped.

"I am not your slave girl," she said.

I stepped back. "I am sorry," I said, "I am sorry, Elizabeth. I am sorry." I shook my head. I wanted to hold her but she stepped back, angrily. "It is too dangerous," I said, "too dangerous."

"No more so for me than for you," she said, "and perhaps less for me." She looked up at Misk and stepped to him. "Send me!" she said.

Misk looked at her, his eyes luminous, his antennae dipping toward her. "Once," said Misk, "I had such a human she as you, many years ago, when humans were slave in the Nest." Misk touched her shoulders with the antennae. "She once saved my life. Sarm, who was my enemy, ordered her slain." Then Misk straightened himself. "It is too dangerous," he said.

"Do you think," demanded Elizabeth, of both myself and Misk, "that a woman cannot be brave? Will you not honor her as you would a man with danger, not permit her to do something worthy of her species, something important and fine, or is all that is significant and meaningful to be reserved for men?" Elizabeth, almost in tears, stepped away from us both and spun about, facing us. "I, too, am a Human!" she said.

Misk looked at her for a long time, his antennae focused. "It will be arranged," said he, "that you will be placed as a slave in the House of Cernus, as a member of the staff of Caprus. Papers will be prepared on you and you will be transmitted to the House of Clark in Thentis, whence you will be taken by tarn caravan to Ar, where you will be sold privately, your purchase to be effected by the agents of the House of Cernus, under the instructions of Caprus."

"There!" said Elizabeth brazenly, facing me, hands on her hips.

"I shall follow her," I said, "probably as a mercenary tarnsman, and attempt to take service with the House of Cernus."

"You are both Humans," said Misk, "noble Humans."

Then he had placed his antennae on us, one on my left shoulder and the other on Elizabeth's right shoulder.

Before we began our dangerous journey, however, at Misk's suggestion, both Elizabeth and I returned to Ko-ro-ba, that we might rest some days and, in a peaceful interlude, share our affections.

My return to the city was affecting, for here it was that my sword had been pledged to a Gorean Home Stone; here it was that I had trained in arms and learned Gorean; it was here that I had met my father, after long years of separation; it was here that I had made dear friends, the Older Tarl, Master of Arms, and small, quick-tempered Torm, he of the Caste of Scribes; and it was from this place that I had, many years before, in tarnflight begun the work that would shatter the Empire of Ar and cost Marlenus of Ar, Ubar of Ubars, his throne; and, too, it was to this place, I could not forget, that I had once brought on tarnback, not as a vanquished slave but as a proud, and beautiful, and free, joyous woman, Talena, daughter of that same Marlenus, Ubar of Ubars, had brought her to this place in love that we might here together drink, one with the other, the wine of the Free Companionship.

I wept.

We crossed the partially rebuilt walls, Elizabeth and I, and found ourselves among cylinders, many of which were in the process of reconstruction. In an instant we were surrounded by Warriors on tarnback, the guard, and I raised my hand in the sign of the city, and drew on the four-strap, taking the tarn down.

I had come home.

In a short time, I found myself in the arms of my father, and my friends.

Our eyes told one another, even in the joy of our meeting, that we, none of us, knew the whereabouts of Talena, once the companion, though she the daughter of a Ubar, of a simple Warrior of Ko-ro-ba.

I remember the days in Ko-ro-ba fondly, though there were certain problems.

Or perhaps one should say, simply, there was Elizabeth.

Elizabeth, besides speaking boldly out on a large number of delicate civic, social and political issues, usually not regarded as the province of the fairer sex, categorically refused to wear the cumbersome Robes of Concealment traditionally expected of the free woman. She still wore the brief, exciting leather of a Tuchuk wagon girl and, when striding the high bridges, her hair in the wind, she attracted much attention, not only, obviously, from the men, but from women, both slave and free.

Once a slave girl bumped into her on one of the bridges and struck at her, thinking she was only slave, but Elizabeth, with a swift blow of her small fist, downed the girl, and managed to seize one ankle and prevent her from tumbling from the bridge. "Slave!" cried the girl. At this point Elizabeth hit her again, almost knocking her once more from the bridge. Then, when they had their hands in one another's hair, kicking, the slave girl suddenly stopped, terrified, not seeing the gleaming, narrow band of steel locked on Elizabeth's throat. "Where is your collar?" she stammered.

"What collar?" asked Elizabeth, her fists clenched in the girl's hair.

"The collar," repeated the girl numbly.

"I'm free," said Elizabeth.

Suddenly the girl howled and fell to her knees before Elizabeth, kneeling trembling to the whip. "Forgive me, Mistress," she cried. "Forgive me!"

When one who is slave strikes a free person the penalty is not infrequently death by impalement, preceded by lengthy torture.

"Oh, get up!" said Elizabeth irritably, jerking the poor girl to her feet.

They stood there looking at one another.

"After all," said Elizabeth, "why should it be only slave girls who are comfortable and can move freely?"

"Aren't you slave?" asked one of the men nearby, a Warrior, looking closely.

Elizabeth slapped him rather hard and he staggered back. "No, I am not," she informed him.

He stood there rubbing his face, puzzled. A number of people had gathered about, among them several free women.

"If you are free," said one of them, "you should be ashamed of yourself, being seen on the bridges so clad."

"Well," said Elizabeth, "if you like walking around wrapped up in blankets, you are free to do so."

"Shameless!" cried a free girl.

"You probably have ugly legs," said Elizabeth.

"I do not!" retorted the girl.

"Don't choke on your veil," advised Elizabeth.

"I am really beautiful!" cried the free girl.

"I doubt it," said Elizabeth.

"I am!" she cried.

"Well then," said Elizabeth, "what are you ashamed of?" Then Elizabeth strode to her and, to the girl's horror, on one of the public high bridges, face-stripped her. The girl screamed but no one came to her aid, and Elizabeth spun her about, peeling off layers of Robes of Concealment until, in a heavy pile of silk, brocade, satin and starched muslin the girl stood in a sleeveless, rather brief orange tunic, attractive, of a sort sometimes worn by free women in the privacy of their own quarters.

The girl stood there, wringing her hands and wailing. The slave girl had backed off, looking as though she might topple off the bridge in sheer terror.

Elizabeth regarded the free woman. "Well," she said, "you are rather beautiful, aren't you?"

The free woman stopped wailing. "Do you think so?" she asked.

"Twenty gold pieces, I'd say," appraised Elizabeth.

"I'd give twenty-three," said one of the men watching, the same fellow whom Elizabeth had slapped.

In fury the free woman turned about and slapped him again, it not being his day in Ko-ro-ba.

"What do you think?" asked Elizabeth of the cringing slave girl.

"Oh, I would not know," she said, "I am only a poor girl of Tyros."

"That is your misfortune," said Elizabeth. "What is your name?"

"Rena," said she, "if it pleases Mistress."

"It will do," said Elizabeth. "Now, what do you think?"

"Rena?" asked the girl.

"Yes," snapped Elizabeth. "Perhaps you are a dull-witted slave?"

The girl smiled. "I would say twenty-five gold pieces," she said.

Elizabeth, with the others, inspected the free girl. "Yes," said Elizabeth, "Rena, I think you're right." Then she looked at the free girl. "What is your name, Wench?" she demanded.

The girl blushed. "Relia," she said. Then she looked at the slave girl. "Do you really think I would bring so high a price—Rena?"

"Yes, Mistress," said the girl.

"Yes, Relia," corrected Elizabeth.

The girl looked frightened for a moment. "Yes—Relia," she said.

Relia laughed with pleasure.

"I don't suppose an exalted free woman like yourself," said Elizabeth, "drinks Ka-la-na?"

"Of course I do," said Relia.

"Well," said Elizabeth, turning to me, who had been standing there, as flabbergasted as any on the bridge, "we shall have some." She looked at me. "You there," she said, "a coin for Ka-la-na."

Dumbfounded I reached in my pouch and handed her a coin, a silver Tarsk.

Elizabeth then took Relia by one arm and Rena by the other. "We are off," she announced, "to buy a bottle of wine."

"Wait," I said, "I'll come along."

"No, you will not," she said, with one foot kicking Relia's discarded Robes of Concealment from the bridge. "You," she announced, "are not welcome."

Then, arm in arm, the three girls started off down the bridge.

"What are you going to talk about?" I asked, plaintively.

"Men," said Elizabeth, and went her way, the two girls, much pleased, laughing beside her.

I do not know whether or not Elizabeth's continued presence in Ko-ro-ba would have initiated a revolution among the city's free women or not. Surely there had been scandalized mention of her in circles even as august as that of the High Council of the City. My own father, Administrator of the City, seemed unnerved by her.

But, long before such a revolution might have been successfully achieved, Al-Ka, from the Nest, arrived in the city. For this mission, he had permitted his hair to grow. I almost did not recognize him, for the humans in the Nest commonly, both men and women, though not now always, shave themselves completely, in accord with traditional practices of sanitation in the Nest. The hair caused him no little agitation, and he must have washed it several times in the day he was with us. Elizabeth was much amused by the forged slave papers prepared for her, giving in detail an account of her capture and exchanges, complete with endorsements and copies of bills of sale. Some of the information such as Physicians' certifications and measurements and marks of identification had been compiled in the Nest and later transferred to the documents. In my compartment, Al-Ka fingerprinted her, adding her prints to the papers. Under a section on attributes I was interested to note that she was listed as literate. Without that, of course, it would be improbable that Caprus could have justified adding her to his staff. I kissed Elizabeth long one morning, and then, with Al-Ka, she, hidden in a wagon disguised to resemble a peddler's wagon, left the city.

"Be careful," I had said to her.

"I will see you in Ar," she had said to me, kissing me. Then she had lain down on a flat piece of rain canvas which Al-Ka and I had rolled about her, and, concealed in this fashion, we had carried her to the wagon.

Beyond the city, the wagon would stop, drawing up in a secluded grove. There Al-Ka would release Elizabeth from the rain canvas and busy himself with the wagon. He would set a central bar, running lengthwise in the wagon, in place, locking it in. Then he would change the white and gold rain canvas to a covering of blue and yellow silk. Meanwhile Elizabeth would have built a fire and in it burned her clothing. Al-Ka would then give her a collar to snap about her throat and she would do so. She would then climb into the wagon where, with two ankle rings, joined by a foot of chain looped about the central bar, she would be fastened in the wagon. Then, whistling, Al-Ka would pull the wagon out of the grove and Elizabeth would be on her way to Thentis, for delivery to the House of Clark, only another slave girl, naked and chained, perhaps lovelier than most but yet scarcely to be noticed among the many others, each day, delivered to so large and important a house, the largest in Thentis, among the best known on Gor.

It was one day to Thentis by tarn, but in the wagon we knew the trip would take perhaps the better part of one of the twenty-five day Gorean months. There are twelve twenty-five day Gorean months, incidentally, in most of the calendars of the various cities. Each month, containing five five-day weeks, is separated by a five-day period, called the Passage Hand, from every other month, there being one exception to this, which is that the last month of the year is separated from the first month of the year, which begins with the Vernal Equinox, not only by a Passage Hand, but by another five-day period called the Waiting Hand, during which doorways are painted white, little food is eaten, little is drunk and there is to be no singing or public rejoicing in the city; during this time Goreans go out as little as possible; the Initiates, interestingly enough, do not make much out of the Waiting Hand in their ceremonies and preachments, which leads one to believe it is not intended to be of any sort of religious significance; it is perhaps, in its way, a period of mourning for the old year; Goreans, living much of their lives in the open, on the bridges and in the streets, are much closer to nature's year than most humans of Earth; but on the Vernal Equinox, which marks the first day of the New Year in most Gorean cities, there is great rejoicing; the doorways are painted green, and there is song on the bridges, games, contests, visitings of friends and much feasting, which lasts for the first ten days of the first month, thereby doubling the period taken in the Waiting Hand. Month names differ, unfortunately, from city to city, but, among the civilized cities, there are four months, associated with the equinoxes and solstices, and the great fairs at the Sardar, which do have common names, the months of En'Kara, or En'Kara-Lar-Torvis; En'Var, or En'var-Lar-Torvis; Se'Kara, or Se'Kara-Lar-Torvis; and Se'Var, or Se'Var-Lar-Torvis. Elizabeth and I had arrived in Ko-ro-ba in the second month, and she departed on the second day of the Second Passage Hand, that following the second month. We estimated that she would surely be in the House of Clark by the Third Passage Hand, which precedes the month of En'Var. If all went well, we expected she would be in Ar, and perhaps in the House of Cernus, by the end of En'Var. It is true that if she, with other girls, were shipped by wagon to Ar, this schedule would not be met; but we knew that the House of Clark, in the case of select merchandise, under which category Elizabeth surely fell, transported slaves by tarn caravan to the markets of Ar, usually binding them in groups of six in slave baskets, sometimes as many as a hundred tarns, with escort, flying at once.

I had decided to wait until the Fourth Passage Hand, that following En'Var, and then take tarn for Ar, where I would pose as a mercenary tarnsman seeking employment in the House of Cernus, but when the Warrior from Thentis, who resembled me, was slain early in En'Var, I decided to go to Ar in the guise of an Assassin, by High Tharlarion, for Assassins are not commonly tarnsmen. Besides, it seemed desirable to let those in Ar think that Tarl Cabot had been killed. Further, I did have the business of vengeance to attend to, for there was a Warrior from Thentis who had died on a Koroban bridge, whose blood surely required the justice of the sword. It was not simply that Thentis was an ally of Ko-ro-ba, but also that this Warrior had been, it seemed, slain in my stead, and that thus his life had been given for mine, and was thus mine to avenge.

* * * *

"I've got it now," said Elizabeth, who, kneeling before the slave ring, had been practicing my signature knot, using the ring as a post.

"Good," I said.

I myself had been spending some time mastering the knot she had invented, which, I was forced to admit, was suitably ingenious. I examined her knot, which I had tied about the handle of one of the chests near the wall.

It is perhaps surprising, but I think there would have been little difficulty telling which knot had been tied by a man and which by a woman; moreover, though this was much subtler, Elizabeth's knot did, in its way, remind me of her. It was intelligent, intricate, rather aesthetically done and, here and there, in little bendings and loopings, playful. In such a small thing as these knots I was again reminded of the central differences in sex and personality that divide human beings, differences expressed in thousands of subtleties, many of which are often overlooked, as in the way a piece of cloth might be folded, a letter formed, a color remembered, a phrase turned. In all things, it seemed to me, we manifest ourselves, each differently.

"You might check this knot," said Elizabeth.

I went over to her knot and she went over to mine, and each began, carefully, movement by movement, to check the other's knot.

Elizabeth's knot was a fifty-five-turn knot. Mine was fifty-seven.

She had threatened to invent a knot with more than fifty-five turns but when I had threatened to beat her she had yielded to reason.

"You have done it perfectly," I told her.

Upon reflection, it did seem to me there might be some purpose in Elizabeth's having her own knot, apart from her delight in inventing and utilizing one. For example, sometime on Gor, she might have her own compartment or her own chests, and such, and might have a use for her own knot. She could have used mine, of course, even in such cases, but, seeing her knot and how it differed from mine, I had little doubt she would find her own more felicitous, more pleasing, it being more feminine, more personal to her. Also, as she was, legally, having submitted in the House of Cernus, a slave girl, any small thing she had or could do which was her own was doubtless rather precious to her. Some slaves, I knew, were even intensely jealous of so little as a dish or a cup which, probably because of use, they had come to regard as their own. Further, having her own knot might have some occasional value, even in our present circumstances. For example, passing the door and seeing her knot in place I would know that she was not in the compartment. This sort of thing was trivial, but one never knew when something less trivial might perhaps be involved. It seemed to me, all things considered, though it was a bother for me, a good thing that Elizabeth had her own knot. Besides, perhaps most importantly, she had wanted her own knot.

"Every girl," she had informed me, loftily, "should have her own knot. Moreover, if you have a knot, I should have a knot."

In the face of such logic, smacking of the contaminations of Earth, there had been little to do but capitulate, bother though it might be.

"Well, Kuurus," said she, from the side of the room, "it seems you have tied my knot correctly, though perhaps somewhat more clumsily than I would have done."

"The important thing," I said, "is that it is done correctly."

She shrugged. "I suppose so," she said.

"Your tying of my knot," I said, a bit disgruntled, "if one is to be critical, was somewhat daintier than I myself would approve."

"I do not tie dainty knots," Elizabeth informed me. "What you mistook for daintiness was mere neatness, simple, common everyday neatness."

"Oh," I said.

"I cannot help it," she said, "if I tie your knot more neatly than you."

"You seem to like knots," I remarked.

She shrugged.

"Would you like me to show you some others?" I asked.

"Signature knots?" she asked.

"No," I said, "simple knots, common Gorean knots."

"Yes," she said, delighted.

"Bring me a pair of sandal thongs," I told her.

She did so and then knelt down opposite me, while I sat cross-legged, and took one of the thongs in my hands.

"This is the basket hitch," I told her, gesturing for her to put out one hand. "It is used for fastening a carrying basket to hooks on certain tarn saddles."

I then illustrated, she cooperating, several other common knots, among them the Karian anchor knot, the Pin hitch, the double Pin hitch, the Builder's bend and the Builder's overhand.

"Now cross your wrists," I said.

She did so.

"So you think your knots are neater than mine?" I asked.

"Yes," she said, "but then you are only a man."

I flipped one of the thongs about her wrists, then again, then turned a double opposite overhand, with a twist following the first overhand.

"My," she said, wiggling her wrists, "you tied that quickly."

I did not tell her, of course, but Warriors are trained to tie that knot, and most can do it in less than three Ihn.

"I wouldn't struggle," I said.

"Oh!" she said, stopping, pinched.

"You will tighten it," I said.

"It is an interesting knot," she said, examining her bound wrists. "What do you call it?"

"It is a Capture Knot," I said.

"Oh," she said.

"It is used for binding slaves and such," I remarked.

"I see," she said.

I took the second thong and flipped it about her ankles, securing them together.

"Tarl!" she said.

"Kuurus," I reminded her.

She sat there. "You tricked me," she said.

"There is even more security," I said, "in this tie," untying her wrists and flipping her on her stomach, crossing her wrists behind her and using the same knot, with an additional knot, binding her wrists behind her back.

She struggled to sit up. "Yes," she said, "I imagine that this tie does provide greater security."

"And this," I said, "provides even greater security," lifting her to the foot of the couch, sitting her down there and snapping the heavy chain and collar, attached to the slave ring fixed there, about her throat.

"Yes," admitted Elizabeth, "I would agree." She looked at me. "Now untie me please," she said.

"I shall have to think about it," I said.

"Please do so," said Elizabeth, wiggling a bit.

"When you returned to the House of Cernus," I asked, "and told the Keeper what had theoretically happened to you, as I instructed you, what happened?"

Elizabeth smiled. "I was cuffed about quite a bit," said Elizabeth. "Was that part of your plan?"

"No," I said, "but I am not surprised."

"Well, that's good," she said. "I certainly would not have wanted you to have been surprised." She looked up at me. "Now," she said, "please untie me."

"I am still thinking about it," I told her.

"Please," she wheedled, "—Master."

"I am now thinking more seriously about it," I informed her.

"Good," she said.

"So you think your knots are neater than mine?" I inquired.

"It is a simple matter of fact," she said. "Now please untie me," she said.

"Perhaps in the morning," I said.

She wiggled about angrily.

"I wouldn't struggle," I said.

"Oh," she cried in frustration, "oh, oh!" Then she sat quietly, looking at me with anger. "All right," she said, "all right! Your knots are very neat, Master."

"Better than yours?" I inquired.

She looked at me irritably. "Of course," she said. "How could the knot of a mere girl, and one who is only slave, compare with the knot of a man, and one who is free, and even of the Caste of Warriors?"

"Then you acknowledge my knots are superior to yours in all respects?" I asked.

"Oh yes," she cried, "yes, Master!"

"Now," I said, satisfied, "I think I will untie you."

"You are a beast," said she, laughing, "Tarl Cabot."

"Kuurus."

"Kuurus, Kuurus!" she said.

I bent to Elizabeth's bonds to free her when suddenly there came a loud knock on the door of the compartment. We looked at one another quickly.

The knock came again.

"Who is it?" I called.

"Ho-Tu, Master Keeper," came the response, muffled, scarcely audible, behind the heavy beams of the door.

I gave Elizabeth a swift kiss and then jerked the slave livery to her waist and turned her about, putting her on her side at the foot of the couch, facing away from the door. She lay there on the stones, half-stripped, turned away, bound hand and foot, her throat fastened to the slave ring by the heavy collar and chain. Drawing her knees up and almost touching her chin to her chest she managed to look about as abject and abused as a poor wench might. Satisfied, I went to the door and removed the two heavy beams, opening it.

Ho-Tu was a short, corpulent man, broad-shouldered, stripped to the waist. He had quick black eyes set in a shaven head, the threads of a mustache dangled at the sides of his mouth. About his neck he wore a rude ornament, a loose iron chain bearing, also in iron, a medallion, the crest of the House of Cernus. He had a broad leather belt, with four buckles. To this belt there hung the sheath of a hook knife, which was buckled in the sheath, the strap passing over the hilt. Also, clipped to the belt, was a slave whistle, used in issuing signals, summoning slaves, and so on. On the other side of the belt, there hung a slave goad, rather like the tarn goad, except that it is designed to be used as an instrument for the control of human beings rather than tarns. It was, like the tarn goad, developed jointly by the Caste of Physicians and that of the Builders, the Physicians contributing knowledge of the pain fibers of human beings, the networks of nerve endings, and the Builders contributing certain principles and techniques developed in the construction and manufacture of energy bulbs. Unlike the tarn goad which has a simple on-off switch in the handle, the slave goad works with both a switch and a dial, and the intensity of the charge administered can be varied from an infliction which is only distinctly unpleasant to one which is instantly lethal. The slave goad, unknown in most Gorean cities, is almost never used except by professional slavers, probably because of the great expense involved; the tarn goad, by contrast, is a simple instrument. Both goads, interestingly, emit a shower of yellow sparks when touched to an object, a phenomenon which, associated with the pain involved, surely plays its role in producing aversion to the goad, both in tarns and men.

Ho-Tu glanced into the room, saw Elizabeth and smiled, a slaver's smile.

"I see you know well how to keep a slave," he said.

I shrugged.

"If she gives you trouble," said Ho-Tu, "send her to the iron pens. We will discipline her for you."

"I discipline my own slaves," I said.

"Of course," said Ho-Tu, dropping his head. Then he looked up. "But with your permission," he said, "we are professionals."

"I will keep it in mind," I said.

"In a quarter of an Ahn," said Ho-Tu, slapping the slave goad at his side, "I could have her begging to be fed from your hand."

I laughed, and snapped my fingers. Elizabeth struggled to her knees, threw back her head turning the collar on her throat, and knelt facing us. She lifted her eyes, glazed and numb, to mine. "Please Master," said she, almost inaudibly, "feed Vella."

Ho-Tu whistled.

"Why have you come to my compartment?" I demanded of Ho-Tu.

At that moment a bar, struck in a certain pattern by an iron hammer somewhere in the house, rang out, the sound taken up by other bars, also struck, on various floors of the House of Cernus. The day, I had discovered, was divided by such signals. There is method in the house of a slaver.

Ho-Tu smiled. "Cernus," said he, "requests your presence at table."

Six

I Sit Table with Cernus

I observed the two men, collared slaves, squaring off against one another in the sand. Both were stripped to the waist. The hair of both was bound back with a band of cloth. Each carried, sheathed, a hook knife. The edges of the sheath were coated with a bluish pigment.

"These men are the champions among male slaves at hook knife," said Cernus. He scarcely glanced up from the game board at which he sat across from Caprus, of the Caste of Scribes, Chief Accountant of the House.

I heard the crack of a whip and the command "Fight!" and saw the two men begin to close with one another.

I glanced at the game board. Cernus had paid me little attention, being absorbed in the game. I had not seen the opening. Judging from the pieces and positions it appeared to be late in the middle game. Cernus was well in command of the board. I assumed he must be skilled at this sport.

A blue line appeared across the chest of one of the slaves fighting between the tables, on a square of sand some twelve feet in dimension. The line was adjudicated as a point. The two men then returned to opposite corners of the ring and crouched down, waiting for the command to fight again.

Without being asked I had taken a position at the table of Cernus himself. No one had objected, at least explicitly, though I did sense some disgruntlement at my action. It had been expected, I gathered, that I would sit at one of the two long side tables, and perhaps even below the bowls of red and yellow salt which divided these tables. The table of Cernus itself, of course, was regarded as being above the bowls. Ho-Tu sat beside me, on my left.

81

There was a shout from the men-at-arms and members of the House who sat at the tables as the second slave, he who had scored the first point, managed to leave a long streak of blue down the inside of the right arm of the first slave. "Point!" called the man-at-arms, he with the whip, and the two slaves separated again, each going to their corners and crouching there in the sand, breathing heavily. The man whose arm had been marked was forced then to carry the sheathed hook knife in his left hand. I heard the odds changing rapidly at the tables as the men of the house of Cernus revised their betting.

I heard Cernus announce "Capture of Home Stone," and turned to see Caprus sit back in defeat, staring at the board. Cernus began to arrange the pieces once more on the board.

"You could have been a Player," said Caprus.

Cernus laughed with pleasure, turning the board. "Take yellow," he offered.

Caprus shrugged and pushed Ubar's Spearman to Ubar Four.

Cernus looked at me eagerly. "Do you play?" he asked.

"No," I said.

He turned again to regard the board. He pushed his Ubara's Initiate's Spearman to Ubara's Initiate's Spearman Four. The Torian Defense.

There was a cry and I looked again to the square of sand and the first slave, with the hook knife in his left hand, had plunged across the sand, taking a stroke across the chest, to strike his own blue line blow at his opponent.

"Point for both," announced the man-at-arms.

The food at the table of Cernus was good, but it was plain, rather severe, like the master of the House. I had tarsk meat and yellow bread with honey, Gorean peas and a tankard of diluted Ka-la-na, warm water mixed with wine. Ho-Tu, I noted, but did not speak to him of it, drank only water and, with a horn spoon, ate only a grain porridge mixed with bosk milk.

At the wall on my right there were fifteen slave rings. To each, on furs, there was chained, by the left ankle, a bare-breasted girl about whose waist there was knotted a scarlet cord, in which was thrust a long, narrow rectangle of red silk. About their throats were matching red-enameled collars. Their lips were rouged and they wore eyeshadow. Some glistening red substance had been sprinkled on their hair. Following the meal, I understood, in the House of Cernus, is a time for the pleasure and recreation of the men. There are games and sports, and wagers and song. Paga and Ka-la-na are then, when Cernus would leave, brought forth.

"A kill!" cried the man-at-arms with the whip. I saw that the second slave, who was doubtless the better man at the sport, had slipped behind the first and, holding his head back with a powerful forearm, had decisively drawn his sheathed hook knife across the throat of the first man.

The first man seemed numb, the heavy blue streak on his throat, and slipped to his knees. Two men-at-arms rushed forward and put him in shackles. For some reason, the man with the whip took the slave's hook knife, unsheathed it, and drew it across the slave's chest, leaving there a smear of blood. It was not a serious wound. It seemed pointless to me. The slave who had lost was then led away in his shackles. The victor, on the other hand, turned about and raised his hands. He was greeted with cheers and was immediately taken to the table on my left, where he was seated at the far end of the table, before a plate heaped with meat, which he began to devour, holding it in his hands, eyes wild, almost lost in the food, to the amusement of the watching men. I gathered the feed troughs in the pens of the male slaves seldom contained viands so choice.

Now that the sport was done some Musicians filed in, taking up positions to one side. There was a czehar player, two players of the kalika, four flutists and a pair of kaska drummers.

The meal was served by slave girls in white tunics, each wearing a white-enameled collar. These would be girls in training, some of them perhaps White Silk Girls, being accustomed to the routines and techniques of serving at table.

One of them carried a large pitcher of the diluted Ka-la-na wine and stepped behind us, climbing the two steps to the broad wooden dais on which our tables were set. She bent over my left shoulder woodenly, her body stiff. "Wine, Master?" she asked.

"She-sleen," hissed Ho-Tu. "How is it that you first serve wine to a strange man at the table of your master?"

"Forgive Lana," said she, tears springing to her eyes.

"You belong in the iron pens," said Ho-Tu.

"He frightens me," she wept. "He is of the black caste."

"Serve him wine," said he, "or you will be stripped and thrown into a pen of male slaves."

The girl turned and withdrew, then approached again, climbing the stairs, delicately, as though timidly, head down. Then she leaned forward, bending her knees slightly, her body graceful, and spoke, her voice a whisper in my ear, an invitation, "Wine, Master?" as though offering not wine, but herself. In a large house, with various slave girls, it is thought only an act of courtesy on the part of a host to permit a guest the use of one of the girls for the evening. Each of the girls considered eligible for this service, at one time or another during the evening, will approach the guest and offer him wine. His choice is indicated by the one from whom he accepts wine.

I looked at the girl. Her eyes met mine, softly. Her lips were slightly parted. "Wine, Master?" she asked.

"Yes," I said, "I will have wine."

She poured the diluted wine into my cup, bowed her head and with a shy smile, backed gracefully down the stairs behind me, then turned and hurried away.

"Of course," said Ho-Tu, "you may not have her tonight, for she is White Silk."

"I understand," I said.

The Musicians had now begun to play. I have always enjoyed the melodies of Gor, though they tend on the whole to a certain wild, barbaric quality. Elizabeth, I knew, would have enjoyed them as well. I smiled to myself. Poor Elizabeth, I thought. She would be hungry tonight and in the morning would have to go to the feed troughs in the quarters of the female staff slaves, probably for water and a porridge of grain and vegetables. When I had left the compartment, Ho-Tu preceding me down the hall, I had turned and blown her a kiss. She had been quite angry, kneeling there bound hand and foot, fastened to the slave ring by chain and collar, while I trotted off to have dinner with the master of the house. She would probably be quite difficult to get on with in the morning, which time it would be, I supposed, before I would return to the compartment. It is not pleasant to be bound all night. Indeed, such is a common and severe punishment for female slaves on Gor. It is less common to bind a girl during the day because then there is much work to be done. I resolved that most of my problems in this matter might be solved if I simply refused to release Elizabeth until she had given her word, which she takes quite seriously, to be at least civil.

But Elizabeth, rightly or wrongly, was banished from my mind for the moment because I heard, from a side door, the rustle of slave bells, and was pleased to note that seven girls hurried in, using the short, running steps of the slave girl, arms to the side, palms out, head to the left, eyes averted, and knelt between the tables, before the men, head down, in the position of Pleasure Slaves.

"Capture of Home Stone," announced Cernus, moving his First Tarnsman to Ubara's Builder One, where Caprus had, at that point in the game, been attempting to protect his Home Stone. The Home Stone, incidentally, is not officially a piece of the game, as it cannot capture, though it can move one square at a time; further, it might be of interest to note that it is not on the board at the beginning of play, but must be placed on the board on or before the seventh move, which placement counts as one move.

Cernus arose and stretched, leaving Caprus to gather up the pieces.

"Let paga and Ka-la-na be served," said Cernus, to a cheer, and turned and left the table, disappearing through a side door, the same through which the shackled slave had been led. Caprus, soon after, carrying the game pieces and board, left also, but he made his exit through a door other than that which had been used by the slave and his guards, and Cernus.

Now the girls in white tunics began to serve the strong beverages of Gor, and the festivities of the evening began. The Musicians began to play, and the girls in Pleasure Silk, hands over their heads, lifted themselves slowly to the melody, their bodies responding to it as though to the touch of a man.

"These girls are not much good yet," said Ho-Tu. "They are only in the fourth month of their training. It is good for them to get the practice, hearing and seeing men respond to them. That is the way to learn what truly pleases men. In the end, I say, it is men who teach women to dance."

I myself would have spoken more highly of the girls than had Ho-Tu, who was perhaps overly negative in his evaluation, but it was true that there were differences between these girls and more experienced girls. The true dancing girl, who has a great aptitude for such matters, and years of experience, is a marvel to behold, for she seems always different, subtle and surprising. Some of these girls, interestingly, are not even particularly beautiful, though in the dance they become so. I expect a great deal has to do with the girl's sensitivity to her audience, with her experience in playing to, and interacting with, different audiences, teasing and delighting them in different ways, making them think they will be disappointed, or that she is poor, and then suddenly, by contrast, startling them, astonishing them and driving them wild with the madness of their desire for her. Such a girl, after a dance, may snatch up dozens of gold pieces from the sand, putting them in her silk, scurrying back to her master.

Suddenly the girls stopped dancing, and the Musicians stopped playing; even those at the table stopped laughing and talking. There was a long, incredibly weird, horrifying scream, coming from far away, and yet seeming to penetrate the very stones of the hall where we enjoyed ourselves.

"Play," ordered Ho-Tu, to the Musicians.

Obediently the music began again, and again the girls moved to the music, though I could see they did so poorly now, and were frightened.

Some of the men laughed. The slave who had won at hook knife had turned white, sitting far below the salt.

"What was that?" I asked Ho-Tu.

"The slave who lost at hook knife," said Ho-Tu, pushing a large spoonful of porridge into his mouth.

"What happened to him?" I asked.

"He was fed to the beast," said Ho-Tu.

"What beast?" I asked.

"I do not know," said Ho-Tu, "I have never seen it."

Seven

The Ship

I could see the black disk now, moving swiftly, but not at great altitude, passing among the night clouds, under the three moons of Gor.

I, and Cernus and Ho-Tu, and others, stood in the lonely darkness of a recessed ledge on a high peak in the Voltai, some pasangs northeast of Ar. The ledge was attainable only on tarnback. There was no fire, no light. There were perhaps a dozen of us there.

About an Ahn following the eerie cry we had heard in the hall Ho-Tu had arisen from the table and gestured for me to accompany him. I did so, and we climbed a long spiral staircase until we came to the roof of the House of Cernus.

Though doubtless Ho-Tu was well known to the guards at the tarn-cot, he nonetheless showed them a small, flat rectangle of glazed clay, white in color, marked with the sign of the House of Cernus.

On the roof we met Cernus and others. Some were tarnsmen, others members of the House. On the roof there were eight tarns, beside five of which there were carrying baskets attached to tarn harness.

Cernus had looked at me. "We did not specifically discuss your wages," he remarked.

"It is not necessary," I said, "it is well known the House of Cernus is generous."

Cernus smiled. "I like you, Killer," said he, "for you do not haggle, but you are silent; you keep your own counsel and then you strike."

I said nothing.

"I am much the same," said Cernus. He nodded his head. "You did well to sit high at the table."

"Who would dispute my place?" I asked.

Cernus laughed. "But not so high as I," he said.

"You are master of the house," I said.

"You will see," said Cernus, "that the house of Cernus is indeed generous, and more generous than you have thought to dream. You will come with us this night and for the first time you will understand how great indeed is my house. You will this night understand how wisely you have invested the use of your sword."

"What will you show me?" I asked.

"Serve me well," said Cernus, "and in time I will make you the Ubar of a City."

I looked at him startled.

"Ha!" laughed Cernus. "So even the equanimity of an Assassin can be shaken! Yes, the Ubar of a city, and you may choose the city, any save Ar, on whose throne I, Cernus, will sit."

I said nothing.

"You think me mad," he said. "Of course. In your place I too should think such. But know that I am not mad."

"I do not believe you mad," I said.

"Good," said Cernus, indicating one of the tarn baskets.

I swung myself into the basket, which I shared with two men-at-arms.

Cernus and Ho-Tu rode together in another basket. The tarn basket may or may not have guidance attachments, permitting the tarn to be controlled from the basket. If the guidance attachments are in place, then the tarn is seldom saddled, but wears only basket harness. If the basket is merely carried, and the tarn cannot be controlled from the basket, then the tarn wears the tarn saddle and is controlled by a tarnsman. The basket of Cernus and my basket both had guidance attachments, similar to those of the common tarn saddle, a main basket ring corresponding to the main saddle ring, and six leather straps going to the throat-strap rings. The other three baskets, however, had no control attachments and those birds wore saddles and were guided by tarnsmen. Tarn baskets, incidentally, in which I had never before ridden, are of many different sizes and varieties, depending on the function for which they are intended. Some, for example, are little more than flat cradles for carrying planking and such; others are long and cylindrical, lined with verrskin, for transporting beverages and such; most heavy hauling, of course, is done by tharlarion wagon; a common sort of tarn basket, of the sort in which I found myself, is a general utility basket, flat-bottomed, square-sided, about four feet deep, four feet wide and five feet long. At a gesture from Cernus the birds took wing, and I felt my basket on its heavy leather runners slide across the roof for a few feet and then drop sickeningly off the edge of the cylinder, only to be jerked up short by the ropes, hover for a moment as the tarn fought the weight, and then begin to sail smoothly behind the bird, its adjustments made, its mighty wings hurling the air contemptuously behind it.

The spires of Ar, depending on the weather, can normally be seen quite clearly from the nearer ranges of the Voltai, or the Red Mountains, the greatest mountain range of known Gor, superior to both those of Thentis and the Sardar itself. We flew for perhaps an Ahn and then, following a lead tarnsman, dipped and, one at a time, the others circling, landed on a rocky shelf on the side of a steep cliff, apparently no different from dozens of other such shelves we had already passed, save that this shelf, due to an overhang of the cliff above, tended to be somewhat more sheltered than most. Once landed the tarns and baskets were moved back beneath the overhang, beneath which we took up our post as well. No one talked. We stood there in the night, in the cold, for perhaps better than two Ahn. Then I heard one of the men-at-arms say, "There!"

The black disk approached, more slowly now, seeming to sense its way. It dropped among the peaks and, moving delicately among the rocks, neared our shelf.

"It is strange," whispered one of the men-at-arms, "that Priest-Kings must act with such secrecy."

"Do not question the will of Priest-Kings," said another.

I was startled.

About a hundred yards from the shelf the ship stopped, stationary, more than two thousand feet from the ground below.

I saw Ho-Tu looking at the ship, marveling. "I have seen it," he said, "a hundred times and yet, each time, it seems to me more strange. It is a ship. But it does not float on water. It floats in the sky. How can it be?"

"It is the power of Priest-Kings," whispered one of the men-at-arms.

Cernus now, from beneath his cloak, removed a small, flat box, and with his finger pressed a button on this box. A tiny light on the box flashed red twice, then green, then red again. There was a moment's pause and then, from the ship, there came an answering light, repeating the signal, except that its signal terminated with two reds.

The men stirred uneasily.

The ship then began to ease toward the shelf, moving perhaps no more rapidly than a man might walk. Then, clearing the shelf by no more than six inches, it seemed to rest there, not actually touching the rock. The ship was disklike, as are the ships of Priest-Kings, but it had observation apertures, which the ships of Priest-Kings lack. It was about thirty feet in diameter, about eight feet in height. There was no evidence of the discharge of energy.

Cernus looked at me. "To speak of what you see is, of course, death," said he.

A panel in the side of the black ship slid back and a man's head appeared.

I do not know what I expected to see, but I was greatly relieved. My hand was on the hilt of my sword, sweating.

"The trip was uneventful, I trust," said Cernus, putting the signal apparatus back in his robes.

The man, who wore a simple dark tunic and sandals, dropped out to the ground. His hair was dark and clipped short; his face intelligent, but hard. On his right cheek, over the cheekbone was the Thief brand of the Caste of Thieves of Port Kar, who use the small brand to identify their members. "Look," said the man to Cernus, leading him about the side of the ship.

There, in the side, was a great smeared wrinkle of erupted metal.

"A patrol ship," said the man.

"You are fortunate," said Cernus.

The man laughed.

"Have you brought the apparatus?" asked Cernus.

"Yes," said the man.

Few of the men on that rocky shelf reacted much to what was going on. I gathered that they had seen this ship, or others like it, before, but that they had little inkling of the nature of the events that were transpiring. Indeed, I suspected that other than Cernus there were none who truly understood the nature of the ship and its mission, and perhaps he only incompletely. I myself, from my conversations with Misk, probably suspected more of its role and purposes than any other on that shelf, with the exception of Cernus himself.

"What do you think?" asked Cernus, turning to me, pleased.

"The power of the House of Cernus is great indeed," I said, "greater than I had dreamed."

Cernus laughed.

The man from the ship, seemingly anxious to be on his way, had now returned to the interior of the ship. Inside I could see four or five others, clad much as he was, all human. They seemed apprehensive, nervous.

Almost immediately the first man, he who wore the tiny Thief's brand, returned to the panel and crouching down, held out a small, obviously heavy box, to Cernus, who, in spite of the fact that he was the master of the House of Cernus itself, took it in his own hands.

Cernus returned to his carrying basket, holding the small box heavily before him. He motioned for Ho-Tu to enter the basket and the Master Keeper did so. Then receiving the box from Cernus, he placed it carefully in the basket. Cernus then himself climbed into the basket. He spoke to one of the men-at-arms. "Unload the cargo," said he. Then, using the one-strap on the basket ring, Cernus signaled the tarn. The bird stalked out from under the overhang, poised itself on the edge of the shelf, and then, with a leap and a beating of its wings, entered its element.

I saw the basket containing Cernus and Ho-Tu flying toward Ar. I gathered that the main cargo, whatever it was, had already been unloaded, that it reposed in the small, heavy box, and that it was now on the way to the House of Cernus.

"Hurry!" called the man with the Thief's scar, and those of the staff of the House, including even the tarnsmen, stood lined before the panel and received various goods which they placed in the carrying baskets. I alone did not participate in this work. I did, however, observe it carefully. Certain of the boxes which were unloaded, to my surprise, bore lettering in various languages of Earth. I recognized English, and French and German, something that was presumably Arabic, and other boxes which were marked with characters doubtless either Chinese or Japanese. I suspected, however, that the goods in these boxes might not all be those of Earth. I suspected rather that in some of these boxes at least might be goods from the ships of Others, transported by way of Earth, in ships to be piloted by men. Some of the goods, however, were surely of Earth. Among them was a high-powered rifle with telescopic sights. To possess such a weapon, of course, on Gor was a capital offense, it being a violation of the weapon laws of Priest-Kings.

"What is this?" asked one of the men-at-arms.

"It is a crossbow," said the man with the Thief's scar. "It shoots a tiny lead quarrel."

The man looked at it skeptically. "Where is the bow and cord?" he asked.

"Inside the quarrel," said the man, impatiently. "It is in a powder. A spark hits the quarrel and the powder cries out and flees, pushing the quarrel before it, down this tube."

"Oh," said the man-at-arms.

The man with the Thief's scar laughed, and turned to accept another box from a man deeper within the ship.

"Surely it is a forbidden weapon," said the man-at-arms.

"Not to Priest-Kings," said the man in the ship.

The man-at-arms shrugged and took the rifle, or crossbow as he thought of it, and surely the stock resembled that of a crossbow, and placed it in one of the carrying baskets.

"Ah," said one of the tarnsmen, seeing the man on the ship hand out the first of several heavy squares of gold. I smiled to myself. This was cargo the men on the shelf could understand. There was a large quantity of this gold, perhaps forty squares, which were distributed among the four tarn baskets remaining on the ledge. It was, I assumed, Earth gold. It was undoubtedly such gold which permitted the House of Cernus to gain significant influence in the city, sponsoring races and games, as well as permitting the house to undersell, when it pleased, other Merchants.

"How many slaves?" asked one of the men-at-arms.

"Ten," said the man with the Thief's scar.

I then watched while ten cylindrical tubes, apparently of transparent plastic, were removed from the ship. Each was marked and sealed, but in each, at two points, there were valve openings, through which in flight I supposed two tubes might pass, one perhaps for oxygen and another gas used to sedate the occupant, and one to draw the carbon dioxide from the cylinder. The valves were now open, permitting a bit of air to enter and leave the cylinders. Each cylinder contained a beautiful girl, unclothed and unconscious. About the left ankle of each there was locked a steel identification band. They were doubtless girls kidnapped on Earth, brought to Gor to be slaves.

With a wrench device each of the cylinders was opened and its occupant drawn forth by the hair and placed on the rocky shelf. The cylinders were then returned to the ship. One of the girls began to stir uneasily, perhaps sensing the difference in temperature and air.

The man with the Thief's scar again emerged from the ship, this time with a syringe. He injected a tiny bit of serum into each girl, entering the needle in the girl's back, on the left side between the hip and backbone, passing the needle each time into a small vial he held in his left hand.

The girl who had been stirring uneasily rolled about once, tossing her head to one side, as though in fever, and then her movements subsided and she lay quietly, sedated.

"They will not awaken now," said the man with the Thief's scar, "for better than an Ahn."

One of the men-at-arms laughed. "When they do," he said, "they will find themselves in the slave kennels." Several of the others laughed.

The man with the Thief's scar then reentered the ship, and the panel slid shut. There had been no bill of lading, or receipts of any kind, exchanged. I gathered that no such checking, common in legitimate exchanges, was felt desirable or necessary. The life of these men, I supposed, was their bond.

The girls had now been placed on their stomachs and two tarnsmen, with short lengths of binding fiber, were fastening the ankles of each together and binding the wrists of each behind her back. Then, because the baskets in which they were to be transported did not have covers, the girls were placed in pairs, head to feet. The throat of each in each pair was tied to the ankles of the other. This is a device used, when transporting slaves in open baskets, to prevent one from struggling to her feet and in flight throwing herself over the side of the basket. The precautions, however, considered that the girls were drugged, seemed to be unnecessary. On the other hand these men were slavers and not accustomed to take chances with merchandise. I supposed it was possible that a girl might awaken, in the rushing cold air, and attempt to hurl herself to the ground. Elizabeth, I had learned, who had been shipped from the House of Clark, had been transported in a covered basket, lashed shut. This was more common. There had been two girls to each of the long sides in her basket, and one at each end. Their wrists had been tied behind them, a loop running through the heavy wicker to hold them in place. Their ankles had been tied together at the center of the basket. A further precaution, and an independent one, was a long strip of leather, looped several times about the throat of each and threaded through the wicker. Even if a girl should manage somehow, incredibly, because certain important knots are outside the wicker, to free herself, she would still be held in place by the loops on her throat. Gorean slavers, it might be mentioned, seldom lose prisoners. A girl enslaved on Gor has little prospect of escape. She is truly slave, and is likely to remain so, unless, as happens upon occasion, she so pleases a master that he, perhaps against his better judgment, consents to free her. I felt sorry for the girls of Earth. Their life would not be easy. Elizabeth Cardwell, I reminded myself, was of Earth. Perhaps once, long ago, she had been brought, like these others, to Gor, on the black ship of a slaver.

I turned and observed the black disk, which had now silently lifted itself from the rocky ledge and was moving horizontally away, vanishing among the peaks of the Voltai.

"We return to the House of Cernus," said a man-at-arms, and I, and the others, entered our baskets or mounted our tarns.

In a moment the tarns left the rocky ledge, and in another moment or two, in the distance, I could see the lights of distant Ar.

94

Eight

Breakfast

It was, predictably, an extremely irritable, and a very stiff and sore Elizabeth Cardwell whom I freed at the eighth Gorean hour, at which time I returned to my compartment. She was, of course, precisely where I had left her, though she had managed to lie on her side on the stones and get one or two Ahn sleep that night.

"It did not seem desirable," I informed her, tongue in cheek, "that I show you particular solicitude in the presence of Ho-Tu, Master Keeper."

"I suppose not," she grumbled, slipping her slave livery over her shoulders, tying the slip knot on the left shoulder, and then, grimacing, rubbing her wrists and ankles.

"In the future," said she, "I recommend, when it becomes necessary to impress someone, you simply strike me a few times with the slave whip."

"That is a thought," I admitted.

She looked at me grimly. "My knots are a great deal neater than yours," she said.

I laughed and swept her into my arms. "You wench!" I cried.

"It's true," she said, irritably, struggling.

I kissed her. "Yes," I said, "it is true—your knots are indeed a great deal neater than mine."

She looked up at me, and smiled, somewhat mollified. "But," she said, suddenly, irritably, "that fingersnapping business was not necessary. Eat from your hand indeed!"

"I thought it a real coup," I said. "It certainly seemed to impress Ho-Tu."

"It did, didn't it," said Elizabeth.

"Yes," I said decisively.

"You try it when we are alone," said Elizabeth, "and I will bite your hand off."

"Hah!" I cried, and Elizabeth jumped. "It seems you must spend another night bound at the slave ring," I announced.

"Don't you dare!" she cried.

I seized her wrist, and she kicked at me, catching me a rather good one under the knee. I stepped behind her and held her. She squirmed furiously, kicking back, trying to hit me with her small fists. I was laughing. My knee, incidentally, also hurt.

"Do not struggle, Slave," I told her.

She stopped struggling, but was fuming. I began to nibble at the loop on the left shoulder of her slave livery. "Do you know what time it is?" she asked.

"No," I admitted.

"If you'd listen to the bars," she said, "you'd know."

"What time is it?" I asked.

"It is past the eighth bar," she informed me.

"So?" I asked.

"So," she said, "I have not had anything to eat since yesterday morning and if I am not at the trough in the quarters for female staff slaves by the small bar after the eighth bar I will miss breakfast. I cannot simply go down to the kitchen like you and demand five vulo eggs!"

I laughed. "But it was my intention to discipline you," I said.

She squared off against me, hitching up the loop on her left shoulder which I had loosened with my teeth. "My discipline," she said, "can wait until after breakfast."

"I think you are simply punishing me," I told her.

She laughed. "After breakfast," she said, blowing me a kiss, much as I had her the evening before, "you can discipline me!" Then she turned and scurried down the corridor.

I kicked the love furs halfway across the room and sat down on the edge of the stone couch.

It was a chipper, fed Elizabeth Cardwell who returned to the compartment, humming and sprightly. "Did you enjoy your wait?" she asked.

"It seems to me," I said, "you lingered long over your breakfast."

"The porridge in the trough this morning," said she, "was simply marvelous."

I closed the door and set the beams in place.

"Now," she said, "it looks like I'm in trouble."

"You certainly are," I agreed.

"I inquired," she said, "but I could not learn exactly when my training is to begin."

"Ah," I said.

"There will apparently be other girls, too," she said.

"Probably," I said. "It would be a waste of time I imagine to train girls one at a time." I did not mention the girls I had seen the night before. I supposed, since they would not speak Gorean, they would not be used in the training. Earth girls, I knew, were usually sold as untrained barbarians at inferior prices. On the other hand, it was certainly not impossible that the girls brought in the other night, or some of them, would be trained with Elizabeth, probably being taught Gorean in the process. The fact that Elizabeth's training was not beginning immediately gave some suggestion that this might be the case.

"Tonight," said Elizabeth, "after the sixteenth bar, I am to report to the smith at the iron pens."

"It seems," I said, "the little Tuchuk slave girl will again wear her nose ring."

"Did you like it?" asked Elizabeth.

"Very much," I admitted.

"I grew rather fond of it, too," said Elizabeth, "after a time."

"This time," I said, "it will probably not hurt much to affix the ring."

"No," she said, "I do not think so." She knelt down in the room, as naturally and easily as a Gorean girl. "What did you learn," she asked, "of the House of Cernus last night?"

"I will tell you," I said, coming close to her and sitting down cross-legged.

"I myself," she said, pointedly, "learned very little." She looked at me. "I was all tied up, so to speak," she said.

"So to speak," I admitted. "But," said I, "I learned enough for both of us."

I then, in great detail, told Elizabeth all that I had seen and learned the night before. She was generally intrigued, though frightened when

I spoke of the thing called the beast, and distressed when I mentioned the girls brought from Earth, to be sold as slaves from the House of Cernus.

"What is our next step?" she asked.

"It is to learn more of the House of Cernus," I said. "Do you know much of the House?"

"I know certain areas quite well," she said. "Further, I can receive a pass tile from Caprus to go most places in the house."

"But there are certain places that are forbidden?"

"Yes," she said.

"I expect," I said, "I should undertake a bit of exploring."

"First," she said, "learn what areas of the House are open. I would suppose you could go many places I could not. On the other hand I would have access to records that you would not, in the office of Caprus. Ho-Tu, I am sure, would be pleased to guide you. That way you would be familiarized with the House and would also, indirectly, have the forbidden areas clearly marked out for you."

I thought about it. "Yes," I said, "that is a good plan. It is simple, natural, deceptive, and likely of success."

"With a good breakfast," said Elizabeth, "I am a pretty shrewd wench."

"That is true," I admitted. "You are not bad before breakfast either."

"But after breakfast," said she, "I am extraordinary."

"It is now after breakfast," I informed her.

"Well," said she, smiling, "I think you will find that after breakfast I am extraordinary."

She leaned closer to me, smiling, putting one finger up to my shoulder.

"But I have not yet had breakfast," I said.

"Oh," she said.

"Show me where the important people eat," I said.

"All you ever think about is food," she said.

"That's not all I ever think about," I said.

"That's true," she admitted.

Elizabeth led me to a room off a kitchen on the third floor of the cylinder. There were some men in the room, mostly men-at-arms but some staff members, a Metal Worker, two Bakers and a pair of Scribes.

The tables were separate and small. I sat behind one, and Elizabeth knelt back of me and to my left.

She lifted her head, sniffing. I did so, too, scarcely believing my nose. She looked at me, and I looked at her.

A girl slave, in a white tunic and white collar, barefoot, came to the table, and knelt before it.

"What is that I smell?" I asked.

"Black wine," said she, "from the Mountains of Thentis." I had heard of black wine, but had never had any. It is drunk in Thentis, but I had never heard of it being much drunk in any of the other cities.

"Bring two bowls," I said.

"Two?" asked the girl.

"The slave," I said, indicating Elizabeth, "will taste it first."

"Of course, Master," said the girl.

"And put bread over the fire," I said, "and honey, and the eggs of vulos, and fried tarsk meat and a Torian larma fruit."

The girl nodded and, rising gracefully, backing away a step or two, head down, turned and went to the kitchen.

"I have heard," I said to Elizabeth, "that black wine is served hot."

"Incredible," she smiled.

In short order two bowls, steam curling out of them, were brought and placed on the table.

I sat there staring down at them, and Elizabeth did, too. Then I picked up one of the thick, heavy clay bowls. Since no one was looking, we knocked the bowls together gently, and put them to our lips.

It was extremely strong, and bitter, but it was hot, and, unmistakably, it was coffee.

I shared the breakfast with Elizabeth, who informed me that it was better than the porridge below in the trough in the feeding room for female staff slaves, marvelous though the latter might have been.

"I envy you free ones," said Elizabeth. "Next time, you be the slave and let me be the Assassin."

"Actually," I said to Elizabeth, "this is very rare. Thentis does not trade the beans for black wine. I have heard of a cup of black wine in Ar, some years ago, selling for a silver eighty-piece. Even in Thentis black wine is used commonly only in High Caste homes."

"Perhaps it is from Earth?" she asked.

"Originally, doubtless beans were brought from Earth," I said, "much as certain other seeds, and silk worms and such, but I doubt very much that the ship I saw last night had in its cargo anything as trivial as the beans for black wine."

"You are probably right," said Elizabeth, taking another sip, her eyes closed.

I was troubled for a moment, but it passed, recalling that the Warrior who had been slain presumably in my stead on the bridge in the vicinity of the Cylinder of Warriors in Ko-ro-ba had been of Thentis.

"It is very good," said Elizabeth.

Breakfast finished we returned to the compartment, where I untied my signature knot, with which I had closed the door. We entered, and I closed the door, put the beams in place, and took off my sword belt.

Elizabeth had gathered up the love furs which I had kicked across the room and had spread them at the foot of the couch. Now, as though suddenly weary, she reclined on them, looked at me, and yawned.

"When do you have to report to Caprus?" I asked.

"He is one of us," she said. "He holds me to no close schedule, and lets me leave the house when I wish. Yet I suppose I should report in upon occasion."

"Are there other assistants to him?" I asked.

"He manages several Scribes," she said, "but they do not work closely with him. There are some other girls, as well, but Caprus is permissive, and we come and go pretty much as we please." She looked up at me. "If I do not report in too regularly," she said, "all will assume I have been detained."

"I see," I said.

"You have been up all night," she said, "you must be tired."

"Yes," I said, reclining on the love furs.

"Poor master," said she, poking me in the neck with one finger.

I rolled over and seized her in my arms, but she turned her head away, and seemed determined that I should not kiss her. She laughed. "Whose knots are neater?" she asked.

"Yours, yours, yours," I mumbled, "yours, yours," in frustration.

"Very well," she said, "you may kiss me."

I did so, grumbling as she laughed. An Ahn later, however, I had my vengeance.

"Will you eat out of my hand?" I inquired.

"Yes, yes!" she cried.

"Even when we are alone?" I inquired.

"Oh yes, yes, yes!" she cried.

"Do you beg to do so?" I asked.

"Yes!" she cried. "Yes!"

"Beg," I told her.

"Vella begs to eat from master's hand!" she cried. "Vella begs to eat from master's hand!"

I laughed.

"You big beast!" she laughed.

We kissed one another much.

"You have always been able to make me eat out of your hand, Tarl Cabot," said she, "you big beast."

I kissed her again.

"But my knots," she said, "are still neater."

"That is true," I admitted.

She laughed.

"There is nothing like coffee and a good wench after breakfast," I told her.

"I told you," she said, "after breakfast I am extraordinary."

"You were right," I said. "You were right."

After we had kissed I rolled over and fell asleep, and Elizabeth busied herself about the compartment, afterward leaving to go to the office of Caprus, perhaps about the twelfth hour. She would tie her signature knot on the outside of the door. On the inside we had cut the loop and with a simple knot tied the two cords together, so that, when we wished, we might let ourselves out of the compartment without cutting the cord on the inside. I slept long and she came and went in the compartment more than once. At last, about the seventeenth hour, she returned, set the beams in place and lay down beside me, putting her head on my shoulder.

I saw that she now wore in her nose the tiny, fine golden ring of the Tuchuk woman.

Nine

I Learn of the House of Cernus

Ho-Tu, as Elizabeth had suggested, was only too willing to show me about the House of Cernus.

He was pleased with the size and complexity of the operation, which was indeed impressive. It was, of course, the largest and most opulent of the slave houses in Ar. The House of Cernus was more than thirty generations old. It had bred slaves as well as handled them for more than twenty-five generations. The breeding lines of the House of Cernus were recognized, with those of the House of Portus, and certain other of the large slave houses, throughout known Gor. To a slaver, certain girls can be recognized at a glance, as being of certain varieties developed by certain houses. The primary goals of the program, of course, wherever found, are beauty and passion. On the other hand, considering the large number of slaves on Gor, only a small fraction are carefully bred; a larger fraction is bred, but more haphazardly, as when a given male of one private house is mated, for a price, with a given female of another house. Often in these matters, conducted under supervision, both slaves are hooded, in order that they not know who it is with whom they are forced to mate, lest they might, in their moment of union, in their common degradation, care for one another, or fall in love. The largest number of slaves, however, far larger than the bred slaves considered as a group, are those who have been born free and have fallen into slavery, a not uncommon fate on this cruel, warlike world, particularly for women. Slave raids are a major business, and from time to time, a city falls. Slavers are angry, incidentally, when a city does fall, for then the market is likely to be depressed for months, due to the influx of new slaves, sometimes numbered in the thousands. The slavers, by the way, indulge in speculation and manipulation whenever possible, trying to anticipate changes in fashion or control them. I suspected that the House of Cernus was attempting to create a need for barbarian girls, if only to add variety to a rich man's Pleasure Gardens—girls of a sort it seemed it could supply in numbers not possible to competing slavers. The major obstacle to this plan, of course, was that barbarian girls tended to be ignorant and untrained. On the other hand, such girls might be trained, and I suspected that Cernus might have in mind some such experiment with Elizabeth.

The House of Cernus, which is a broad, many-storied cylinder, has a number of facilities which any large slave house must have. The only difference between these facilities in the House of Cernus and such facilities in other houses would probably have been in size, numbers of staff and lavishment of appointment. I have already mentioned the baths in the House of Cernus, which can rival some of the pools in the gigantic Capacian Baths, the finest of known Gor. Less impressive perhaps but even more essential to the operation of the House were its kitchens, its laundries, commissaries and storerooms; its medical facilities, in which dental care is also provided; its corridors of rooms for staff members, all of whom live in the House; its library, its records and files; its cubicles for Smiths, Bakers, Cosmeticians, Bleachers, Dyers, Weavers and Leather Workers; its wardrobe and jewelry chambers; its tarncots, two of them, opening by means of vast portals to tarn perches fixed in the side of the cylinder; its training rooms, both for slaves and for guards, and for those learning the trade of the slaver; recreation rooms for the staff; eating places; and, of course, deep in the cylinder, various pens, kennels and retention facilities; as well as a chamber in which slaves are processed, collared and branded; deliveries to the House of Cernus, both of foodstuffs and materials, and slaves, are frequent; it is not unusual that a hundred slaves be received in a given day; the total number of slaves in the house at any one time, a shifting population, of course, tends to be between four and six thousand. Many of these, of course, are simply put in pens and retained there until removed for sale; some lots are wholesaled to minor slavers, usually coming in from distant cities to pick up merchandise, which tends in Ar to be abundant and, on the whole, reasonably priced. Ar is the slave capital of known Gor. Although there are some private show and sales rooms in the House of Cernus, and private auctions and exhibitions, intended to interest prospective clients, are held, most slaves, of the House of Cernus and others, are sold in one of the five public auction houses, licensed and taxed by the Administrator of Ar. The major auction house, the Curulean, contains the great block. It is a great mark of prestige among slave girls to be selected for sale from the great block in the Curulean, and girls tend to compete viciously among themselves for this honor. To be sold from the Curulean great block is almost a guarantee of a rich master, and a luxurious pleasant life, though it be, of course, only that of a slave. As at many of the larger markets, there are Musicians near the block, and a girl is given enough time to present herself well. At the minor blocks in the small houses, or even the minor blocks in the Curulean, sales are conducted with a swiftness and dispatch that gives the girl little time to interest and impress buyers, with the result that even a very fine girl, to her indignation and shame, may be sold for only an average price to an average buyer, who may use her for little more than, as it is said, kettle and mat. This type of thing is at its worst when large numbers of girls must be sold, as when a city has fallen. Then, stripped, chained by the throat, in a long chain of girls, each separated from the other by about ten feet, secured not even by the dignity of a collar but only by a loop of the communal chain bolted or padlocked about her neck, each is dragged up the steps of the minor block, bid upon while a one-Ehn sand clock is turned, sold for the highest bid that comes forth in one Ehn, and then dragged down the steps on the other side, making room for the next girl.

"This is the best of our private auction rooms," said Ho-Tu.

I looked into one of the private salesrooms in the House of Cernus. It would seat no more than a hundred buyers. The tiers in the room were of marble. The room itself was draped in rich purple. The block itself, interestingly, as tradition required, was rounded and of wood. On its surface there was sprinkled, again in one of the conventions of Gorean tradition, some sawdust. Female slaves, incidentally, are always sold barefoot. It is good for the girl to feel wood and sawdust beneath her feet, it is said.

I was a bit sad as I looked at the block. I knew that in such places private auctions were sometimes conducted, discreetly, for favored clientele, many times slavers themselves. At such private auctions, conducted secretly, Gorean slavers sometimes find it convenient to dispose of important, High Caste women without trace, sometimes even from the city of Ar itself, perhaps women who have lived proudly, luxuriously, not more than a pasang or two from the rounded, wooden block from which they now find themselves, to their horror, being sold. Who knows what women, freshly branded, hooded and braceleted, chained in the slave wagons, pass to and from Ar?

Passing down a corridor, trailing after Ho-Tu, we stopped briefly to peer into a large room. In this room I saw two slave girls, clad in yellow livery with yellow collars, as Elizabeth normally was, kneeling opposite one another. One girl was dictating from a piece of record paper held in her hand and the other girl was copying it rapidly on a second piece of record paper. The speed with which this was done informed me that some form of shorthand must be being used. Elsewhere in the room there were some free men, Scribes I gathered though they were stripped to the waist, who were inking, using a silk-screen process, large sheets of layered, glued rag paper. One of them held the sheet up inspecting it, and I saw that it was a bill, which might be pasted against the wall of a public building, or on the public boards near the markets. It advertised a sale. Other such sheets, hanging on wires, proclaimed games and tarn races. The common thread in these various matters was that the House of Cernus was involved, either in presenting the sale or in sponsoring the races or games.

"This may interest you," said Ho-Tu, turning down a side corridor. There was a door at the end of this corridor, and two guards posted. They recognized Ho-Tu immediately, of course, and unlocked and opened the door. I was much surprised when I saw, about four feet inside this door, a second door. In this second door there was an observation panel, which slid back. A woman looked through the panel, saw Ho-Tu and nodded. In a moment I heard two iron bolts being withdrawn and we entered another corridor. I heard the door being bolted again behind us. In the corridor we passed another woman. Both, interestingly, wore long, rather graceful white gowns, and had their hair bound back with bands of white silk. Neither had worn collars.

"Are they slaves?" I asked Ho-Tu.

"Of course," he said.

We saw another woman. We had not yet seen a man in this corridor.

Ho-Tu turned into a side corridor and we found ourselves, to my surprise, looking through a huge rectangle of glass, some twelve feet high and perhaps fifteen feet wide; it was one of a dozen such panels I could see in the corridor.

Beyond the glass I looked into what seemed to be a Pleasure Garden, lit by energy bulbs radiant in its lofty ceiling. There were various hues of grass, some secluded pools, some small trees, a number of fountains and curving walks. I heard the music of a lute from somewhere. Then I stepped back for I noted, coming along one of the curving walks, two lovely girls, clad in white, their hair bound back with white silk; they were quite young; perhaps less than eighteen.

"Do not fear," said Ho-Tu. "They cannot see you."

I studied the glass that separated us. The two girls strolled near the glass and one of them, lifting her hands behind her head, studied her reflection gravely in the mirror, retying the band of silk which confined her hair.

"On their side of the glass," said Ho-Tu, "it seems a mirror."

I looked suitably impressed, though of course, from Earth, I was familiar with the principles of such things.

"It is an invention of the Builders," said Ho-Tu. "It is common in slave houses, where one may wish to observe without being observed."

"Can they hear us?" I whispered.

"No," said Ho-Tu.

Now one of the girls laughed and pushed the other and then turned and fled, pursued by the other, also laughing.

I looked at Ho-Tu sharply.

"There is a system of sound baffles," said he. "We can hear them but they cannot hear us."

I regarded the two girls running off. Beyond them I could see some others. Two of them were playing catch with a red ball.

There seemed to me something strange about these girls, though they were beautiful. They seemed, in a way, simple, very childlike.

"Are they slaves?" I asked Ho-Tu.

"Of course," said Ho-Tu, adding, "but they do not know it."

"I do not understand," I said.

I could now see the girl playing the lute. She was lovely, as were the others. She was strolling about one of the pools. Two other girls, I now saw, were lying by the pool, putting their fingers in the water, making circles in the water.

"These are exotics," said Ho-Tu.

That expression is used for any unusual variety of slave. Exotics are generally quite rare.

"In what way?" I asked. I myself had never cared much for exotics, any more than I cared much for some of the species of dogs and goldfish which some breeders of Earth regarded as such triumphs. Exotics are normally bred for some deformity which is thought to be appealing. On the other hand, sometimes the matter is much more subtle and sinister. For example it is possible to breed a girl whose saliva will be poisonous; such a woman, placed in the Pleasure Gardens of an enemy, can be more dangerous than the knife of an Assassin.

Perhaps Ho-Tu guessed my line of thought, for he laughed. "No, No!" he said. "These are common wenches, though more beautiful than most."

"Then in what way are they exotic?" I asked.

Ho-Tu looked at me and grinned. "They know nothing of men," said he.

"You mean they are White Silk?" I asked.

He laughed. "I mean they have been raised from the time they were infants in these gardens. They have never looked on a man. They do not know they exist."

I then understood why only women had been seen in these rooms.

I looked again through the glass, at the gentle girls, sporting and playing together by the pool.

"They are raised in complete ignorance," said Ho-Tu. "They do not even know they are women."

I listened to the music of the lute, and was disturbed.

"Their life is very pleasant, and very easy," said Ho-Tu. "They have no duties other than to seek their own pleasure."

"And then?" I asked.

"They are very expensive," said Ho-Tu. "Normally the agent of a Ubar who has been victorious in battle will purchase one, for his high officers, to be brought to the victory feast." Ho-Tu looked at me. "The attendants, when the girl is purchased, give her a drug in her food that night, and remove her from the gardens. She is kept unconscious. She will be revived at the height of the Ubar's victory feast, commonly to find herself unclothed in a cage of male slaves set up among the tables."

I looked back at the girls through the glass.

"Not infrequently," said Ho-Tu, "they go mad, and are slain the following morning."

"And if not?" I asked.

"Commonly," said Ho-Tu, "they will seek out a female slave, one who reminds them of the attendants in the garden, and this woman will comfort them, and explain to them what they are, that they are women, that they are slaves, that they must wear a collar and that they must serve men."

"Is there more to the House of Cernus?" I asked, turning away.

"Of course," bowed Ho-Tu, leading me away from the area.

One of the women looked at me as I left and smiled. I did not smile back.

Ten

To the Pens

We had soon passed through the two doors, the first being locked behind us by one of the white-gowned women, the second by the two guardsmen.

In the hallway we passed four female slaves, naked, on their hands and knees, with sponges, rags and buckets, cleaning the tiles of the corridor. A male slave stood near, a heavy band of iron about his throat, a whipping strap dangling from his right hand.

"This is an interesting room," said Ho-Tu, opening a door and leading me through. "Sometimes it is guarded, but now it is empty."

Once again I found myself staring through a large rectangle of glass, but this time there was only one such panel.

"Yes," said Ho-Tu, "on the other side it is a mirror."

On our side of the glass there was a metal grillwork, with rectangular openings about twelve inches long and four inches high. I gathered this was in case someone on the other side would attempt to break the mirror. In the room, which now had no occupant, I saw an open wardrobe closet, some chests of silks, a silken divan of immense size, several choice rugs and cushions about, and a sunken bath to one side. It might have been the private compartment of a lady of High Caste save that, of course, in this house it was a cell.

"It is used for Special Captures," said Ho-Tu. "Sometimes," he added, "Cernus amuses himself with the women kept in this room, leading them to believe that if they serve him well they will be well treated." Ho-Tu laughed. "After they yield to him they are sent to the iron pens."

"And if they do not yield?" I asked.

"Then," said Ho-Tu, "they are strangled in the chain which bears the crest of the House of Cernus." I looked down into the room.

"Cernus," said Ho-Tu, "does not like to lose."

"I gather not," I said.

"When using a woman," said Ho-Tu, "Cernus is in the habit of placing the chain about her neck."

I looked at him.

"It encourages docility and effort," said Ho-Tu.

"I expect it does," I said.

"You do not seem much pleased with the House of Cernus," observed Ho-Tu.

"Are you," I asked, "Ho-Tu?"

He looked up at me, surprised. "I am well paid," he said. Then he shrugged. "Most of the House you have seen," said he, "with the exception of training areas, the iron pens, the processing rooms, and such."

"Where are the women who were brought to the Voltai last night on the black ship?"

"In the kennels," he said. "Follow me."

On the way down the stairs to the lower portions of the cylinder, several floors of which, incidentally, are below ground level, we passed the office of Caprus. I saw Elizabeth there, in the hallway outside, carrying an armful of scrolls.

Seeing me she fell to her knees and put down her head, managing somehow to retain her hold on the several scrolls.

"I see your training has not begun even yet," I said, rather sternly.

She did not speak.

"Her training," said Ho-Tu, "will begin soon."

"What are you waiting for?" I asked.

"It is an idea of Cernus," said Ho-Tu. "He wants to train a first small set of barbarian slaves. She will be numbered among those in the first set."

"The girls who were brought in last night?" I asked.

"Only two of them in her set," said Ho-Tu. "The remaining eight will be divided into two larger sets and trained separately."

"Barbarians, I have heard," I said, "do not train well."

"It is our belief," said Ho-Tu, "that much can be done with a barbarian girl—it remains to be proven, of course."

"But such would not be likely to bring a high price," I observed.

"Who knows what may be the case by the month of En'Var?" asked Ho-Tu. "Or perhaps even by En'Kara?"

"Should the experiment be successful," I said, "it seems the House of Cernus will have the largest supply of such girls."

Ho-Tu smiled. "Of course," he said.

"You already have several in the pens?" I speculated.

"Yes," said Ho-Tu. "And more are obtained each rendezvous."

Elizabeth looked up, as though puzzled at this, as though she did not understand the reference, and then dropped her head again.

"When will you begin the training?" I asked.

"When the two new girls chosen for the first set grow weary of the kennels, and of the gruel of the iron pens."

"Do girls in training not eat such gruel?" I asked.

"Girls in training," said Ho-Tu, "partake of the finest of slave porridges. They are given mats to sleep on, and later in their training, furs. They are seldom chained. Sometimes they are even permitted, under guard, to leave the house, that they may be stimulated and pleased by the sights of Ar."

"Do you hear that, little Vella?" I asked.

"Yes, Master," said Elizabeth, not lifting her head.

"Further," said Ho-Tu, "after the first few weeks of training, if sufficient progress is made, they will be permitted foods other than slave porridges." Elizabeth looked up brightly.

"One might even say," said Ho-Tu, "that they will be well fed." Elizabeth smiled.

"In order that they may bring," added Ho-Tu, looking at Elizabeth, "a higher price."

Elizabeth looked down.

At that time we heard the fifteenth bar. Elizabeth looked up at me. "You are permitted to leave," I told her. She sprang up and returned to the office of Caprus, who was closing the top of the desk before which he stood. She replaced the scrolls in the pigeonholes of a scroll bin and Caprus slid the cover over the bin and locked it, and then, with a word to him, she lightly ran past us and disappeared down the hall.

"With speed like that," said Ho-Tu, smiling, "she will not be the last to arrive at the porridge trough."

I looked at Ho-Tu and smiled.

111

He lifted his shaved head to mine, and the black eyes met mine. He scratched his left shoulder. He stood squarely there before me, and then he grinned.

"You are a strange one for an Assassin," he said.

"Are we now to go to the pens?" I asked.

"It is the fifteenth bar," said Ho-Tu. "Let us go to table. After we have eaten, I will show you the pens."

Here and there, down the hall, I could see slaves hurrying in one direction or another, depending on the location of their feeding quarters. I could also see members of the staff moving about, and could hear doors being closed and locked.

"All right," I said, "let us eat."

There were various matches in the pit of sand that evening. There was a contest of sheathed hook knife, one of whips and another of spiked gauntlets. One of the slave girls spilled wine and was fastened to a slave ring, stripped and beaten. Later the Musicians played and a girl I had not seen before, whom I was told was from Cos, performed the collar dance, and creditably. Cernus, as before, was lost in his game with Caprus, this time lingering at the board even long after paga and full-strength Ka-la-na were served.

"Why is it?" I asked Ho-Tu, whom I felt I had come to know somewhat better in the day, "that when others have Ka-la-na and meat and bread and honey you eat only this porridge?"

Ho-Tu pushed back the bowl.

"It is not important," he said.

"Very well," I said.

The horn spoon snapped in his hands, and he angrily threw the pieces into the bowl.

"I am sorry," I said.

He looked at me puzzled, his black eyes glinting. "It is not important," he repeated.

I nodded.

He rose. "I will take you to the pens now," he said.

I indicated the door to one side through which, the night before, the shackled slave had been led, through which Cernus had left as well. This night, I had been pleased to note that none of the slaves who had come out poorly in their contests had been shackled and led through the door. The slave who had won at hook knife the night before, I

112

observed, was again eating at the foot of the table. The collar had been taken from his throat. I gathered he might now be free. There was a whipping strap looped about his belt, and in the belt, sheathed, was a hook knife, the hilt buckled down in the sheath, as was the case with that of Ho-Tu. "The thing you call the beast," I said, "lies through that door."

Ho-Tu looked at me, narrowly. "Yes," he said.

"I would like to see it," I said.

Ho-Tu paled. Then he smiled. "Pray to the Priest-Kings," he said, "that you never see it."

"You know nothing of the beast?" I asked.

"Cernus, and certain others," said he, "can look upon it—they alone." He looked at me closely. "Do not be curious, Killer," said he, "for commonly those who look upon the beast do so only in death."

"I trust," I said, "it is safely caged."

Ho-Tu smiled. "I trust so," he said.

"How often is it fed?" I asked.

"It can eat many times a day," said Ho-Tu, "but it can also endure long periods without food. Normally we feed it a slave every ten days."

"A live slave?" I asked.

"It likes to make its own kills," said Ho-Tu.

"As long as it is safely caged," I remarked, "I gather there is no danger."

"Fear of the beast keeps good order in the House of Cernus," said Ho-Tu.

"I expect it does," I admitted.

"Come," said Ho-Tu. "I will show you the pens."

Eleven

Two Girls

After having passed through several doors of iron, each with an observation panel, descending on a spiral ramp deeper and deeper beneath the ground level, I could at last, clearly, smell the stink of the pens.

In the cylinder there are several varieties of retention areas, ranging from the luxuriousness of the cell shown to me earlier by Ho-Tu, in which Cernus was accustomed to keep Special Captures, to the iron pens. Some of the facilities were simply lines of reasonably clean cells, some with windows, usually a lavatory drain and something in the way of a mat to sleep on. Other rows of cells were rather more ornate, with heavy intricate grillwork taking the place of bars, hung with red silks, floored with furs and perhaps lit by a small tharlarion-oil lamp set in a barred recess. But the pens, of which there were several sorts, boasted no such luxuries. The expression "The Iron Pens," incidentally, generally refers to all of the subterranean retention facilities in the house of a slaver, not simply cages, but pits, steel drums, wall chains and such; it is the name of an area, on the whole, rather than a literal description of the nature of the only sort of security devices found there. The expression "kennels" is sometimes used similarly, but more often it refers to a kind of small, cement cell, customarily about three feet by three feet by four feet, with an iron gate, which can be raised and lowered; similar cells, but entirely of bars, are also common, and are to be found in the house of slavers; the smaller cells can function as separate units, and may be used to ship slaves, but they can also be locked together in groups to provide tiers of cells, usually bolted into a wall, conserving space.

Ho-Tu led the way, moving from catwalk to catwalk, spanning cages below. In these cages, through the bars, male slaves, crowded together, naked and wearing heavy collars, glared sullenly up at us.

"It would not be well to lose your footing," advised Ho-Tu.

I supposed it was from this sort of facility that the general expression "The Iron Pens" took its origin. On each cage we passed, as we took our way over it, I saw a thin metal plate covered with numbers. Some of these numbers referred to the occupants within the cage, but other numbers were coded to instruct the keepers in such matters as diet, special precautions, date of the lot's acquisition, and its intended disposition. Some of the numbers had been scratched out, and others had been hammered into the plates, which were changed from time to time. The pens seemed humid and, though we were below ground, warm from the heat of the bodies. The only sanitation facility was an open metal mesh, supported by close-set horizontal bars, in the bottom of the cages, beneath which, some five feet below, was a cement floor, washed down and cleaned by slaves once daily. There was a feed trough at one side of each cage and a low watering pan on the other, both filled by means of tubes from the catwalk. The cages of female slaves were mixed in with those of the male slaves, presumably on no other basis than what cage happened to be empty at a given time. The female slaves, like the men, were unclothed, and wore collars; their collars, however, were not the typical locked collar of the female slave but, since they were only in the iron pens, a narrow band of iron, with a number, hammered about their neck.

I noted that the females tended to remain near the center of their cage. Their food and water areas were protected from the wall of bars shared with the next cage, which might contain male slaves, by a heavy iron mesh rather like that of the flooring, riveted by hammer to the bars. Sometimes I supposed a girl might wander too close to the bars and be seized, but, because of the bars, little could be done with her. Mating among slaves is carefully supervised. One or two girls I noted lay on the flooring mesh, their heads near the bars separating them from the males, their hair cruelly tied to the bars. They had been careless.

I did not try to count the pens over which we passed, and we descended two more levels, which were similarly tenanted. We stopped on the fourth subterranean level, beneath which I was told there were three more levels, retention levels, on the whole similar to those we had just passed. The fourth level, though containing many retention facilities, is used for the processing, assignment, interrogation and examination of slaves; it can be reached independently by a spiral ramp and tunnel which does not pass through the area of the iron pens. The kitchen for the pens is on this level, and the infirmary, and certain facilities for smiths; Ho-Tu kept his chair of office on this level; also, discipline was administered on this level, I gathered, seeing certain racks and chains, certain stone tables with straps, certain carefully arranged instruments designed for the exaction of pain; certain irons and high-heat-level fires in perforated metal drums.

"I will show you the girls brought in from the Voltai," said Ho-Tu.

I followed him into a large room, barred by a heavy iron door.

There was a drum fire near the center of the room on the floor. There was a littered look about the room, some pieces of chains about. Two smiths were in the room. There was a guard talking with the smiths. There was also a man in the green of the Caste of Physicians, standing at one side, writing notes on a slip of record paper. He was a large man, smooth-shaven. I saw a branding rack, noted that there were irons in the drum fire. There was also an anvil in the room, resting on a large block of wood. Against the far wall there were thirty kennels, five rows of six each, tiered, with iron runways and iron stairs giving access to them. They reached to the ceiling of the room. Elsewhere in the room there were some slave cages, but they were now empty. Slave rings were mounted on one wall. Hanging from the ceiling, worked from a windlass, dangled a chain, attached to which was a pair of slave bracelets. Against one wall I noted a variety of slave whips, of different weights and leathers.

The Physician looked up from the paper. "Greetings, Ho-Tu," said he.

"Greetings, Flaminius," said Ho-Tu. "May I introduce Kuurus, of the black caste, but of our employ?"

Coldly Flaminius nodded his head, and I did the same.

Then the Physician looked at Ho-Tu. "It is a good lot," he said.

"It should be," said Ho-Tu, "they have been selected with great care."

I then understood for the first time that it is not just any girl who is picked up by the Gorean slavers, but that the acquisition of each of these doubtless had been planned with the same diligence and care that is given to a slave raid on Gor itself. They had doubtless been watched, without their knowledge studied and investigated, their habits noted, their common movements and routines recorded, for months prior to the strike of the slaver at a predetermined place and time. I supposed the requirements of the slaves were high. Each of the girls, I suspected, would be vital and much alive. Each of them I knew was beautiful. Each of them I suspected would be intelligent, for Goreans, as the men of Earth commonly do not, celebrate quickness of mind and alertness in a girl. And now they were in the kennels.

"Let's look at them," said Ho-Tu, picking up a small metal hand torch with a wick of twisted, tarred straw from the floor and thrusting it into the drum fire.

I and the Physician, and the guardsman, followed him up the iron ramp to the second level.

A blond girl, wearing the steel band locked on her left ankle, crouched at the barred gate, and extended her hands through. "Meine Herren!" she cried. The guard, with a heavy stick he carried, struck the bars viciously before her face and she cried out, jerking back and crouching at the rear of the cage.

"These next two," said Flaminius, indicating two cages separated by a cage from the last, "refuse to eat."

Ho-Tu lifted the torch to first one cage, and then the other. Both girls were Oriental—my guess would have been Japanese.

"Feed this one," said Ho-Tu, pointing to the cage on his left.

The girl was dragged out and her hands were braceleted behind her back. One of the smiths from below was summoned with a bowl of slave porridge, which he mixed half with water, and stirred well, so that it could be drunk. There are various porridges given to slaves and they differ. The porridges in the iron pens, however, are as ugly and tasteless a gruel, and deliberately so, as might be imagined. As the girl knelt the guardsman pulled back her head and held her nose while the smith, with thumb and forefinger, forced open her jaws and, spilling it a bit on her chin and body, poured a half cup of gruel into her mouth. The girl tried to hold her breath but when it became necessary for her to breathe she must needs swallow the gruel; twice more the smith did this, and then the girl, defeated, swallowed the gruel as he poured it into her mouth, half choking on it.

"Put her back in the kennel," said Ho-Tu.

"Will you not remove the bracelets from her?" I asked.

"No," said Ho-Tu, "that way she will not be able to rid herself of the gruel."

The second girl had been watching what had gone on. Ho-Tu, with his foot, kicked her gruel pan toward her, which slid under the bars of the gate. She lifted it to her lips and began to eat, trembling.

The last girl on the second row might have been Greek. She was quite beautiful. She sat with her chin on her knees, looking at us.

We began to go up to the third level. "They seem very quiet," I observed.

"We permit them," said Flaminius, deigning to offer a bit of explanation, "five Ahn of varied responses, depending on when they recover from the frobicain injection. Mostly this takes the form of hysterical weeping, threats, demands for explanation, screaming and such. They will also be allowed to express their distress for certain periods at stated times in the future."

"It is important for them," added Ho-Tu, "from time to time to be able to cry and scream."

"But this is now a silent period, it seems," I said.

"Yes," said Ho-Tu, "until tomorrow morning at the fifth bar."

"But what if they are not silent?" I asked.

"They would be lashed," said Ho-Tu.

"It has only been necessary to lift the whip," said the guard. "They do not speak the language, but they are not fools. They understand."

"Each girl in her processing," said Ho-Tu, "after her fingerprinting, is given five strokes of the lash, that she may feel it and know what it means. After that, to ensure prompt obedience, it is commonly enough to merely move one's hand toward the leather."

"I imagine," I said, "they can understand very little of what has happened to them."

"Of course not," said Flaminius. "Right now several of them doubtless believe they have gone insane."

"Do you lose many girls to madness?" I asked.

"Surprisingly," said Flaminius, "no."

"Why is that?" I asked.

"It probably has much to do with the selection of the girls, who tend to be strong, intelligent and imaginative. The imagination is important, that they can comprehend the enormity of what has occurred to them."

"How could you convince them they are not insane?" I asked.

Flaminius laughed. "We explain what has happened to them. They are intelligent, they have imagination, they will have understood the possibility before, though not considering it seriously, and will, in time, accept the reality."

"How can you explain to them?" I asked. "They do not speak Gorean?"

"There is no girl here," said Flaminius, "for whom there is not at least one member of our staff who can speak their language."

I looked at him, bewildered.

"Surely," said Flaminius, "you do not think we lack men who are familiar with the world from which these slaves have been brought. We have men of their world in the House and men of our world on their planet."

I said nothing.

"I myself," said Flaminius, "have visited their world and speak one of its languages."

I looked at him.

"It is called English," he said.

"Oh," I said.

We had now paused before the two last cages on the right side of the third tier. There was a black girl in each of them, both beautiful. One was sullen and quiet, sitting hunched over in the back of the kennel; the other was curled on the floor, crying softly. We continued on down the walkway until we came to the third cell from the left side of the tier.

"Why are this girl's hands braceleted through the bars?" asked Ho-Tu.

"The guard," said Flaminius, "liked her. He wanted to look on her face."

Ho-Tu, holding the torch close, lifted the girl's head. She stared at him, her eyes glazed. She was quite beautiful. Italian, I supposed.

He dropped her head. "Yes," said Ho-Tu. "She is superb."

We then climbed up the stairs to the fourth level.

When Ho-Tu held his torch to the third cell from the end, above that of the girl below, the Italian, the girl inside cried out and scrambled to the back of the cage, weeping, pressing herself against the cement, scratching at it. I could see the marks of a lash on her back. She was a short girl, dark-haired. I would have guessed French or Belgian.

"This one," said Flaminius, "started to go into shock. That can be quite serious. We lashed her that she would feel, that she would come alive under the lash, come to her senses in the pain."

I looked into the cage. The girl was terrified, and doubtless in pain, but certainly she was not in shock.

"Sometimes," said Flaminius, "shock cannot be so easily prevented. Indeed, sometimes the lash itself drives the girl into shock. Then sedations and drugs are called for. This lot, however, has been excellent."

"Have you prepared the initial papers on them?" asked Ho-Tu.

"Yes," said Flaminius.

"How many are white silk?" asked Ho-Tu.

"Six," said Flaminius.

"So many?" asked Ho-Tu.

"Yes," said Flaminius.

"Good," said Ho-Tu. The Master Keeper turned to me. "The two last girls," said he, gesturing with his head to the last two cages on the fourth level, "will be of interest to you."

"Why is that?" I asked.

"They have been selected to train with the girl Vella, who keeps your quarters."

We went to the last two cages on the tier. Flaminius turned to us. "I can communicate with these two," he said. Ho-Tu lifted the torch closer to the two cages. "Slaves," said Flaminius. He spoke in English.

The two girls lifted their eyes to him startled. "You speak English," said one of them, slowly, staring at him, dumbfounded. The other scrambled to the bars, thrusting her hands through. "Help us!" she cried. "Help us!" Then the first girl, too, knelt at the bars, putting her hands through. "Please!" she wept. "Please! Please!"

Flaminius stood back, expressionlessly accepting their supplications.

Then they knelt there, holding the bars, their faces stained with tears.

"Please," whispered the one on the left, "Please."

"You are slaves," said Flaminius, again in English.

They shook their heads. Both, I noted, were, like Elizabeth, dark-haired. I suspected they had been chosen to train with her, at least in part, in order that they might form a matched set. The girl on the left had her hair cut rather short; the slavers would, in all probability, not permit her to continue to wear her hair in that fashion; her face was delicate, fragile, rather thin and intellectual; her body was thin; I expected her new masters would put some weight on her; her eyes were gray; the thin face was marked with several blemishes; the other girl was perhaps an inch or so shorter, though it was difficult to tell; she was more full-bodied than the first girl but not excessively so; she had fair, exciting shoulders, a good belly and wide, sweet, well-turned hips; her hair had been cut at the shoulders; her eyes, like Elizabeth's, were brown; the second girl, I supposed, if sold separately, might bring a somewhat higher price than the first. I found both extremely attractive, however.

Flaminius turned to Ho-Tu and the rest of us. "I have just told them," he said, in Gorean, "that they are slaves."

The girl on the left, the thinner one with the blemishes, spoke. "I am not a slave," she said.

Flaminius turned to us again. "She has just denied that she is a slave," he told us.

The guard with us laughed.

Tears sprang into the girl's eyes. "Please!" she said.

"You are mad!" said the second girl. "All of you are mad!"

"What is your name?" asked Flaminius of the first girl.

"Virginia," said the first girl, "Virginia Kent."

"Where are we!" demanded the second girl. "I demand that you release us! I demand an explanation! Get us out of here immediately! Hurry! Hurry, I tell you!"

Flaminius paid the second girl no attention. "Eat your gruel, Virginia," said he, soothingly, to the first girl.

"What are you going to do with us?" asked the first girl.

"Eat," said Flaminius, kindly.

"Let us out!" cried the second girl, shaking the bars. "Let us out!"

Virginia Kent picked up the gruel pan and put it to her lips, taking some of the stuff.

"Let us out!" cried the second girl.

"Now drink," said Flaminius.

Virginia lifted the pan of water, and took a sip. The pan was battered, tin, rusted.

"Let us out!" cried the second girl yet again.

"What is your name?" asked Flaminius of the second girl, very gently.

"You are mad!" cried the girl. "Let us out!" She shook the bars.

"What is your name?" repeated Flaminius.

"Phyllis Robertson," said the girl angrily.

"Eat your gruel, Phyllis," said Flaminius. "It will make you feel better."

"Let me out!" she cried.

Flaminius gestured to the guard and he, with his club, suddenly struck the bars in front of Phyllis Robertson's face and she screamed and darted back in the cage, where she crouched away from the bars, tears in her eyes.

"Eat your gruel," said Flaminius.

"No," she said. "No!"

"Does Phyllis remember the lash?" asked Flaminius.

The girl's eyes widened with fear. "Yes," she said.

"Then say so," said Flaminius.

I whispered in Gorean to Ho-Tu, as though I could not understand what was transpiring. "What is he doing with them?"

Ho-Tu shrugged. "He is teaching them they are slaves," he said.

"I remember the lash," said Phyllis.

"Phyllis remembers the lash," corrected Flaminius.

"I am not a child!" she cried.

"You are a slave," said Flaminius.

"No," she said. "No!"

"I see," said Flaminius, sadly, "it will be necessary to beat you."

"Phyllis remembers the lash," said the girl numbly.

"Excellent," said Flaminius. "Phyllis will be good. Phyllis will eat her gruel. Phyllis will drink her water."

She looked at him with hatred.

His eyes met hers and they conquered. She dropped her head, turning it to one side. "Phyllis will be good," she said. "Phyllis will eat her gruel. Phyllis will drink her water."

"Excellent," commended Flaminius.

We watched as the girl lifted first the gruel pan and then the water pan to her lips, tasting the gruel, taking a swallow of the water.

She looked at us with tears in her eyes.

"What are you going to do with us?" asked the first girl.

"As you probably have suspected, noting the difference in gravitational field," said Flaminius, "this is not Earth." He regarded them evenly. "This is the Counter-Earth," he said. "This is the planet Gor."

"There is no such place!" cried Phyllis.

Flaminius smiled. "You have heard of it?" he asked.

"It is only in books!" cried Phyllis. "It is an invention!"

"This is Gor," said Flaminius.

Virginia gasped, drawing back.

"You have heard, as many others," he asked, "of the Counter-Earth?"

"It is only in stories," she said.

Flaminius laughed.

"I read of Gor," said Virginia. "It seemed to me very real."

Flaminius smiled. "In the books of Tarl Cabot you have read of this world."

"They are only stories," said Phyllis numbly.

"There will be no more such stories," said Flaminius.

Virginia looked at him, her eyes wide.

"Tarl Cabot," said he, "was slain in Ko-ro-ba." Flaminius indicated me. "This is Kuurus, who for gold seeks his killer."

"He wears black," said Virginia.

"Of course," said Flaminius.

"You're all mad!" said Phyllis.

"He is of the Caste of Assassins," said Flaminius.

Phyllis screamed and held her head in her hands.

"This is Gor," said Virginia. "Gor."

"Why have we been brought here?" asked Phyllis.

"Strong men," said Flaminius, "have always, even in the course of your own planet's history, taken the females of weaker men for their slaves."

"We are not slaves," said Virginia numbly.

"You are the females of weaker men," said Flaminius, "the men of Earth." He looked at her intently. "We are the stronger," he said. "We have power. We have ships which can traverse space to Earth. We will conquer Earth. It belongs to us. When we wish we bring Earthlings to Gor as our slaves, as was done with you. Earth is a slave world. You are natural slaves. It is important for you to understand that you are natural slaves, that you are inferior, that it is natural and right that you should be the slaves of the men of Gor."

"We are not slaves," said Phyllis.

"Virginia," said Flaminius. "Is what I say not true? Is it not true that the women of weaker, conquered men, if permitted to live, have been kept only as the slaves of the conquerors, permitted to live only that they may serve the pleasures of victorious masters?"

"I teach classics and ancient history," said Virginia, scarcely whispering. "It is true that in much of the history of the Earth the sort of thing you say was done."

"Does it not seem natural?" asked Flaminius.

"Please," she whispered, "let us go."

"You are upset," said Flaminius, "because you deemed yourself superior. Now you find yourself in the position of the female of weaker men, taken as slave." He laughed. "How does it feel?" he asked. "To suddenly understand that you are a natural slave?"

"Please," said Virginia.

"Do not torture her so!" cried Phyllis.

Flaminius turned to Phyllis. "What is the band of steel locked on your left ankle?" he asked.

"I don't know," stammered Phyllis.

"It is the anklet of a slave," said Flaminius. Then he turned again to Virginia, putting his face close to the bars, speaking as though confidentially.

"You are intelligent," he said. "You must know two of the ancient languages of Earth. You are learned. You have studied the history of your world. You have attended important schools. You are perhaps even brilliant."

Virginia looked at him hopelessly.

"Have you not noticed," asked Flaminius, "the men of this world? Do they seem like those of Earth to you?" He pointed to the guard, who was a tall, strong fellow, rather hard-looking. "Does he seem like a man of Earth to you?"

"No," she whispered.

"What in all your femaleness do you sense of the men of this world?" asked Flaminius.

"They are men," she said, in a whisper.

"Unlike those of Earth?" asked Flaminius.

"Yes," said Virginia, "unlike them."

"They are true men, are they not?" asked Flaminius.

"Yes," she said, looking down, confused, "they are true men."

It was interesting to me that Virginia Kent, as a woman, was apparently intensely aware of certain differences between Gorean men and the men of Earth. I suspected that these differences clearly existed, but I would not, as Flaminius seemed to wish, have interpreted these differences as suggesting an inferiority of Earth stock. After all, Gorean males were surely, at one time at any rate, of the same stock as the men of Earth. The differences were surely primarily cultural and not physical or mental. I do think, of course, that the Gorean population tends to be more physically fit and mentally acute than that of Earth, but I would rate them provisionally rather than essentially superior in these respects; for example, Goreans live much out of doors and, as a very natural thing, celebrate the beauty of a healthy, attractive body; further, Goreans tend to come from intelligent, healthy stock, for such was brought over many generations to this world by the Priest-Kings' Voyages of Acquisition, curtailed now, as far as I knew, following the Nest War. The primary differences, I suspect, to which Virginia Kent was reacting, were subtle and psychological. The male of Earth is conditioned to be more timid, vacillating and repressed than the males of Gor; to be subject, to achieve social controls, to guilts and anxieties that would be as incomprehensible to the Gorean male as a guilt over having spoken to one's father-in-law's sister would be to most of the men of Earth. Moreover, the Gorean culture tends, for better or worse, to be male oriented and male dominated, and in such a culture men naturally look on women much differently than they do in a consumer-oriented, woman-dominated culture, one informed by an ethos of substantially feminine values; the women then, in coming to Gor, would naturally sense that they are looked on differently, and it was not improbable to suppose that something in them, submerged and primitive, would tend to respond to this.

"In the presence of such a man," said Flaminius, indicating the guard, "how do you sense yourself?"

"Female," she said, looking down and away.

Flaminius put his hand through the bars, his fingers gently touching her chin and throat as she looked away. Her body tensed, but she did not move. Her cheek was pressed against the bars.

"You wear on your left ankle," said Flaminius, "a locked band of steel."

The girl tried to move her head but could not. A tear coursed down her right cheek, running against the bar.

"What is it?" asked Flaminius.

"It is the anklet of a slave," she said, not facing him.

He turned her head to him. Her eyes, wide with tears, faced his. She regarded him, herself held. "Pretty slave," he said.

"Yes," she said.

"Yes what?" he asked, kindly.

"Yes," she said, "—Master." Then suddenly she cried out and broke free and knelt in the back of the kennel, her face in her hands, weeping.

Flaminius laughed.

"You beast!" cried out the second girl. "You beast!"

Flaminius suddenly reached into the cage and, taking the girl by the wrists, jerked her against the bars, painfully so, holding her at arm's length cruelly against them. "Please," she wept.

"From the time you were first anesthetized and hooded," said Flaminius, "you had but one purpose in life—to give pleasure to men."

"Please," she wept, "please."

"Bracelets," said Flaminius, in Gorean, to the guard, who produced a set of bracelets.

Flaminius then locked one on the girl's right wrist and then, her arms through the bars, bent her arms back, put the other bracelet around one of the bars in the gate, above the horizontal bar at the top of the gate, and, on the outside of the gate, about her other wrist, the left, snapped shut the second bracelet, so that her hands were now braceleted outside the gate, at its top, that she might be, on the inside, held cruelly against the bars. "Please," she wept, "Please."

"It would be pleasant to tame you," said Flaminius.

"Please let me go," she wept.

"But there are other things in store for you, pretty slave."

The girl looked at him, tears in her eyes.

"You will be trained as a slave girl," said Flaminius, "you will be taught to kneel, to stand, to walk, to dance, to sing, to serve the thousand pleasures of men." He laughed. "And when your training is complete you will be placed on a block and sold."

The girl cried out in misery, pressing her head against the bars.

Flaminius then looked into Virginia's eyes. "You, too," said he, "will be trained as a slave girl."

She looked at him, red-eyed.

"Will you train?" asked Flaminius.

"We must do whatever you wish," said Virginia. "We are slaves."

"Will you train?" asked Flaminius of the girl Phyllis, braceleted against the bars.

"What if I do not?" she asked.

"Then you will die," said Flaminius.

The girl closed her eyes.

"Will you train?" asked Flaminius.

"Yes," she said, "I will train."

"Good," said Flaminius. Then he reached into the cage and took her by the hair, twisting it. "Do you beg to be trained as a slave girl?" he asked.

"Yes," she said, in pain, "yes!"

"Yes what?" inquired the Physician.

"Yes," she said, weeping, "—Master!"

Flaminius then stood up and faced us. He was instantly again the Physician, cool and professional. He regarded Ho-Tu and spoke in Gorean, swiftly. "They are both interesting girls," he said. "They resemble one another in several ways and yet each is quite different. The results of the tests I have just conducted are quite affirmative, much better than merely satisfactory, decidedly promising."

"How will they train?" asked Ho-Tu.

"It is impossible to tell," said Flaminius, "but my prognosis is that each, in her own way, will do quite well in training. I do not think drugs will be necessary, and I expect that a sparing use of the whip and slave goad will be sufficient. My prognosis is on the whole extremely favorable. Excellent merchandise, some risk, but every likelihood of achieving a status of considerable value. In short I think they are both decidedly worth development, and should prove a quite profitable investment."

"They are, however, barbarians," pointed out Ho-Tu.

"That is true," said Flaminius, "and doubtless they will always be barbarians—but that quality, for some buyers, may exercise its own fascination."

"That is the hope of Cernus," said Ho-Tu.

Flaminius smiled. "Few of the hopes of Cernus are disappointed," he said.

Ho-Tu grinned. "That is true," he said.

"If there is a demand for such girls," said Flaminius, "our house will profit handsomely indeed."

Ho-Tu slapped his thigh. "Cernus will see," said he, "that there is such a demand."

Flaminius shrugged. "I do not doubt it," he said.

I regarded the girls, piteous in their cages.

Virginia, her face stained with tears, knelt at the bars, looking up at us, holding them. Phyllis, on her knees, her wrists braceleted outside the cage, held pressed against the bars, looked at us and then turned her face away.

"I promise you, Ho-Tu," Flaminius was saying, "that each of these girls, properly trained, will provide a master with the most exquisite of delights."

I was pleased that neither of the girls understood Gorean. I suspected that what Flaminius said was true. The Gorean slaver knows his business. Both girls, I expected, would be trained as exquisite female slaves.

We then, following Ho-Tu, retraced our steps on the iron walkway, descended the steps, and, taking our way between the metal branding rack and the glowing, perforated steel drum containing irons, left the room. As we left I could hear one of the girls weeping. I did not, of course, turn back to see which one it might be.

Twelve

The Peasant

The shrill pain scream of the racing tarn pierced the roar of the frenzied crowd.

"Blue! Blue!" screamed the man next to me, a blue patch sewn on his left shoulder, a pair of glazed blue clay plates clutched in his right hand.

The tarn, screaming, its wing useless, tumbled uncontrollably from the edge of the large, open, padded ring suspended over the net on the track, plunging into the net, its rider cutting the safety straps and leaping from its back in order that he not be slain beneath the bird struggling in the net.

The other bird, which had buffeted it against the edge of the ring, spun awkwardly through, turned in the air, and under the savage command of its control straps, and responding to a yellow flash of the tarn goad, regained its control and sped toward the next ring.

"Red! Red! Red!" I heard from nearby.

The next seven tarns, strung out, sped through the ring and wheeled in flight to take the next ring. Their leader was a brown racing tarn, whose rider wore red silk, and whose small saddle and tight control straps were of red leather.

This was only the third lap in a ten-lap race, and yet already two tarns were down in the net. I could see the netmen expertly moving across the broad stands approaching them, loops in their hands to tie together the bird's beak, to bind its curved, wicked talons. The wing of one bird was apparently broken, for the netmen, after binding it, quickly cut its throat, the blood falling through the net, staining it, soaking into the sand below in a brownish red patch. Its rider took the saddle and control straps from the still-quivering bird and dropped

129

with them through the broad strands of the net, to the sand some six feet below. The other bird was apparently only stunned, and it was being rolled to the edge of the net where it would be dropped into a large wheeled frame, drawn by two horned tharlarion, onto a suspended canvas, where it was immediately secured by broad canvas straps.

"Gold! Gold!" cried a man two tiers away from me. Already the birds had turned the twelve-ring track and were again approaching. A bird of the Yellow faction was in the lead, followed by Red, then Blue, Gold, Orange, Green and Silver.

In the crowd I heard the shrill screams of slave girls and free women alike, the differences between them lost in the moment of their excitement. During the time of the race the hawkers of candies, sweetmeats, Kal-da, pastries and paga were quiet, standing with their goods in the aisles watching. Many of them, too, were much involved in the race, for concealed in their trays or about their persons were doubtless the glazed clay tablets, purchased from the track merchants, redeemable at odds should their favorites finish in one of the four privileged positions.

The birds swept past us again. "Oh Priest-Kings," cried a man nearby, a Leather Worker, "speed the wings of red!" Everyone in the crowd seemed to be on their feet, even those who sat in the marbled tiers beneath the awnings of purple silk. I rose also that I might see. Near the finishing perches, nine of which were standing for this race, were the areas reserved for the Administrator, the High Initiate, and members of the High Council. These areas were almost porches, extending beyond the regular stands, covered with awnings, on which were mounted sets of curule chairs, at different levels. Flanked by two guards, in the red of Warriors, I could see the throne of the Administrator, on which, intent, leaning forward, sat the member of the Hinrabian family who now stood highest in Ar. Nearby, but lofty, as though disinterested, on a throne of white marble, but between two Warriors as well, sat the High Initiate. Before him sat two rows of Initiates, who were intoning prayers to the Priest-Kings, not watching the race.

I noted that a green banner hung over the wall before both the thrones of the Administrator and the High Initiate, indicating they favored the greens.

The Warriors who flanked the Administrator and High Initiate, incidentally, were Taurentians, members of the palace guard, an elite corps of swordsmen and bowmen, carefully selected, specially trained, independent of the general military organizations of the city. Their leader, or Captain, was Saphronicus, a mercenary from Tyros. I could see him a few feet behind the throne, wrapped in a scarlet cloak, a tall, spare man, long-armed and narrow-faced, whose head moved restlessly, surveying the crowd.

There were other favored areas, too, about the stands, in the front, each covered by awnings, in which there sat members of the numerous high families of the city; I noted that some of these areas were now occupied by Merchants; I had no objection to this for I have always thought higher of the Merchants than many of my caste, but I was surprised; in the time of Marlenus, when he was Ubar of Ar, I think even his friend, Mintar, that great brilliant toad of a man, of the Caste of Merchants, would not have had so choice a vantage point from which to observe the races.

Across the track, on the far side, I heard a judge's bar clang indicating that one of the birds had missed a ring, and a colored disk, silver, was hauled to the top of a pole. There was a groan from many in the crowd and others cried out with delight. The rider was wheeling the bird, trying to bring it under control, and returning to the ring. By this time the other birds had flashed through it.

Below me I saw a hawker of sweetmeats angrily discarding four silver-glazed, numbered clay tiles.

The birds were now flashing through the great rings before me.

Yellow held the lead, followed by Red. Green had now moved up to third.

"Green! Green!" a woman was crying out, not far from me, her veil awry, her fists clenched.

The Administrator leaned forward even more on his throne. He was said to wager heavily on the races.

On the low wall, some seven or eight feet in height, some forty feet in width, which divided the track, I could see that only three of the great wooden tarn heads remained on their poles, indicating that only three laps remained in the race.

In a few moments, with a cry of victory, the rider of the Yellow brought his tarn to the first perch, followed closely by the Red and the

Green. Then, one after another, Gold, Blue, Orange and Silver took their perches. The last two perches remained empty.

I looked to the area of the Administrator and saw the Hinrabian disgustedly turning away, dictating something to a scribe, who sat cross-legged near the throne, a sheaf of record papers in his hand. The High Initiate had risen to his feet and accepted a goblet from another Initiate, probably containing minced, flavored ices, for the afternoon was warm.

The crowd was now engaged in various pursuits, no fixed center now holding their attention. Several were going about seeking the odds Merchants, several of whom wandered in the stands, but others of whom kept their tables at the foot of the stands, on the sand itself, almost under the nets beneath the rings. The hawkers of candies and such were now crying their wares. I heard a slave girl wheedling her master for a pastry. Free women, here and there, were delicately putting tidbits beneath their veils. Some even lifted their veils somewhat to drink of the flavored ices. Some low-caste free women drank through their veils, and there were yellow and purple stains on the rep-cloth.

I heard a judge's bar sound twice, indicating that the next race would begin in ten Ehn.

There was some scurrying about to find the odds Merchants.

Almost everyone in the crowd wore some indication of the faction he favored. Generally, it was a small faction patch sewn on the left shoulder; the faction patches of the High-Caste women tended to be fine silk, and tastefully done; those of low-caste women merely a square of crudely stitched, dyed rep-cloth; some of the masters had dressed their slave girls in slave livery of the color of the faction they favored; others had twined a colored ribbon about their hair or in their collar.

"The races were better in the days of Marlenus of Ar," said a man behind me, leaning forward to speak to me.

I shrugged. I did not find it strange that he had spoken to me. When I had left the House of Cernus I had removed the livery of the black caste and had washed the sign of the dagger from my forehead. I wore a worn, red tunic, that of a Warrior. It was thus easier for me to move about the city. I would not be likely to be noticed, or feared. Men would more willingly speak to me.

"But," said the man glumly, "what can you expect with a Hinrabian on the throne of the Ubar."

"On the throne of the Administrator," said I, not turning about.

"There is only one who is first in Ar," said the man. "Marlenus, who was Ubar of Ar, he, the Ubar of Ubars."

"I would not speak so," I said. "There are those who might not care to hear such words."

I heard the man make a noise of amusement and lean back.

Marlenus, who had been Ubar of Ar many years ago, had founded the Empire of Ar, and had extended the hegemony of luxurious Ar over several of the cities of the north. He had fallen when I had purloined the Home Stone of the city. Later he had helped to free Ar after it had fallen to the horde of Pa-Kur, master of the Assassins, who had wished to become Ubar of the City, inheriting the medallion of office and putting about his shoulders the purple cloak of empire. Marlenus, because he had lost the Home Stone and because the men of Ar feared him and his ambitions, had been publicly denied bread, salt and fire, exiled from the city and forbidden to return on pain of death. He had become an outlaw in the Voltai, whence he could see, with loyal followers, the spires of Ar, Glorious Ar where once he had ruled as Ubar. I knew that there were many in Ar who had not wished for the exile of Marlenus, particularly the lower castes, which he had always championed. Kazrak, who had been Administrator of the City for several years, had been popular but his straightforward attention, after he had put aside the Red of the Warrior and donned the Brown of the Administrator, to numerous and complex civil and economic matters, such as reform of the courts and laws and controls and regulations pertaining to commerce, had not been such as to inspire the general enthusiasm of the common citizens of Ar, in particular those who remembered with nostalgia the glories and splendors of the reign of Marlenus, that larl of a man, that magnificent Warrior, vain and self-centered, powerful, conceited, yet a dreamer of dreams, of a world undivided and safe for men, a world united, be it at the point of the swords of Ar. I remembered Marlenus. He had been such that standing before men and lifting his hand, a thousand swords would be unsheathed in the sun, a thousand throats would cry his name, a thousand men would march or a thousand tarns would fly. Such a man needed to be exiled from Ar. Such a man could never be second in a city.

I heard the judge's bar ring three times and I could now see the tarns coming forth. There was a cry of expectancy from the crowd. Last-minute bets were being placed. Cushions were being rearranged.

Eight tarns were flying in this race, and, hooded, they were brought forth on low, sideless wheeled platforms, drawn by horned tharlarion. The carts were painted in faction colors. The rider rode on the cart beside his bird, dressed in the silk of his faction.

The tarns were, of course, racing tarns, a bird in many ways quite different from the common tarns of Gor, or the war tarns. The differences among these tarns are not simply in the training, which does differ, but in the size, strength, build and tendencies of the bird. Some tarns are bred primarily for strength and are used in transporting wares by carrying basket. Usually these birds fly more slowly and are less vicious than the war tarns or racing tarns. The war tarns, of course, are bred for both strength and speed, but also for agility, swiftness of reflex, and combative instincts. War tarns, whose talons are shod with steel, tend to be extremely dangerous birds, even more so than other tarns, none of whom could be regarded as fully domesticated. The racing tarn, interestingly, is an extremely light bird; two men can lift one; even its beak is narrower and lighter than the beak of a common tarn or a war tarn; its wings are commonly broader and shorter than those of the other tarns, permitting a swifter takeoff and providing a capacity for extremely abrupt turns and shifts in flight; they cannot carry a great deal of weight and the riders, as might be expected, are small men, usually of low caste, pugnacious and aggressive. Racing tarns are not used by tarnsmen in war because they lack the weight and power of war tarns; meeting a war tarn in flight, a racing tarn would be torn to pieces in moments; further, the racing tarns, though marvelous in their particular ways, lack the stamina of the common tarn or the war tarn; their short wings, after a flight of perhaps only fifty pasangs, would begin to fail; in a short-distance dash, of course, the racing tarn would commonly be superior to the war tarn.

The tarns were now being unhooded and they leaped up, with a snap of their wings, to their perches, numbered and chosen by lot. Possession of the inside perch is regarded, of course, as an advantage. I noted Green had the inside perch this race. This would swing some silver to Green surely, for men, though they have their factions, yet will purchase the tiles of the bird they feel has the best chance of winning. The same perches that are used in starting the race, incidentally, are the perches which the tarns will take after the race. The winning perch, or the first perch after the race, is that closest to the stands, rather than that closest to the dividing wall, the inside perch, which is first with respect to the beginning of the race, most desirable at the beginning, least desirable at the end.

I noted that two of the tarns in this race were not of given factions, but were the property of private owners, not associated with the faction corporations; their riders, similarly, were not faction riders; the rider, incidentally, is quite as important as the bird, for an experienced rider often manages to bring a new bird to the first perch, whereas even a fine bird, controlled poorly or timidly, is likely to be far outdone.

"Candies!" whined a small voice some yards below me. "Candies!"

I looked down and was startled to see, some four tiers below, not seeing me, the pathetic, stubby, bulbous little body of Hup the Fool, limping and hopping about in the aisle, his large head on the fat little body lolling one way or another, the tongue occasionally, suddenly, unexpectedly, protruding uncontrollably. His knobby hands were clutching a candy tray which was fastened behind his neck with a strap. "Candies!" he whined. "Candies!"

Many of the people he passed turned away. The free women drew their hoods about their faces. Some of the men angrily gestured for the little fool to hurry from their area, lest he spoil the races for their women. I did note that a young slave girl, however, perhaps about fifteen, with a coin given her by her master, did purchase a small candy from the little Hup. I might have bought some myself but I did not wish him to recognize me, assuming that his simple mind might hold the remembrance of our first meeting, that at the tavern of Spindius, where I had saved his life.

"Candies!" called the little fellow. "Candies!"

I supposed Hup, though he doubtless spent much of his time begging, made what money he could, and vending candies at the races might help him to live. I wondered if the golden tarn disk, that of

Portus, which I had given to him at the tavern had been used to buy a vending license.

"I think I shall have a candy," said the man behind me.

I arose and turned away, leaving my place on the tier, that I might not be seen by Hup, should he approach the man. I looked neither to the left or right, but moved away.

"Candy!" called the man behind me.

"Yes, Master!" I heard Hup call and begin to make his way toward the man.

I found a seat several yards away, and, after a bit, noted Hup making his way down another aisle in the opposite direction.

"What is your faction?" asked the fellow whom I had sat down beside, a Metal Worker.

"I favor the Greens," I said, saying the first thing that came into my mind.

"I'm a Gold myself," he said. He wore a patch of golden cloth on his left shoulder.

The judge's bar rang once and there was a cry from the crowd and all leaped to their feet as, with a flurry of beating wings, almost at the instant the white cord was whipped away from in front of them, the tarns took flight.

The Green, which had had the inside perch, took the lead.

The track flown by the tarns is one pasang in length. In English measure the two sides of the track are each about seventeen hundred feet in length, and the measure at the corners would be something under a hundred and fifty feet in width. The flight track itself, of course, is rather like a narrow, aerial rectangle with two rounded ends. The course is determined by twelve rings, hung on chains from great supporting towers; six of these "rings" are rectangular and six are round; the large rectangular "rings" are three on a side; the smaller, round rings are set at the corners of the dividing wall, and one at each of the narrowest portions of the dividing wall. Thus, in leaving the perches at the beginning of the race, the tarns pass first through three rectangular "rings," then come to the first turn, where they negotiate three round rings, two of which are at the corners; and then they encounter three more rectangular "rings" and then come to the second turn, where they again encounter three round rings, two at the corners and one in the center; skill is required in flying such a course, particularly in making the turns and passing through the small round rings. If four tarns were flown perfectly, one above, one below, and one on each side, four could just pass through one of the round rings; one of the objects of course is to maneuver the tarn in such a way that it takes the center of the ring, or forces the following bird to strike the ring or miss it altogether; I doubt that this fierce form of racing would be practical were it not for the almost uncanny agility in flight of the short-winged racing tarns.

This race was a short one, only five pasangs in length, and one of the nonfaction birds won, much to the displeasure of the crowd, saving those who had dared to accept the long odds on such a bird.

One man near me had apparently been one of the lucky few for he was leaping up and down screaming with delight. Then, stumbling, and brushing through spectators, few of whom shared his pleasure, he was making his way down to the tables of the odds Merchants.

I noted that Minus Tentius Hinrabius now chose to leave the races. He did so, irritation in his every movement, followed by his guards, Saphronicus, the Captain of the guards, and the rest of his retinue. To my surprise hardly anyone in the stands even noted his going.

There were various races to follow but the afternoon sun was now below the roof of the central cylinder in the distance and I decided to leave the races.

As I did so I passed several chained slave girls kneeling on a stone tier. They were doubtless girls in training, and reasonably well advanced in training. They had been brought to see the races, that they might be pleased and stimulated, that they might return to their training refreshed and recreated. They were clearly enjoying themselves, and some were making bets, the stakes being pleasure beads from the contents of the jewelry and cosmetic box allotted to each, usually kept in her cell. They were fastened together on a common chain, each by wrist rings, each by both wrists, each ring separated by about a yard of chain. As they knelt the chain was over their calves, behind their backs. At each end of the line there was a guard. The slaves wore light, hooded cloaks, the length of which, when they stood, would fall slightly above the hem of their brief slave livery. The garments had rather large sleeves and fastened with a cord under the chin. It protected them from the sun to some extent but even more from the glances of the curious. Some of the girls, judging by the stripes on the hoods and cloaks, were White Silk, and others Red Silk. The White Silk Girls, of course, having been released from the house, would have been placed in locked, iron belts. The girls were neither of the House of Cernus nor of Portus, but of one of the several lesser houses on the Street of Brands.

I heard the judge's bar ring twice, informing the crowd that the next race would begin in ten Ehn.

I rose from my seat and began to make my way to the exit. Some of the spectators looked at me with ill-concealed reproach, even something amounting to disdain. The racing fan of Ar commonly remains to the last race, and sometimes even later, discussing the races and commenting on how he would have flown such and such a race better than the bird's rider. I did not even wear a faction patch.

It was my intention to relax at the Capacian Baths, have a leisurely supper at some paga tavern and then return to the House of Cernus. There was a little wench named Nela, usually in the Pool of Blue Flowers, whom I enjoyed sporting with. By the time I returned to the House of Cernus Elizabeth would have finished her slave porridge and be in the compartment, and I would hear about her day, and she would hear about mine, or most of it. When she was permitted, later in her training, to leave the house more often, I was eager to take her to the races and the baths, though perhaps not to the Pool of Blue Flowers.

It was now some twenty days after the girls had been brought in from the Voltai. Yet Elizabeth, and the two others, Virginia and Phyllis, had only been in training for five days. This had to do with certain decisions of Flaminius and Ho-Tu, and the two girls Virginia and Phyllis. I myself had been there that night that both, interrogated in their cages, had agreed to train as slave girls. I would have expected their training to have begun immediately. But it had not.

For about fifteen days Virginia and Phyllis, while the other captive Earth girls had been removed to an iron pen, remained in the tiny cement, iron-gated cages, so constructed that the inmate cannot at any one time fully stretch her body; over a period of time this builds up a considerable amount of body pain; and Phyllis, on the instructions of Flaminius, was further tormented in being braceleted to the bars, as she had been the first night, for several Ahn a day, being fed her gruel by hand, taking her water from a tin bottle thrust between her lips.

At last even Phyllis had asked again and again, irrationally, the guard not even understanding English, if they were truly to be trained. This question, insistently and irrationally pressed, received no answer. The guard, under instructions, did not even address a word in Gorean to them. In so far as was possible he ignored them. They were fed and watered as animals, which in Gorean eyes, being slaves, they were. Flaminius would not visit them. For days they remained in the cages, cramped and miserable, alone, neglected, apparently overlooked, forgotten. They came to look eagerly for the sound of the bolt on the door. At last Flaminius visited them, informing them that they were not to be trained, and left. Both at this point had become hysterical. The next day Flaminius reentered the chamber, but apparently only to pick up some records which he had left behind the day before. Piteously, hysterically, they had cried out to him, begging to be taken from the cages, begging to be trained. Flaminius, apparently moved by their entreaties, told them he would speak to Cernus, master of the house, and to Ho-Tu, Master Keeper. He did not return until late the next day when the girls, with tears of relief, heard that Cernus, who was moved to kindness, would permit them an opportunity to train; they were sternly warned, however, that if their training did not proceed well, they would be promptly returned to the kennels. Flaminius then accepted their tearful gratitude for his intercession on their behalf.

Since Elizabeth was to be the lead girl in the set she was summoned to the kennel chamber when Virginia and Phyllis were to be released. I accompanied her. When the small iron gates were raised, the guard with a whip standing over them, Virginia and Phyllis crawled painfully out onto the iron walkway. They could not stand. The guard braceleted one of Phyllis' wrists to the rail and then snapped bracelets on Virginia, confining her wrists behind her back; he carried Virginia down to the main level and set her on her knees there, before Flaminius and Ho-Tu; Elizabeth and I were in the background; then the guard went back up to the walkway, freed Phyllis only to bracelet her hands behind her back, as he had done with Virginia, and then he carried her, too, down the iron stairs and placed her beside Virginia. He shoved the heads of both to the stones of the floor.

"Is the iron ready?" asked Ho-Tu of the guard, and the man nodded.

At a signal from Ho-Tu the guard carried Virginia to the branding rack and placed her in the rack, spinning the lever that locked her thigh in place. She said nothing but stood there, wrists braceleted behind her back, locked in place, watching the approach of the iron, observing the graceful, white-hot character at the iron's termination; she screamed uncontrollably when the iron marked her, firmly, decisively for about three Ihn; and then she sobbed, beside herself, while the guard spun the lever releasing her; he lifted her from the rack and put her on the stones at the feet of Ho-Tu and Flaminius; Phyllis' eyes were wild with fear, but she, like Virginia, did not so much as whimper as the guard lifted her, carried her to the rack and locked her in place.

"We still do hand branding," said Ho-Tu to me. "Mechanical devices brand too uniformly. Buyers like a hand-branded girl. Besides it is better for a female slave to be branded by a man; it makes them better slaves. The rack, however, is a useful device, preventing a blurred brand." He indicated the guard. "Strius," said he, "has one of the finest irons in Ar. His work is almost always exact and clean."

Phyllis Robertson threw back her head and screamed helplessly, and then she, too, began to sob, trembling, when the guard, Strius, released her from the rack and put her with Virginia.

Both girls were weeping.

Flaminius, gently, stretched out their legs, and rubbed them. I'm sure, in the pain of branding, they scarcely felt the pain which might be attendant on his massage, trying to restore some feeling and strength to their aching limbs.

I heard a woman moving close to me, heard the sound of slave bells.

I looked to one side and was startled. Watching us was a woman in Pleasure Silk, of remarkable beauty, yet with a certain subtle hardness and contempt about her. She wore a yellow collar, that of the House of Cernus, and yellow Pleasure Silk. The slave bells, a double row, were locked on her left ankle. About her throat there hung a slave whistle. From her right hand, looped about the wrist, there dangled a slave goad. She was fairly complected but had extremely dark hair and dark eyes, very red lips; the movement of her exquisite body was a torment to observe; she looked at me with a slight smile, regarding the black of the tunic, the mark of the dagger; her lips were full and magnificently turned, probably a characteristic bred into her; I had no doubt this black-haired, cruelly beautiful woman was a bred Passion Slave. She was one of the most rawly sensuous creatures on which I had ever looked.

"I am Sura," she said, looking at me, "I teach girls to give pleasure to men."

"These are the three," said Ho-Tu, indicating the two branded girls, and Elizabeth.

Flaminius rose to his feet, leaving the two girls lying on the stones, sobbing.

"Kneel," said Sura to the girls, in Gorean.

"Kneel," said Flaminius to them, in English.

The two girls, freshly branded, tears in their eyes, struggled to their knees.

Sura walked around them, and then she regarded Elizabeth. "Take off your clothes," she said.

Elizabeth did so, drawing at the loop on the left shoulder of her garment.

"Join them," ordered Sura, and Elizabeth went to kneel between Virginia and Phyllis.

"Bracelet her," said Sura, and the guard snapped slave bracelets on Elizabeth, confining her hands behind her back, like the other girls.

"You are lead girl?" asked Sura of Elizabeth.

"Yes," said Elizabeth.

Sura's finger flicked the slave goad on. She rotated the dial. The tip began to glow, a bright yellow.

"Yes, Mistress," said Elizabeth.

"You are barbarian?" asked Sura.

"Yes, Mistress," said Elizabeth.

Sura spat on the stones before Elizabeth.

"They are all barbarians," said Ho-Tu.

Sura turned about and looked at him with disgust. "How does Cernus expect me to train barbarians?" she asked.

Ho-Tu shrugged.

"Do what you can," said Flaminius. "These are all intelligent slaves. They all have promise."

"You know nothing of such matters," said Sura.

Flaminius looked down, angry.

141

Sura walked over to the girls, lifted Virginia's head and looked into her eyes, and then stepped back. "Her face is too thin," she said, "and there are blemishes, and she is thin, too thin."

Ho-Tu shrugged.

Sura looked at Elizabeth. "This one," she said, "was Tuchuk. She will know nothing except the care of bosk and the cleaning of leather."

Elizabeth, wisely, refrained from response.

"Now this one," said Sura, examining Phyllis, "has a slave's body, but how does she move? I have seen these barbarians. They cannot even stand straight. They cannot even walk."

"Do what you can," said Flaminius.

"It is hopeless," said Sura, stepping back to us. "Nothing can be done for them. Sell them off a minor block and be done with it. They are kettle girls, only that." Sura dialed the slave goad down, and then switched it off.

"Sura," said Flaminius.

"Kettle girls," snapped Sura.

Ho-Tu shook his head. "Sura is right," he said, rather too agreeably. "They are only kettle girls."

"But," protested Flaminius.

"Kettle girls," insisted Ho-Tu.

Sura laughed in triumph.

"No one could do anything with such barbarians," said Ho-Tu to Flaminius. "Not even Sura."

Something about the back of Sura's neck informed me she had noted what Ho-Tu had said and hadn't cared for the sound of it.

I saw Ho-Tu grimace at Flaminius.

A smile broke out on the Physician's face. "You're right," he said, "no one could do anything with such barbarians. They could not be trained by anyone, except perhaps Tethrite of the House of Portus."

"I had forgotten about her," said Ho-Tu.

"Tethrite is an ignorant she-tharlarion," said Sura irritably.

"She is the best trainer in Ar," said Ho-Tu.

"I, Sura, am the best in Ar," said the girl, not pleasantly.

"Of course," said Ho-Tu to Sura.

"Besides," said Flaminius to Ho-Tu, "even Tethrite of the House of Portus could not train such barbarians."

Sura was now inspecting the girls more closely. She had pushed one thumb under Virginia's head. "Do not be frightened, little bird," said Sura soothingly in Gorean to Virginia. Sura removed her thumb and Virginia kept her fine head on its delicate neck high. "Some men might like a thin, pocked face," said Sura. "And her eyes, the gray, that is very good." Sura looked at Elizabeth. "You are probably the stupid one," she said.

"I scarcely think so," said Elizabeth, adding acidly, "Mistress."

"Good," said Sura to herself, "good."

"And you," she said to Phyllis, "you with the body of a Passion Slave, what of you?" Sura then took the slave goad, which was off, and moved it along the left side of Phyllis' body, touching her with the cold metal. Instinctively, even in her pain from the branding and with her aching limbs, Phyllis made a small noise and pulled away from the cold metal. The movement of her shoulders and belly was noted by Sura. She stood up, and again the slave goad dangled from her right wrist.

She indicated Virginia and Phyllis. "How do you expect me to train uncollared slaves?" she asked.

Ho-Tu grinned. "Call the smith!" said he to the guard. "Plate collars!"

To their surprise, the guard then released the two girls, and Elizabeth, as well, from their slave bracelets.

Flaminius gestured that the two girls should try to rise and walk a bit about the room.

Awkwardly, painfully, they did so, stumbling to the edge of the room, then leaning against the wall, taking a step at a time. Elizabeth, now also free, went to their side, trying to help them. She did not speak to them, however. As far as they knew she could speak only Gorean.

When the smith arrived, he took, from a rack in the wall, two narrow, straight bars of iron, not really plates but narrow cubes, about a half inch in width and fifteen inches in length.

The girls were then motioned to the anvil. First Virginia and then Phyllis laid their heads and throats on the anvil, head turned to the side, their hands holding the anvil, and the smith, expertly, with his heavy hammer and a ringing of iron, curved the collar about their throats; a space of about a quarter of an inch was left between the two ends of the collar; the ends matched perfectly; both Virginia and Phyllis stepped away from the anvil feeling the metal on their throats, both now collared slave girls.

"If your training goes well," said Flaminius to the girls, "you will in time be given a pretty collar." He indicated Elizabeth's yellow enameled collar, bearing the legend of the House of Cernus. "It will even have a lock," said Flaminius.

Virginia looked at him blankly.

"You would like a pretty collar, wouldn't you?" asked Flaminius.

"Yes, Master," said Virginia numbly.

"And what of you, Phyllis?" asked Flaminius.

"Yes, Master," said the girl, a whisper.

"I will decide if and when they receive a lock collar," said Sura.

"Of course," said Flaminius, backing away a step, bowing his head.

"Kneel," said Sura, pointing to the stones before her feet.

This time Virginia and Phyllis needed no translation, and they, with Elizabeth, knelt before Sura.

Sura turned to Ho-Tu. "The Tuchuk girl," she said, "keeps quarters with the Assassin. I do not object. Take the others to cells of Red Silk."

"They are White Silk," said Ho-Tu.

Sura laughed. "Very well," she said, "to cells of White Silk. Feed them well. You have almost crippled them. How you expect me to train crippled barbarians I am not clear."

"You will do splendidly," said Flaminius warmly.

Sura glared at him, coldly, and the Physician dropped his eyes.

"In the first weeks," she said, "I will also need one who speaks their tongue. Further, when not in training, they must learn Gorean, and quickly."

"I will send one who speaks their tongue," said Flaminius. "Also I will arrange that they are taught Gorean."

"Translate for me," said Sura, to Flaminius, as she turned and faced the three kneeling girls.

She then spoke to them in short sentences, pausing for Flaminius to translate.

"I am Sura," she said. "I will train you. In the hours of training you are my slaves. You will do what I wish. You will work. You will work and you will learn. You will be pleasing. I will teach you. You will work and you will learn."

Then she looked at them. "Fear me," she said. Flaminius translated this, as well.

Then without speaking she flicked on the slave goad and rotated the dial. The tip began to glow brightly. Then suddenly she struck at the three kneeling girls. The charge must have been high, judging by the intense shower of fiery yellow needles of light and the screams of pain from the three girls. Again and again Sura struck and the girls, half stunned, half crazed with pain, seemed unable to even move, but could only scream and cry. Even Elizabeth, whom I knew was swift and spirited, seemed paralyzed and tortured by the goad. Then Sura dialed the goad down, and turned it off. The three girls lying in pain on the stones looked up at her in fear, even the proud Elizabeth, their bodies trembling, their eyes wide. I read in their eyes, even those of Elizabeth, a sudden terror of the goad.

"Fear me," said Sura softly. Flaminius translated. Then Sura turned to Flaminius. "Have them sent to my training room at the sixth Ahn," she said, and turned, and walked away, the slave bells flashing on her ankle.

* * * *

I left the tiers of the racing stadium and began to walk down the long, sloping stone ramp, level by level. There were few leaving the races but I did pass some late comers, moving up the ramps, who had perhaps been detained or had been released from their shops only late in the day. At one corner in the descending ramp there was a small knot of young men, weavers by their garments, who were gambling with the inked knucklebones of verr, shaking them in a small leather cup and spilling them to the stones. On the ground level, beneath the lofty stands, there was much more life. Here there were lines of booths in an extended arcade, where merchandise of various sorts might be purchased, usually of an inexpensive and low-quality variety. There were poorly webbed, small tapestries; amulets and talismans; knotted prayer strings; papers containing praises of Priest- Kings, which might be carried on one's person; numerous ornaments of glass and cheap metal; the strung pearls of the Vosk sorp; polished, shell brooches; pins with heads carved from the horn of kailiauk tridents; lucky sleen teeth; racks of rep-cloth robes, veils and tunics in various caste colors; cheap knives and belts and pouches; vials containing perfumes, for which extraordinary claims were made; and small clay, painted replicas of the stadium and racing tarns. I also saw a booth where sandals were sold, cheap and poorly sewn, which the seller was proclaiming were of the same sort as those worn by Menicius of Port Kar. He, riding Yellow, had won one of the races I had just witnessed. He claimed over six thousand wins and was, in Ar and certain of the northern cities generally, a quite popular hero; he was said in private life to be cruel and dissolute, venal and petty, but when he climbed to the saddle of a racing tarn there were few who did not thrill to the sight; it was said no man could ride as Menicius of Port Kar. The sandals, I noted, were selling quite well.

I was approached twice by men who had small scrolls to sell, reputedly containing important information on forthcoming races, the tarns to be flown, their riders, their times recorded in previous races and such; I supposed this would be little more than what was publicly available on the large track boards, and was copied from them; on the other hand, such men always claimed to have important information not contained on the public boards. I knew that when there was such information it would not be to such men that it would be known. "I am lonely," said a kneeling slave girl by one of the booths, lifting her hands to me. I looked at her, a comely wench in soiled Pleasure Silk. She was leashed and her master, who wished to rent her for the quarter Ahn, held the chain with its leather loop wound in his fist. "Use her," said he, "the poor wench is lonely, only a copper tarn disk." I turned and, pressing through the crowd, walked away.

As I was passing under the main arch of the stadium, going to the broad street beyond, called The Street of Tarns because of its proximity to the stadium, I heard a voice behind me. "Perhaps you did not enjoy the races?"

It was the voice of the man who had sat behind me in the tiers, before I had changed my seat to avoid recognition by the small fool Hup, he who had spoken poorly of the Hinrabian on the throne of Ar, and who had purchased a candy from the fool.

It struck me that there was something familiar about the voice.

I turned.

Facing me, clean-shaven, but with a massive, regal face concealed in the hood of a peasant, his gigantic body broad and powerful in the coarse rep-cloth garment of what is thought to be Gor's lowest caste, there stood a man whom I could not mistake, even though it had been years since I had looked upon him, even though his great beard was now gone, even though his body now wore the hood and garment of a peasant. In his right hand there was a heavy peasant staff, some six feet in height and perhaps two inches in width.

The man smiled at me, and turned away.

I reached out and began to walk after him but I stumbled into the body of Hup the Fool, spilling his tray of candies. "Oh, oh, oh!" cried the fool in misery. Angrily I tried to step about him, but then there were others pressing between myself and the large man in the peasant's garments, and he had disappeared. I ran after him but could not find him in the crowd.

Hup hobbled angrily after me, jerking on my tunic. "Pay! Pay!" he whined.

I looked down at him and I saw, in those wide, simple eyes, of uneven size, no recognition. His poor mind could not even recall the face of the man who had saved his life. Irritably I gave him a silver forty-piece, far more than enough to pay for the spilled candies, and strode away. "Thank you, Master," whined the fool, leaping about from one foot to the other. "Thank you, Master!"

My mind was reeling. What did it mean, I asked myself, that he was in Ar?

I strode away from the stadium, my mind confused, unsettled, breathing deeply, wildly.

There had been no mistaking the man in the garments of a peasant, he with the great staff.

I had seen Marlenus of Ar.

Thirteen

Mip

"I do not see how it could have happened," Nela was saying, bending over me as I lay sleepily on my stomach on the heavy striped piece of toweling, about the size of a blanket, her strong, dutiful hands rubbing the oils of the bath into my body.

"The daughter of Minus Tentius Hinrabius, if none other," said she, "should be safe."

I grunted, not too concerned.

Nela, like most of the others at the baths, could talk of little but the startling disappearance, and presumed abduction, of Claudia Tentia Hinrabia, the proud, spoiled daughter of the Administrator of the City. It seemed she had vanished from the central cylinder, in those portions of it devoted to the private quarters of the Administrator and his family and closer associates, almost under the very noses of Taurentian guardsmen. Saphronicus, Captain of the Taurentians, was reportedly, and understandably, beside himself with frustration and rage. He was organizing searches of the entire city and surrounding countryside, and gathering all possible reports which might bear on the case. The Administrator himself, with his consort, and many others of the high family, had locked themselves in their quarters, secluding themselves in their outrage and sorrow. The entire city was humming with the news and a hundred rumors ran rampant through the alleys and streets and on the bridges of Glorious Ar. On the roof of the Cylinder of Initiates the High Initiate, Complicius Serenus, offered sacrifices and prayers for the speedy return of the girl and, failing that, that she might be found slain, that she might not be reduced to the shames of slavery.

"Not so hard," I murmured to Nela.

"Yes, Master," she responded.

I supposed it quite probable that Claudia Hinrabia had been abducted, though it would not be the only possible explanation for her absence. The institution of capture is universal, to the best of my knowledge, on Gor; there is no city which does not honor it, provided the females captured are those of the enemy, either their free women or their slaves; it is often a young tarnsman's first mission, the securing of a female, preferably free, from an enemy city, to enslave, that his sisters may be relieved of the burden of serving him; indeed, his sisters often encourage him to be prompt in the capture of an enemy wench that their own tasks may be made the lighter; when the young tarnsman, if successful, returns home from his capture flight, a girl bound naked across the saddle, his sisters welcome her with delight, and with great enthusiasm prepare her for the Feast of Collaring.

But I suspected that the lofty Claudia Hinrabia, of the Hinrabians, would not dance in pleasure silk at a Collaring Feast. Rather she would be returned for ransom. What puzzled me about the matter was that she had been abducted. It is one thing to drop a loop about a girl on a high bridge in streaking over the walls and quite another to pick up the daughter of an Administrator in her own quarters and make off with her. I knew the Taurentians to be skilled Warriors, wary and swift, and I would have thought the women of the Hinrabians would have been the safest of the city.

"Probably tomorrow," Nela was saying, "an offer of ransom will be made."

"Probably," I grunted.

Although I was sleepy from the swim and the oiling I was more concerned with wondering about Marlenus of Ar, whom I had seen in the arcade of the races this afternoon. Surely he knew the danger in which he stood once within the environs of Ar? He would be slain in the city if discovered. I wondered what it was that would bring him to Glorious Ar.

I did not suppose that his appearance in Ar had anything to do with the disappearance of the Hinrabian girl because she would have been abducted about the same time that I had seen him in the arcade. Further, abducting a wench from the Hinrabians, if a rather arrogant gesture, would not have brought Marlenus closer to the throne of Ar, nor would it have much hurt the city. If Marlenus had wished to strike the Hinrabians he presumably would have flown his tarn to the central cylinder itself and cut his way to the throne of the Administrator. Marlenus, I was confident, had nothing to do with the disappearance of the Hinrabian girl. But still I wondered what had brought him to the city.

"How much ransom do you think so great a woman would bring?" asked Nela.

"I don't know," I admitted. "Maybe the Hinrabian brick works," I ventured.

Nela laughed.

I felt her hands hard about my spine, and could sense her thought. "It would be amusing," said she, rather bitterly, "if whoever captured her would collar her, and keep her as a slave."

I rolled over and looked at Nela, and smiled.

"I forget myself, Master," said she, dropping her head.

Nela was a sturdy girl, a bit short. She had wrapped about her a piece of toweling. Her eyes were blue. She was a magnificent swimmer, strong and vital. Her blond hair was cut very short to protect it from the water; even so, in swimming, such girls often wrapped a long broad strap of glazed leather about their head, in a turban of sorts. Beneath the toweling Nela wore nothing; about her neck, rather than the common slave collar, she, like the other bath girls, wore a chain and plate. On her plate was the legend: I am Nela of the Capacian Baths. Pool of Blue Flowers. I cost one tarsk.

Nela was an expensive girl, though there were pools where the girls cost as much as a silver tarn disk. The tarsk is a silver coin, worth forty copper tarn disks. All the girls in the Pool of Blue Flowers cost the same, except novices in training who would go for ten or fifteen copper tarn disks. There were dozens of pools in the vast, spreading Capacian Baths. In some of the larger pools the girls went as cheaply as one copper tarn disk. For the fee one was entitled to use the girl as he wished for as long as he wished, his use, of course, limited by the hours of the pool's closing.

The first time I had seen Nela, several days ago, she had been playing in the pool alone, rolling about. It took but one glance and I dove into the water, swam to her, seized her by the ankle and dragged her under, kissing her, rolling about beneath the surface. I liked the lips and feel of her and when we broke surface, she and I laughing, I asked her how much she went for. "For a tarsk," she laughed, and turned about, looking at me, "but you will have to catch me first."

I knew this game of bath girls, as though they, mere slaves, would dare to truly flee from one who pursued them, and I laughed, and she, too, sensing my understanding, laughed. The girl commonly pretends to swim away but is outdistanced and captured. I knew that few men could, if a bath girl did not wish it, come close to them in the water. They spend much of the day in the water and, it is said, are more at ease in that element than the Cosian song fish.

"Look," I said, pointing to the far end of the curving pool, some hundred and fifty yards away, "if I do not catch you before you reach the edge you will have your freedom for the day."

She looked at me, puzzled, her feet and hands moving.

"I will pay the tarsk," I said, "and I will not use you, nor make you serve me in any way."

She looked over to the side of the pool where a small man in a tunic of toweling was standing about, a metal box with a slot strapped over his shoulder.

"Is Master serious?" she asked.

"Yes," I said.

"You cannot catch me if I do not wish it," she said, warning me.

"Then," I said, "you will have your freedom for a day."

"Agreed," she said.

"Go!" I said.

She looked at me and laughed, and then, on her back, began to move gracefully toward the opposite end of the pool. Once she stopped, seeing that I was not yet following. She, I noted, had not been hurrying. I knew that she could, if she wished, swim like a water lizard making a strike. Yet it was enough for her to play with me, to tease me, if I should follow her, keeping just out of my reach. She was puzzled that I was not yet thrashing after her.

She was about half of the way to the far edge of the pool when she straightened herself in the water, and looked back at me.

At that moment I began to swim.

I gather, from the sound of a fellow watching us, that she began to swim again when I began to follow her. Apparently, from what I later learned, she began to swim slowly on her back until it became clear to her that I was gaining with some swiftness. Then she rolled onto her stomach and began to stroke easily toward the far edge, looking back now and then. In a matter of about ten Ihn, however, seeing me approach ever more closely, she began to move with a deliberate, swift ease. But still I gained. I swam as I never had before, knifing through the water. The thought went through me, bubbling to the roar of water passing my ears, that tomorrow I would scarcely be able to move; each breath was a cruel explosion in my lungs. At that point, looking back once more, and noting that I was still moving quickly toward her, and not willing to lose a possible rare day's freedom, she began, with the marvelous, strong trained stroke of her legs and arms, to slice swiftly through the water. Still I gained. Now she was moving as rapidly as she could, determinedly, a fury of beauty in the water. Yet I pressed on, ever gaining, each of my muscles suddenly charged with the excitement of the pursuit of her. I now sensed her but feet from me, swimming desperately, the pool's edge long yards away. Faster yet I swam. I knew now I would overtake her. Suddenly she, sensing this too, became like a maddened, terrified water animal. She cried out in frustration. She lost her stroke. She threw all her energies now into her panic-stricken flight; but the beauty of the rhythm, that powerful, even rhythm, was gone; her stroke was uneven; she lifted too much water; she missed a breath; she thrashed; but still she fled wildly for safety, kicking madly, trying to escape. And then my hands closed on her waist and she cried out in rage, struggling, trying to break free. I turned her about on her back and put my hand in the chain about her throat, staying behind her. She tried to put her hands back but could not remove my hand from the chain. Then, slowly, in triumph, my hand in the chain, I towed her on her back, she helpless, to the other end of the pool.

In a secluded place, among the planted grasses and ferns, sheltered from view, I had lifted Nela from the pool and placed her on a large piece of orange toweling on the grass, near which I had left my clothes and pouch.

"It seems you have lost your freedom for the day," I said.

I liked the feel of her wet body. There were tears in her eyes.

"It will be a silver tarsk for that one," said a thin voice behind me. I motioned that the man should get the coin from my pouch and he did so. I heard the coin drop into the metal box, and heard him leave.

"What is your name?" I asked.

"Nela," said she, "if it pleases Master."

"It pleases me," I said.

I took the girl into my arms, and pressed my lips to hers, as she lifted her arms and placed them about my neck.

After we had kissed we swam together, and then again kissed and swam. Afterwards, Nela gave me the first rubbing, with coarse oils, loosening dirt and perspiration, and scraped me with the thin, flexible bronze strigil; then she gave me the second rubbing, vigorous and stimulating, with heavy toweling; then she gave me the third rubbing, that with fine, scented oils, massaged at length into the skin. After that we lay side by side for a long time, looking up at the bluish translucent dome of the Pool of Blue Flowers. There are, as I mentioned, many pools in the Capacian Baths, and they differ in their shapes and sizes, and in their decor, and in the temperatures and scents of their waters. The temperature of the Pool of Blue Flowers was cool and pleasing. The atmosphere of the pool was further charged with the fragrance of Veminium, a kind of bluish wildflower commonly found on the lower slopes of the Thentis range; the walls, the columns, even the bottom of the pool, were decorated with representations of Veminium, and many of the plants themselves were found in the chamber. Though the pool was marble and the walkways about it, much of the area was planted with grass and ferns and various other flora were in abundance. There were many small nooks and glades, here and there, some more than forty yards from the pool, where a man might rest. I had heard the Pool of the Tropics was an excellent pool in the Capacian; and also the Pool of Ar's Glories, and the Pool of the Northern Forests; there was even, of recent date, a Pool of the Splendor of the Hinrabians; I myself, however, with one arm about Nela, who nestled against me, felt content with the Pool of Blue Flowers.

"I like you," she said to me.

I kissed her, and looked again to the ceiling.

I recalled Harold of the Tuchuks. The pools were beautiful, and yet I knew that somewhere, chained in darkness, were gangs of male slaves who cleaned them each night; and there were of course the Bath Girls of Ar, of which Nela was one, said to be the most beautiful of all Gor. Harold, as a boy, had once been a slave in the baths, those of the city of Turia, before he had escaped. He had told me that sometimes a Bath

Girl, to discipline her, is thrown to the slaves in the darkness. I held Nela a bit more closely to me, and she looked at me, puzzled.

Nela had been a slave since the age of fourteen. To my surprise she was a native of Ar. She had lived alone with her father, who had gambled heavily on the races. He had died and to satisfy his debts, no others coming forth to resolve them, the daughter, as Gorean law commonly prescribes, became state property; she was then, following the law, put up for sale at public auction; the proceeds of her sale were used, again following the mandate of the law, to liquidate as equitably as possible the unsatisfied claims of creditors. She had first been sold for eight silver tarsks to a keeper of one of the public kitchens in a cylinder, a former creditor of her father, who had in mind making a profit on her; she worked in the kitchen for a year as a pot girl, sleeping on straw and chained at night, and then, as her body more adequately developed the contours of womanhood, her master braceleted her and took her to the Capacian Baths where, after some haggling, he received a price of four gold pieces and a silver tarsk; she had begun in one of the vast cement pools as a copper-tarn-disk girl and had, four years later, become a silver-tarsk girl in the Pool of Blue Flowers.

Now, days after I had first met Nela, I lay thinking on the thick square of striped toweling and felt her massage the final oils of the bath into my body.

"I hope," said Nela, kneading my flesh rather harder than was necessary, "Claudia Tentia Hinrabia is made a slave."

I lifted my head and got up on my elbows, looking at her.

"Are you serious?" I asked.

"Yes," said Nela, bitterly, "let her be branded and collared. Let her be forced to please men."

"Why do you hate her so?" I asked.

"She is free," said Nela, "and of high birth and rich. Let such women, I say, feel the iron. Let it be they who dance to the whip."

"You should feel sorry for her," I recommended.

Nela threw back her head and laughed.

"She is probably an innocent girl," I said.

"She once had the nose and ears of one of her girls cut off for having dropped a mirror," said Nela.

"How do you know that?" I asked.

The girl laughed. "Everything that goes on in Ar," she said, "is heard in the Capacian." Then she looked at me bitterly. "I hope she is made a slave," she said. "I hope she is sold in Port Kar."

I gathered that Nela must hate the Hinrabian girl much indeed.

"Are the Hinrabians popular in Ar?" I asked.

Nela stopped massaging my back.

"Do not answer if you do not wish," I said.

"No," she said, and I could sense her looking about. "They are not popular."

"What of Kazrak?" I asked.

"He was a good Administrator," she said. "He is gone now."

She began again to massage my back. The oil was fragrant. It felt warm from her hands.

"When I was a little girl," she said, "when I was free I once saw Marlenus of Ar."

"Oh?" I asked.

"He," she said, "was the Ubar of Ubars." There was something of awe in her voice.

"Perhaps," I said, "someday Marlenus will return."

"Do not speak so," she whispered. "Men have been impaled in Ar for less."

"I understand he is in the Voltai," I said.

"Minus Tentius Hinrabius," she said, "has a dozen times sent prides of a hundred Warriors to the Voltai to seek him out and slay him, but never have they found him."

"Why should he wish to slay him?" I asked.

"They fear him," she said. "They fear he will return to Ar."

"Impossible," I said.

"In these days," she said, "much is possible."

"Would you like to see him again in Ar?" I asked.

"He was," said the girl, her voice proud, "the Ubar of Ubars." Her hands were powerful now, and I could feel the thrill in her. "When he was publicly refused bread, salt and fire on the height of the central cylinder, when he was exiled from Ar, not to return on pain of death, do you know what he said?"

"No," I said, "I do not."

"He said, 'I will come again to Ar.'"

"Surely you do not believe it," I said.

"I could speak to you of things I have heard," she said, "but it is better that you not know of them."

"As you wish," I said.

I heard her voice, something of awe in it. "He said," she repeated, "'I will come again to Ar.'"

"Would you like to see him once more upon the throne?" I asked.

She laughed. "I am of Ar," she said. "He was Marlenus. He was the Ubar of Ubars!"

I rolled over, took Nela by the wrists, drew her to me and kissed her. I saw no reason to tell her that this very afternoon, in the arcade of the stadium, I had seen Marlenus of Ar.

Upon leaving the baths I encountered by chance the Tarn Keeper whom I had met briefly when observing the game outside the tavern of Spindius, that fought between the blind Player and the Vintner. He was short, small, with close-cropped brown hair. He had a rather heavy, squarish face, large considering his size. I saw he wore a patch of green on his shoulder, indicating he was of the Greens.

"I see you now wear the red of the Warrior," said he, "rather than the black of the Assassin."

I said nothing.

"I know disguises are useful," said he, "in hunting." He grinned at me. "I liked what you did at the game, when you gave the double tarn to the Player."

"He did not accept it," I said. "To him it was black gold."

"And so it was," said the Tarn Keeper, "so it was."

"It will buy as much as yellow gold," said I.

"True," said the Tarn Keeper, "and that is what must be kept in mind."

I turned to go.

"If you are intending to go to table in the neighborhood," said he, "may I accompany you?"

"Of course," said I.

"I know a good tavern," said he, "which favors the Greens. Many of the faction eat and drink there after the races."

"Good," I said. "I am hungry and would drink. Take me to this place."

The tavern, like the Capacian Baths, was within fair walking distance of the stadium. It was called, appropriately enough, the Green

Tarn, and the proprietor was a genial fellow, bald and red-nosed, called Kliimus. The Pleasure Slaves who served wore green Pleasure Silk, and the tops of the tables and the walls were also painted green; even the curtains on the alcoves by one wall were green. About the walls, here and there, were lists and records, inked on narrow boards; there were also, here and there, hanging on the walls, some memorabilia, such as saddle rings and tarn harnesses, suitably labeled as to their origin; there were also representations of tarns and some drawings of famous riders, who had brought victory to the Greens.

Tonight, however, the tavern was relatively subdued, for the day had not been a good one for the Greens. And, instead of racing, many were discussing the case of the daughter of the Hinrabian Administrator, speculating on her whereabouts, arguing about how the abduction, if abduction it was, could possibly have taken place within earshot of dozens of Taurentian guardsmen. There had apparently been no tarns near the central cylinder during the time, and, according to report, no strangers were known to have entered the cylinder. It was a mystery suitable to start all Ar conjecturing.

The Tarn Keeper, who was called by those in the tavern Mip, bought the food, bosk steak and yellow bread, peas and Torian olives, and two golden-brown, starchy Suls, broken open and filled with melted bosk cheese. I bought the paga, and several times we refilled our cups. Mip was a chipper fellow, and a bit dapper considering his caste and his close-cropped hair, for his brown leather was shot with green streaks, and he wore a Tarn Keeper's cap with a greenish tassel; most Tarn Keepers, incidentally, crop their hair short, as do most Metal Workers; work in the tarncots and in training tarns is often hard, sweaty work.

Mip, for some reason, seemed to like me, and he spoke much during the evening, as we drank together, of the factions, of the organizations of the races, of the training of tarns and riders, of the hopes of the greens and the other factions, of given riders and given birds. I suspected few knew as much of the races of Ar as Mip.

After we had eaten and drunk together, clapping me on the shoulders, Mip invited me to the tarncot where he worked, one of the large cots of the Greens.

I was pleased to accompany him for I had never seen a faction cot before.

We walked through the dark streets of Ar, and though such was perhaps dangerous, none approached us, though some who passed did so with circumspection, their weapons drawn. I expect the fact that I walked as a Warrior, a sword at my side, perhaps dissuaded individuals who might otherwise have attempted to cut a purse or threaten a throat were they not rewarded for leniency. There are few on Gor who will take their lives into their hands by confronting a Gorean Warrior.

The cot was one of six in a vast and lofty cylinder containing many of the offices and dormitories of those associated professionally with the Greens. Their records and stores, and treasures, are kept in this cylinder, though it is only one of four they maintain in the city. The tarncot in which Mip worked was the largest and, I was pleased to note, he was the senior Tarn Keeper in the place, though there were several employed there. The cot was a huge room beneath the roof of the cylinder, taking up what normally would be four floors of the cylinder. The perches were actually a gigantic, curving framework of tem-wood four stories high, and following the circular wall of the cylinder. Many of the perches were empty, but there were more than a hundred birds in the room; each was now chained to its area of the perch; but each, I knew, at least once in every two days, was exercised; sometimes, when men do not wander freely in the cot, and the portals of the cot, opening to the sky, are closed, some of the birds are permitted the freedom of the cot; water for the birds is fed from tubes into canisters mounted on triangular platforms near the perches, but there is also, in the center of the cot, in the floor, a cistern which may be used when the birds are free. Food for the tarns, which is meat, for that is their diet, is thrust on hooks and hauled by chain and windlass to the various perches; it might be of interest to note that, when any of the birds are free, meat is never placed on the hooks or on the floor below; the racing tarn is a valuable bird and the Tarn Keepers do not wish to have them destroy one another fighting over a verr thigh.

As soon as Mip entered the cot he picked a tarn goad from a hook on the wall over a small table with a lamp and papers on it. He then took a second goad, from a hook nearby, and handed it to me. I accepted it. Few dare to walk in a tarncot without a goad. Indeed, it is foolish to do so. Mip, receiving and acknowledging the salutations of his men, made his rounds. With an agility that could come only from years in the cots he clambered about the tem-wood beams, sometimes forty feet from the floor, checking this bird and that; perhaps because I was slightly drunk I followed him; at last we had come to one of the four great round portals which give access to the open air from the tarncot. I could see the large, beamlike tarn perch extending from the portal, out over the street far below. The lights of Ar were beautiful. I stepped out on the tarn perch. I looked up. The roof was only about ten feet above. A person could, I noted, if sufficiently bold or foolish, leap from the roof, seize the tarn perch and enter the tarncot. I have always been amazed at the grandeur of Ar at night, the bridges, the lanterns, the beacons, the many lamps in the windows of countless cylinders. I stepped farther out on the tarn perch. I could sense Mip a bit behind me, back in the shadows, yet also on the perch. I looked down and shook my head. The street seemed to loop and swing below me. I could see the torches of two or three men moving together far below. Mip moved a bit closer.

I turned about and smiled at him, and he stepped back.

"You'd better come in from there," he said, grinning. "It's dangerous."

I looked up and saw the three moons of Gor, the large moon and the two small ones, one of the latter called the Prison Moon, for no reason I understood.

I turned about and walked back on the perch and again stood on the thick, beamed framework of tem-wood that formed the vast housing for numerous racing birds.

Mip was fondling the beak of one bird, an older bird I gathered. It was reddish brown; the crest was flat now; the beak a pale yellow, streaked with white.

"This is Green Ubar," said he, scratching the bird's neck.

I had heard of the bird. It had been famous in Ar a dozen years ago. It had won more than one thousand races. Its rider, one of the great ones in the tradition of the greens, had been Melipolus of Cos.

"Are you familiar with tarns?" asked Mip.

I thought for a moment. Some Assassins are, as a matter of fact, skilled tarnsmen. "Yes," I said, "I am familiar with tarns."

"I am drunk," said Mip, fondling the bird's beak. It thrust its head forward.

I wondered why the bird, as is usual, it now being rather old, surely past its racing prime, had not been destroyed. Perhaps it had been preserved as an act of sentiment, for such is not unknown among the partisans of the factions. On the other hand, the business managers of the factions have little sentiment, and an unprofitable tarn, like an unprofitable or useless slave, is customarily sold or destroyed.

"The night," I said, "is beautiful."

Mip grinned at me. "Good," he said. He moved over the tem-wood beams until he came to two sets of racing saddles and harness, and he threw me one, indicating a brown, alert racing tarn two perches away. The racing harness, like the common tarn harness, works with two rings, the throat ring and the main saddle ring, and six straps. The major difference is the tautness of the reins between the two rings; the racing saddle, on the other hand, is only a slip of leather compared to the common tarn saddle, which is rather large, with saddle packs, weapon sheaths and paired slave rings. I fastened the saddle on the bird and, with a bit of difficulty, the bird sensing my unsure movements, the tarn harness. Mip and I, moving the lock levers, removed the hobble and chain from the two birds and took the saddle.

Mip rode Green Ubar; he looked well in the worn saddle; his stirrups were short.

We fastened the safety straps.

On the racing saddle there are two small straps, rather than the one large strap on the common saddle; both straps fasten about the rider and to the saddle, in a sense each duplicating the work of the other; the theory is that though smaller straps can break more easily the probability of both straps breaking at the same time is extremely small; further the two straps tend to divide strain between them, thereby considerably lessening the possibility of either breaking; some saving in weight, of course, is obtained with the two smaller straps; further, the broad strap would be a bit large to fasten to the small saddle; even beyond this, of course, since races take place largely and most often over a net there is normally not as much danger in a fall as there would be in common tarn flight; the main purpose of the straps is simply to keep the rider in the saddle, for the purpose of his race, not primarily to protect his life.

"Do not try to control the tarn until you are out of the cot," said Mip. "It will take time to accustom yourself to the harness." He smiled. "These are not war tarns."

Mip, scarcely seeming to touch the one-strap with his finger, almost a tap, took the old bird from the perch and in a whiplike flurry of its wings it struck the outside perch and stood there, its old head moving alertly, the wicked black eyes gleaming. My bird, so suddenly I was startled, joined the first.

Mip and I sat on tarnback on the lofty perch outside the tarncot. I was excited, as I always was, on tarnback. Mip too seemed charged and alive.

We looked about, at the cylinders and lights and bridges. It was a fresh, cool summer evening. The stars over the city were clear and bright, the coursing moons white with splendor against the black space of the Gorean night.

Mip took his tarn streaking among the cylinders and I, on my tarn, followed him.

The first time I attempted to use the harness, though I was aware of the danger, I overdrew the strap and the suddenness of the bird as it veered in flight threw me against the two narrow safety straps; the small, broad, rapid-beating wings of the racing tarn permit shifts and turns that would be impossible with a larger, heavier, longer-winged bird. With a tap on the two-strap I took the bird in a sudden breathtaking sweep to the high right and in an instant had joined Mip in flight.

The lights of Ar, and the lanterns on the bridges, flew past below me, the roofs of cylinders looming up out of the darkness of the streets far below.

Then Mip turned his bird and it seemed to veer and slide through the air, the cylinders below slicing to the right, and he brought it to rest on a great rail above and behind the highest tier on Ar's Stadium of Tarns, where that afternoon I had watched the races.

The stadium was empty now. The crowds had gone. The long, curving terraces of tiers gleamed white in the light of Gor's three moons. There was some litter about in the tiers, which would be removed before the races of the next day. The long net under the rings had been removed and rolled, placed with its poles near the dividing wall. The painted, wooden tarn heads, used for marking laps of the race, stood lonely and dark on their poles. The sand of the stadium seemed white in the moonlight, as did the broad dividing wall. I looked across to Mip. He was sitting on his tarn, silent.

"Wait here," he said.

I waited on the height of the stadium, looking down into that vast, open structure, empty and white.

Mip on his tarn, Green Ubar, seemed a swift, dark movement against the white sand and tiers, the shadow coursing behind them, seeming to break geometrically over the tiers.

I saw the bird stop on the first perch.

They waited there for a moment. The judge's bar, hanging on its chain from a pole on the dividing wall, was silent.

Suddenly with a snap of its wings I could hear more than two hundred yards away the tarn exploded from the perch, Mip low on its back, and streaked toward the first "ring," the first of three huge metal rectangles, before the round "rings" mounted at the corners and at the end of the dividing wall. Startled, I saw the bird flash through the three first rings, veer and speed through the first of the round "rings," and in the same motion, still turning, pass through the second and third of the round "rings," and then, wings beating with incredible velocity, its beak forward, Mip low on its back, pass in a moment through the three rectangular "rings" on the other side of the dividing wall, then whip about the end of the dividing wall, negotiating the three round "rings" in one swift, fierce trajectory and alight, wings snapping, talons extended, on the last perch of the line, that of the winner.

Mip and the bird remained there for some moments, and then I saw the bird lift itself and turn toward me. In a moment Mip had alighted beside me on the high rail circling the top of the stadium.

He stayed there for a moment, looking back over the stadium. Then he took his bird from the rail and I followed him. In a few Ehn we had returned to the perch outside the portal of the tarncot.

We returned the birds to their perches and put the tarn hobble on them there. We removed the small saddles and control straps from the birds, and hung them on vertical beams, a portion of the perch framework.

When we were finished I stepped again out onto the perch extending from the portal in the cot, that perch fixed far above the street below. I wanted once more to feel the air, the beauty of the night.

Mip stood somewhat behind me and I walked out to the end of the perch.

"I have enjoyed myself this night," said I, "Mip."

162

"I am pleased," said Mip.

I did not face him. "I shall ask you a question," I said, "but do not feel obliged to answer if you do not wish."

"Very well," said Mip.

"You know I hunt," I said.

"Those of the black caste often hunt," said Mip.

"Do you know of any," I asked, "of the Greens who were in Ko-ro-ba in En'Var this year."

"Yes," said Mip.

I turned to face him.

"Only one that I know of," said Mip.

"And who would he be?" I asked.

"I," said Mip. "I was in Ko-ro-ba in En'Var this year."

In Mip's hand I saw a small dagger, a throwing knife, of a sort manufactured in Ar; it was smaller than the southern quiva; it was tapered on only one side.

"It is an interesting knife," I said.

"All Tarn Keepers carry a knife," said Mip, playing with the blade.

"This afternoon," I said, "at the races, I saw a rider cut the safety straps and free himself from a falling bird."

"It was probably with such a knife as this," said Mip. He now held it by the tip.

I felt the breeze pick up, moving past me, cool and fresh that summer evening.

"Are you skilled with such a knife?" I asked.

"Yes," said Mip. "I think so. I could hit the eye of a tarn at thirty paces."

"You are skilled indeed," I said.

"Are you familiar with such knives?" asked Mip.

"Not particularly," I said. My body was apparently relaxed, but each nerve was alive and ready. I knew he could throw the knife before I could reach him, before I could hope to unsheath the sword at my side. I was keenly aware of the height of the perch, the street far below. I heard two men hailing one another below. The sound drifted up.

"Would you like to examine the knife?" asked Mip.

"Yes," I said. I tensed myself.

Mip tossed the knife underhanded to me, and I caught it. My heart had nearly stopped beating.

I examined the knife, the balance of it, the hilt, the tapered blade.

"You had better come in from the tarn perch," said Mip. "It is dangerous."

I tossed him back the knife and retraced my steps along the narrow perch. In a few Ehn I had left the cylinder and was returning to the House of Cernus.

Fourteen

The Prisoner

When I had returned to the House of Cernus I passed the heavy, bolted door which led to the hallway off which was the luxurious cell in which Cernus was accustomed to keep his Special Captures, which cell had been shown to me earlier by Ho-Tu. I was surprised to see that now four guards were posted at this door.

When I returned to our compartment I found Elizabeth sleeping on a mat, wrapped in a rep-cloth blanket, under the slave ring. The collar and chain had been snapped about her throat. It is a rule in the House of Cernus that all slaves, save those who may be on house business, be secured by the eighteenth bar. This precaution is implemented by guards who make the rounds shortly before that bar. When I was in the compartment, however, as I normally was at that time, she would not be secured, my presence being taken as a sufficient guarantee of her custody. On such nights we would double beam the door and sleep in one another's arms.

I entered the compartment, closed the door and put the beams in place.

Elizabeth, with a rustle of chain, sat up, rubbing her eyes.

She was attired in a brief gown of red Pleasure Silk, prescribed for her because she was a Red Silk Girl and in training. Virginia and Phyllis, in their cells, would wear similar gowns, but of white silk.

Elizabeth's collar had also been changed. She now wore a red-enameled collar. Virginia and Phyllis, however, Elizabeth had told me, still wore the simple iron collars which had been hammered about their necks by the smith days before.

165

I turned up the lamp and noted that the floor of the compartment had been washed down with sponge and towel, that the chests and cabinets had been dusted and straightened, that cleaned furs lay neatly folded on the stone couch. I had insisted that the girl keep the compartment spotless. I think it was not so much I minded an occasional bit of silk lying on the floor as that I derived great pleasure from the fact that the lovely Miss Elizabeth Cardwell, slave in the House of Cernus, must keep my quarters. Elizabeth's puttering about, dusting, a cloth about her hair, serving me with these small domesticities, was a sight I relished. She had had the temerity to suggest that such chores be shared but, when threatened with thong and slave ring, she had irritably understood that she must conform to my wishes. Interestingly, one evening, after learning that she would be forced to do these things, and alone, she had been unusually submissive, responsive, passionate. Women, I suspected, even proud, beautiful, intelligent women like Elizabeth Cardwell, secretly wish their men to be strong, and upon occasion to prove it to them, commanding them as mere females, giving them no choice but to do precisely as he wishes.

I released Elizabeth from the slave ring, the chain and collar.

She sniffed suspiciously. "You have been to the baths again," she said.

"It is true," I said.

"The Pool of Blue Flowers?" she asked.

"Yes," I said.

"Are the girls pretty there?" she asked.

"Not so pretty as you," I said.

"You are a sweet beast," she said. She looked up at me. "You will take me to the Pool of Blue Flowers sometime, will you not?"

"There are many lovely pools in the Capacian," I said.

"But you will take me to the Pool of Blue Flowers, won't you?" she asked.

"Perhaps," I said.

"You beast," she smiled, kissing me. Then she knelt down on the mat, and I sat across from her cross-legged. "While you were sporting about at the Pool of Blue Flowers," she said, "I was spoken to by Caprus."

I was immediately attentive. To this point the tall, angular, dour Scribe had given us no information.

"He tells me," said she, "that he has at last bribed the chamber slave in the compartments of Cernus to allow him access to the compartments at given times. The records you seek are not, of course, kept in the office of Caprus."

"It will be extremely dangerous," I said.

"He says he may need time," she said. "He has found numerous notes and maps, but it may take months to copy them. He does not wish to appear to be absent from his duties for long periods."

"Are the maps clear?" I asked. "Are the notes in Gorean?"

"He says they are," she said.

"That is interesting," I said. I did not mention it to Elizabeth but I would have expected the maps to be oriented only by key, and the notes to have been in some form of code.

"Our problem," said Elizabeth, "will be to get the copies to the Sardar."

"That should not be difficult," I said, "for I have free exit from the house and you, when you are working with Caprus after your training, may upon occasion leave."

"I did not realize the matter would be so easy," she said.

"Nor did I," I said. The reason that Elizabeth and I had been placed in the House of Cernus had been because Caprus, according to report, could not obtain the documents we believed must exist in the house. It was thought that I, as a mercenary in the house, or Elizabeth, as a staff slave, might be able to locate and seize the documents in question. This was prior to the slaying of the Warrior of Thentis, who resembled me, which had given me independent reason for coming to Ar, and in the guise of an Assassin.

"Still," I said, "it seems like a very long time to wait—months."

"Yes," she admitted. "It does."

"In that time," I said, "the Others might carry their work far, establish new bases of influence, new stations, storehouses perhaps for arms."

She nodded.

"The best we can do," I said, "is to convey the materials which Caprus copies in portions to the Sardar. As he finishes a fair portion we must arrange for it to be transmitted. I have much freedom. I can arrange for the Older Tarl to be summoned from Ko-ro-ba, and to act as our messenger between Ar and the mountains of Priest-Kings. He is already known to Al-Ka, who brought you to the House of Clark in Thentis."

"Unfortunately," said Elizabeth, "Caprus has said he will not turn over any materials to us until he is finished."

"Why is that?" I asked, angry.

"He fears there may be discovery in sending them from the House. Also he fears there may be spies of Others in the Sardar itself who, if they found out about the information being sent from the House of Cernus, would investigate and, doubtless, find us."

"I think that is not a likely possibility," I said.

"But Caprus believes so," she said.

I shrugged. "It seems we must do what Caprus wishes."

"We have no other choice," she said.

"When the information is complete," I said, "I gather that we three will depart for the Sardar."

She laughed. "Caprus will certainly not wish to be left behind. Indeed, I am sure he will carry the documents on his very person."

I smiled. "I suppose Caprus is wise to trust no one."

"He is playing a dangerous game, Tarl."

I nodded.

"So," said she, "we must wait."

"Also," I said, "I would like to find out who slew the Warrior from Thentis, he who died on the high bridge in Ko-ro-ba near the Cylinder of Warriors."

"You did not even know him," she said. Then, as I gazed sternly upon her, she dropped her eyes. "I'm sorry," she said. She looked up. "It is only that I fear for you."

I took her hands gently in mine. "I know," I said.

"Tonight," she said, "hold me. I'm frightened."

I took her gently in my arms and kissed her, and she put her head against my left shoulder.

* * * *

About the third bar, unable to sleep, I left the side of Elizabeth and drew on my tunic, that of the Assassin. My mind was concerned with the appearance of Marlenus in Ar. I knew the former Ubar, still to his followers, years after the days of his glory, the Ubar of Ubars, was not in Ar for the sport of the races. Also, in the Baths, Nela, who doubtless heard much in the Capacian, had been evasive about matters pertaining to the Ubar. This suggested to me there might be movements afoot in Ar of which I knew nothing. I had not known, for example, and I gathered it was not common knowledge, about the many sorties to the Voltai to find and slay Marlenus, sorties which had invariably failed. I gathered that those now high in Ar had good reason for such desperate attempts to locate and slay the former Ubar.

I left the compartment and walked the halls of the House of Cernus, lost in thought. I passed occasional guards in the corridors but none challenged me. I had, for most practical purposes, the freedom of the house.

I was angry and frustrated that Caprus would not surrender the results of his labors before their completion, but I could understand his reasoning, his fears; and, on the other hand, the fact that he had himself located the documents we wished and was copying them gave me great satisfaction, for it meant that the work of Elizabeth and I in the house would now be little other than to convey, some months from now, Caprus and his documents to the Sardar. I anticipated little difficulty in this portion of the business. I could buy a tarn, with carrying basket, easily and in five days, with Caprus and Elizabeth, be in the black Sardar, safe with Misk, Kusk, Al-Ka, Ba-Ta and my other friends. I puzzled on the fact that the maps and documents which Caprus was copying were not coded, but in simple Gorean. I supposed that it was thought by Others that the materials were safe in the keeping of Cernus. Once as I walked about I heard the wild cry, a howling roar, of an animal, apparently large and fierce; I supposed it to be the Beast of which Ho-Tu, and others, seemed so frightened; they seemed to know as little of it as I; when I heard the cry an involuntary shiver coursed my spine; I felt the hair on my nape and forearms lift and stiffen; I stopped; I heard nothing more, and so I continued to walk about. I did not fear it, but, like Ho-Tu, I was pleased that it was doubtless safely caged; I would not have cared to meet it in the lonely halls of the House.

I found that my steps had inadvertently brought me to the corridor with the heavy bolted door, that door leading to the hallway off which lay the cell for Special Captures, earlier shown to me by Ho-Tu. The four guards were still posted near the door. To my surprise at the door I encountered none other than Cernus, Master of the House of Cernus.

He wore his long, black, coarse, woolen robe, that which bore the three stripes of silk, two blue enclosing a yellow, on the left sleeve. About his neck hung the golden medallion of the House of Cernus, the tarn with slave chains grasped in its talons. His stone gray eyes regarded me. But a small smile touched his heavy mouth.

"You are up late, Killer," said he.

"I could not sleep," I said.

"I thought those of the black caste slept the soundest of all men," said Cernus.

"It was something I ate," I said.

"Of course," said Cernus. "Was your hunt successful?"

"I have not yet found the man," I said.

"Oh," said Cernus.

"It was bad paga," I said.

Cernus laughed. "It is just as well you are here. I have something to show you."

"What?" I asked.

"The downfall of the House of Portus," said he.

I knew the House of Portus was the greatest remaining rival to the House of Cernus, fighting it for the control of the slave trade in Ar. Between them they handled better than seventy percent of the flesh purchased, exchanged and sold in the city. Several minor houses had shut down; there were others, but small houses, scrabbling for the thirty percent of the trade still left them.

"Follow me," said Cernus, leading the way through the door which the guards had thrown open for him. We found ourselves in the hallway giving access to the large one-way glass, backed by metal grillwork.

I was not clear as to the meaning of the remark of Cernus.

Once again I found myself looking through the glass, which on the other side was a mirror, into the luxurious compartment, with wardrobe, chests of silk, rugs and cushions, a silken divan and a scented, sunken bath, now drawn.

But this time, in that room rich with hangings, with lamps set behind ornate mesh in the ceiling, there was a prisoner.

It was a strikingly, but cruelly beautiful girl, who walked from one end of the room to the other, in fury, like a young, caged she-larl. The hood to her ornate, marvelous robes of concealment had been taken from her; and her veil. Otherwise, given the splendor of her robes, she might have been on the highest bridges the envy of all the free women of Ar.

"Behold the downfall of the House of Portus," said Cernus.

I looked into the room. The girl had black hair, swirling and long, beautiful, which had never been cut, and flashing black eyes, high cheekbones.

On each small wrist, locked, she wore a slave bracelet, of simple, unadorned steel. The two bracelets were joined by a light, gleaming chain of perhaps a yard in length. It did not restrict her movements to any appreciable extent.

"I want her," said Cernus, "to feel steel on her wrists, the weight of a chain."

The girl spun about and threw her head back, staring wildly at the ceiling, throwing the chain back over her head. Then she sobbed in rage and flung the chain forward, striking it on the chests, on the divan, again and again. Then crouching over, with first one hand and then the other, she tried madly to push and slip the encircling, resisting steel over her other hand. She ran even to the bath and took oils, rubbing them on her wrists, but still the steel would not release her. Then she sobbed and ran back to the center of the room, striking again and again the divan with the chain. Then, still chained, she knelt on the divan, pounding it with her fists.

I heard a movement near us. I turned and saw a female slave, in a rep-cloth kitchen tunic, stained with food, approaching, bearing a tray of fruit with a flask of wine. She was followed by a guard.

The slave knocked timidly on the door of the cell.

The girl sprang up from the divan, wiped oil from her wrists on a towel, threw back her hair, and stood regally in the center of the room.

"Enter," she said.

The guard unlocked the door and the kitchen slave, deferentially, entered, her head down, and placed the tray of fruit and wine on a small low table near the divan. She then, head down, began to back lightly away.

"Wait, Slave," ordered the girl.

The slave sank to her knees, head down.

"Where is your master?" demanded the chained girl.

"I do not know, Mistress," said the kitchen slave.

"Who is your master?" demanded the chained girl.

"I am not permitted to say, Mistress," whined the kitchen slave.

The girl in chains strode to her and seized her by the collar, at which point the kitchen slave began to whine and weep, trying to draw back, to turn her head away. The chained girl, half crouching, scrutinized the collar and laughed, and then, with disdain, her hands in the slave's collar, flung her to one side, where the slave lay, fearing to rise. The chained girl kicked her savagely in the side with her slipper. "Begone, Slave," she snarled, and the kitchen slave leaped to her feet and sped through the door, which was closed behind her and locked by the guard.

Outside Cernus gestured for the kitchen slave not to leave. Immediately the kitchen slave knelt in the hallway, not speaking. There were tears in her eyes.

Cernus then drew my attention again to the interior of the cell.

The prisoner now seemed in a better mood. There was a new haughtiness in her movements. She looked down at the tray of fruit and wine and laughed, and picked up a fruit and bit into it, smiling.

"I have plans for this girl," said Cernus, regarding the prisoner through the glass. "I had intended to have her used by a male slave before she leaves the house, but I shall not do so. This afternoon, following her capture, I sent uncollared serving slaves to groom and bathe her. I observed her, and she interests me. I shall, therefore, before she leaves the house, use her myself, but she will not know who it is whom she serves, for when I visit her from time to time she will be locked in a slave hood."

"What do you intend eventually to do with her?" I asked.

"Her hair is very beautiful, is it not?" asked Cernus.

"Yes," I said, "it is."

"I expect she is quite vain about it," speculated Cernus.

"Doubtless," I said.

"I will have her hair shaved off," said Cernus, "and have her bound and hooded and sent by tarn to another city, Tor perhaps, where she will be publicly sold."

"Perhaps her sale could be private?" I said.

"No," said Cernus, "it must be public."

"What has all this to do with the House of Portus?" I asked.

Cernus laughed. "You, Killer," said he, "would not make a Player."

I shrugged.

"This girl," said he, "will in time make her way back to Ar. I will arrange it, if necessary."

"I do not understand," I said.

Cernus gestured for the kitchen slave to approach, and she did so immediately.

"Look at her collar," said Cernus.

I read the collar aloud. "I am the property of the House of Portus."

"She will find her way back to Ar," said Cernus. "And it will be the downfall of the House of Portus."

I looked at him.

"She is, of course," said Cernus, "Claudia Tentia Hinrabia."

Fifteen

I observed Phyllis Robertson performing the belt dance, on love furs spread between the tables, under the eyes of the Warriors of Cernus and the members of his staff. Beside me Ho-Tu was shoveling porridge into his mouth with a horn spoon. The music was wild, a melody of the delta of the Vosk. The belt dance is a dance developed and made famous by Port Kar dancing girls. Cernus, as usual, was engaged in a game with Caprus, and had eyes only for the board.

As the weeks had worn on, becoming months, I had grown more and more apprehensive and impatient. More than once I had called on Caprus myself, though it was perhaps not wise, to urge him to speed in his work, or to permit me to transmit portions of the documents he was copying to the Sardar. Always he refused. I had been bitter at these delays, complaining and chafing, but there seemed little I could do. He would not inform me of the location of the maps and papers and I did not feel that any direct attempt to steal them and carry them away would be likely to be successful; further, if simply stolen, the Others, through Cernus, would doubtless be informed at the first opportunity and alternate plans put into effect. I reminded myself, again and again, as the month clock rotated, that Caprus was a trusted agent of Priest-Kings, that Misk himself had spoken in the highest terms of him. I must trust Caprus. I would trust him. Yet I could not help my anger.

Ho-Tu pointed with his spoon at Phyllis. "She is not bad," he said.

The belt dance is performed with a Warrior. She now writhed on the furs at his feet, moving as though being struck with a whip. A white

174

silken cord had been knotted about her waist; in this cord was thrust a narrow rectangle of white silk, perhaps about two feet long. About her throat, close-fitting and snug, there was a white-enameled collar, a lock collar. She no longer wore the band of steel on her left ankle.

"Excellent," said Ho-Tu, putting aside his spoon.

Phyllis Robertson now lay on her back, and then her side, and then turned and rolled, drawing up her legs, putting her hands before her face, as though fending blows, her face a mask of pain, of fear.

The music became more wild.

The dance receives its name from the fact that the girl's head is not supposed to rise above the Warrior's belt, but only purists concern themselves with such niceties; wherever the dance is performed, however, it is imperative that the girl never rise to her feet.

The music now became a moan of surrender, and the girl was on her knees, her head down, her hands on the ankle of the Warrior, his sandal lost in the unbound darkness of her hair, her lips to his foot.

"Sura is doing a good job with her," said Ho-Tu.

I agreed.

In the next phases of the dance the girl knows herself the Warrior's, and endeavors to please him, but he is difficult to move, and her efforts, with the music, become ever more frenzied and desperate.

A girl in a tunic of white silk, gracefully, carrying a large pitcher of diluted Ka-la-na wine, approached our table from the rear, and climbed the stairs, delicately, and as though timidly, head down. Then she leaned forward behind me, bending her knees slightly, her body graceful. Her voice in my ear was a whisper, an invitation. I looked at her. Her eyes met mine, beautiful, deep, gray. Her lips were slightly parted. "Wine, Master?" asked Virginia Kent.

"Yes," I said, "I will have wine."

Virginia served me, bowed her head and backed gracefully down the stairs behind me, then turned and hurried away.

"She is White Silk, of course," said Ho-Tu.

"I know," I said.

Another girl approached similarly, though she was attired in a tunic of red silk.

"Wine, Master?" asked Elizabeth Cardwell.

"Again," snapped Ho-Tu, angrily.

175

Flustered, Elizabeth retreated and again approached. It was only on the third time that she managed to satisfy Ho-Tu, when her eyes, her lips, the carriage of her body, the words she whispered seemed to him adequate. "That is a stupid one," said Ho-Tu. Elizabeth, angry, backed down the stairs and hurried away.

I glanced at Virginia Kent, who was now moving about the tables, in the incredibly brief silken slave livery, the pitcher on her left shoulder, held there gracefully with her left hand. Her hair was now about three inches longer than it had been when she had come to the House of Cernus. She walked gracefully, insolently, the movement of her firing my blood. Her ankles were slender, beautiful. The left, as was the case with Phyllis, was now no longer encircled with the steel band, the identification band. About her throat, however, as was the case with Phyllis also, there was now a lock collar, snugly fitting, white-enameled. Both girls, branded and collared, were well marked as slave.

The belt dance was now moving to its climax and I turned to watch Phyllis Robertson.

"Capture of Home Stone," I heard Cernus say to Caprus, who spread his hands helplessly, acknowledging defeat.

Under the torchlight Phyllis Robertson was now on her knees, the Warrior at her side, holding her behind the small of the back. Her head went farther back, as her hands moved on the arms of the Warrior, as though once to press him away, and then again to draw him closer, and her head then touched the furs, her body a cruel, helpless bow in his hands, and then, her head down, it seemed she struggled and her body straightened itself until she lay, save for her head and heels, on his hands clasped behind her back, her arms extended over her head to the fur behind her. At this point, with a clash of cymbals, both dancers remained immobile. Then, after this instant of silence under the torches, the music struck the final note, with a mighty and jarring clash of cymbals, and the Warrior had lowered her to the furs and her lips, arms about his neck, sought his with eagerness. Then, both dancers broke apart and the male stepped back, and Phyllis now stood, alone on the furs, sweating, breathing deeply, head down.

I noted Sura standing somewhat behind the tables. She would not eat with the staff, of course, for she was slave. I did not know how long she had been standing there.

Cernus had watched the ending of the dance, his game having been finished. He glanced to Ho-Tu, who nodded affirmatively to him.

"Give her a pastry," said Cernus.

One of the men at the tables threw a pastry to Phyllis, which she caught. She stood there for an instant, the pastry clutched in her hands, her eyes suddenly brimming with tears, then she turned and fled from the room.

Ho-Tu turned to Sura. "She is coming along nicely," he said.

Sura tossed her head. "Tomorrow," said she, "we will work on it further," and turned and left.

I took a deep drink of the diluted Ka-la-na wine I had been served.

In the past months I had spent my time variously. During the season of the races I had often attended them, and, on several occasions, had met the small Tarn Keeper Mip afterwards, with whom I had occasionally sat table. Several times we had taken racing tarns from the cot. He had even showed me, at night in the empty Stadium of Tarns, certain tricks of racing, about which he seemed to know a great deal, doubtless because of his connection with the Greens. I learned such things as the pacing of the bird, the model trajectories for negotiating the rings, techniques of avoiding birds and blocking others, sometimes forcing them to hit or miss the rings; racing could be, and often was, as dangerous and cruel as the games in the Stadium of Blades, where men met men and beasts, and often fought to the death. Sometimes in the races, in pressing through the rings, fighting for position, riders used goads on one another, or tried to cut the safety or girth straps of others; more than one man had been stabbed as the birds, jammed at the corner rings, had fought for passage and position. Also, I had sometimes called at the Capacian Baths, even after the races were finished, seeing if Nela was available at that hour. I had come to be fond of the sturdy little swimmer, and I think she of me. Also, the girl seemed to know everything that transpired in Ar. The games in the Stadium of Blades finished their season at the end of Se'Kara, a month following the season of races. I attended the games only once, and found that I did not much care for them. To the credit of the men of Ar I point out that the races were more closely followed.

I do not choose to describe the nature of the games, except in certain general detail. There seems to me little of beauty in them and much of blood. Matches are arranged between single armed fighters, or teams of such. Generally Warriors do not participate in these matches, but men of low caste, slaves, condemned criminals and such. Some of them, however, are quite skillful with the weapons of their choice, surely the equal of many Warriors. The crowd is fond of seeing various types of weapons used against others, and styles of fighting. Buckler and short sword are perhaps most popular, but there are few weapons on Gor which are not seen over a period of three or four days of the games. Another popular set of weapons, as in the ancient *ludi* of Rome, is net and trident. Usually those most skilled with this set of weapons are from the shore and islands of distant, gleaming Thassa, the sea, where they doubtless originally developed among fishermen. Sometimes men fight locked in iron hoods, unable to see their opponents. Sometimes men wrestle to the death or use the spiked gauntlets. Sometimes slave girls are forced to fight slave girls, perhaps with steel claws fastened on their fingers, or several girls, variously armed, will be forced to fight a single man, or a small number of men. Surviving girls, of course, become the property of those whom they have fought; men who lose are, of course, slain. Beasts are also popular in the Stadium of Blades, and fights between various animals, half starved and goaded into fury by hot irons and whips, are common; sometimes the beasts fight beasts of the same species, and other times not; sometimes the beasts fight men, variously armed, or armed slave girls; sometimes, for the sport of the crowd, slaves or criminals are fed to the beasts. The training of slaves and criminals for these fights, and the acquisition and training of the beasts is a large business in Ar, there being training schools for men, and compounds where the beasts, captured on expeditions to various parts of Gor and shipped to Ar, may be kept and taught to kill under the unnatural conditions of the stadium spectacle. Upon occasion, and it had happened early in Se'Kara this year, the arena is flooded and a sea fight is staged, the waters for the occasion being filled with a variety of unpleasant sea life, water tharlarion, Vosk turtles, and the nine-gilled Gorean shark, the latter brought in tanks on river barges up the Vosk, to be then transported in tanks on wagons across the margin of desolation to Ar for the event.

Both the games and the races are popular in Ar, but, as I have indicated, the average man of Ar follows the races much more closely. There are no factions, it might be mentioned, at the games. Further, as might be expected, those who favor the games do not much go to the races, and those who favor the races do not often appear at the games. The adherents of each entertainment, though perhaps equaling one another in their fanaticism, tend not to be the same men. The one time I did attend the games I suppose I was fortunate in seeing Murmillius fight. He was an extremely large man and a truly unusual and superb swordsman. Murmillius always fought alone, never in teams, and in more than one hundred and fifteen fights, sometimes fighting three and four times in one afternoon, he had never lost a contest. It was not known if he had been originally slave or not, but had he been he surely would have won his freedom ten times over and more; again and again, even after he would have won his freedom had he first been slave, he returned to the sand of the arena, steel in hand; I supposed it might be the gold of victory, or the plaudits of the screaming crowd that brought Murmillius ever again striding helmeted in the sunlight onto the white sand. Yet Murmillius was an enigma in Ar, and little seemed to be known of him. He was strange to the minds of those who watched the games. For one thing he never slew an opponent, though the man often could never fight again; the afternoon I had seen him the crowd cried for the death of his defeated opponent, lying bloodied in the sand, pleading for mercy between his legs, and Murmillius had lifted his sword as though to slay the man, and the crowd screamed, and then Murmillius threw back his head and laughed, and slammed the sword into its sheath and strode from the arena; the crowd had been stunned and then furious, but by the time Murmillius had turned before the iron gate to face them they were on their feet crying his name, cheering him wildly, for he had spurned them; the will of the vast multitude in that huge stadium had been nothing to him, and the crowd, their will rejected, roared his praises, adoring him; and he turned and strode into the darkness of the pits beneath the stadium; even the face of Murmillius was unknown for never, even when the crowd cried out the loudest, would he remove the great helmet with its curving steel crest that concealed his features; Murmillius, at least until he himself should lie red in the white sand, held the adherents of the games in Ar, and perhaps the city itself, in the gauntleted palm of his right hand, his sword hand.

Claudia Tentia Hinrabia, though she had now been gone months from the House, had been kept for better than two months in the cell for Special Captures. In this time her head had been shaved at various times. She was commonly permitted to wear lavish and luxurious robes of concealment, save for hood and veil. The bracelets and chain on her wrists, during this time, save in dressing and in the bath, were never removed. And during such times, before the bracelets and chain were removed, a steel slave anklet would be placed on her left ankle, in order that there be no time that her body would be completely free of slave steel; this anklet she wore even in her bath; it would be removed only after the bracelets and chain had been replaced. Each evening five lovely, long-haired, uncollared serving slaves would come to her cell, to bathe her and perfume her, to prepare her for love. These girls, under the instructions of Cernus, were extremely deferential, save that they were continually to amuse themselves at the prisoner's expense, making sport of her shaved head, laughing and joking about it among themselves. Four times Claudia Tentia Hinrabia had attempted to kill one of the girls but the others would easily overpower her; and the Hinrabian must endure her bath and her perfuming; when finished the girls would lock her raiment in a chest and then draw a slave hood over her head, locking it in place, and the Hinrabian, stripped, perfumed, hooded, chained, must wait for he for whom she has been prepared. After two months of such treatment, Cernus, perhaps because he wearied of her body, or because he felt she was now ready, now at the height of her hatreds and miseries, ordered her sent to Tor, where, I heard, she was collared, marked and publicly sold during the ninth passage hand, that preceding the winter solstice. It was thought she would probably return to Ar within two months. There had been nothing clandestine about her sale, and it was unlikely that she would not be able to convince her master, eventually, that she was of high family in Ar and might be richly ransomed. If he were not convinced of her story one of the agents of Cernus would make a good offer for the girl, pretend to be convinced of her identity and hastily return her to Ar. It would be better, of course, if her master, bound to be ignorant of the intrigue, would undertake this business himself.

The time, during this period, seemed to me to pass with incredible slowness. Ar lies in Gor's northern hemisphere; it is rather low in her temperate latitudes; the long cold rains of the winter, the darkness of the days, the occasional snows, turning to black slush in her streets, depressed me. Each day I became more and more angry at the time that was passing. I spoke to Caprus again but he, now irritated, reiterated his position, and would speak with me no more.

Sometimes, to while away the time I would watch the girls in training.

Sura's training room lay directly off her private compartment, which might have been that of a free woman, save that the heavy door locked only on the outside and, at the eighteenth bar, it became her cell.

The training room was floored with wood, laid diagonally across beams for additional strength; one twelve-foot area of the room was a shallow pit of sand; against one wall were various chests of raiment, cosmetics and retention devices, for girls must be trained to wear chains gracefully; certain dances are performed in them, and so on. To one side there was a set of mats for Musicians, who almost invariably were present at the sessions, for even the exercises of the girls, which were carefully selected and frequently performed, are done to music; against one wall were several bars, also used in exercise, not unlike a training room in ballet except that there were four parallel bars fastened in the wall, which are used in a variety of exercises. Near the chests of raiment and such were several folded mats and sets of love furs. One entire side of the room, the left, facing the front, was a mirror. This mirror was, as might be expected, a one-way mirror. Various members of the House might observe the training without being noted from behind this glass. I used it sometimes myself, but at other times, sometimes alone, sometimes with others, would enter the room and sit near the back. Sura encouraged males to observe, wanting the girls to sense their presence and interest. And, though I do not think I would have told Elizabeth, her performances with men clearly present, and she knowing it, were almost invariably superior to those in which she did not know herself observed.

There were several men, including myself, who visited the training area with some frequency. In the past two months, in particular, I noted two young Warriors, guards, recent additions to the staff of the House. Their names were Relius and Ho-Sorl. They seemed likable, capable young men, something above the average cut of the men in the employ of Cernus the Slaver. I supposed they had succumbed to gold, for slavers pay high for their hired swords. The staff, incidentally, had been increased in the last month, largely due to the increasing number of slaves being processed by the House but perhaps also, in part, in preparation for the approaching spring, which is the busiest season on the Street of Brands, for then, after the winter, slave raids are more frequent and buyers wish to celebrate the New Year, beginning with the Vernal Equinox, by adding a girl or two to their household. On the other hand, the single greatest period for the sale of slaves is the five days of the Fifth Passage Hand, coming late in summer, called jointly the Love Feast. I recalled a girl once known, named Sana, who had been sold in Ar during those days, who had become the consort of Kazrak, once Administrator of Ar. I knew that Cernus intended to market Elizabeth, and the two other girls, on that feast. It is thought to be good luck to buy a girl on that feast, so prices tend to be high. Long before that time, however, I hoped, with Elizabeth and Caprus, to be free of the House.

The training of a slave girl, like the training of an animal, tends to be a grueling task, calling for patience, time, good judgment and sternness. These numerous latter qualities Sura possessed in plenty. Many were the evenings, particularly in the beginning, when Elizabeth would return to my quarters, and Virginia and Phyllis to their cells, in tears, stinging from the slave goad, confused, convinced that they could never please their harsh mistress. Then they would make some small progress and be rewarded with a kind word, which they found they could not help themselves from receiving with joy. The techniques employed were relatively transparent, much as the kennel technique had been with Virginia and Phyllis, and the girls objectively, rationally recognized what was being done to them, but yet, to their frustration and anger, they could not help, in the moment, responding as they did.

"I fear the goad," Elizabeth had told me one night. "I am afraid of it. I know it is foolish, but I am afraid. I will do anything that woman tells me, if only she will not touch me with the goad. I hate her. I know what they are doing. But yet I cannot help myself. I want desperately to please her."

"It is not irrational to fear the goad," I said. I had once been struck with a tarn goad and knew substantially what her pain must be; further, the shower of yellow sparks, though perhaps in itself innocuous, was, conjoined with the sudden pain, terrifying.

"I'm being trained like an animal," said Elizabeth, putting her head to my shoulder.

I held her head on my shoulder. What she said was to a large extent true, for she was being conditioned to certain responses by pain and rewards. Indeed, sometimes the girls would be forced to compete among themselves, with small candies as prizes, and each would find herself, to her subsequent horror, striving eagerly to outdo the others, that it might be she to whom Sura would throw the sugared pellet. Sometimes Sura would let the men observing determine which girl should receive the pellet, that they might learn how to win men's pleasure.

The conditioning, of course, was subtle, as well as gross, being a combination not simply of torment and reward, but including the intended inculcation of an image and understanding of themselves as well. In its most primitive expression this was begun in the first two weeks of the girls' training. The first week, surprisingly, consisted of nothing but the girl kneeling before the great mirror, in the position of a Pleasure Slave, for several Ahn a day. During this time they wore only their collars, and in the case of Virginia and Phyllis the slave anklets on their left ankles. The point of this, as Elizabeth and I supposed, was simply to accustom them to seeing themselves as slave girls. In the second week, they knelt in the same fashion, but had been forced to repeat, out loud, incessantly, the ritual phrase, "I am a slave girl. I am a slave girl. I am a slave girl." Virginia and Phyllis must needs do this in English, Elizabeth in Gorean. In the third week, the education became somewhat more subtle and Flaminius visited the girls for their training hours, and discussed, with ingenious subtlety, first in English and then in Gorean, certain views of history, of natural right, of orders of human beings and of relations among the sexes. The upshot of these disquisitions, predictably, was that what had happened to them was appropriate given certain laws of intraspecific competition, of conflict and dominance, of the rightful orders of nature. They were the women of inferior men who had been unable to protect them; such men would be conquered when one wished; their women belonged to those who could take them, who would be the victorious; hence they were of slave stock, by nature; that this sort of thing had occurred always, and would always occur; that it was right and just; that as natural slaves they must now bend all their efforts and intelligence to the pleasures of their masters; there was also a strong dose of masculine superiority thrown in, and the common Gorean contention, and arguments relating to it, that women are by nature slaves, deserve to be such and are fully content and pleased only when this is so. Flaminius, for a time, accepted and encouraged counter-arguments, patiently, as though waiting for the girls, when their simple minds permitted it, to understand the truth of what he said. Phyllis, I learned from Elizabeth, was particularly wrathful, when permitted to be so, with Flaminius. Phyllis, it seemed, to Elizabeth's amusement, had actually, on Earth, been a rather serious, ardent feminist. She had, as a matter of fact, hated and resented men. Virginia, on the other hand, had been a shy girl, fearing men. Needless to say, both presented Sura with different problems, which in a Gorean girl seldom occur.

Elizabeth would sometimes, in these weeks, come back to the compartment and relate, with amusement, the subtle exchanges between Phyllis and Flaminius. In her opinion, and perhaps rightly, the positions of both were subtle combinations of truths and half-truths; Phyllis seemed to regard men and women as unimportant differentiations off a sexless, neuter stock, whereas Flaminius argued for a position in which women were hardly to be recognized as belonging to the human species. I expect both, and I am certain that Flaminius, recognized the errors and exaggerations of their own position, but neither was concerned with the truth; both were concerned only with victory, and pleasing themselves. At any rate, to my satisfaction, but Elizabeth's irritation, Flaminius commonly had the best of these exchanges, producing incredibly subtle, complex arguments, quoting supposedly objectively conducted studies by the Caste of Physicians, statistics, the results of tests, and what not. Phyllis, unconvinced, was often reduced to tears and stuttering incoherence. Flaminius, of course, was practiced and skillful in what he was doing, and Phyllis was not difficult to catch and tangle in his well-woven nets of logic and supposed fact. During this time Virginia would usually remain silent, but she would occasionally volunteer a fact, a precedent or event which would support Flaminius' position, much to the anger of Phyllis. Elizabeth chose, wisely, not to debate with Flaminius. She had her own ideas, her own insights. She had learned on Gor that women are marvelous, but that they are not men, nor should they be; that they are themselves; that they are independent, magnificent creatures;

that it takes two sexes for the human race to be whole; and that each is splendid.

Following some two weeks of these discussions, which seemed to me at the time, at any rate, to be a waste of training time, Virginia Kent, who had feared men, had come to weigh seriously, if not to accept, certain of the theories of Flaminius, Phyllis to fight them and reject them as hateful slanders, and Elizabeth to regard them as an entertaining and stimulating hodgepodge of sophistry, reality, nonsense and propaganda. All three girls, in the last week, were taught certain standard answers to certain standard questions put to them by Flaminius, whether they agreed with them or not. These questions, to which simple, standard, memorized answers were to be promptly volunteered, were put to them over and over, until they, even Phyllis, responded without thinking. Certain of these questions and answers, suggesting their nature, would be:

Q: What are you?

A: I am a slave girl.

Q: What is a slave girl?

A: A girl who is owned.

Q: Why do you wear a brand?

A: To show that I am owned.

Q: Why do you wear a collar?

A: That men may know who owns me.

Q: What does a slave girl want more than anything?

A: To please men.

Q: What are you?

A: I am a slave girl.

Q: What do you want more than anything?

A: To please men.

There is, beyond these, an entire set of questions and answers, some of them considerably more detailed, and involving standard responses to simple questions pertaining to such matters as history and psychology.

The truly sinister aspect of even this portion of the girls' training did not become evident to me, or to Elizabeth, until the entire next week was spent again before the mirror, seeing themselves as slave girls, and repeating, aloud, these questions and answers, as though putting them to themselves; as though, with Flaminius gone, it was they themselves, the girls, who were putting these questions to themselves, and responding with almost hypnotic automatism; it was probably easiest on Elizabeth, who knew that she was playing a part, that she would be, sooner or later, carried to safety, but even Elizabeth, more than once, awakened with a cry in the night, clutching me, whimpering, "No, no, no." The sixth week of the training was spent, as several of the former, before the mirror, but this time repeating over and over, aloud, "I love being a slave girl. I love being a slave girl." At last, after this cruel and almost interminable repetition, utilizing simple psychological principles, intended to brand into the girls' psyche the identity of a Pleasure Slave, the girls began the period of exercises, many of which would, for certain periods of the day, be carried through the next months. During the next weeks and months the lessons of Flaminius were never again touched upon, except occasionally, for her amusement, by Sura, who would suddenly cry to one of the girls, at the same time brandishing the slave goad, such a query as "What do you want more than anything?" to which the girl, to her shame and astonishment, would find herself crying out in fear, "To please men!" Then Sura would say, "Then learn what I am teaching you," and they would respond, fearing the goad, "Yes, Mistress!"

In the hours that Virginia and Phyllis were not in training, and the training hours are only five Ahn a day, they were, particularly in the beginning, intensively drilled in Gorean. Elizabeth, on the other hand, usually assisted Caprus in his office. Later, when the girls became reasonably proficient at Gorean, they were permitted the freedom of the House baths, which they enjoyed, and the liberty to move about the House rather as they pleased, saving that they must be locked in their cells by the eighteenth bar. The foods given them also changed with the advance in their training, and the desire to have varied, tasty fare, and sometimes a small bowl of Ka-la-na with their supper, drove them to perform well. Further, each must eat the same, so pressure was brought on each to come to a given level, for the food of all remained the same until each had attained the desired next level of training. By the end of the twelfth week of their training they were eating well, and by the end of the fifteenth, very well, generally low-calorie foods, nourishing, a good amount of protein, diets supervised as carefully as those of racing tarns or hunting sleen; Elizabeth was the only girl who had, so to speak, a compartment of her own, with a door that might be shut, rather than simple bars, and so the three girls often, when possible, would come to the compartment, for some moments of privacy. At these times they would, as well as possible, converse in Gorean; Elizabeth taught them much; she did not permit them to know she spoke English; I would often leave the compartment at these times but sometimes I would remain. Elizabeth led them, to some extent, not to fear me, leading them to believe that she had so well served me that she had, to some degree, engaged my affections. I think she did not realize how true her words were.

In the beginning, when moving about the house, the girls had been permitted only the garb customarily worn in the sweat and motion of the training, a rectangle of silk, about a foot long, thrust into a silken string knotted about the waist; Virginia and Phyllis would not even leave their cells so clad until Elizabeth called upon them, so clad herself, ordering them forth; Phyllis had been tearfully furious that she should be so seen, Virginia terrified; but, on the orders of Elizabeth, who spoke with authority, they followed her forth, frightened, but heads high and shoulders back, and soon they were delighting in the sights of the house, for they had seen little but the kennels, the training room and their cells; it had been a good day for them; each was female and Elizabeth had taught them that this was a permissible thing to be.

"These men are slavers," Elizabeth confided to them. "They have seen women before."

Later, in the eighteenth week of their training, they were given brief silken slave livery, sleeveless, fastened by the loop on the left shoulder. Virginia and Phyllis were given white livery, Elizabeth red. It was at this time also that Virginia and Phyllis had been given their lock collars, white-enameled, and that the slave anklets, the identification bands, had been removed from their left ankles. Elizabeth, at the beginning of her training, had simply exchanged her yellow collar for a red one. She had already been a lock-collar girl.

By the twentieth week of their training the girls could converse rather adequately in Gorean, and Virginia and Phyllis continued to improve. Elizabeth, of course, was totally fluent in the language. Elizabeth's accent was interesting, for it was, in effect, Tuchuk; the accent of the girls was that of Ar. I noted, however, that Sura had insisted that the girls not refine their accents overly much, for it must remain clear they were barbarians; further, Virginia and Phyllis were encouraged to slur and lisp certain sounds, it being thought appealing in female slaves; on the other hand Sura, who did not slur and lisp these sounds herself, did not insist on it, for some reason, with the girls; accordingly Elizabeth, Phyllis and Virginia, not being forced to do so, did not adopt this affectation. I learned independently, from Ho-Tu, that this particular form of speech defect was, however, no longer in style; perhaps if it had been Sura would have been more adamant.

Once Virginia had, in our compartment, with Elizabeth and Phyllis, shyly looked up at me, and asked if I knew the name of the blond guard, he with blue eyes, who came upon occasion to observe the training.

"Relius," said I.

"Oh," said she, dropping her head.

"The fellow with him often," I volunteered, "is Ho-Sorl."

"The ugly one?" asked Phyllis. "The one with the black hair and the scar on the side of his face?"

"I do not think he is ugly," I said, "but I think you mean the same one as I. He does have black hair and there is a scar on the side of his face."

"I know him," said Phyllis. "He keeps looking at me. I detest him."

"I thought," said Elizabeth, "you were dancing to him this morning."

"I was not!" snapped Phyllis.

"And yesterday," laughed Elizabeth, rocking back, clapping her hands, "when Sura asked him to stand forth that one of us might approach him to administer the First Kiss of the Captive Slave Girl, it was you who first sprang to your feet."

"I have scarcely ever seen anyone move so fast," commented Virginia.

"It's not true!" cried Phyllis. "It's not true!"

"Perhaps he will buy you," suggested Elizabeth.

"No!" cried Phyllis.

"Do you think we will be sold at the Curulean?" asked Virginia of me.

"It is apparently the plan of Cernus," I said.

188

"I wonder," said Virginia, "if someone like Relius will buy me."

"Perhaps," said Elizabeth.

"I doubt it," said Phyllis. "You are too skinny and your face has pocks."

"I am not ugly," said Virginia. "And I cannot help it that I do not have a body like yours."

Phyllis tossed her head, sniffing.

"I was afraid of men," said Virginia, her head down. "But now I find I am curious about them. I did not know what to do, or how to act with men. But now I am a slave, and I am being taught. I am being shown what to do. I am not so afraid of men now." She looked at Phyllis. "I want a man," she said.

"Slave!" jeered Phyllis.

"Don't you want a man?" asked Virginia, tears in her eyes.

"I will have nothing to do with men," said Phyllis.

"Oh yes you will, Pleasure Slave," Elizabeth assured her, "oh yes you will!"

Phyllis cast her a withering glance.

"I wonder what it would be like to be in the arms of a man," said Virginia.

"Like Relius?" asked Elizabeth.

"Yes!" said Virginia.

Phyllis laughed.

Virginia dropped her head. "I am ugly," she said. "I am unworthy of being sold at the Curulean."

"You're a slave!" laughed Phyllis. "Only a slave! Virginia the little slave!"

"I am a slave," said Virginia. And she added, "And so are you!"

"I am not a slave!" cried Phyllis.

"Pretty little slave!" laughed Virginia, pointing her finger at her.

"Never say that to me!" screamed Phyllis, leaping to her feet.

"Pretty little slave!" screamed Virginia.

Phyllis leaped upon her and in an instant the two girls were rolling and scratching on the stones, screaming at one another.

"Stop them!" cried Elizabeth. "Stop them!"

I spoke calmly. "Free men do not much interfere in the squabbles of slaves."

The two girls stopped fighting. Phyllis stood up, breathing heavily. Virginia rose to her feet, and stepped back. She brushed back her hair with her right hand. Both girls looked at me.

"Thank you," said Virginia.

"It is time that you returned to your cells, Slaves," said I.

Virginia smiled. Phyllis, not speaking, turned and went to the door, but there she turned once more, looking at me, waiting for Virginia.

Virginia regarded me. "You are a man," she said. "Does Master find the slave Virginia ugly?"

"No," I said, "the slave Virginia is not ugly. The slave Virginia is beautiful."

There were tears in her eyes. "Could such a man as Relius, do you think," she asked, "desire such a slave as Virginia?"

"Doubtless," I said, as though irritated with her question, "were the slave Virginia not White Silk the man Relius would have asked for her long ago."

She looked at me gratefully.

It is, incidentally, one of the perquisites of employment in the house of a slaver that a member of the guard or staff may ask for, and generally receive, the use of whatever Red Silk Girls he pleases. Elizabeth had not been bothered in this particular because she was, by general recognition, solely mine while I remained in the house.

"And," I said, rather loudly, looking at Phyllis, "were the slave Phyllis not White Silk she would have found herself used frequently, and well, by the man Ho-Sorl."

Phyllis looked at me in fury and turned, leaving the room. She walked beautifully, sinuous in her rage.

"The slave Phyllis," I said, rather loudly again, "has learned much from Mistress Sura."

Phyllis cried out and turned in the hall, her fists clenched. Then she spun about with a cry of rage and ran weeping down the corridor.

Elizabeth clapped her hands and laughed.

I glared at Virginia, who still stood in the room. "Go to your cell, Slave," I said.

Virginia dropped her head, smiling. "Yes," she said, "Master," and then turned and left. She, too, walked beautifully.

"It is hard to believe," said Elizabeth, "that she once taught classics and ancient history in a college."

"Yes," I said, "it is."

"On Earth," said Elizabeth, "I do not think a woman would dare walk so beautifully."

"No," I said, "I do not think so."

The training of the slave girls progressed. It had begun, following the period entirely consumed with exercises, with such small things as instruction on how to stand, to walk, to kneel, to recline, to eat, to drink. Grace and beauty, following Sura, and I would scarcely dare dispute such an authority, is mostly a matter of expression, both that of the face and body. I could, week to week, see the change in the girls, even Elizabeth. Some of the things they were taught seemed to me very silly, but I, at the same time, found it difficult to object.

One thing of that sort I recall is a trick where the girl feeds the master a grape held between her teeth. She may or may not have her wrists braceleted behind her back for this particular feat. One leg is folded beneath her and the other is extended behind her, toes pointed, and then she lifts the grape delicately to your mouth. Elizabeth and I used to laugh heartily over this one, but I think it was effective, as I seldom got beyond the third grape.

"Observe," once had said Elizabeth to me, to my amusement, in the secrecy of our compartment, "the twelfth way to enter a room."

I had observed. It was not bad. But I think I preferred the tenth, that with the girl's back against the side of the door, the palms of her hands on the jamb, her head up, lips slightly parted, eyes to the right, smoldering at just the right temperature.

"How many ways are there," I asked, sitting cross-legged in the center of the compartment, on the stone couch, "to enter a room?"

"It depends on the city," said Elizabeth. "In Ar we are the best; we have the most ways to enter a room. One hundred and four."

I whistled.

"What about," I asked, "just walking straight through?"

She looked at me. "Ah," said she, "one hundred and five!"

A good deal of the training of the slave girl, surprisingly, to my naive mind, was in relatively domestic matters. For example, the Pleasure Slave, if she is trained by a good house, must also be the master of those duties commonly assigned to Tower Slaves. Accordingly, they must know how to cut and sew cloth, to wash garments and clean various types of materials and surfaces, and to cook an extensive variety of foods, from the rough fare of Warriors to concoctions which are exotic almost to the point of being inedible. Elizabeth would regularly bring her efforts back to the compartment, and the nights were not infrequent when I longed for the simple fare at the table of Cernus, or perhaps a bowl of Ho-Tu's gruel. One dish I recall was composed of the tongues of eels and was sprinkled with flavored aphrodisiacs, the latter however being wasted on me as I spent, to Elizabeth's consternation, the night lying on my side in great pain. Elizabeth was, however, to my satisfaction, taught a large number of things which, to my mind, were more appropriate to the training of slave girls, including a large number of dances, dozens of songs, and an unbelievable variety of kisses and caresses. The sheer mechanics of her repertoire, theoretically outfitting her to give exquisite pleasure to anyone from an Ubar to a peasant, are much too complex and lengthy to recount here. I do not think, however, that I have forgotten any of it. One thing that I thought was nice was that Elizabeth had asked Sura about the dance she had begun to perform but could not finish, when we had first come to the house of Cernus, the dance which is accompanied by the Tuchuk slave song. Sura, who seemed to know everything, taught the rest of it, song and all, to her, and to the other girls. For good measure she also taught them the independent dance, sometimes called the Dance of the Tuchuk Slave Girl, which I had once seen performed at a banquet in Turia.

"Know that you are beautiful," Sura had once said to them. "Now I will teach you to dance."

My own duties during these months in the House of Cernus remained light, consisting of little more than accompanying Cernus on infrequent occasions on which he left the house, a member of his guard; in the city Cernus traveled in a sedan chair, borne on the shoulders of eight men. The chair was enclosed and, under the blue and yellow silk which covered it, there was metal plating.

The night that Phyllis Robertson, under the torches in the hall of Cernus, while we supped, performed the belt dance, was the last day of the Eleventh passage hand, about a month before the Gorean New Year, which occurs on the Vernal Equinox, the first day of the month of En'Kara. The training of the girls, over the months, had been substantially completed, and would be for all practical purposes finished by the end of the twelfth passage hand. Many houses would doubtless have put them up for sale in En'Kara, but Cernus, as I had heard, was saving them for the Love Feast, which occupies the five days of the fifth passage hand, falling late in the summer. There was a variety of reasons why he was postponing their sale. The most obvious was that good prices are commanded on the Love Feast. But perhaps more importantly he had been spreading rumors throughout the city of the desirability of trained barbarians, of which he now had several in training, those who had been brought to Gor with Virginia and Phyllis, some who had been brought to the pens earlier and not sold off immediately, and a large number who had been brought in subsequent trips to the Voltai by the ship of the slavers; I had sometimes but not always accompanied Cernus on these missions; to the best of my knowledge one or another of the black ships had come seven times to the point of rendezvous, since the one I had first seen; the House of Cernus now, altogether, had better than one hundred and fifty barbarians in training, under the tutelage of various Passion Slaves; I gathered that the reports of Sura and Ho-Tu on the progress of the first group, that of Elizabeth, Virginia and Phyllis, had been extremely encouraging. In postponing the sales until the Love Feast, of course, there would be time to complete, at least substantially, the training of a large number of barbarian girls. Also, as Cernus doubtless intended, the delay would give his delicately seeded rumors, pertaining to the desirability of barbarians, time to circulate, time to stimulate the imagination and inflame the curiosity of potential buyers. I gather his planning must have been successful, for sales generally in Ar during the first two months of the New Year were down somewhat from seasonal norms, as though Ar's gold for slaves was being held somewhat, in anticipation of the Love Feast.

I recall one incident worthy of note from that night Phyllis performed the belt dance.

It was rather late in the evening, but Cernus had remained long at table, playing game after game with Caprus the Scribe.

At one point he had lifted his head, listening. Outside, in the air overhead, we heard a storm of wings, tarnsmen aflight. He smiled, and returned to his game. Later we heard the marching of men's feet outside in the streets, the clanking of weapons. Cernus listened, and once again turned to his game. A few minutes later we heard a great deal of shouting, and running about. Again Cernus listened, and smiled, and then returned to the study of the board.

I myself was curious to know what was occurring, but I did not leave the table. I had made it a practice normally to eat beside Ho-Tu, to come to the table with him and leave with him, and Ho-Tu was not yet ready to leave. He had finished his gruel but he was sitting there listening to a slave girl, sitting on furs between the tables, playing a kalika. Several of the guards and staff had left the tables, retiring. Even the girls at the wall had been unchained and returned, after the evening's sport, to their cells. Phyllis and Virginia, and Elizabeth, had long since left the hall. Ho-Tu was fond of the music of the kalika, a six-stringed, plucked instrument, with a hemispheric sound box and long neck. Sura, I knew, played the instrument. Elizabeth, Virginia and Phyllis had been shown its rudiments, as well as something about the lyre, but they had not been expected to become proficient, nor were they given the time to become so; if their master, at a later date, after their sale, wished his girls to possess these particular attributes, which are seldom involved in the training of slave girls, he himself could pay for their instruction; the time of the girls, I noted, was rather fully occupied, without spending hours a day on music. The slave girl sitting on the furs, for the kalika is played either sitting or standing, bent over her instrument, her hair falling over the neck of it, lost in her music, a gentle, slow melody, rather sad. I had heard it sung some two years ago by the bargemen on the Cartius, a tributary of the Vosk, far to the south and west of Ar. Ho-Tu's eyes were closed. The horn spoon lay to the side of the empty gruel bowl. The girl had begun to hum the melody now, and Ho-Tu, almost inaudibly, but I could hear him, hummed it as well.

The door to the hall suddenly burst open and two guards, followed by two others, burst in. The first two guards were holding between them a heavy man, with a paunch that swung beneath his robes, wild-eyed, his hands extended to Cernus. Though he wore the robe of the Metal Workers, though now without a hood, he was not of that caste.

"Portus!" whispered Ho-Tu.

I, too, of course, recognized him.

"Caste sanctuary!" cried Portus, shaking himself free of the guards and stumbling forward and falling on his knees before the wooden dais on which sat the table of Cernus.

Cernus did not look up from his game.

"Caste sanctuary!" screamed Portus.

The Slavers, incidentally, are of the Merchant Caste, though, in virtue of their merchandise and practices, their robes are different. Yet, if one of them were to seek Caste Sanctuary, he would surely seek it from Slavers, and not from common Merchants. Many Slavers think of themselves as an independent caste. Gorean law, however, does not so regard them. The average Gorean thinks of them simply as Slavers, but, if questioned, would unhesitantly rank them with the Merchants. Many castes, incidentally, have branches and divisions. Lawyers and Scholars, for example, and Record Keepers, Teachers, Clerks, Historians and Accountants are all Scribes.

"Caste sanctuary!" again pleaded Portus, on his knees before the table of Cernus. The girl with the kalika had lightly fled from between the tables.

"Do not disturb the game," said Caprus to Portus.

It seemed incredible to me that Portus had come to the House of Cernus, for much bad blood had existed between the houses. Surely to come to this place, the house of his enemy, must have been a last recourse in some fearful set of events, to throw himself on the mercies of Cernus, claiming Caste Sanctuary.

"They have taken my properties!" cried Portus. "You have nothing to fear. I have no men! I have no gold! I have only the garb on my back! Tarnsmen! Soldiers! The very men of the street! With torches and ropes! I barely escaped with my life. My house is confiscated by the state! I am nothing! I am nothing!"

Cernus meditated his move, his chin on his two fists, one above the other.

"Caste sanctuary!" whined Portus. "Caste sanctuary, I beg of you. I beg of you!"

The hand of Cernus lifted, as though to move his Ubar, and then drew back. Caprus had leaned forward, with anticipation.

"Only you in Ar can protect me," cried Portus. "I give you the trade of Ar! I want only my life! Caste Sanctuary! Caste Sanctuary!"

Cernus smiled at Caprus and then, unexpectedly, as though he had been teasing him, he placed his first tarnsman at Ubara's Scribe Two.

Caprus studied the board for a moment and then, with an exasperated laugh, tipped his own Ubar, conceding the board and game.

Cernus now, while Caprus replaced the pieces of the game, regarded Portus.

"I was your enemy," said Portus. "But now I am nothing. Only a caste brother, nothing. I beg of you Caste Sanctuary."

Caprus, looking up from his work, regarded Portus. "What was your crime?" he asked.

Portus wrung his hands, and his head rolled wildly. "I do not know," he cried. "I do not know!" Then, piteously, Portus lifted his hands to Cernus, Master of the House of Cernus. "Caste Sanctuary!" he pleaded.

"Put him in chains," said Cernus, "and take him to the cylinder of Minus Tentius Hinrabius."

Portus cried out for mercy as he was dragged away by two guards, two others following.

Cernus stood up behind the table, ready now to retire. He looked at me and smiled. "By the end of En'Var," said he, "Killer, I will be Ubar of Ar."

He then left the table.

Ho-Tu and I looked at one another, each as puzzled as the other.

Sixteen

The Tarn

Less than a month following the downfall of the House of Portus, Cernus had become the undisputed master of the slave trade in Ar. He had purchased from the state the facilities and chattels of the House of Portus, at a comparatively small price. The men of the House of Portus, who had been Slavers and mercenaries the equals of those of the House of Cernus, had now been disbanded, some leaving the city, some taking their gold from new masters, some even hiring their swords to the House of Cernus.

I would have expected the price of slaves to rise in Ar, but Cernus did not permit it, but continued, when necessary, to undersell the minor houses to keep the general prices in the range he wished. This was hailed as generosity on his part by those of Ar, who were familiar with and had experienced to their sorrow, particularly since the deposition of Kazrak, the effect of a number of monopolies, in particular those in salt and tharlarion oil.

Further, because of his services to the state, including the sponsorship of games and races, Cernus was, upon the petition of Saphronicus, Captain of the Taurentians, invested in the scarlet of the Warrior, thus honoring him with High Caste. He did not, of course, give up the House of Cernus nor any other of his widely ranging interests in Ar and beyond it. I do not suppose the Hinrabian Administrator much cared to approve this raising of caste in the case of Cernus, but he lacked the courage to go against the wishes of the Taurentians, and of the city generally. The High Council, with scarcely a murmur, agreed to the investiture. That he was now of the Caste of Warriors did not change much with Cernus, of course, save that a strip of red silk, with those of blue and yellow, now adorned his left sleeve. I did know that

Cernus had been, for years, trained in the use of weapons. Indeed, he was said to be, and I do not doubt it, first sword in the house. He had doubtless hired masters of arms because he wished to acquire skill in weapons, but I think, too, he may, even for years, have had in mind his investiture as Warrior. It perhaps need only be added that now being a Warrior, and thus of High Caste, he was now eligible for a seat on the High Council of the city, and even for the throne itself, whether it be that of Administrator or Ubar. Cernus celebrated his investiture by sponsoring the first games and races of the new season, which began in En'Kara.

It had been a long, hard winter for me and I think I, as well as the common citizens of Ar, rejoiced in the coming of En'Kara. The girls had finished their training during the Twelfth Passage Hand. Little then remained for them except to review their lessons, eat and sleep well, and be in prime condition for their sale in the late summer, during the Fifth Passage Hand, on the Love Feast. On the first day of the Waiting Hand, the last five days of the old year, the portals of Ar, including even that of the House of Cernus, had been painted white, and in many of the low-caste homes had been sealed with pitch, not to be opened until the first day of En'Kara. Almost all doors, including that of the House of Cernus, had nailed to them some branches of the Brak Bush, the leaves of which, when chewed, have a purgative effect. It is thought that the pitch and the branches of the Brak Bush discourage the entry of bad luck into the houses of the citizens. During the days of the Waiting Hand the streets are almost deserted, and in the Houses there is much fasting, and little conversation, and no song. Rations even in the House of Cernus were halved during this period. Paga and Ka-la-na were not served. The slaves in the pens received almost nothing. Then, at dawn, on the first day of En'Kara, in the name of the city, the Administrator of Ar, or a Ubar if it be Ubar, greets the sun, welcoming it to Ar on the first day of the New Year. The great bars suspended about the walls of the city then ring out for more than an Ahn with their din, and the doors of the city burst open and the people crowd out onto the bridges, clad in the splendor of their finest, singing and laughing. The doors are painted green and the pitch washed away, and the branches of the Brak Bush burned in a small ceremony on the threshold. There are processions in the city that day, and songfests, and tournaments of the game, and recitations by poets, and contests and exhibitions. When the lanterns on the bridges must be lit the people return home, singing, carrying small lamps, and give the night over to feasting and love. Even the slaves in the iron pens in the House of Cernus received that day a small cake with oil and had their troughs filled with water mixed with paga. It was also the day that, before the High Council and the Administrator, Cernus, of the House of Cernus, accepted the red of the Warrior from the hands of Saphronicus, Captain of the Taurentians. The following day would begin the races and games sponsored by the House of Cernus.

On the first day of En'Kara much of the old year had been forgotten, but there were three who could not forget it; Portus, who lay chained in the dungeons of the Central Cylinder; Claudia Tentia Hinrabia, now free, but who had endured the shame of slavery, and would perhaps never again permit herself to walk on the high bridges of the city; and Tarl Cabot, who seemed as far now from his goal as he had been months before, when first he came to the House of Cernus.

I had, during the Waiting Hand, cornered Caprus, angered, demanding that he now turn over what he had, that it would be enough, and that we would fly during En'Kara. But he had assured me that just recently Cernus had received a large batch of new documents and maps, which were perhaps crucial, and that the Priest-Kings would surely be angry if he did not obtain copies of them as well; moreover, he reminded me, he would refuse to let any documents leave the house unless they all did, himself being carried to safety at the same time. I was furious but it seemed to me I could do nothing. I turned and strode away from him, enraged.

The games and the races began with great enthusiasm and excitement. Murmillius, in the games, returned with more brilliance than ever and, on the second day of En'Kara, with superb swordsmanship downed two foes, wounding them again and again, until even the crowd did not regard them as worth slaying, at which time Murmillius sheathed his sword, turned his back, and left the two bleeding men standing in the sand, staring after him, only to collapse a moment later, weak from the loss of blood. The Yellows carried the first day of the races, led by Menicius of Port Kar, claiming more than six thousand wins, perhaps the most famed rider since the days of Melipolus of Cos, who even in his own time had been a legend, said to have accumulated more than eight thousand wins. The Greens came in second, carrying three of the eleven races. The Yellows had won seven, five of them ridden by Menicius.

I remember this first day of the races well.

The girls, too, would have special reason, as I would, to recall it. For them, it was the first time since the beginning of their training that they were permitted to leave the house. Normally, late in their training, girls are permitted the sights of the city, that they may be stimulated and refreshed, but such had not been the case with Elizabeth, Virginia and Phyllis. According to Ho-Tu, whom I had once asked about this, there were two main reasons for this; first, their training was peculiarly full and intensive; second, the prospect of being permitted to leave the house, particularly attractive to Virginia and Phyllis, who had known nothing of Gor save the House of Cernus, was a powerful inducement to be diligent in their lessons. Further, as Ho-Tu pointed out, their sale was not to be until the late summer; thus there was plenty of time to use the sights and scenes of Ar, judiciously mixed with review and practice, diet and rest, to bring them to a height of vitality, interest and excitement before putting them on the block. Timing in such matters, following Ho-Tu, is extremely important. A bored, jaded or overstimulated girl does not perform as well as one whose appetites, whetted, stand at their peak.

At any rate, regardless of the reasoning, or the stratagems of Slavers, Elizabeth, Virginia and Phyllis were permitted to attend the first day of the races, under, of course, suitable guard.

We met in Sura's training room and I, who was to be in charge of this expedition, given that I would let no other guard Elizabeth, was given a leather sack of silver and copper coins by Ho-Tu, for the expenses of the day. Each of the girls would wear brief silken slave livery, sleeveless, the disrobing loop on the left shoulder. Elizabeth wore red, Virginia and Phyllis white. Each of the girls was also issued a light slave cloak, the hem of which fell a bit above the hem of her livery, but which had a hood. Elizabeth's was red with white stripes, Virginia and Phyllis' white with red stripes. To their consternation, before being permitted to leave the training room, Virginia and Phyllis, beneath their livery, had locked on their bodies, by Sura, the iron belt. The other two guards, who arrived carrying slave bracelets and slave leashes, the latter of light, gleaming chain, were Relius and

Ho-Sorl. Virginia, seeing Relius, merely lowered her head; Phyllis, seeing Ho-Sorl, seemed beside herself with anger.

"Please," she said to Sura, "let it not be he."

"Be silent, Slave," said Sura.

"Come here, Slave," said Ho-Sorl to Phyllis. She looked at him angrily, and went to him.

Relius, who had walked over to Virginia, placed his large hands on her hips. She did not raise her head.

"She wears the iron belt," said Sura. Relius nodded.

"And I will hold the key," said Sura.

"Of course," said Relius. Virginia did not raise her head.

"This one does, too," said Ho-Sorl, a bit irritably.

"Of course I wear the iron belt," said Phyllis, even more irritably. "What did you expect?"

"I will hold the key to her belt as well," said Sura.

"Let me hold the key," suggested Ho-Sorl, and Phyllis blanched.

Sura laughed. "No," she said, "I will hold it."

"Bracelets!" snapped Ho-Sorl suddenly, and Phyllis flung her wrists behind her back, threw back her head and turned it to one side, the instantaneous response of a trained girl.

Ho-Sorl laughed.

Tears appeared in Phyllis' eyes. Her response, automatic, unthinking, had been that of a trained animal. Before she could recover, Ho-Sorl had snapped the bracelets on her. He then said, "Leash," and she looked at him angrily, then lifted her chin. He snapped the leash on her collar.

Meanwhile Virginia had turned her back to Relius, extending her wrists, and he had put bracelets on her; then she turned and faced him, her head still down. "Leash," said he, quietly. She lifted her head, the chin delicately high. There was a metallic snap and Virginia Kent, the slave girl, had been leashed by Relius, guard in the House of Cernus, Slaver of Ar.

"Do you want leash and bracelets for her?" asked Sura, pointing to Elizabeth.

"Oh yes," I said. "Yes, of course."

They were brought. Elizabeth glared at me while I braceleted her, and leashed her. Then, together, we left the House of Cernus, leading our girls.

Outside the House of Cernus, and around the first corner, I took the bracelets and leash from Elizabeth.

"Why did you do that?" asked Ho-Sorl.

"She will be more comfortable," I said. "Besides," I said, "she is only Red Silk."

"He is probably not afraid of her," said Phyllis pointedly.

"I do not understand," said Ho-Sorl.

"You may remove the bracelets from me," said Phyllis. "I will not attack you." Phyllis turned about and held her braceleted hands to Ho-Sorl, her head irritably in the air.

"Well," said Ho-Sorl. "I would certainly not want to be attacked."

Phyllis stamped her foot.

Relius was looking at Virginia, and with his hand he lifted her chin, and for the first time, she met his eyes, with her deep gray, timid eyes. "If I remove the bracelets from you," said Relius, "you will not attempt to escape, will you?"

"No," she said, softly, "Master."

In an instant her bracelets had been removed. "Thank you," said she, "Master." The Gorean slave girl addresses all free men as "Master" and all free women as "Mistress."

Relius looked deeply into her eyes, and she dropped her head.

"Pretty slave," he said.

Without looking up, she smiled. "Handsome Master," she said.

I was startled. That seemed rather bold for the timid Virginia Kent.

Relius laughed and set off down the street, giving Virginia a tug that almost pulled her off her feet, and she stumbled and caught up with him, then remembered herself, and followed him, head down, two paces behind, but he gave her another tug and took up the slack in her leash, so that she must walk at his side, and she did so, barefoot, beautiful, and, I think, happy.

Ho-Sorl was speaking to Phyllis. "I will take off the bracelets, but in order that you may attack me if you wish. That might be amusing."

The bracelets were removed from Phyllis. She rubbed her wrists and stretched in the leash.

"I think I will tear the iron belt from her," commented Ho-Sorl.

Phyllis stopped stretching. She looked at Ho-Sorl irritably. "Perhaps you wish me to promise that I shall not attempt to escape?" she inquired.

"That will not be necessary," responded Ho-Sorl, starting off after Relius. "You will not escape."

"Oh," cried Phyllis, nearly thrown from her feet. Then she was angrily walking beside Ho-Sorl. But he stopped and turned and regarded her. Not speaking, but biting her lip, she stepped back two paces, and thus, leashed, furious, followed him.

"Let us not be late for the races," said Elizabeth.

I extended her my arm, and together we followed the guards and their prisoners.

At the races Relius and Ho-Sorl unsnapped the slave leashes and, though in the stands, amid thousands of people, Virginia and Phyllis were free. Virginia seemed rather grateful, and knelt quite close to Relius, who sat on the tier; in a moment she felt his arm about her shoulders and thus they watched race after race, or seemed to watch the race, for often I observed them looking rather more at one another. Ho-Sorl, after several races, gave Phyllis a coin, ordering her to find a vendor and buy him some Sa-Tarna bread smeared with honey. A sly look came over her face and in an instant, saying "Yes, Master," she was gone.

I looked at Ho-Sorl. "She will try to escape," I said.

The black-haired, scarred fellow looked at me, and smiled. "Of course," he said.

"If she escapes," I said, "Cernus will doubtless have you impaled."

"Doubtless," said Ho-Sorl. "But she will not escape."

Pretending not to be particularly observant, but watching very closely, Ho-Sorl and I observed Phyllis picking her way past two vendors with bread and honey. He smiled at me. "See," he said.

"Yes," I said. "I see."

Phyllis then, darting a look about her, suddenly turned and fled down one of the dark ramps at the races.

Ho-Sorl leaped nimbly to his feet and started after her.

I waited a moment or so and then I arose also. "Wait here," I said to Elizabeth.

"Don't let him hurt her," said Elizabeth to me.

"She is his prisoner," I told Elizabeth.

"Please," said Elizabeth.

"Look," I said, "Cernus would not be much pleased if she were slain or disfigured. The most Ho-Sorl will do to her is give her a good drubbing."

"She doesn't know any better," said Elizabeth.

"And that," I said, "would probably do her good."

I then left Elizabeth, and Relius and Virginia, and started off after Ho-Sorl and Phyllis, picking my way through the bustling crowd. The judge's bar rang three times, signaling that the tarns were coming to the track for the next race.

I had hardly walked more than fifty yards through the crowd when I heard a frightened scream, that of a girl, coming from the dark ramp down which Phyllis had disappeared. I then pushed and shoved my way through men and women, tumbling a vendor to the left, and raced to the passageway. I could now hear some angry cries of men, the sound of blows.

I bounded down the ramp, three turns, and managed to seize a fellow by the neck and arm and fling him some dozen feet to the next landing below, who had been rushing on Ho-Sorl from behind. Ho-Sorl meanwhile was lifting one fellow over his head and hurling him down the ramp. On both the left and the right side there lay a battered, senseless fellow. Phyllis, wild eyed, the clothing half torn from her, the iron belt revealed, was trembling by the iron banister on the ramp, on her knees shuddering, her left wrist braceleted to the railing, breathing spasmodically. The fellow Ho-Sorl had flung down the ramp rolled for some feet, struck the wall at the turn, struggled to his feet and drew a knife. Ho-Sorl immediately took a step toward him and the fellow screamed, threw down his knife, and ran.

Ho-Sorl strode over to Phyllis. The bracelet that fastened her to the railing was his. I gather he had come on the men, who had apparently seized the girl, beaten them away, braceleted her to keep her there, and then turned to fight them again as they had regrouped and attacked.

He glared down at Phyllis, who, this time, did not meet his eyes but looked down at the stones of the ramp on which she knelt.

"So," said Ho-Sorl, "the pretty little slave girl would run away?"

Phyllis swallowed hard, looking down, not speaking.

"Where did the pretty little slave girl think to run?" asked Ho-Sorl.

"I don't know," she said numbly.

"Pretty little slave girls are foolish, aren't they?" asked Ho-Sorl.

"I don't know," she said. "I don't know."

"There is no place to run," said Ho-Sorl.

Phyllis looked up at him, then, I think, feeling the true hopelessness of her plight.

"Yes," she said numbly, "there is no place to run."

Ho-Sorl did not beat her but rather, after removing the slave bracelets from the railing of the ramp and from her wrist, putting the bracelets in his belt, simply pulled her to her feet. He found the ripped slave cloak and hood which had been torn from her and helped her to tie together the parts of her slave livery. When she stood ready to return to the tiers she put her back to him and extended her wrists behind her. But he did not bracelet her, nor leash her. Rather he looked about on the ramp until he found the small coin he had given her to buy him bread and honey, which coin she had dropped when the four men had seized her. To her astonishment he gave her the coin. "Buy me bread and honey," he told her. Then he said to me, "We have missed the sixth race," and together we turned about and went back into the stands, finding our seats. Some minutes later Phyllis came to our seats, bringing Ho-Sorl his bread and honey, and the two copper tarn disks change. He became absorbed in the races. He may not have noticed that she knelt on the tier below us, her head down, her face in her hands, sobbing. Virginia and Elizabeth knelt with her, one on each side, holding her about the shoulders. "I only regret," Ho-Sorl was saying to me, "that I never saw Melipolus of Cos ride."

Race followed race, and, eventually, we heard the judge's bar ringing three times, signaling that the tarns were being brought out for the eleventh race, the last of the day.

"What do you think of the Steels?" asked Relius, leaning toward me.

The Steels were a new faction in Ar, their patch a bluish gray. But they had no following. Indeed, there had never yet been a Steel in a race in Ar. I had heard, however, that the first tarn would fly for the Steels in this very race, the eleventh race, that which was shortly to begin. I did know, further, that a tarncot for the Steels had been established during Se'Var and riders had been hired. The backing of the faction was a bit mysterious. What gold there was behind the Steels was not clear, either as to quantity or origin. It might be noted, however, that a serious investment is involved in attempting to form a faction. There are often attempts to found a new faction, but generally they are unsuccessful. If a substantial proportion of races are not won in the first two seasons the law of the Stadium of Tarns discontinues its recognition of that faction. Moreover, to bring a new faction into competition is an expensive business, and involves considerable risk to the capital advanced. Not only is it expensive to buy or rent tarncots, acquire racing tarns, hire riders and Tarn Keepers, and the entire staff required to maintain a faction organization, but there is a large track fee for new factions, during the first two probation years. This fee, incidentally, can be levied even against older factions if their last season is a very poor one; moreover, a number of substandard seasons, even for an established faction, will result in the loss, permanently or for a ten-year period, of their rights on the track. Further, the appearance of new factions is a threat to the older factions, for each win of the new counts as a loss against the old. It is to the advantage of any given faction that there should be a small number of factions in competition and so the riders of an older faction, if unable to win themselves in given races, will often attempt to prevent a good race being flown by the riders of the new faction. Further, it is common among older factions not to hire riders who have ridden for the new factions, though sometimes, in the case of a particularly excellent rider, this practice is waived.

"What do you think of the Steels?" asked Relius again.

"I don't know," I said. "I know nothing of them." There had been something in his voice which puzzled me. Also, Ho-Sorl gave me a look at about this time. Neither of them, incidentally, had ever seemed much taken aback by the fact that I commonly wore the black of the Assassin. Now, of course, as I usually did when I was outside the house, I wore the red of the Warrior. They had not exactly attempted to become friends with me, but they had not avoided me; and often where I was I found them about.

"Now that is a bird!" cried Ho-Sorl, as the low, wheeled platforms were being drawn on the track.

I heard several in the crowd cry out in amazement.

I looked down to the track, and could not speak. I sat frozen on the tier. I could not breathe.

Throughout the stands, startling those multitudes, unsettling the other birds being drawn by the horned tharlarion on the low carts, there was heard the sudden shrill, ringing challenge scream of a tarn, unhooded, a giant tarn, black, a wild mountain cry of one of Gor's fiercest, most beautiful predators, that might have been heard in the sharp crags of the Mountains of Thentis, famed for its tarn flocks, or even among the red peaks of the lofty, magnificent Voltai itself, or perhaps in battle far above the swirling land below as tarnsmen met in duels to the death.

"It is not even a racing tarn," said a man nearby.

I now stood on my feet, stupefied, staring down at the wagons, the birds being brought to the perches.

"They tell me," said Relius, "that the bird is from the city of Ko-ro-ba."

I stood there, not speaking, my limbs weak. Behind me I heard Virginia and Phyllis cry out with pain. I turned a bit to see that Ho-Sorl had a fist in the hair of each, twisting it, pulling their heads back to him. "Slaves," said he, "will not speak of what they see today."

"No, Master!" said Virginia.

"No, no!" cried Phyllis. Ho-Sorl's hand twisted her head and hair cruelly. "No, Master!" cried Phyllis. "No, Master! Phyllis will not speak!"

I turned to my left and began to follow the tier, until I came to a narrow set of stairs, leading to the lower portions of the stands, which I then followed, descending.

I heard Relius behind me. "Take this," he said. He pushed something into my hand, something like a folded cloth of leather. I scarcely noticed. Then he was left on the stairs, and I was descending again, alone. Near the railing of the front tier, I stopped.

I was now some forty yards from the birds. I stood still.

Then, as though searching for me in those multitudes, that turbulence of faces and cloth, of sound, of cries, I saw the gleaming eyes of the tarn cease their scanning and fasten upon me. The wicked, black eyes, round and blazing with light, did not leave me. The crest on its head seemed to lift and each muscle and fiber in that great body seemed filled with blood and life. The vast, long black wings, broad and mighty, opened and struck against the air, hurling a storm of dust and sand on all sides, almost tumbling the small, hooded Tarn Keeper from the low wagon. Then the tarn threw back its head and once more screamed, wild, eerie, fierce, savage, a cry that might have struck terror into the heart of a larl, but I did not fear it. I saw the talons of the tarn were shod with steel. It was, of course, a war tarn.

I looked down at the wad of leather in my hand. I opened it, and drew on the hood concealing my features. I leaped over the rail and strode to the bird.

"Greetings, Mip," said I, mounting to the platform, seeing the small Tarn Keeper.

"You are Gladius of Cos," said he.

I nodded. "What is the meaning of this?" I asked.

"You ride for the Steels," said he.

I reached up and touched the fierce, curved beak of that mighty bird. And then I held it, and pressed my cheek to its fierce surface. The tarn, that predator, gently lowered its head, and I put my head against its head, below its round, gleaming right eye, and, within the leather hood, unseen, I wept. "It has been long, Ubar of the Skies," I said. "It has been long."

Vaguely I was aware about me of the sounds of men, tense, speaking curt words, mounting into the high saddles of tarns.

I sensed Mip near me.

"Do not forget what I have taught you in the Stadium of Tarns," said Mip, "as we have ridden together so many nights."

"I will not," I said.

"Mount," said Mip.

I climbed to the saddle of the tarn, and when Mip unlocked the hobble from its right foot, took it to the starting perch.

Seventeen

Kajuralia

"Kajuralia!" cried the slave girl hurling a basket of Sa-Tarna flour on me, and turning and running. I had caught up with her in five steps and kissed her roundly, swatted her and sent her packing.

"Kajuralia yourself!" I said laughing, and she, laughing, sped away.

About that time a large pan of warm water splashed down on me from a window some sixteen feet above the street level. Wringing wet I glared upward.

I saw a girl in the window, who blew me a kiss, a slave girl.

"Kajuralia!" she cried and laughed.

I raised my fist and shook it and her head disappeared from the window.

A Builder, whose robes were stained with thrown fruit, hastily strode by. "You had better be indoors," said he, "on Kajuralia."

Three male house slaves stumbled by, crowned with odorous garlands woven of the Brak Bush. They were passing about a bota of paga and, between dancing and trying to hold one another up, managed to weave unsteadily by. One of them looked at me and from his eyes I judged he may have seen at least three of me and offered me a swig of the bota, which I took. "Kajuralia," said he, nearly falling over backwards, being rescued by one of his fellows, who seemed fortunately to be falling in the opposite direction at the same time. I gave him a silver coin for more paga. "Kajuralia," I said, and turned about, leaving, while they collapsed on one another.

At that time a slave girl, a blond girl, sped by and the three slaves, stumbling, bleary-eyed, bumping into one another, dutifully took up her pursuit. She turned, laughing in front of them, would run a bit, then stop, and then when they had nearly caught up with her, she would run on again. But, to her astonishment, coming up from behind, catching her by surprise, another male seized her about the waist and held her, while she screamed in mock fear. But in a moment it was determined, to the rage of all save the girl, that she wore an iron belt. "Kajuralia!" she laughed, wiggled free and sped away.

I dodged a hurled larma fruit which splattered on the wall of a cylinder near me.

The wall itself was covered with writing and pictures, none of it much complimentary to the masters of the area.

I heard some breaking of pottery around the corner, some angry cries, the laughing of girls.

I decided I had better return to the House of Cernus.

I turned down another street. Here, unexpectedly, I ran into a pack of some fifteen or twenty girls who, shrieking and laughing, surrounded me in a moment. I found myself wishing that masters belled their girls for Kajuralia, so that they might be heard approaching. Their silence in the street a moment before I had turned into it told me they had been hunting. They had probably even had spies, advance scouts. Now they crowded about me, laughing, seizing my arms.

"Prisoner! Prisoner!" they shrieked.

I felt a rope thrown about my throat; it was drawn unpleasantly tight.

It was held in the hand of a black-haired girl, collared of course, long-legged, in brief slave livery.

"Greetings," said she, "Warrior." She jerked menacingly on the rope. "You are now the slave of the girls of the Street of Pots," she informed me.

I felt five or six more ropes suddenly looped about me, drawn tight. Two girls had even, behind me, darted unseen to my ankles, and in an instant had looped and drawn tight ropes on them. My feet could be thus jerked from beneath me should I attempt to run or struggle.

"What shall we do with this prisoner?" asked the black-haired girl of her fellows.

Numerous suggestions were forthcoming. "Take off his clothes!" "Brand him!" "The whip!" "Put him in a collar!"

"Now look here," I said.

But they had now set off down the street, dragging me along amongst them.

We stopped when I was pushed stumbling into a large room, in which there were numerous baskets and harnesses hanging about, apparently a storeroom of sorts in an unimportant cylinder. A wide area had been cleared in the center of the room, on which, over straw, had been spread some rep-cloth blankets. Against one wall there were two men, bound hand and foot. One was a Warrior, the other a handsome young Tarn Keeper. "Kajuralia," said the Warrior to me, wryly.

"Kajuralia," I said to him.

The black-haired girl, the tall girl, walked back and forth before me, her hands on her hips. She also strode over to the other two men, and then she returned to me.

"Not a bad catch," said she.

The other girls laughed and shrieked. Some leaped up and down and clapped their hands.

"Now you will serve us, Slaves," announced the black-haired girl.

We were freed, save that two ropes apiece were kept on our throats, and a rope on each ankle, each rope in the care of one of the girls.

We were given some small cups of tin, containing some diluted Kala-na that the girls had probably stolen.

"After we have been served wine," announced the girl, "we will use these slaves for our pleasure."

Before we were permitted to serve the wine, garlands of talenders were swiftly woven about our necks.

Then each of us gave some of the girls wine, asking each "Wine, Mistress?" to which each of the girls, with a laugh, would cry out, "Yes, I will have wine!"

"You will serve me the wine, Slave!" said the long-legged, black-haired girl. She was marvelous in the brief slave livery.

"Yes, Mistress," I said, as humbly as I could manage.

I reached out to hand her the small, tin cup.

"On your knees," she said, "and serve me as a Pleasure Slave!"

The girls gasped in the room. The two men cried out in anger.

"I think not," I said.

I felt the two ropes on my throat tighten. Suddenly the two girls on the ankle ropes jerked on their ropes and I fell heavily forward, spilling the wine to the stones.

"Clumsy slave," jeered the long-legged girl.

The other girls laughed.

"Give him more wine," ordered the long-legged girl.

Another small tin cup was placed in my hands. I no longer much cared for their foolery. The long-legged girl, doubtless a miserable slave most of the year, seemed intent on humiliating me, taking revenge probably on her master, for whom I now stood as proxy.

"Serve me wine," she ordered harshly.

"Kajuralia," I said, humbly.

She laughed, and so did the other girls as well. My eye strayed to a room off the storeroom, in which I could see some boxes, much dust.

Then the room was very still.

I put down my head, kneeling, and extended the small tin cup to the girl.

The other girls in the room seemed to be holding their breath.

With a laugh the long-legged girl reached for the tin cup, at which point I seized her wrists and sprang to my feet, swinging her off balance and, not releasing her, whirled her about, tangling her in the ropes, preventing them from being drawn tight. Then while the girls shrieked and the long-legged girl cried out in rage I swept her into my arms and leaped into the small room, where I dropped her to the stones and spun about, throwing the door shut and bolting it. I heard the angry cries of the girls and their fists on the door for a moment, but then I heard them suddenly begin shrieking, and crying out, as though slavers might have fallen upon them. I glanced about the room. There was one window high in one wall, narrow, barred. There was no escape for the girl locked within with me. I removed the ropes from my body, coiled them neatly, and dropped them inside the door. I put my ear to the door, listening. After about five Ehn I heard only a number of sobs, frustrated noises of girls in bonds.

I opened the door and, not to my surprise, discovered that the Warrior and Tarn Keeper, preventing the girls from escaping, and having freed themselves in the moment of surprise and tumult in which I had seized the long-legged girl, had, probably one by one, while the other girls had looked on miserably, cuffed away if they tried to interfere, bound the girls of the Street of Pots. A long rope, or set of ropes knotted together, ran behind the kneeling girls, with which their wrists were bound; another rope, or set of ropes tied together, fastened them by the throat, as in a slaver's chain. The long-legged girl was pushed into the larger room to observe her helpless cohorts.

The black-haired girl sobbed.

There were tears in the eyes of several of the girls.

"Kajuralia!" said the Warrior, cheerfully, getting to his feet, after checking the knots that bound the wrists of the last girl on the ropes.

"Kajuralia!" I responded to him, waving my hand. I took the black-haired, long-legged girl by the arm and dragged her to the line of bound girls. "Behold the girls of the Street of Pots," I said.

She said nothing, but tried to turn away. I permitted her to go to the center of the room, where she stood, facing me, tears in her eyes, near the rep-cloth blankets spread over straw.

Then she looked down, defeated. "I will serve you wine," said she, "Master."

"No," I said.

She looked at me, puzzled. Then she nodded her head, and, reached to the disrobing loop on her left shoulder.

"No," I said gently.

She looked at me, startled.

"I," I said, "will serve you wine."

She looked at me in disbelief while I filled one of the small tin cups with diluted Ka-la-na and handed it to her. Her hand shook as she took the cup. She lifted it to her lips, but looked at me.

"Drink," I said.

She drank.

I then took the cup from her and threw it to the side of the room, and took her into my arms, that lovely, long-legged, black-haired beast, provocative in the brevity of her slave livery, and kissed her, and well, and at length.

Then she was lying on the rep-cloth blankets, spread over the straw, beneath me, kissing me helplessly.

"Do not let me escape," she begged.

"You will not escape," I told her, reaching to the loop on her left shoulder.

I heard one of the girls bound in the line whisper to the Warrior, and another to the Tarn Keeper, "Do not let me escape, Master."

They removed these girls from the line, later returning them to it.

The Warrior, the Tarn Keeper and I remained the greater part of the day with the girls of the Street of Pots. When I had finished with the long-legged girl I had bound her hand and foot and put her to one side. When we were preparing to leave, she begged again to be used, and was.

This time when I finished with her I did not bind her but stood her before me, my hands on her arms above the elbows. I would not truss her, that she might free her fellows.

The Warrior, followed by the Tarn Keeper, was moving down the line of bound girls, lifting their heads, taking their final wages for the sport, saying "Kajuralia," to each and moving to the next.

Once more I kissed the black-haired, long-legged girl, and she me.

"Kajuralia," I said to her gently, and turned, and with the Warrior and the Tarn Keeper, arm in arm, with garlands of talenders, which had been several times replaced, woven about our necks, left the Street of Pots.

"Kajuralia!" called the girls to us.

"Kajuralia!" we responded.

"Kajuralia!" I heard the long-legged girl call after me. "Kajuralia, Warrior!"

"Kajuralia!" I responded, well satisfied with the day's sport.

The Kajuralia, or the Holiday of Slaves, or Festival of Slaves, occurs in most of the northern, civilized cities of known Gor once a year. The only exception to this that I know of is Port Kar, in the delta of the Vosk. The date of the Kajuralia, however, differs. Many cities celebrate it on the last day of the Twelfth Passage Hand, the day before the beginning of the Waiting Hand; in Ar, however, and certain other cities, it is celebrated on the last day of the fifth month, which is the day preceding the Love Feast.

It had been a strange and eventful summer, fantastic in many ways. Week by week Ar became ever more wild, ever more lawless. Gangs of men, often armed, roamed streets and bridges, apparently undisturbed by Warriors, their depredations not curbed; and, startlingly, when captured and sent to the Central Cylinder, or to the Cylinder of Justice, pretexts would be found for their release, customarily on legal technicalities or an alleged lack of evidence against them. But, as this lawlessness grew, and it became such that men would not walk the bridges without arms, the frenzy over the races and the games grew more rabid; it became rare on the streets and bridges to pass a person who would not, either for himself or for someone he knew, wear a faction patch, even on those rare days in which the Stadium of Tarns stood empty. People seemed to care little for anything save the races and the games. Their neighbor's compartment might be despoiled by ruffians but, if they themselves were unharmed, they would think little of it and hasten to their chosen entertainment, fearing only that they might be late.

The duel for the lead in racing hung suspended among three factions, the Greens, the Yellows and the Steels, the new faction. The progress and startling rise of the Steels as a faction dated from the first day of the races, when, in the eleventh race, Gladius of Cos, astride a great tarn, initiated the Steels as a faction with a surprising, but resounding, win over a strong field of competitors. The great bird he rode was no racing tarn but its size, its swiftness, its sureness, its incredible power and ferocity made it a terrible foe in the wars of the suspended rings; indeed, never had it lost; many of the other tarns of the Steels, as well, were not bred racing tarns, but war tarns, ridden by unknown riders, mysterious men hailing supposedly from far cities; the excitement of a new faction not only competing but dangerously challenging the established factions of Ar provided a spectacle that inflamed the imaginations of the men and women of Ar; thousands of fans, for one reason or another, discouraged with their factions, or seeking novelty, or wishing to feel a part of the great battle of the races, sewed or pinned on their garments the small rectangle of bluish-gray cloth, faction patch of the Steels.

I, masked in a leather hood, wearing bluish-gray silk, had again and again ridden the great black tarn for the Steels. The name of Gladius of Cos was a watchword in the city, though surely few knew his identity. I rode with the Steels because my tarn was there, and Mip, whom I had come to know and like, wished it to be so. I knew myself involved in games of a dangerous sort, but I had agreed to play, not clearly understanding the object or the goal of what I did. Relius and Ho-Sorl often assisted me. I gathered that it had not been coincidence that had brought them to the House of Cernus. After each race Mip, in detail, would discuss my riding, making suggestions; before each race, he would explain to me what he knew of the habits of the riders and tarns I faced, which was almost invariably a great deal; he taught me to recognize for myself certain faults in other riders, certain exploitable characteristics in the flight patterns of the birds they rode; one rider, for example, had a tendency to take the third corner ring at the three-strap point, thus permitting a probable block at that point without slackening speed near the ring to effect it; one bird, a swift, reddish tarn, which raced for the blues, flown at least twice every ten days, would, in approaching its perch, brake with its wings an instant before necessary, thus making it possible, if following it closely, to strike the very perch it intended to take, rather than the next perch below it, as one would normally do.

Equaling and perhaps exceeding the fame of Gladius of Cos was that of the swordsman Murmillius, of the cruel games observed in the Stadium of Blades. Since the beginning of En'Kara he had fought more than one hundred and twenty times, and one hundred and twenty foes had fallen before him, which, following his unusual custom, he had never slain, regardless of the will of the crowd. Some of the best swordsmen of Ar, even Warriors of High Caste, eager to be the one to best the mysterious Murmillius, had dared to enter the arena against him, but each of these bold gentlemen he seemed to treat with more scorn than his common foes, playing with them and then, it seemed when he wished, disabling their sword arm, so cruelly that perhaps they might never again be able to lift the steel. Condemned criminals and men of low caste, fighting for gold or freedom in the arena, he treated with the harsh courtesies obtaining among sword brothers. The crowd, each time he fought, went mad with pleasure, thrilling to each ringing stroke of steel, and I suspected that that man most adored in Ar was the huge, mysterious Murmillius, superb and gallant, a man whose very city was unknown.

Meanwhile the intrigues of Cernus, of the House of Cernus, threaded their way through the days and events of the spring and summer in Ar. Once in a paga tavern I heard a man, whom I recognized to be one of the guards from the iron pens, though now in the tunic of a Leather Worker, declaring that the city needed for its Administrator not a Builder but a Warrior, that law would again prevail.

"But what Warrior?" inquired a fellow at the table, a Silversmith.

"Cernus, of the House of Cernus," said the disguised guard, "is a Warrior."

"He is a Slaver," said one.

"He knows the business and needs of Ar," said the guard, "as would a Merchant, but he is yet of the Caste of Warriors."

"He has sponsored many games," said a Tharlarion Keeper.

"He would be better than a Hinrabian," said another fellow.

"My admission to the races," said another man, a Miller, "has been paid a dozen times by the House of Cernus." He referred to a practice of handing out passes, dated *ostraka* bearing the print of the House of Cernus, outside the gate of the Slaver's house, which were dispensed on a first-come-first-served basis, a thousand a day, each day of the races. Some men spent the night at the walls of the house of Cernus, that they might obtain their *ostrakon* at dawn.

"I say," said the disguised guard, "Ar could do worse than have such a man as Cernus on the throne!"

To my amazement, several about the table, who were undoubtedly common citizens of Ar, began to nod their heads.

"Yes," said the Silversmith, "it would be good if a man such as Cernus were Administrator of the city."

"Or Ubar?" said the guard.

The smith shrugged. "Yes," he said, "or Ubar."

"Ar is at war with itself," said one man, who had not spoken before, a Scribe. "In these times perhaps what one needs is truly a Ubar."

"I say," said the guard, "Cernus should be Ubar of Ar."

The men about the table began to grunt affirmatively. "Bring paga!" called the disguised guard, summoning a belled slave girl to him, one carrying a large vessel of paga, that drinks might be dispensed yet once again. I knew the moneys spent so lavishly by the guard had been counted out carefully from the office of Caprus, for such information I had from Elizabeth. I turned and left when I heard the men at the table, led by the guard, lifting their cups to Cernus, of the House of Cernus. "May Cernus, of the House of Cernus," said they, "become Ubar of Ar!"

I saw one other man rise up when I did, and also leave the tavern.

Outside I stopped and turned, regarding Ho-Tu.

"I thought you did not drink paga," I said.

"I do not," said Ho-Tu.

"How is it that you are in a paga tavern?" I asked.

"I saw Falarius leave the house," said he, "in the garb of a Leather Worker. I was curious."

"It seems he was on the business of Cernus," I said.

"Yes," said Ho-Tu.

"Did you hear them speak of Master Cernus," I asked, "as a possible Ubar?"

Ho-Tu looked at me sharply. "Cernus," he said, "should not be Ubar."

I shrugged.

Ho-Tu turned and strode away between the buildings.

While the men of Cernus did their work in the paga taverns, and on the streets and in the market squares, and on the ramps and in the tiers of the games and races, the gold of Cernus, and the steel of Cernus, was apparently plied elsewhere. His loans to the Hinrabians, a wealthy family in itself but surely unable to carry the incessant burdens of supporting games and races, became fewer and then stopped. Then, with great reluctance, claiming need, Cernus petitioned for the repayment of certain minor, but significant, portions of his loans. As these might be repaid from the private treasuries of the Hinrabians, he required ever larger payments, greater and greater portions of the moneys owed to his house by the Hinrabians. Further, games and races which he had sponsored in the name of the Hinrabians now ceased, and those they had jointly sponsored ceased to bear the name of the Administrator. The name of Cernus, as patron and benefactor, was now what appeared on the placards and the boards of announcements. Then, interestingly, minor omens, recorded by the High Initiate, and others, began to turn against the Hinrabian dynasty. Two members of the High Council, who had spoken out against the influence of Merchants in the politics of Ar, presumably a veiled reference to Cernus, were found slain, one cut down by killing knife and another throttled and found dangling from a bridge near his home. The first sword of the military forces of Ar, Maximus Hegesius Quintilius, second in authority only to Minus Tentius Hinrabius himself, was relieved of his post. He had shortly before expressed reservation concerning the investiture of Cernus in the Caste of Warriors. He was replaced by a member of the Taurentians, Seremides of Tyros, nominated by Saphronicus of Tyros, Captain of the Taurentians. Shortly thereafter Maximus Hegesius Quintilius was found dead, poisoned by the bite of a girl in his Pleasure Gardens, who, before she could be brought before the Scribes of the Law, was strangled by enraged Taurentians, to whom she had been turned over; it was well known that the Taurentians had greatly revered Maximus Hegesius Quintilius, and that they had felt his loss perhaps as deeply as the common Warriors of Ar. I had known Maximus Hegesius Quintilius only briefly several years ago, when he had been a captain, in 10,110 from the Founding of Ar, in the time of Pa-Kur and his horde. He had seemed to me a good soldier. I regretted his passing. He was given a full military funeral; his ashes had been scattered from tarnback over a field where, as a general some years before, he had led the forces of Ar to victory.

The demands of Cernus for repayment of moneys owed to him by the Hinrabians became increasingly persistent and unavoidable. Claiming need, he was implacable. The citizens of Ar, generally, found it distasteful that the private fortunes of the Hinrabians should be in such poor state. Then, as I would have expected, within the month, there were rumors of peculation, and an accounting and investigation, theoretically to clear the name of the Hinrabian, was demanded by one of the High Council, a Physician whom I had seen upon occasion in the house. The Scribes of the Central Cylinder examined the records and, to their horror, discrepancies were revealed, in particular payments to members of the Hinrabian family for services it was not clear had ever been performed; most outstandingly there had been a considerable disbursement for the construction of four bastions and tarncots for the flying cavalry of Ar, her tarnsmen; the military men of Ar had waited patiently for these cylinders and were now outraged to discover that the moneys had actually been disbursed, and had apparently disappeared; the parties, presumably of the Builders, to which the disbursements had been made were found to be fictitious. Further, at this time, the Odds Merchants of the Stadium of Tarns made it known that the Administrator was heavily in debt, and they, not to be left out, demanded their dues.

It seemed almost to be a foregone conclusion that Minus Tentius Hinrabius would surrender the brown robes of office. He did so late in spring, on the sixteenth day of the third month, that month which in Ar is called Camerius, in Ko-ro-ba Selnar. The day before he surrendered his robes the High Initiate, reading the liver of a sacrificial bosk, had confirmed what all by then were anticipating, that the omens stood strongly against the Hinrabian dynasty.

The High Council receiving the promise of Minus Tentius Hinrabius to depart from the city, did not inflict officially the penalty of exile. He, with his family and retainers, left the city on the seventeenth day of Camerius. By the end of that month the other Hinrabians of Ar, in the face of widespread public anger, hastily liquidated their assets at considerable loss and fled from the walls of Ar, joining Minus Tentius Hinrabius some pasangs beyond the city. Then, together, the Hinrabians, with an armed retinue, set forth in caravan for Tor, envoys of which city had granted their petition for refuge. Unfortunately the caravan, not more than two hundred pasangs from the Great Gate of Ar, was attacked and plundered by a large armed force, but of unknown origin. Strangely, with perhaps one exception, each of the Hinrabians had had his throat cut, even the women; this was unusual, for the women of a captive caravan, regarded as portions of its booty, are almost always enslaved; the one Hinrabian whose body was not found among the dead, scattered on the plains and among the burning remains of the wagons, was, interestingly, Claudia Tentia Hinrabia.

On the twentieth day of Camerius the great signal bars suspended about the walls of the city rang out the enthronement of a Ubar of Ar. Cernus had been proclaimed, as the Taurentians lifted their swords in salute and the members of the High Council had stood on the tiers of the Council Chamber and cried out and applauded, Ubar of Ar. Processions took place on the bridges; there were tournaments of the game organized; poets and historians vied in praising the day, each more ecstatically than the last; but, perhaps most importantly, holiday was declared, and great games and races were sponsored without cessation for the next several days, extending even through the Third Passage Hand.

I saw more in this, of course, than the work of Cernus. I saw in his elevation a portion of the plan of Others being unfolded; with one of their own on the throne of Ar, they would have a remarkable base in Ar for the advancement of their schemes, in particular the influencing of men, the recruitment of partisans in their cause; as Misk had pointed out, a human being, armed with a significant weapon, can be extremely dangerous, even to a Priest-King.

There was one point, however, in this strange summer which seemed to give me clear and adequate reason to rejoice. Elizabeth, with Virginia and Phyllis, would be extricated from the house and carried to safety. Caprus, who had become more affable, and apparently somewhat bolder, following the enthronement of Cernus, perhaps because Cernus was less often then in the House, informed me that he had made contact with an agent of Priest-Kings. The girls, even though I had not yet received the documents and maps, would be rescued.

His plan was a simple one, but ingenious. The plan was to arrange to have the girls purchased by an agent of Priest-Kings on the Love Feast, which began tomorrow, an agent who would have the resources to outbid any conceivable competition. They would then be as naturally and neatly removed from the House as Elizabeth had originally been introduced into it. It was true that Elizabeth was no longer needed in the House, nor had she been for a long time; Caprus had located the important materials and was copying them; I was needed, of course, to take the documents and Caprus from the house. Elizabeth, predictably, did not care to leave without me, but she recognized the plan as a good one; if she could be independently removed from the House there would be less for Caprus and me to worry about; further, she naturally wished Virginia and Phyllis to have the same opportunity for freedom as she had for herself, an opportunity they might not be likely to obtain elsewhere; further, of course, she recognized that it might well be complex and difficult for me to attempt to convey the documents, Caprus, herself and myself, and two others as well, from the house.

All things considered, Caprus' plan seemed not only suitable, but ideal. Neither Elizabeth nor I, of course, said anything to Virginia or Phyllis. The fewer people who knew of the plan the better. Surely, if kept in ignorance, their behavior would be more natural. Let them think that they were to be sold from the block. It would be a fine surprise for them later to discover that they were actually being whisked to safety and freedom. I chuckled. I was further cheered by the thought that Caprus had informed me his work was coming along very well and he hoped to have the documents and maps copied by the beginning of Se'Kara; I gathered that now with Cernus spending much of his time in the Central Cylinder as Ubar, Caprus' opportunities for work had been substantially increased. Se'Kara was, of course, a long wait. Still it was better than nothing. Other dates he had set similarly, I reminded myself, had not turned out. But still I was pleased. Elizabeth, with Virginia and Phyllis, would be rescued. And Caprus seemed in a good humor; that perhaps was significant, betokening an end in sight for my mission. In thinking about this I realized what a brave man Caprus was, and how little I had respected his courage and his work. He had risked much, probably much more than I. I felt ashamed. He was only a Scribe, and yet what he had done had taken great courage, probably more courage than that possessed by many Warriors.

I found myself whistling. Things were working out. I regretted only that I had not yet learned who it was that had slain the Warrior from Thentis.

* * * *

Cernus, upon occasion, though Ubar of Ar, would return to sit table in his own house, where, as he had invariably done before, he would play with Caprus, losing himself in the movements of the red and yellow pieces on the large board of red and yellow squares.

This was the evening of Kajuralia.

There was much hilarity in the hall of the House of Cernus, and, though it was early in the evening, paga and full-strength Ka-la-na were flowing.

Ho-Tu threw down his spoon in disgust, grinning at me wryly.

His gruel had been salted to the point of being inedible; he stared disgustedly down at the wet mash of porridge and salt.

"Kajuralia, Master," said Elizabeth Cardwell to Ho-Tu, smiling sweetly, as she passed by with a pitcher of Ka-la-na. Ho-Tu seized her by the wrist.

"What is wrong, Master?" inquired Elizabeth innocently.

"If I thought it was you," growled Ho-Tu, "who dared to salt my porridge, you would spend the night sitting on a slave goad."

"I would never think of such a thing," protested Elizabeth, wide-eyed.

Ho-Tu grunted. Then he grinned. "Kajuralia, Little Wench," said he.

Elizabeth smiled. "Kajuralia, Master," said she, and turning quickly about, still smiling, went on with her work.

"Little pock-face," called Relius. "I would be served!"

Virginia Kent, with her pitcher of Ka-la-na, ran light-footedly to Relius, guard in the House of Cernus.

"Let Lana serve Relius wine," said another girl, a Red Silk Girl, first to the guard, leaning toward him, lips parted.

Relius put out his cup but before the girl could pour the wine she seemed suddenly to fly off the back of the dais, the seat of her tunic firmly grasped in the small hand of Virginia Kent. Lana landed with a considerable bump on the stones of the hall, the wine flying backward.

"Relius guards Virginia," the young slave girl from Earth informed collared Red Silk Lana.

Lana scrambled to her feet, angry, her pitcher of wine set aside on the wet, red stones. The two girls stood facing one another.

"I wear the leash of Relius," said Virginia. "I wear his bracelets!"

Lana looked at Relius. "Leash Lana," she said. "Lana is Red Silk." She extended her wrists provocatively to Relius. "Put your bracelets on Lana. She is Red Silk. She will serve you better than a silly little White Silker."

"No!" cried Virginia.

Lana turned and faced her contemptuously. "Why should you," she asked, "wear the leash of a man such as Relius?"

"He has chosen to guard me," said Virginia.

Lana turned and looked at Relius. "Guard Lana," she said.

At this point Virginia Kent put down her pitcher of wine, seized Lana by the shoulder, spun her about and struck her a rather severe blow near the left eye. Several of the men and girls at and about the tables approvingly observed the two girls rolling and scratching, biting and tearing on the floor, first White Silk on top, and then Red Silk, and then White Silk again. At last Virginia Kent, to the cheers of several of those present, sat atop Lana and was pummeling her mercilessly, until Lana, throwing up her arms and shrieking, crying out, begged for mercy.

"Who wears the leash of Relius?" demanded Virginia.

"Ginia!" screamed Lana.

"And who his bracelets?"

"Ginia!"

"And who does Relius guard?"

"Ginia! Ginia!" wept Lana, trying to cover her face. "Ginia!"

Then Virginia Kent, breathing hard, climbed to her feet.

Lana scrambled up and stood some feet from her, tears in her eyes. "You will be sold tomorrow!" cried Lana. "Then Relius will guard another!" Then the girl looked at Relius. "I hope it will be Lana who will wear the leash of Relius," she said, and then, as Virginia Kent cried out and leaped toward her, Lana turned about and sped as though for her life from the room.

"It seems I am not going to be served," said Relius, as though rather bored with the whole matter.

Virginia Kent straightened herself, bent down and picked up her pitcher of Ka-la-na, smiled shyly, and approached her guard.

He put forth his goblet but, suddenly, unexpectedly, she drew back the pitcher.

"What is the meaning of this?" he cried.

"Kajuralia!" she laughed.

"Will you not serve me?" asked Relius in anger.

Virginia Kent, to my amazement, put aside the pitcher of wine.

"I would serve you," she said, and put her hands behind his neck and suddenly pressed her lips, to the delight of those present, boldly to his.

"Kajuralia," she whispered.

"Kajuralia," mumbled he, closing his arms upon her, devouring her.

But when he permitted her to draw back her lips there were tears in her eyes.

"What is wrong, little pock-face?" asked Relius.

"Tomorrow," she said, "I will be sold."

"Perhaps you will find a kind master, Little Slave," said Relius.

The girl put her head to his shoulder and wept. "I do not want Virginia to be sold," she wept, "unless it be Relius who will buy her."

"Do you wish truly to be my slave, little pock-face?" asked Relius.

"Yes," wept Virginia, "yes!"

"I cannot afford you," said Relius, holding her head against him.

I turned away.

Near the pit of sand several slave girls, dancers, in Pleasure Silk were kneeling back on their heels and clapping their hands with glee. In the pit of sand one of the guards, utterly drunk, was performing a ship dance, the movement of his legs marvelously suggesting the pitch and roll of a deck, his hands moving as though climbing rope, then hauling rope, then splicing and knotting it. I knew he had been of Port Kar. He was a cutthroat but there were drunken tears in his eyes as he hopped about, pantomiming the work of one of the swift galleys. It is said that men once having seen Thassa are never willing to leave it again, that those who have left the sea are never again truly happy. A moment later another guard leaped into the pit of sand and, to the amusement of the girls, began a dance of larl hunters, joined by two or three others, in a file, dancing the stalking of the beast, the confrontation, the kill.

The man who had been dancing the ship dance had now left the pit of sand and, over against one wall, in the shadows of the torchlight, largely unnoted, danced alone, danced for himself the memories of gleaming Thassa and the swift black ships, the Tarns of the Sea, as the galleys of Port Kar are known.

"Serve me wine," Ho-Sorl ordered Phyllis Robertson, though she was far across the room, and there were several girls nearer. This was not unusual, however, for Ho-Sorl invariably demanded that the proud Phyllis, who professed to despise him, serve him as table slave, which service she would ultimately, irritably, head in the air, have to render him, whether it be merely the pouring of his wine or the offering of a grape held delicately between her teeth.

I heard Caprus say, as though marveling, "I shall capture your Home Stone in three moves!"

Cernus grinned and clapped his hands on the Scribe's shoulders.

"Kajuralia!" he laughed. "Kajuralia!"

"Kajuralia," mumbled Caprus, rather depressed, making the first essential move, but now without zest.

"What is this?" cried Ho-Sorl.

"It is bosk milk," Phyllis informed him. "It is good for you."

Ho-Sorl cried out in rage.

"Kajuralia," said Phyllis, and turned and moved away, with a triumphant twitch that might have shocked even Sura.

Ho-Sorl bounded over the table and caught her four paces from the dais, spilling the milk about. He threw her bodily over his shoulder, her small fists pounding on his back, and carried her to Ho-Tu's place.

"I will pay," said Ho-Sorl, "the difference between what she will bring as Red Silk and White Silk."

Phyllis shrieked in fear, wiggling on his shoulder, pounding.

Ho-Tu apparently gave the matter very serious thought.

"Don't you want to be Red Silk?" he asked Phyllis, who, from her position, could not see him.

"No, no, no!" she cried.

"By tomorrow night," pointed out Ho-Sorl, neatly, "she may be Red Silk anyway."

"No, no!" wept Phyllis.

"Where would you make her Red Silk?" asked Ho-Tu.

"The pit of sand will do," said Ho-Sorl.

Phyllis shrieked with misery.

"Would you not like Ho-Sorl to make you Red Silk?" asked Ho-Tu of Phyllis.

"I detest him!" she screamed. "I hate him! I hate him! I hate him!"

"I wager," said Ho-Sorl, "I can have her leaping to my touch in a quarter of an Ahn."

That seemed to me like not much time.

"An interesting wager," mused Ho-Tu.

Phyllis shrieked for mercy.

"Put her in the sand," said Ho-Tu.

Ho-Sorl carried the struggling Phyllis Robertson to the square of sand, and flung her to his feet. He then stood over her, hands on hips. She could roll neither to the left nor right. She lay on her back between his sandals, one knee slightly raised, as though she would flee, and lifted herself on her elbows, terrified, looking up at him. He laughed and she screamed and tried to escape but he took her by the hair and, crouching over her, pressed her back weeping to the sand.

His hand moved to the disrobing loop and she shuddered, turning her head away.

But instead of tugging on the loop, he simply, holding her under the arms, lifted her up, and then dropped her on her seat in the sand, where she sat foolishly, bewildered, looking up at him.

"Kajuralia!" laughed Ho-Sorl and turned, and, to the laughter of all, returned to his place at the table.

Ho-Tu was laughing perhaps the loudest of all, pounding the table with his fists. Even Cernus looked up from his game and smiled.

Phyllis had now struggled to her feet, blushing a red visible even under the torches, and, unsteady, trembling slightly, was trying to brush the sand from her hair, her legs and her slave livery.

"Don't look so disappointed," said a Red Silk Girl passing near her, carrying Ka-la-na.

Phyllis made an angry noise.

"Poor little White Silk slave," said another Red Silk Girl passing between the tables.

Phyllis clenched her fists, crying out in rage.

Ho-Sorl regarded her. "You are rather fat," he said.

That was an appraisal I surely did not agree with.

"I'm glad I'm going to be sold," cried Phyllis. "It will take me from the sight of you! You black-haired, scarred—tarsk!" There were tears in her eyes. "I hate you!" she screamed. "I hate you!"

"You are all cruel!" cried Virginia Kent, who was standing now a bit behind Ho-Tu.

The room was extremely silent for a moment.

Then, angrily, Virginia Kent picked up Ho-Tu's bowl of gruel and, turning it completely upside down, dumped it suddenly on his head.

"Kajuralia," she said.

Relius nearly leaped up, horror on his face.

Ho-Tu sat there with the porridge bowl on his head, the gruel streaming down his face.

Once again there was an extremely still moment in the room.

Suddenly I felt a large quantity of fluid, wine, surely at least half a pitcher, being poured slowly over my head. I began to sputter and blink. "Kajuralia, Master," said Elizabeth Cardwell, walking regally away.

Now Ho-Tu was laughing so hard that his eyes were watering. He took the bowl from his bald head and wiped his face with his forearm. Then he began to pound the table with his fists. Then everyone in the room, amazed at the audacity of the slave girl, to so affront one of the black caste, after a moment, began to roar with amusement, even the slave girls. I think so rich a treat they had never expected on Kajuralia. I maintained a straight face, and tried to frown convincingly, finding myself the butt of their laughter. I saw that even Cernus had now looked up from his board and was roaring with laughter, the first time I had ever seen such amusement in the person of the Master of the House of Cernus. Then, to my horror, I saw Elizabeth, her back straight, her step determined, walk straight to Cernus and then, slowly, as his mouth flew open and he seemed scarcely to understand what was occurring, pour the rest of the contents of the vessel of Ka-la-na directly on his head.

"Kajuralia," said Elizabeth to him, turning away.

Ho-Tu then, to my great relief, rose to his feet, lifting both hands. "Kajuralia, Ubar!" he cried.

Then all at the tables, and even the slaves who served, stood and lifted their hands, laughing, saluting Cernus. "Kajuralia, Ubar!" they cried. And I, too, though the words nearly stuck in my throat, so acclaimed Cernus. "Kajuralia, Ubar!" I cried.

The face of Cernus relaxed, and he leaned back. And then, to my relief, he, Ubar of Ar, smiled, and then he, too, began to laugh.

Then the slave girls about the table began to go wild, throwing things and where possible pouring liquids on the heads of the guards and members of the staff, who, leaping up, seized them when they could catch them, kissing them, holding them, making them cry out with delight. And more than one was thrown to the love furs under the slave rings at the wall. Revel filled the hall of the House of Cernus. I made sure I got my hands on Elizabeth Cardwell, though she dodged well and was a swift wench, and taking her in my arms carried her to one side. She looked up at me.

"You did well," I said.

"It was a close one," she said.

"Closer than I like," I admitted.

"You have captured me," she said.

I kissed her. "You will be free tomorrow night," I said.

"I'm happy," she said.

"Was it you," I asked, "who salted the gruel of Ho-Tu?"

"It is possible," she admitted.

"Tonight," I said, "will be the last night together in our compartment."

She laughed. "Last night was," she informed me. "Tonight I am to be sent to the Waiting Cells, where girls are kept who will be sent to the market tomorrow."

I groaned.

"It is easier than rounding them up all over the House," she pointed out.

"I suppose so," I said.

"Between the tenth and the fourteenth Ahn," she pointed out, "we can be examined nude in the cages."

"Oh?" I asked.

"It is sometimes difficult to make an appraisal from the high tiers," she said.

Beyond us, as though in a world apart, we could hear the laughter and shrieks of the men and girls sporting in the hall, celebrating Kajuralia.

"Are you frightened?" I asked.

"No," she said. "I'm looking forward to it."

"Why is that?" I asked.

"It should be quite thrilling," she said, "the lights, the sawdust, being so utterly naked, the men bidding for you."

"You are a little mad fool," I told her.

"Every girl," she said, "should be sold at least once in her life."

"You are utterly, utterly mad," I told her, kissing her again.

"I wonder what I'll bring," she mused.

"Probably two copper tarn disks," I said.

"I hope I will be purchased by a handsome master," she said.

I kissed her irritably to silence.

We heard the voice of Ho-Tu booming in the hall. "It is past the eighteenth bar," he called. "Slaves to cells!"

There were cries of disappointment from both men and women in the hall.

I kept kissing Elizabeth. "Slaves to cells," she mumbled. When I released her she lifted her head to me, standing on her toes, and kissed me on the nose. "Perhaps," she said, "I will see you even tomorrow night."

I doubted it, but it was possible. I assumed the agent of Priest-Kings, who would purchase the girls, might be eager to take them to the Sardar, or perhaps to Ko-ro-ba. Yet again he might wait, and perhaps I could learn of her whereabouts in the city before she took flight, and see her once more. After the work of Caprus and myself was finished I would be able to join her, probably in Ko-ro-ba, for a time, before we arranged to return her to Earth; I assumed, naturally, she would wish to return to her native planet. Gor is harsh and cruel. And surely no woman bred to the civilities and courtesies of Earth would care to remain on a world so barbaric, a world perhaps beautiful but yet threatening and perilous, a world in which a woman is seldom permitted to be other than a woman, a world in which even the exalted Free Companion sleeps upon a couch with a slave ring set at its foot.

She kissed me one last time and turned about and ran off. She would spend the night in the Waiting Cells, and, at dawn, with hundreds of others, be sent as slave cargo to the pens of the Curulean.

"You there, Slaves," called Ho-Tu, "to your cells!"

He was speaking to Virginia Kent, and to Lana, who had both lingered in the vicinity of Relius, who was finishing a cup of wine.

"You there, little White Silker," said Ho-Tu, "who are so adept with the porridge bowl, hasten to the Waiting Cells. You will need your sleep. You are to ascend the block tomorrow. You must make a good showing for the House of Cernus."

Virginia choked back a tear. "Yes, Master," she said.

Lana laughed and went to Relius, taking his arm, looking at Virginia. "Tomorrow, White Silker," she said, "you will be sold but Lana will still be in the House of Cernus." She looked at Relius, snuggling up to him, kissing him on the side of the neck. "If Lana is permitted to leave the House tomorrow," she wheedled the guard, "Lana wants to wear the leash of Relius."

Virginia stood there, helpless, her fists clenched, fighting back tears.

"What is your name?" demanded Ho-Tu of the Red Silk Girl.

"Lana," she said, "if it pleases Master."

"Lana," said Ho-Tu, "you will indeed leave the House tomorrow."

"Thank you, Master," said Lana, looking up then at Relius.

"Now, Lana," said Ho-Tu, "go to the Waiting Cells."

She spun about. "The Waiting Cells!" she cried.

"Yes," said Ho-Tu, "you will be sold tomorrow on the Love Feast."

"No!" she cried. "No!"

Virginia laughed and clapped her hands with joy.

"No!" cried Lana.

"To the Waiting Cells, Slave!" commanded Ho-Tu. He slapped the slave goad that hung at his belt.

Terror came into the eyes of the girl. She threw one wild look at Relius and then, as Ho-Tu removed the slave goad from his belt, she ran weeping from the room.

Virginia Kent dropped to her knees before Ho-Tu, in the position of the Pleasure Slave, and lowered her head. "Thank you, Master," she said.

He shook her head with his heavy hand. "You are a brave little wench," he said. "And you are very dangerous with a bowl of porridge."

She dropped her head even more.

"Hurry, Slave!" barked Ho-Tu. "To the Waiting Cells!"

Virginia Kent, who had taught classics and ancient history in a college on Earth, leaped to her feet and, barefoot, a slave girl, raced from the room, hurrying to the Waiting Cells, whence at dawn, with others, she would be sent to the Curulean, where, in the evening, she would, with Elizabeth and Phyllis, ascend the block, her purchased flesh, like theirs, to bring gold to the House of Cernus.

Ho-Tu looked after her and grinned. "A very brave little wench," he muttered.

"And dangerous with a bowl of porridge," I reminded him.

"Yes," said he, "that is true."

I looked about the room. Now only guards and members of the staff remained in the room. I supposed I might as well return to my compartment. I would miss Elizabeth.

Suddenly two guards entered the room, thrusting a woman before them.

I saw Ho-Tu look up and turn white. His hand moved to the hook knife at his belt.

The woman stumbled to the place before the table of Cernus, where she stood. A bit of scarlet cord had been knotted about her waist, into which was thrust a long rectangle of red silk; her hair had been unbound; her wrists were braceleted behind her back; the key hung on a string about her neck; the slave bells were still locked on her left ankle, but her finery was gone; no longer did the slave goad dangle from her wrist.

"Kajuralia, Sura," said Cernus to the woman.

"Kajuralia, Master," said she bitterly.

Ho-Tu spoke. "Let her return to her compartment," said he. "Sura has served us well. She is the finest trainer in Ar."

"She will be reminded," said Cernus, "that she is only a slave."

"I beg your favor," cried Ho-Tu.

"It is denied," said Cernus. "Let the gambling begin."

A number of men crowded between the tables then and some dice, inked knucklebones of the verr, were soon rattling in a metal goblet. Sura knelt before the table of Cernus, her head down. One of her guards snapped a slave leash on her collar. The leash key was on a tiny loop of wire. The guard twisted this wire about the red-enameled steel of her collar. Behind her the men began crying out, watching the tumbling of the knucklebones on the stones of the floor. I understood to some extent what was taking place. It was merely another of the turnabouts of Kajuralia, but in it was perhaps more; Sura's pride and her position in the House, though she was slave, had been resented by many of the men and staff; perhaps even Cernus felt she had over-stepped herself; surely he seemed pleased that she would now be humbled, now used as a common Red Silk Girl.

"I use her first!" cried one man.

Then there were more shouts and the men continued to gamble. I had not understood until then that the beautiful, proud Sura would, in order of the gambling, serve each of the men in that room.

I looked to Ho-Tu. To my astonishment there were tears in his fierce, dark eyes. His hand was on the hilt of the hook knife.

I looked to Sura. She was kneeling on the stones, bent over, her head down, the hair falling forward, clad only in the bit of red silk, her wrists braceleted behind her back. I saw her shoulders move, and, startled, realized that she wept.

I then moved into the center of the gambling men and, not speaking, as they looked up, angry at the intrusion, I took the metal goblet containing the knucklebones from the man who held it.

Bitterly, yet not daring to object, he surrendered it.

I looked from face to face, and then I shook the knucklebones and scattered them, the four of them, on the stones at my feet.

It had been a low cast, not high. Several of the men laughed with relief. But then my sword was out of the sheath and delicately, turning each bone with the tip of the blade, I placed the side marked with the highest number on each of the bones facing the ceiling.

232

The men looked on angrily. One or two of them muttered in rage. On their knees from the gambling, they looked up at me, in fury.

"I will use her," I said. "And I alone will use her."

"No!" cried a guard, springing to his feet.

I looked at him and he stepped back, turned, and angrily left the room.

"Dispute her with me who will," I said.

Angrily the men rose to their feet and, muttering, dispersed.

I turned to face Cernus. He smiled and expansively lifted his hand. "If none dispute you," said he, "she is surely yours." He laughed and grinned down at Sura. "Kajuralia, Slave," said he.

"Kajuralia, Master," said Sura, whispering.

I spoke harshly to Sura. "Lead me to your quarters, Slave."

She struggled to her feet, the leash dangling from her collar. I did not pick up the leash and she moved past me, tears in her eyes, leaving the room, the sound of bells marking her movements. But she did not walk as a trained Pleasure Slave. She walked numbly, her head down, a defeated woman. I heard Cernus laugh. "I have heard," jeered Cernus, "that the Killer knows well how to use slaves!"

Sura stopped at that moment, and put her head back, though she did not turn to face him, and then she hurried through the door.

"Killer," I heard.

I turned to face Ho-Tu. His hand was still on the hook knife.

"She is not a common slave," he said.

"Then," said I, "I shall expect from her uncommon pleasures," and turned and left.

Sura preceded me through the halls of the House of Cernus, and then we passed through her training room, and entered her own quarters where we stopped. As she stood in the room I took the key on its string from about her neck and removed the bracelets. I threw them with the key to one side of the room; then I unlocked the slave leash and threw it, with its key, also to the side of the room.

She stood there, rubbing her wrists a bit. There were red marks on them. The bracelets need not have been fastened so tightly. She looked at me with hatred. I turned about to examine the room. There were several chests there, doubtless containing silks, cosmetics, jewelry; there were also rich furs, on which I gathered she slept; in one corner there leaned a six-stringed kalika, long-necked, with its hemispheric sound box; I knew she played the instrument; on one wall, some feet away, hanging over a hook, I saw her slave goad.

I looked at her. She had not moved, though she now no longer rubbed her wrists. I could still see the red circles on them. Her black hair was quite marvelous, long and unbound, falling as it did over her shoulders; her eyes were dark and deeply beautiful; her body, as the slave masters had intended, was tormentingly magnificent; the features of her face and lips showed to my eye, which had become more discerning in the past several months, the breeding lines of the House of Cernus.

I turned away again, wondering if there might be some Ka-la-na or perhaps even paga, though I doubted the latter, hidden away in the room. I began to rummage through one of the chests, and then another. Still she had not moved.

I came to another chest. "Please do not open that chest," she said.

"Nonsense," said I, thinking that in this one must be the beverage I sought, flinging up the lid.

"Please!" she cried out.

This must be the one, I thought to myself. I poked around in the chest but I could find nothing, so far, but tangles of beads and jewelry, some silks. Sura certainly had a great deal of such things. That I was forced to admit. Were they her own, she would have been the envy of many of the free women of Ar.

"Do not look further!" she cried.

"Be silent, slave," said I, poking about, and then I saw in the bottom of the chest, almost colorless, ragged, not more than a foot high nor a few ounces heavy, a small worn, tattered doll, dressed in faded Robes of Concealment, of a sort little girls might play with on the bridges or in the corridors of cylinders, dressing it or singing to it.

"What is this?" I asked in amusement, lifting it up and turning to face Sura.

With a cry of rage the Pleasure Slave ran past me and tore the slave goad from the wall, flicked it to on. I saw the dial rotate to the end of the red band, to the Kill Point. The tip of the goad, almost instantly, seemed incandescent. I could not even look directly upon it.

"Die!" she screamed, hurling herself toward me, striking with the goad.

I dropped the doll, spun and managed to catch her wrist as she struck downward with the burning goad. She screamed out in frustration, weeping. My hand closed on her wrist and she cried out in pain, the goad falling to the floor, rolling. I hurled her some feet across the room and retrieved the goad; it had stopped rolling and now, burning, had begun to sink through the stone. I rotated the dial back to its minimal charge and then flicked it off.

I let the goad, on its leather strap, dangle from my left wrist and then I went to the doll and picked it up. I approached Sura, who backed against the wall, closing her eyes, turning her head to one side.

"Here," I said. I handed her the doll.

She reached out and took it.

"I am sorry," I said.

She stood there, looking at me, holding the doll.

I walked away from her and then took the slave goad from my wrist and hung it up again on its hook, where she might take it again if she wished.

"I am sorry," said I, "Sura." I looked upon her. "I was looking for Ka-la-na."

She looked at me, bewildered.

"It is in the last chest," she whispered.

I went to the last chest along the wall and opened it, finding a bottle and some bowls. "You are a fortunate slave," I said, "to have Ka-la-na in your quarters."

"I will serve you," she whispered.

"Is it not Kajuralia?" I asked.

"Yes," said she, "Master."

"Then," said I, "if Sura will permit, I shall serve her."

She looked at me blankly, and then, still clutching the doll, put out one hand, trembling, to take the bowl of wine from me. It began to spill, and I steadied it, lifting it with her hand to her lips.

She drank, as had the black-haired girl, the leader of the girls of the Street of Pots.

Then, when she had lowered the bowl, I took my drink, that she should have drunk first.

"Kajuralia," said I to her.

"Kajuralia," she whispered, "—Master."

"Kuurus," I said.

"Kajuralia," said she, whispering, "Kuurus."

I turned about and went back to the center of the room, where I sat down cross-legged. I had taken the bottle with me, of course.

She placed her bowl on the floor near me and then went back to the chest where the doll had been kept.

"How is it," I asked, "that you have such a doll?"

She said nothing, but returned the doll to its hiding place, beneath some silks and jewelry, at the back of the chest, in the right corner.

"Do not answer if you do not wish," I said.

She returned to where I sat and knelt there across from me. She lifted her bowl again to her lips and drank. Then she looked at me. "It was given to me," she said, "by my mother."

"I did not know Pleasure Slaves had mothers," I said. I was sorry I had said this, immediately, for she did not smile.

"She was sold when I was five," she said. "It is all that I have left from her."

"I'm sorry," I said.

She looked down.

"My father," she said, "I never knew, though I suppose he was a handsome slave. My mother knew little of him, for they were both hooded when mated."

"I see," I said.

She lifted her cup again to her lips.

"Ho-Tu," I said, "loves you."

She looked across to me. "Yes," she said.

"Are you often victimized on Kajuralia?" I asked.

"When Cernus remembers," she said. "May I clothe myself?" she asked.

"Yes," I said.

Sura went to one of the chests and drew forth a long cloak of red silk, which she drew on. She tied the string at the neck, closing the high collar.

"Thank you," she said.

I refilled her bowl.

"Once," she said, "for Kajuralia, many years ago, I was mated."

"Do you know with whom?" I asked.

"No," she said. "I was hooded." She shuddered. "He was brought in from the streets," she said. "I remember him. The tiny body, swollen. The small, clumsy hands. His whining and giggling. The men at table laughed very loudly. It was doubtless quite amusing."

"What of the child?" I asked.

"I bore it," she said, "but, once more hooded, I never saw it. It was surely, considering its sire, a monster." She shuddered.

"Perhaps not," I said.

She laughed sadly.

"Does Ho-Tu visit you often?" I asked.

"Yes," said she. "I play the kalika for him. He cares for its sound."

"You are Red Silk," I said.

"Long ago," said she, "Ho-Tu was mutilated, and forced to drink acid."

"I did not know," I said.

"He was once a slave," said Sura, "but he won his freedom at hook knife. He was devoted to the father of Cernus. When the father of Cernus was poisoned and Cernus, then the lesser, placed upon his neck the medallion of the House, Ho-Tu protested. For that he was mutilated, and forced to drink acid. He has remained in the house these many years."

"Why should he remain here?" I asked.

"Perhaps," she said, "because it is in this house that Sura is slave."

"I would not doubt it," I said.

She looked down, smiling.

I looked about the room. "I am not anxious to return immediately to my compartment," I said. "Further, I am confident that the men of the house will expect me to remain some time here."

"I will serve your pleasure," she said.

"Do you love Ho-Tu?" I asked.

She looked at me, thoughtfully. "Yes," she said.

"Then," I said, "let us find something else to do."

She laughed.

"Your room," I said, "seems to offer little in the way of diversions."

She leaned back, and smiled. "Little save Sura," she admitted.

I, glancing about once again, saw the kalika in the corner.

"Would you like me to play for you?" asked Sura.

"What would you like to do?" I asked.

"I?" she asked, amused.

"Yes," I said, "you—you Sura."

"Is Kuurus serious?" she asked skeptically.

"Yes," I affirmed. "Kuurus is serious."

"I know what I would like," she said, "but it is very silly."

"Well," I said, "it is, after all, Kajuralia."

She looked down, flustered. "No," she said. "It is too absurd."

"What?" I asked. "Would you like me to try and stand on my head, or what? I warn you I would do it very poorly."

"No," she said. Then she looked at me very timidly. "Would you," she asked, "teach me to play the game?"

I looked at her, flabbergasted.

She looked down, immediately. "I know," she said. "I am sorry. I am a woman. I am slave."

"Have you a board and pieces?" I asked.

She looked up, happily. "Will you teach me?" she asked, delighted.

"Have you a board and pieces?" I asked.

"No," she said, miserably.

"Do you have paper?" I asked. "A pen, ink?"

"I have silk," she said, "and rouge, and bottles of cosmetics!"

In a short time we had spread a large square of silk on the floor between us, and, carefully, finger in and out of a rouge pot, I had drawn the squares of the board. I put a dot in the center of the squares that would normally be red on a board, leaving those squares that would normally be yellow blank. Then, between us, we managed to find tiny vials, and brooches, and beads, to use as the pieces. In less than an Ahn we had set up our board and pieces, and I had shown Sura the placing of the pieces and their moves, and had explained some of the elementary techniques of the game to her; in the second Ahn she was actually negotiating the board with alertness, always moving with an objective in mind; her moves were seldom the strongest, but they were always intelligent; I would explain moves to her, discussing them, and she would often cry out "I see!" and a lesson never needed to be repeated.

"It is not often," I said, "that one finds a woman who is pleased with the game."

"But it is so beautiful!" she cried.

We played yet another Ahn and, even in that short amount of time, her moves had become more exact, more subtle, more powerful. I became now less concerned to suggest improvements in her play and more concerned to protect my own Home Stone.

"Are you sure you have never played before?" I asked.

She looked at me, genuinely delighted. "Am I doing acceptably?" she asked.

"Yes," I said.

I began to marvel at her. I truly believe, also, that she had never played before. I realized, to my pleasure, if danger, that I had come upon one of those rare persons who possesses a remarkable aptitude for the game. There was a rawness in her play, a lack of polish, but I sensed myself in the presence of one for whom the game might have been created.

Her eyes sparkled.

"Capture of Home Stone!" she cried.

"I do not suppose you would care to play the kalika," I proposed.

"No! No!" she cried. "The game! The game!"

"You are only a woman," I reminded her.

"Please, Kuurus!" she said. "The game! The game!"

Reluctantly I began to put out the pieces again.

This time she had yellow.

To my astonishment, this time I began to see the Centian Opening unfold, developed years ago by Centius of Cos, one of the strongest openings known in the game, one in which the problems of development for red are particularly acute, especially the development of his Ubar's Scribe.

"Are you sure you have never played before?" I asked, thinking it well to recheck the point.

"No," she said, studying the board like a child confronting something never seen before, something wonderful, something mysterious and challenging, a red ball, some squares of brightly colored, folded orange cloth.

When it came to the fourteenth move for red, my color, I glanced up at her.

"What do you think I should do now?" I asked.

I noted that her lovely brow had already been wrinkled with distress, considering the possibilities.

"Some authorities," I told her, "favor Ubar's Initiate to Scribe Three at this point, others recommend the withdrawal of Ubara's Spearman to cover Ubar Two."

She studied the board closely for a few Ihn. "Ubar's Initiate to Scribe Three is the better move," she said.

"I agree," I said.

I placed my Ubar's Initiate, a perfume vial, on Scribe Three.

"Yes," she said, "it is clearly superior."

It was indeed a superior move but, as it turned out, it did not do me a great deal of good.

Six moves later Sura, as I had feared, boldly dropped her Ubar itself, a small rouge pot, on Ubar Five.

"Now," she said, "you will find it difficult to bring your Ubar's Scribe into play." She frowned for a moment. "Yes," she mused, "very difficult."

"I know," I said. "I know!"

"Your best alternative at this point," she explained, "would be, would it not, to attempt to free your position by exchanges?"

I glared at her. "Yes," I admitted. "It would."

She laughed.

I, too, laughed.

"You are marvelous," I told her. I had played the game often and was considered, even among skilled Goreans, an excellent player; yet I found myself fighting for my life with my beautiful, excited opponent. "You are simply incredible," I said.

"I have always wanted to play," she said. "I sensed I might do it well."

"You are superb," I said. I knew her, of course, to be an extremely intelligent, capable woman. This I had sensed in her from the first. Also, of course, had I not even known her I would have supposed her a remarkable person, for she was said to be the finest trainer of girls in the city of Ar, and that honor, dubious though it might be, would not be likely to have been achieved without considerable gifts, and among them most certainly those of unusual intelligence. Yet here I knew there was much more involved than simple intelligence; I sensed here a native aptitude of astonishing dimension.

"Don't move there," she told me, "or you will lose your Home Stone in seven."

I studied the board. "Yes," I said at last, "you are right."

"Your strongest move," she said, "is First Tarnsman to Ubar One."

I restudied the board. "Yes," I said, "you are right."

"But then," she said, "I shall place my Ubara's Scribe at Ubar's Initiate Three."

I tipped my Ubar, resigning.

She clapped her hands delightedly.

"Wouldn't you like to play the kalika?" I asked, hopefully.

"Oh Kuurus!" she cried.

"Very well," I said, resetting the pieces.

While I was setting them up I thought it well to change the subject, and perhaps to interest her in some less exacting pastime, something more suitable to her feminine mind.

"You mentioned," I said, "that Ho-Tu comes here often."

"Yes," she said, looking up. "He is a very kind man."

"The Master Keeper in the House of Cernus?" I asked, smiling.

"Yes," she said. "And he is actually very gentle."

I thought of the powerful, squat Ho-Tu, with his hook knife and slave goad.

"He won his freedom at hook knife," I reminded her.

"But in the time of the father of Cernus," she said, "when hook knives were sheathed."

"The fights with hook knife I saw," I said, "were contests with sheathed blade."

"That is since the beast came to the house," she said, looking down. "The knives are sheathed now that the loser will survive to be fed to the beast."

"What manner of beast is it?" I asked.

"I do not know," she said.

I had heard it cry out and knew that it was not a sleen, nor a larl. I could not place the roar, the noise.

"I have seen the remains of its feeds," she said, shuddering. "There is little left. Even the bones are broken open and splintered, the marrow sucked out."

"Is it only those who lose at hook knife who are fed to the beast?" I asked.

"No," she said. "Anyone who displeases Cernus might be given to the beast. Sometimes it is a guard even, but normally a slave.

Generally it is a male slave from the pens. But sometimes a girl is bloodied and fed to it."

I remembered that the slave who had lost in hook knife had been wounded slightly before being taken to the beast.

"Why bloodied?" I asked.

"I do not know," she said. Then she looked down again at the board, that square of silk marked with rouge. "But let us forget the beast," she said. She smiled looking at the silk, the vials and beads. "The game is so beautiful," she said.

"Ho-Tu," I observed, "seldom leaves the house."

"In the last year," said Sura, "he left it only once for an extended period."

"When was that?" I asked.

"In last year's En'Var," she said, "when he was gone from the city on the business of the house."

"What business?" I asked.

"Purchases of slaves," she said.

"To what city did he go?" I asked.

"Ko-ro-ba," she said.

I stiffened.

She looked up at me. "What is wrong, Kuurus?" she asked. Then suddenly her eyes widened and she threw out her hand. "No, Ho-Tu!" she screamed.

Eighteen

The End of Kajuralia

I leaped across the rouged square of silk, scattering the vials and beads that were the pieces of our game, flinging Sura to the floor, pressing myself across her body that she might be protected. In the same instant the hurled knife struck a chest behind us and I had rolled over throwing my legs under me, trying to draw the sword from my sheath, when Ho-Tu, running, hook knife in hand, leaped upon me, the curved blade streaking for my throat; I threw my left hand between the knife and my throat and felt the sudden hot flash of pain in my cut sleeve, the sudden splash of blood in my eyes, but then I had my hands on Ho-Tu's wrist, trying to force the knife back, and he, with his two hands, leaning his weight on his hands, his feet slipping on the floor, stepping on the square of silk, pressed down again toward my throat.

"Stop it!" cried Sura. "Ho-Tu, stop!"

I pressed up and then, knowing his full weight was on the knife, I suddenly ceased resistance, removing my counter-pressure, and rolled from under him. Ho-Tu fell heavily on the floor and I slipped free, rolled and had the sword from my sheath, standing.

He scrambled to his feet, his face a mask of hate, looked about, saw the slave goad, ran to it and whipped it from the wall.

I did not pursue him, not wanting to kill him.

He turned and I saw, in almost one motion of his finger, the goad switch to on, the dial rotate to the Kill Point. Then crouching, the goad blazing in his hand, he approached me warily.

But Sura stood between us. "Do not hurt him," said Sura.

"Stand aside," said Ho-Tu.

"No!" cried Sura.

I saw the dial rotate back from the Kill Point and Ho-Tu swept the goad toward her, angrily. There was an intense eruption of needle-like sparks and Sura screamed in pain and fell stumbling to one side, weeping, crying out on the stones of the floor.

For an instant the face of Ho-Tu seemed in agony, and then he turned again to me. Again I saw the dial rotate and the goad now seemed a jet of fire in his hand.

I had backed to the chest, resheathed my sword, and drawn forth the knife which had been thrown. It was a killing knife, short, well-balanced for throwing, tapered on one side.

It reversed itself in my hand.

With a cry of rage and anger Ho-Tu hurled the goad at me. It passed to the left of my head, struck the wall with an explosion of sparks and lay burning on the stones.

"Throw!" ordered Ho-Tu.

I looked at the knife, and the man. "It was with a knife such as this," I said, "that you slew a Warrior of Thentis on a bridge in Ko-ro-ba, in En'Var, near the tower of Warriors."

Ho-Tu looked puzzled.

"You struck him from behind," I said, "the blow of a coward."

"I killed no one," said Ho-Tu. "You are mad."

I felt a cold fury moving through me. "Turn around," I told him, "your back to me."

Woodenly, Ho-Tu did so.

I let him stand that way for a moment. Sura had now, shaken, still feeling the pain of the goad, risen to her hands and knees.

"Do not kill him!" she whispered.

"When will it strike, Ho-Tu?" I asked.

He said nothing.

"And where?" I probed. "Where?"

"Please do not kill him!" cried Sura.

"Throw!" cried Ho-Tu.

Sura leaped between us, standing with her back to Ho-Tu. "Kill Sura first!" she screamed.

"Stand aside!" cried Ho-Tu, not turning, his fists clenched. "Stand aside, Slave!"

"No!" cried Sura. "No!"

"Do not fear," I said. "I will not kill you with your back turned." Ho-Tu turned to face me, with his arm pushing Sura to one side.

"Pick up your hook knife," I said.

Ho-Tu, not taking his eyes much from me, found the hook knife and lifted it.

"Do not fight!" screamed Sura.

I crouched down, the killing knife now held by the hilt in my hand.

Ho-Tu and I began to circle one another.

"Stop!" cried Sura. Then she ran to the slave goad and picked it up; it was still incandescent, brilliant; one could not look on it without pain. "The goad," said she, "is at the Kill Point. Put down your weapons!" Her eyes were closed and she was sobbing. The goad was clenched in her two hands, moving toward her throat.

"Stop!" I cried.

Ho-Tu flung away his hook knife and rushed to Sura, tearing the goad away from her. I saw him rotate it to minimum charge, turn it off, and fling it away. He took Sura in his arms weeping. Then he turned to face me. "Kill me," he told me.

I did not wish to kill a man who was unarmed.

"But," said Ho-Tu, "I killed no man—in Ko-ro-ba or elsewhere."

"Kill us both," said Sura, holding the squat, ugly Ho-Tu to her, "but he is innocent."

"He killed," I told her.

"It was not I," said Ho-Tu. "I am not he whom you seek."

"You are he," I said.

"I am not," said he.

"A moment ago," I charged, "you attempted to kill me."

"Yes," said Ho-Tu. "That is true. And I would do so again now."

"You poor fool," said Sura, sobbing, to Ho-Tu, kissing him. "You would kill for a simple slave?"

"I love you," cried Ho-Tu. "I love you!"

"I, too," said she, "love you, Ho-Tu."

He stood as though stunned. A strong man, he seemed shaken. His hands trembled on her. In his dark eyes I saw tears. "Love," asked he, "for Ho-Tu, less than a man?"

"You are my love," said Sura, "and have been so for many years."

He looked at her, hardly daring to move.

"Yes," she said.

"I am not even a man," said he.

"In you, Ho-Tu," said she, "I have found the heart of a larl and the softness of flowers. You have been to me kindness, and gentleness and strength, and you have loved me." She looked up at him. "No man on Gor," said she, "is more a man than you."

"I killed no one," he said to her.

"I know that," said Sura. "You could not."

"But when I thought of him with you," sobbed the Master Keeper, "I wanted to kill—to kill."

"He did not even touch me," said Sura. "Do you not understand? He wanted to protect me, and so brought me here and freed me."

"Is this true?" asked Ho-Tu.

I did not speak.

"Killer," said Ho-Tu, "forgive me."

"He wears the black tunic," said Sura, "and I do not know who he is, but he is not of the black caste."

"Let us not speak of such matters," I said, sternly.

Ho-Tu looked at me. "Know," said he, "whoever you are, that I killed no one."

"I think I shall return to my compartment," I said, feeling it well to be on my way.

"I wanted to hurt you," said Ho-Tu, looking at me.

"But," said Sura to Ho-Tu, "it was I whom you hurt, Ho-Tu."

There still was the trace of pain in her voice, the memory in her nerves of the strike of the slave goad.

"Forgive me," sobbed Ho-Tu. "Forgive me!"

She laughed. "A Master Keeper begging the forgiveness of a slave for touching her with a slave goad!"

Ho-Tu looked down at the square of silk, the tumbled vials and beads.

"What were you doing here?" he asked.

"He was teaching me to play the game," she laughed, "with such things."

Ho-Tu grinned. "Did you like it?" he asked.

"No, Ho-Tu," laughed Sura. She kissed him. "It is too difficult for me," she said.

Ho-Tu spoke to her. "I will play with you, if you like," he said.

"No, Ho-Tu," said she. "I would not like that." Then she left his arms, to pick up the kalika in the corner of her quarters. Smiling at him she then returned to the center of the compartment and sat down, cross-legged, for the instrument is commonly played that way, and bent over it. Her fingers touched the six strings, a note at a time, and then a melody, of the caravans of Tor, a song of love.

They did not notice me as I left the compartment.

* * * *

I found Flaminius, the Physician, in his quarters, and he, obligingly, though drunk, treated the arm which Ho-Tu had slashed with the hook knife. The wound was not at all serious.

"The games of Kajuralia can be dangerous," remarked Flaminius, swiftly wrapping a white cloth about the wound, securing it with four small metal snap clips.

"It is true," I admitted.

Even from the Physician's quarters we could hear, at various points in the House, the laughing and sporting of drunken slaves in their cells, drunken guards running down one hall or another playing jokes on each other.

"This is the sixth hook-knife wound I have treated today," said Flaminius.

"Oh?" I asked.

"Your opponent is, I suppose," said Flaminius, "dead."

"No," I said.

"Oh?" asked Flaminius.

"I received this wound," I said, "in the quarters of Mistress Sura."

"Ha!" laughed Flaminius. "What a wench!" Then he looked at me, grinning. "I trust Mistress Sura was taught something this evening."

I recalled instructing her in the game. "Yes," I said, dourly, "this evening Mistress Sura learned much."

Flaminius laughed delightedly. "That is an arrogant slave," he said. "I would not mind getting my hands on her myself, but Ho-Tu would not permit it. Ho-Tu is insanely jealous of her, and she only a slave! By the way, Ho-Tu was looking for you this evening."

"I know," I said.

"Beware of Ho-Tu," said Flaminius.

"I do not think Ho-Tu will bother Kuurus, of the black caste," said I, rising to my feet.

Flaminius looked at me, with a certain drunken awe. Then he rose in his green quarters tunic and went to a chest in his room, from which he drew forth a large bottle of paga. He opened it and, to my surprise, poured two cups. He took a good mouthful of the fluid from one of the cups, and bolted it down, exhaling with satisfaction.

"You seem to me, from what I have seen and heard," I said, "a skilled Physician."

He handed me the second cup, though I wore the black tunic.

"In the fourth and fifth year of the reign of Marlenus," said he, regarding me evenly, "I was first in my caste in Ar."

I took a swallow.

"Then," said I, "you discovered paga?"

"No," said he.

"A girl?" I asked.

"No," said Flaminius, smiling. "No." He took another swallow. "I thought to find," said he, "an immunization against Dar-Kosis."

"Dar-Kosis is incurable," I said.

"At one time," said he, "centuries ago, men of my caste claimed age was incurable. Others did not accept this and continued to work. The result was the Stabilization Serums."

Dar-Kosis, or the Holy Disease, or Sacred Affliction, is a virulent, wasting disease of Gor. Those afflicted with it, commonly spoken of simply as the Afflicted Ones, may not enter into normal society. They wander the countryside in shroudlike yellow rags, beating a wooden clapping device to warn men from their path; some of them volunteer to be placed in Dar-Kosis pits, several of which lay within the vicinity of Ar, where they are fed and given drink, and are, of course, isolated; the disease is extremely contagious. Those who contract the disease are regarded by law as dead.

"Dar-Kosis," I said, "is thought to be holy to the Priest-Kings, and those afflicted with it to be consecrated to Priest-Kings."

"A teaching of Initiates," said Flaminius bitterly. "There is nothing holy about disease, about pain, about death." He took another drink.

"Dar-Kosis," I said, "is regarded as an instrument of Priest-Kings, used to smite those who displease them."

"Another myth of Initiates," said Flaminius, unpleasantly.

"But how do you know that?" I queried.

"I do not care," said Flaminius, "if it is true or not. I am a Physician."

"What happened?" I asked.

"For many years," said Flaminius, "and this was even before 10,110, the year of Pa-Kur and his horde, I and others worked secretly in the Cylinder of Physicians. We devoted our time, those Ahn in the day in which we could work, to study, research, test and experiment. Unfortunately, for spite and for gold, word of our work was brought to the High Initiate, by a minor Physician discharged from our staff for incompetence. The Cylinder of Initiates demanded that the High Council of the Caste of Physicians put an end to our work, not only that it be discontinued but that our results to that date be destroyed. The Physicians, I am pleased to say, stood with us. There is little love lost between Physicians and Initiates, even as is the case between Scribes and Initiates. The Cylinder of the High Initiate then petitioned the High Council of the City to stop our work, but they, on the recommendation of Marlenus, who was then Ubar, permitted our work to continue." Flaminius laughed. "I remember Marlenus speaking to the High Initiate. Marlenus told him that either the Priest-Kings approved of our work or they did not; that if they approved, it should continue; if they did not approve, they themselves, as the Masters of Gor, would be quite powerful enough to put an end to it."

I laughed.

Flaminius looked at me, curiously. "It is seldom," he said, "that those of the black caste laugh."

"What happened then?" I asked.

Flaminius took another drink, and then he looked at me, bitterly. "Before the next passage hand," said he, "armed men broke into the Cylinder of Physicians; the floors we worked on were burned; the Cylinder itself was seriously damaged; our work, our records, the animals we used were all destroyed; several of my staff were slain, others driven away." He drew his tunic over his head. I saw that half of his body was scarred. "These I had from the flames," said he, "as I tried to rescue our work. But I was beaten away and our scrolls destroyed." He slipped the tunic back over his head.

"I am sorry," I said.

Flaminius looked at me. He was drunk, and perhaps that is why he was willing to speak to me, only of the black caste. There were tears in his eyes.

"I had," he said, "shortly before the fire developed a strain of urts resistant to the Dar-Kosis organism; a serum cultured from their blood was injected in other animals, which subsequently we were unable to infect. It was tentative, only a beginning, but I had hoped—I had hoped very much."

"The men who attacked the Cylinder," I said, "who were they?"

"Doubtless henchmen of Initiates," said Flaminius. Initiates, incidentally, are not permitted by their caste codes to bear arms; nor are they permitted to injure or kill; accordingly, they hire men for these purposes.

"Were the men not seized?" I asked.

"Most escaped," said Flaminius. "Two were seized. These two, following the laws of the city, were taken for their first questioning to the courts of the High Initiate." Flaminius smiled bitterly. "But they escaped," he said.

"Did you try to begin your work again?" I asked.

"Everything was gone," said Flaminius, "the records, our equipment, the animals; several of my staff had been slain; those who survived, in large part, did not wish to continue the work." He threw down another bolt of paga. "Besides," said he, "the men of Initiates, did we begin again, would only need bring torches and steel once more."

"So what did you do?" I asked.

Flaminius laughed. "I thought how foolish was Flaminius," he said. "I returned one night to the floors on which we had worked. I stood there, amidst the ruined equipment, the burned walls. And I laughed. I realized then that I could not combat the Initiates. They would in the end conquer."

"I do not think so," I said.

"Superstition," said he, "proclaimed as truth, will always conquer truth, ridiculed as superstition."

"Do not believe it," I said.

"And I laughed," said Flaminius, "and I realized that what moves men is greed, and pleasure, and power and gold, and that I, Flaminius, who had sought fruitlessly in my life to slay one disease, was a fool."

"You are no fool," said I.

"No longer," said he. "I left the Cylinder of Physicians and the next day took service in the House of Cernus, where I have been for many years. I am content here. I am well paid. I have much gold, and some power, and my pick of Red Silk Girls. What man could ask for more?"

"Flaminius," I said.

He looked at me, startled. Then he laughed and shook his head. "No," said he, "I have learned to despise men. That is why this is a good house for me." He looked at me, drunkenly, with hatred. "I despise men!" he said. Then he laughed. "That is why I drink with you."

I nodded curtly, and turned to leave.

"One thing more to this little story," said Flaminius. He lifted the bottle to me.

"What is that?" I asked.

"At the games on the second of En'Kara, in the Stadium of Blades," said hc, "I saw the High Initiate, Complicius Serenus."

"So?" said I.

"He does not know it," said Flaminius, "nor will he learn for perhaps a year."

"Learn what?" I asked.

Flaminius laughed and poured himself another drink. "That he is dying of Dar-Kosis," he said.

* * * *

I wandered about the house. It was now past the twentieth hour, the midnight of the Gorean day, yet still, here and there, I could hear the revels of Kajuralia, which are often celebrated until dawn.

My steps, as I was lost in thought, brought me back to the hall of Cernus, in which we had sat table. Curious I opened the door off the hall, through which the slave taken to the beast had been led. I found a long set of stairs, and I followed them. I came to a landing, and there was a long corridor. At the end I saw two guards. They immediately sprang up, seeing me. Neither was drunk. Both were apparently perfectly sober, rested and alert.

"Kajuralia," I said to them.

Both men drew their weapons. "Do not pass this point," said they, "Killer."

"Very well," I said. I looked at the heavy beamed door behind them. It was not locked on this side, which interested me. I would have thought it would have been bolted shut, for fear of the beast locked within. There were, however, the means for shutting it at hand, two large beams which might be placed in iron brackets.

Suddenly I heard an enraged roar from somewhere behind the door.

"I was wounded," I said to them, "in the sport of hook knife."

I shoved back the sleeve of my tunic, revealing the bandage. Some blood had soaked through it.

"Leave!" cried one of the guards.

"I will show you," I said, drawing down the white cloth, revealing the wound.

Suddenly there was a wild cry from behind the door, of almost maniacal intensity, and I thought I heard something moving on the stones behind it, uncontrollable, clawed.

"Go!" cried the second guard. "Go!"

"But it is not a serious wound," I said, pinching it a bit, letting some blood move from it, trickling down my forearm.

To my horror I heard something behind the door fumbling with a bolt. It seemed to draw it open, and then, wildly, to thrust it back, keeping the door locked; and then I heard the bolt rattling in its brackets as though something had seized it and trembling was trying to hold it in place. The door I then realized had been locked on the inside, and could be opened from the inside.

There was another wild, eerie cry, an uncanny almost demented roaring noise, and the bolt on the other side was dashed free of the door, and the two guards, with a cry of fear, hurled the beams in the two brackets, fastening the door, which was made to swing outward, shut. The two guards leaned against the door. Behind it I heard an enraged, frustrated roaring, weird and terrible; I heard clawing at the wood; I saw the heavy door, as if struck with great force, buckle out against the beams.

"Go!" screamed the first guard. "Go!"

"Very well," I said, and turned and walked away down the corridor.

I could hear the guards cursing, and hear the door being thrust against the heavy beams. Then, when I was far down the corridor, I fixed the bandage again in place, shoved down my sleeve, and looked back. The thing behind the door was no longer making noise, and the door was no longer pressing against the beams; from where I stood I could hear the bolt on the inside being thrust back in place, locking it from the inside. Then, after a minute or two, I saw the guards remove the beams. What was inside was then apparently quiet.

* * * *

I continued to wander about the House, here and there bumping into inebriated guards or staff members, who would invariably hail me with "Kajuralia!" to which greeting I would respond in turn.

A given thought kept going through my mind, for no reason that I was clearly aware of. It seemed unrelated to anything. It was Cernus saying to me, outside the Cell for Special Captures, "You, Killer, would not make a Player." His remark kept burning its way through my brain.

But as I walked the halls it seemed to me that, on the whole, things were not proceeding badly, though I regretted the amount of time lost, apparently necessarily, in the House of Cernus. Elizabeth, and Virginia and Phyllis, by tomorrow at this time, would be free. And Caprus, now that Cernus was often in the Central Cylinder, attending to the numerous duties of Ubar of the city, had more time for his work. By Se'Var he hoped to be finished. Caprus, I said to myself, a good man. Caprus. Thought well of by Priest-Kings. Trusted. He himself had arranged for an agent of Priest-Kings to purchase the girls. Caprus who seldom left the house. Brave Caprus. You, Killer, would not make a Player. Brave Caprus.

I turned suddenly into the kitchen in which the food for the hall of Cernus is prepared. Some startled slaves leaped up, each chained by one ankle to her ring; but most slept, drunk; one or two, too drunk to notice me, were sitting against the wall, their left ankles chained to their slave rings, a bottle of Ka-la-na in their grasp, their hair falling forward.

"Where is the paga?" I demanded of one of the girls. Startled, I saw, now that she stood forth from the shadows, that she had no nose.

"There, Master!" said she, pointing to a basket of bottles under the large cutting table in the center of the room.

I went to the basket and took out a bottle, a large one.

I looked about myself.

There was the odor of food in the kitchen, and of spilled drink. There were several yards of sausages hung on hooks; numerous canisters of flour, sugars and salts; many smaller containers of spices and condiments. Two large wine jugs stood in one corner of the room. There were many closed pantries lining the walls, and a number of pumps and tubs on one side. Some boxes and baskets of hard fruit were stored there. I could see the bread ovens in one wall; the long fire pit over which could be put cooking racks, the mountings for spits and kettle hooks; the fire pit was mostly black now, but, here and there, I could see a few broken sticks of glowing charcoal; aside from this, the light in the room came from one small tharlarion-oil lamp hanging from the ceiling, near the side where the kitchen slaves were chained, presumably to facilitate the guard check which, during the night, took place each second Ahn; the other lamps in the room were now extinguished.

I took another bottle of paga from the basket and tossed it to the girl without a nose, who had directed me to the paga.

"Thank you, Master," said she, smiling, going back to her ring. I saw her nudge the girls on the left and right of her. "Paga," I heard her whisper.

"Kajuralia," I said to her.

"Kajuralia," she said.

Again the thought went through me. You, Killer, would never make a Player. You, Killer, would never make a Player. Grimly, the paga bottle in my hand, I went back into the corridor and found the stairs that took one to lower floors in the cylinder, and eventually to its depths.

Lower and lower I went into the cylinder, the thought pounding in my brain: You, Killer, would never make a Player.

I was beginning to feel sick with fear, with anger. A realization that horrified me seemed to claw at the back of my brain, as the beast had torn at the door, unseen, in the corridor far above. You, Killer, would never make a Player.

Now, paga bottle in hand, I was passing guards and found myself walking down the narrow iron runways over the pens below, now filled with drunken slaves, some sleeping, some sitting stupefied in the center of their pen, some singing brokenly to themselves, some trying to crawl again to the trough to lap there at the paga mixed with their water. I saw one girl, drunk, putting her hands through the bars which separated the cage which she shared with other female slaves, from the cage adjacent to it, filled with male slaves. "Touch me," she begged. "Touch me!" But the males lay in drunken sleep on the stones.

I passed through the level on which interrogations take place, the level of the kennels, and went lower in the cylinder, now far below ground, past even more iron pens and levels. When I would pass a guard I would hail him with "Kajuralia!" and pass by.

Always the thought burned through me, You, Killer, would never make a Player, and always I seemed driven by the black fear that would not speak itself but whose presence I could clearly sense.

Descending a last spiral of iron stairs I came to the lowest level of the cylinder.

"Who goes there?" cried a startled guard.

"It is I, Kuurus, of the black caste," said I, "on the orders of Cernus bringing paga to prisoners on Kajuralia!"

"But there is only one prisoner here," said he, puzzled.

"The more for both of us then," I said.

He grinned and put out his hand and I bit the cork from the bottle, which was a very large bottle, and handed it to him.

"I have spent Kajuralia," he grumbled, between guzzles, "sitting here without paga—they did not even send a girl down to me."

I gathered from what he said that the guard was intended to remain sober, and from this that he had valuable materials under his care, and gathered also that the guard, from his disgruntlement, was ignorant of their value. It could of course be that he had merely been forgotten, overlooked in the general revels of Kajuralia.

Then the guard sat down heavily, not willing to try to remain upright longer.

"It is good paga," said he. He took two or three more swallows, and then simply held the bottle, looking at it.

I left him and looked about. There were several corridors lined with small cells with iron doors, each with an observation panel. The corridors were damp. Here and there some water had gathered in recesses in the flooring. They were dark, save that each, at intervals of some thirty yards, was lit with a small tharlarion-oil lamp. I picked up a torch and lit it in the light of a lamp near the swirling iron stairs.

I heard the guard take another swallow of the paga, a long swallow, and then he sat there again, holding the bottle.

I walked down a corridor or two. The cells were locked but, by sliding back the panel, and holding the torch behind me I could see dimly into the cells. Each seemed piled with boxes; I recognized the boxes as being of the general sort which I had seen unloaded from the Slavers' ship in the Voltai. I gathered that most, or a great many of the cells, on this level, might be filled with such merchandise, whatever it might be. Each of the cells was locked.

I heard the guard calling out from near the stairs. "The prisoner is in Nine Corridor."

I strode back to him, stepping aside not to brush against a wet, silken, blazing-eyed urt scampering along the edge of the corridor wall.

"My thanks," said I to the guard. I put my hand on the bottle but he retained it long enough to take yet another swallow, and then two more, and then he reluctantly surrendered it.

"I will bring it back," I assured him.

"There is too much paga there for one prisoner," mumbled the guard, rather groggily.

"True," I said. "I will return the bottle to you."

I saw him close his eyes and slump a bit against the wall.

"The Forty Cell," he said.

"Where is the key?" I asked. The other cells had all been locked.

"Near the door," he said.

"The other keys," I said, "were not near the doors."

"The other keys," he mumbled, "are kept somewhere above. I do not know where."

"My thanks," said I.

I began moving down the Nine Corridor. Soon, in the flickering light of the torch, I could read the Forty on the tiny metal plate over one of the cells.

I slid back the observation panel. It, like the others, was about six inches in width and about an inch high. A man could do little more than thrust his fingers through. Inside, very dimly, I could see a slumped, dark figure lying near the back wall, chained.

256

The key box was about a yard to the left of the keyhole; and about four feet from the observation panel; it is a small, heavy metal box bolted to the stone of the wall; it opens and shuts to the left, by means of a round-knobbed screw, which must be turned several times before the small metal door opens. I rotated the screw and opened the box, and removed the key. I inserted the key into the keyhole and swung back the door. Lifting the torch I entered.

Startled by the light an urt scurried from my path, disappearing through a small crevice in the wall. It had been nibbling at the scrapings of dried gruel caked in a tin pan near the prisoner's foot.

I could smell wet straw in the place, and the excrement of urts and a human being.

The slumped figure, that of a small man, naked, white-haired, stinking, skeletal, haggard, covered with sores, awakening, cried out in misery, whimpering. He crawled to his knees, squinting against the torch, trying to shelter his eyes with manacled clawlike hands from the sudden, fierce, painful blaze of fire that his world must have then been for him.

"Who are you?" he whispered.

I saw that he was not actually an old man, though his hair was white. One ear had been partly bitten away. The white hair was long, white, yellowish.

"My name is Kuurus," said I, speaking to him from the light of the torch.

Each of his limbs, and his throat, was separately confined, each chained individually to the wall, each chain running to a separate ring bolted in the stone; any one of the chains would have been sufficient to hold a man; I gathered that this prisoner must be unusual indeed; I observed, further, that the chains gave him some run, though not much, just enough to permit him to feed himself, to scratch his body, to defend himself to some extent against the attacks of urts; I gathered it was intended that this prisoner should, at least for a time, survive. Indeed, it seemed probable that he had lived under these miserable conditions for a long time.

I rose and found a torch rack in the room and set the torch in the rack. As I did so I saw four or five urts run for various small crevices in the stone.

I returned to the prisoner.

"You are of the black caste," he whispered. "At last they are done with me."

"Perhaps not," I said.

"Am I to be tortured again?" he asked, piteously.

"I do not know," I said.

"Kill me," he whispered.

"No," I said.

He moaned.

I looked on that small, trembling, skeletal body, the straggly hair, the sores; the mutilated ear; angrily I rose to my feet and searched about, finding some loose stone which, with my foot, I wedged into the several crevices through which the urts had darted.

Unbelievingly the prisoner with his sunken eyes, now accustoming themselves to the light of the torch, regarded me.

I returned to him; beneath the iron on his ankles and wrists, and on his throat, there were scars, like white bands, pale shadows of the dark metal; it would take months to form such scars, superseding the fearful sores that must first have been inflicted.

"Why have you come?" he asked.

"It is Kajuralia," I said to him, simply.

I held the bottle to him.

"Kajuralia?" he asked.

"Yes," I said.

He began to laugh, softly, hoarsely. "I was right," he said. "I was right."

"I do not understand," I said.

He began to suck at the bottle. There were few teeth left in his mouth; most had rotted and, apparently, snapped away, or had been broken off by him and discarded.

I forcibly drew the bottle from his mouth. I had no wish that he kill himself on the paga. I did not know what its shock would be to his system, after apparently months of torture, confinement, fear, poor food, the water, the urts.

"I was right," he said, nodding his head.

"About what?" I asked.

"That today was Kajuralia," said he.

He then indicated behind himself, on the wall, a large number of tiny, regularly formed scratches in the stone, perhaps cut there by a pebble or the edge of the tin drinking dish. He indicated the last of the scratches. "That is Kajuralia," he said.

"Oh," I said, regarding his crude calendar. There were a very large number of scratches.

"Like any other day," he laughed.

I let him have another small swig at the paga bottle.

"Some days," he said, "I was not sure that I marked the wall, and then I would forget; sometimes I feared I had marked it twice."

"You were accurate," I said, regarding the carefully drawn scratches, the rows methodically laid out, the months, the five-day weeks, the passage hands.

I counted back the rows. Then I said, pointing to the first scratch, "This is the first day of En'Kara before the last En'Kara."

The toothless mouth twisted into a grin, the sunken eyes wrinkled with pleasure. "Yes," he said, "the first day of En'Kara, 10,118, more than a year ago."

"It was before I came to the House of Cernus," I said, my voice trembling.

I gave him another drink of the paga.

"Your calendar is well kept," I said. "Worthy of a Scribe."

"I am a Scribe," said the man. He reached under himself to hold forth for my inspection a shred of damp, rotted blue cloth, the remains of what had once been his robes.

"I know," I said.

"My name is Caprus," he said.

"I know," I said.

I heard a laugh behind me, and spun. Standing in the doorway, four guards armed with crossbows with him, stood Cernus, of the House of Cernus. With him also was the guard to whom I had given the paga. In the background I could see the lean Scribe whom I had thought for these many months to be Caprus. He was grinning.

The men stepped within the room.

"Do not draw your weapon," said Cernus.

I smiled. It would have been foolish to do so. The four men with crossbows leveled their weapons on me. At this distance the bolts would pass through my body, shattering against the stones behind me.

The guard to whom I had first given paga came over to Caprus and tore the bottle from his hand. Then, with the sleeve of his tunic, the guard distastefully wiped the rim of the bottle. "You were to have returned this paga to me," said the guard, "were you not?"

"It is yours," I said, "you have earned it."

The man laughed and drank.

"You, Killer," said Cernus, mocking, "would never make a Player."

"Apparently it is true," I said.

"Chain him," said Cernus.

One of the guards, putting his crossbow in the hall, brought forth heavy steel manacles. My hands were thrown behind my back. I felt the heavy steel close on my wrists.

"May I introduce to you, Caprus," said Cernus, looking down at the piteous chained figure by the wall, "Tarl Cabot of Ko-ro-ba?"

I stood stunned.

"Tarl Cabot," I said, numbly, "was slain in Ko-ro-ba."

"No," said Cernus, "the Warrior Sandros of Thentis was slain in Ko-ro-ba."

I looked at him.

"Sandros thought he was to be your Assassin," said Cernus. "It was for that purpose he thought himself sent to Ko-ro-ba. Actually he was sent there to die himself by the knife of a killer. His resemblance to a certain Koroban Warrior, perhaps Tarl Cabot, would make it seem clear, in the darkness of the night, that the knife had been intended for that Warrior, and a convenient clue, a patch of green, would lead to Ar, and doubtless then to the House of Cernus."

I could not speak.

"Sandros was a fool," said Cernus. "He was sent to Ko-ro-ba only to be slain, that you would be lured to this house, where in effect you have been my prisoner for more than a year."

"There must be some reason why you would want me here?" I said.

"Let us not jest, Tarl Cabot," said Cernus. "We knew that Priest-Kings would suspect our House, as we intended that they should; so simple a ruse, and profitable a one, as selling barbarian Earth girls under the auspices of the House would guarantee their investigation.

For this investigation they would need men. Surely they would wish, if possible, to choose a man such as Tarl Cabot."

"You play well," I said.

Cernus smiled. "And to guarantee that it should be Tarl Cabot, whom we know, and with whom we, so to speak, have an old score to settle, the matter of the egg of Priest-Kings, we sent Sandros of Thentis to Ko-ro-ba where he, poor fool, was to be slain in your stead, that you would be brought here."

"You play brilliantly," said I.

Cernus laughed. "And so we arranged to have you arrive in our house, the trusted spy and agent of Priest-Kings, who would thus think themselves moving secretly and intelligently against us. And here, while we have through the months advanced our cause you have stood by, patiently and cooperatively, a dupe and a fool, our guarantee that Priest-Kings would not send another."

Cernus threw back his head and laughed.

"You speak of 'we' and 'our cause,'" I said.

Cernus looked on me, unpleasantly. "Do not mock me," said he, "Warrior." He looked at me then and smiled. "I serve those who are not Priest-Kings."

I nodded.

"It is war, Tarl Cabot," said he. "And there will be no quarter given." He smiled. "Not then, nor now."

I nodded once more, accepting his words. I had fought. I had lost.

"Will you kill me?" I asked.

"I have an amusing fate in store for you," said Cernus, "which I have considered these many months."

"What?" I asked.

"But first," said Cernus, "we must not forget the little beauty."

I stiffened.

"Sura reports that she has trained superbly, that she is now capable of giving the most exquisite of pleasures to a master."

I tensed in the manacles.

"I understand she expects, with the other two barbarians, to be purchased by an agent of Priest-Kings, and carried to safety and freedom."

I looked at him angrily.

"I expect," said Cernus, "that she will put on an excellent performance."

I wished that I might break the steel from my wrists and seize his
throat.

"It should be worth seeing," said Cernus. "I will see that you have
a chance to see it."

I choked with rage.

"What is the matter?" asked Cernus, concerned. "Do you not wish
to see the little beauty presenting herself on the block? I expect she,
with the others, will bring much gold to the House of Cernus, which
we may then invest in our cause." He laughed. "It will be time enough,
afterward," said he, "for her to learn that she has been truly sold."

"You sleen!" I cried. I hurled myself at Cernus but two men seized
me, threw me back, then held my arms.

"You, Tarl Cabot," said Cernus, "would never make a Player."

"Sleen! Sleen!" I cried.

"Kajuralia," said Cernus, smiling, and turned and left the cell.

I stared after him. My wrists fought the steel. Two of the guards
laughed.

"Kajuralia," I said bitterly. "Kajuralia."

Nineteen

The Curulean

The sale of Elizabeth Cardwell, Virginia Kent and Phyllis Robertson, with that of Cernus' other trained barbarians, did not take place on the first night of the Love Feast, though they had been transported to the cages of the Curulean early in the first day. The Love Feast, incidentally, as I may have mentioned, occupies the full five days of the Fifth Passage Hand, occurring late in summer. It is also a time of great feasting, of races and games. Cernus, sensing the temper and curiosity of the crowds, had determined to make them wait for his surprise delights, over a hundred of them, whose supposed qualities of beauty and skill, enhanced by the mysterious aura of barbaric origin, had been for months the object of ever more eager rumors and excited speculations. Many were the furious Gorean slave girls who found themselves, early in the Love Feast, forced to ascend the block while buyers were still waiting, before the larger quantities of gold would be spent, to be sold for prices less than they might otherwise have won for themselves under the conditions of a more normal market. The evening of the fourth day of the Love Feast is usually taken as its climax from the point of view of slave sales. The fifth day, special races and games are celebrated, regarded by many Goreans as the fitting consummation of the holidays. These games are among the most heavily attended and important of the year. It was on the evening of the fourth day of the Love Feast that Cernus decided to bring Elizabeth Cardwell, Virginia Kent and Phyllis Robertson, with his other barbarian slave girls kidnapped from Earth, before the buyers, not only of Ar but of all the cities of known, civilized Gor.

It was now the fourth day of the Love Feast.

Hooded, a chain on my throat, my wrists in steel behind my back, I stumbled after a tharlarion wagon, to the back of which my throat chain had been bolted, through the streets of Ar. On the wagon there rode some eight guards. Behind me, prodding me upon occasion with the butts of their spears, there walked two others. On the seat of the wagon, which was drawn by a horned tharlarion, sat the driver and the Scribe whom I had known as Caprus, whose real name, as I had been informed, was Philemon of Tyros, an island some hundreds of pasangs west of Port Kar. In the House of Cernus, however, to all, he had been known simply as Caprus, having been introduced to the staff and guards in this fashion by Cernus. He had been a member of the staff of Caprus, the agent of Priest-Kings, until the latter had disappeared, presumably because he had displeased Cernus; Philemon of Tyros had then assumed Caprus' position and duties.

I was barefooted and not used to so walking the stone streets of Ar. Hooded, it was further difficult to pick my way. Particularly was I angered by the occasional large, flat blocks of stone placed across the streets, low enough to permit a wagon to pass over them, and separated by enough distance to allow the passage of a wagon's wheels, but surely a threat to a tethered fool, shackled and hooded, led on a chain behind a wagon. The purpose of the blocks, which are used where the streets are curbed, is to provide stepping stones for crossing the street when there have been heavy rains.

Occasionally, unexpectedly, I would be struck by a stone or a strap and hear a jeer or mocking cry.

It was hot in the slave hood, of several layers of thick leather, stifling, locked under my chin and about my throat; further, this hood, like many, was so constructed as to ensure silence in a prisoner; I could not spit out the thick leather wad that was packed in my mouth nor, because of the straps that held it in place, dislodge it.

Another strap stung my legs, across the calves. "Slave!" I heard.

It had been a girl's voice, she perhaps a slave herself.

In Ar, as on Gor generally, a slave, on threat of torture and impalement, must endure whatever abuse a free person cares to inflict on him.

In my position, bound and hooded, anyone might strike me with impunity, even slaves.

Those who jeered me or sported with their straps and stones would have little reason for not thinking me slave. I was barefooted; my only garment was a short woolen, sleeveless tunic; on both the back and the front of this tunic was sewn a large block letter, the initial letter of the Gorean expression "Kajirus," which means a male slave.

I fell down several times but the cart did not stop; each time I managed to regain my feet, though sometimes I was dragged for several yards before, nearly strangling, I managed to get up once more. Twice children tripped me; at least twice one of the guards with the butt of his spear did so. They laughed.

I knew that I was on my way to the Curulean.

I supposed that Elizabeth Cardwell would be pleased and excited at this hour.

In my heart I laughed bitterly.

"Slave!" I heard, and felt again the sting of a strap in someone's hand. And then the strap fell twice again. "Slave! Slave!"

When a girl first arrives at the Curulean, there is, on a ticket wired to her collar, a lot number. Elizabeth, Virginia and Phyllis would have the same lot number. The papers of most of the girls, including those of Elizabeth, Virginia and Phyllis, had been transmitted days before to the staff of the Curulean, to be checked for authenticity, and for the updating of certain endorsements. The papers are correlated with the lot number and the girls' fingerprints are taken and checked against those on the papers. Some girls, whom the House had determined late would be sold, arrive at the Curulean with a small leather cylinder tied about their collar, which contains their papers, which girl is then, by the staff of the Curulean, assigned a lot number. Lana, whom Ho-Tu, who held considerable power in the House of Cernus, had decided to sell at the Love Feast, so arrived at the Curulean. Virginia, thanks to Ho-Tu, need not fear that the forward Lana would be likely to soon grace the leash of her Relius. When the members of the staff of the Curulean are satisfied that the girl's papers are in order the ticket with her lot number is stamped approved.

I stumbled again, on one of the large, broad, flat stepping stones, and fell forward and was jerked by the chain tearing at the back of my neck, and struggled again to my feet, hearing through the thick layers of leather in the slave hood the laughter of the guards, as though far away.

The girls, when brought to the Curulean, are braceleted and naked; they have been chained in slave wagons; they are brought to a large, heavy, barred gate in the rear of the large building, through which they are led; the bracelets are, of course, to secure them; the lack of clothing is simply to save the trouble of transporting numerous sets of slave livery back to the House; by the time the girls arrive at the Curulean the slave livery which had been theirs may already have been washed and be drying, soon to be ready for issue to another.

"This is the Curulean," I heard Philemon of Tyros say, the words sounding far off, blurred through the hood.

The wagon stopped, and I felt the heavy, slack chain dragging at my collar.

This was the evening of the fourth day of the Love Feast, the climax of the feast insofar as the sales of slaves was concerned; this was the night Cernus would put his barbarian beauties on the block; tomorrow would be the concluding races and games, wild, dizzying hours in the Stadium of Tarns and that of Blades, bringing the Love Feast to its frenzied conclusion; it was tomorrow, in the Stadium of Blades, that Cernus had informed me I would die.

I heard two girls laugh and I felt my ankles seized and held while small hands thrust on my back, taking me by surprise and throwing me heavily forward; I struck my shoulder on the back of the cart and the booted foot of a Warrior thrust me from the cart and I fell to my knees on the stones; when I wished to rise a Warrior's hand on my shoulder prevented me. Then another Warrior, with his two hands, thrust my hooded head to the sandal of one of my unseen tormentors; I heard her laugh; then my head was jerked up and thrust down again, to the sandal of another; I heard her laugh.

"You have had your sport," said Philemon. "Be gone, Slaves."

I heard the two girls laugh and dart away.

I was conscious of a crowd about me, not that I was the center of it, but that many men, and some women, were passing about me, probably on the way into the Curulean; there was much bustle, some shouting, much talking and moving. Most were doubtless on their way to the ticket booths, for there is a small charge to enter the Curulean; the fee, though minimal, helps to defray the expenses of the market, most of which are met by commissions on sales transacted on its premises;

the fee also tends to some extent, but I suspect not greatly, to discourage attendance at the market by the merely curious or the indigent.

I heard my neck chain being unbolted from the back of the wagon. When it was free I was jerked to my feet and, stumbling in the midst of my guards, was led from the street, around the back of the building, where we entered through a small, private gate. Within, the hood was, to my satisfaction, removed; when the large wad of soured leather was removed from my mouth I threw up against one wall; the guards laughed and struck me; the lights, lamps, though they were feeble, seemed very bright, and ringed with many colors; the hood had been dark and hot and wet, stifling; now even the close, humid air of the Curulean seemed welcome and cold. My wrists pulled futilely against the circles of steel that confined them; I felt the point of a short sword in my back.

"This way," said Philemon.

We began to walk down a long, slowly bending passageway. I had seen the Curulean from the outside before, but I had never been inside. From the outside it resembles several tiers of disks, surrounded by a circling portico with lofty, fluted columns; the predominant colors are blue and yellow, the traditional colors of the Gorean slaver; around the outside there are large numbers of well-wrought mosaics set in the walls, and on the floor of the circling portico; various scenes, stories and events are depicted, primarily having to do with, as would be expected, the trade of the Slaver and his merchandise; there are hunting scenes, for example, and those of capture, enslavement, training, the sale, the dance, submission, and so on. One striking set of mosaics details a slave raid from its initial planning phases through the successful return of the Slavers, on tarnback, to Ar with their stunning victims; another picks up this story from the registration and training of prizes to the block of the Curulean itself; another records the theoretical history of certain of these prizes, fortunate enough to be sold to men of Ar, who find eventual rapture in the arms of their masters, of Ar, naturally. There is another set of interesting mosaics, each portraying a chained beauty, identified as being of a given city, kneeling before a Warrior, identified as being of Ar.

The men of Ar, like those of most other Gorean cities, regard themselves as being the best and finest on Gor, and the women of other cities as being worthy of being only the slave girls of such men. I would suppose that the Slavers, many of them sophisticated, rather cosmopolitan men, who come to Ar from many distant cities, must find such mosaics delightful; I am sure they have seen similar representations in their own cities, only there it is perhaps a wench of Ar who kneels, frightened, obedient, at the feet of one of their own warriors. How seriously the men of Gor understand these representations depends doubtless on the man; but even those who, upon reflection, laugh at them, I have found, do generally regard the women of other cities rather differently than they regard their own, thinking of them almost automatically, particularly if of a hostile city, in terms of slave steel and silk; women on Gor, like gold and weapons, tend to be categorized as spoils. Outside the Curulean also, on sale days, actual slave girls are exhibited, some in suspended plastic cages fastened to the roof of the portico, others in a tier of cages lining the interior wall of the portico; these are not, however, the exposition cages within the Curulean; they are merely, so to speak, advertisements and attractions to lure customers; on the other hand, of course, such displays, along with many others, will be offered for sale.

Now, following Philemon, and surrounded by guards, one of whom held my heavy leash, we passed by the heavy, barred gate in the back of the Curulean, through which deliveries are made; some days ago Elizabeth, and Virginia and Phyllis, would have entered through that gate. We passed tables on one side, and rooms where medical examinations could be held; there were also facilities for washing prisoners; here and there I saw the office of a market official; there were also rooms where I saw silks, cosmetics, vials of perfumes, chains and such. The sale at the Curulean is carefully planned, and the lots prepared and scheduled with much attention to such matters as variety and the attention of the buyers; for example, two consecutive lots are not likely to wear the same first silks upon ascending the block, yet each girl, given her complexion and hair color, must be attractively silked; similarly, the adornments initially worn must be apt and dissimilar; and further, of course, the merchandise itself must have great variety in its presentation; for example, women of the same general type and hair color seldom follow one another on the block. Cosmetics and their utilization present further problems. The sale of women, like that of any other merchandise, can be a difficult and time-consuming business, calling optimally for good judgment, experience and imagination.

I saw no merchandise in my passage through the rear halls of the Curulean; the girls are generally kept, prior to their sale, in holding cells, lit by energy bulbs, beneath the ground level; soon, however, I was passing by the exposition cages, which are accessible to the public; these cages were now empty; they are used, from the tenth to the fourteenth Ahn of a given day, to display the goods that will be sold that evening; access to the exposition cage area is free to the public prior to the sale, but, after the fourteenth Ahn, the Curulean is cleared and made ready for the evening's work; after that time a citizen must pay to enter the market; the cells themselves, and the corridors on each side surrounding them, are carpeted; the bars are set rather widely; inside the cells there are cushions and silks; on each cell there is a lot number and its date of sale; in the cells the girls are exhibited unclothed; moreover, they must be shown precisely as they are, absolutely without makeup; the only exception to this, interestingly, is that perfume is permitted; even the slave collars are removed, lest they be used to conceal a scar or blemish; the girl is simply washed, brushed and combed, and perfumed, and turned into the cage where, at the prospective bidder's pleasure, she may be examined; she is also expected, upon command, to walk, to assume postures, or otherwise to present the properties of her beauty for discernment and comparison; as Elizabeth had once said to me, it is sometimes difficult to make an assessment from the high tiers; on the block, of course, the girl is under the command of the auctioneer; moreover, on the block, she will customarily be made up; if the bidder does not recall that a particularly dazzling girl on the block was actually rather less dazzling in the exhibition cage, that is the responsibility of the bidder and not of the house; I suspect that, in the excitement of the sale, and in the marvelous presentation on the block of the Slaver's wares, the more careful, more dispassionate assessments of the exhibition cages are often forgotten.

I supposed that now Elizabeth, and Virginia and Phyllis, would be in the holding cells beneath the ground level, perhaps being fed, some two or three Ahn prior to the sale; later they would be moved, with others, to the tunnel of ready cells, which leads to the block; there they would be adorned, made up and silked; each of these cells gives access to the one on its left and right; as the sale begins the lots move through the cells, one by one, until reaching that which opens at the foot of the block; as the lots move through the cells other lots are summoned from the holding cells and prepared for sale, these lots then moving through the tunnel of ready cells as did those before them.

Here in the area of the exhibition cages there were various citizens of Ar milling about, some meeting their friends, before taking their seats in the tiers; some seats in the tiers, the better ones, are reserved by number, but many are simply available on a first-come-first-served basis; those citizens wandering about, I gathered, had reserved seats.

Philemon, I and the guards emerged from the exposition area to the interior of the sales amphitheater; the entire house was now lit by energy bulbs; later, the block alone would be illuminated; the seats rose in tier after tier, largely circling the block, though a passage lay open behind the block; there were exits from the amphitheater available on several of the levels of tiers; certain specially favored portions of the tiers were boxed, seating areas reserved for important clients of the Curulean, often important Slavers from distant cities; the blue and yellow of the Slavers was much in evidence in the amphitheater, worked into intricate patterns of fantastic designs, but the background color of the amphitheater was a rich, deep red; the block itself, lying in the pit of the amphitheater, was perhaps seven or eight feet in height, round, and with a diameter of some twenty feet; it was doubtless incredibly heavy, being formed of huge beams, shaped and fitted together with long wooden pegs; it was of simple wood, plain and unvarnished; the broad, heavy stairs, without banisters, leading to its height were shining and concave, polished, shaped and worn smooth by the bare feet of countless wenches who had climbed them; the surface of the block itself was similarly worn smooth and was slightly concave; its broad surface had now been sprinkled, as is traditional, with sawdust; it is a Gorean custom that the girl, no matter how richly silked she may be when she ascends the block, must from the very first feel the wood with her feet.

"This way," said Philemon.

Philemon led the way to the box of Cernus, the largest and most impressive in the amphitheater, shielded on both sides and the back from the rest of the boxes and seats by heavy wooden screens; there, on a marble dais on which sat a low, thronelike chair of marble, I was forced to kneel. My throat chain was then locked to a heavy ring set in the side of the chair.

I had seen that many of the seats in the higher tiers, those not reserved, had already been filled with citizens, many of whom were doubtless prospective buyers. This was surprising because the hour was still early; I supposed the crowd this night would be unusually large, even for the fourth night of the Love Feast; none of the citizens had paid much attention to my being brought under guard to the box of Cernus; he was Ubar; it is not unusual on Gor for a powerful victor to force his enemy to witness the sale of his own women, before he is either sold or slain himself.

Philemon looked at me with his narrow ferret eyes and smiled. He pursed his thin, sour mouth.

"Cernus will not arrive until the sales begin," said he, "so we have something of a wait."

I said nothing.

"Hood him," said Philemon.

I struggled but the huge wad of soured leather was thrust again in my mouth and the heavy hood, with its thick layers of leather, drawn over my head and locked.

Hooded, my wrists locked in steel, my throat chained to the chair of my enemy, I knelt for perhaps two Ahn. During this time I was conscious of noise, the movement of men, the filling of the amphitheater. I wondered if Elizabeth, and Virginia and Phyllis, were yet in the ready cells, being prepared; I judged it unlikely, for they would probably be sold late, and would not be prepared until the sales were in progress; the last touches of their makeup might not even be made until minutes before they ascended the block. I felt rage and sorrow, rage at the twisting of events, the brilliance of my enemies, my own failures, and sorrow for Elizabeth, and the other girls; for Elizabeth in particular my heart cried out, for her hopes would be so cruelly dashed; she might not even discover that she was not on her way to safety and freedom, or how we had been tricked and used, until she found herself, to her horror, beneath the lash of a master to whom she would be only another slave.

I heard movement about me and sensed that Cernus had now arrived.

In a few moments I heard his voice. "Unhood the fool," said he.

The hood was peeled over my head and I shook my head and hair, gasping for breath.

I saw Cernus in his chair, who smiled down at me. Beside me stood a man with pliers and a hook knife.

"Do not raise your voice during the sale," said Cernus, "or your tongue will be cut out."

I looked down at the block bitterly, not speaking.

Cernus laughed to himself and turned his attention to his right, where stood Philemon, and conversed with the Scribe.

As well as I could, given the wooden screens about the box of Cernus, I examined the interior of the amphitheater. It was now packed with the various caste colors of Gor. The aisles and passageways themselves were jammed with men, and some free women. The individual sounds of their conversations were undistinguishable, blurring into a melded roll of gray thunder, low-keyed, far-off. There was, however, a kind of tensity in the noise, reflecting, I suppose, an eagerness, an expectancy. I'm not sure what the seating capacity of the amphitheater was, theoretically, but I would guess that it would be in the neighborhood of four to six thousand; counting those crowded into the tiers, and standing and sitting in aisles, it might now have held twice that many; the air was hot with bodies; the faces of many of the men were streaked with sweat.

A number of Musicians now filed out from the door at the foot of the block and took their places about it, sitting cross-legged on the floor. Those with string instruments began to tune them; there was a czehar player, the group's leader, some kalika players, some flutists, players of the kaska, small drums, and others. Each of these, in his way, prepared himself for the evening, sketching out melodies or sound patterns, lost with himself.

Even more individuals began to crowd into the amphitheater. Slaves on catwalks opened metal, shuttered vents in the ceiling, which is domed, and in the curved walls; I caught a breath of the cool air; outside I could see stars in the black Gorean sky; I could not see any of her moons.

"It will soon begin," said Cernus, turning in my direction, pleasantly.

I did not deign to speak to him.

He chuckled.

There were vendors in the crowd. They had great difficulty in moving about. Still, given the size of the crowd, they seemed to have little difficulty retailing their goods in short order; they would then disappear down an exit, soon returning with more.

Among the crowd, though it was predominantly male, there were, as I might have mentioned, several women, perhaps one in ten or fifteen; many of these were doubtless rich, and of High Caste; some of them were probably interested in picking up a serving slave; kettle wenches, so to speak, would probably be purchased at one of the minor markets; their bids would be made by a male agent; others of the women were perhaps just curious, interested in observing the beauty of the girls of other cities, wondering if it might match their own; others perhaps merely enjoyed the excitement and color of the sales, possibly thrilling to the sight of their sisters being sold nude into bondage; perhaps some, in the lights and shouts, imagined that it was they themselves who stood brazen and marvelous on the block, exciting men, driving them into frenzies of bidding, bringing higher and ever higher prices, beautiful women, slaves, sold at auction.

Then the crowd stilled and the Musicians, too, were silent, as the energy lights in the amphitheater dimmed and went out, and another set of energy bulbs, to a pleased shout of the crowd, suddenly lit the block with a blaze of light.

The block, in the light, looked very stark and massive. It was empty.

I wondered how much the girls would be able to see from the block. I could make out, in the reflected light, the faces of those about me, and, as the moments passed, could make out more and more. The girls would be, of course, keenly aware of the crowd, its moods and responses, for this is extremely important in stimulating and tantalizing it, manipulating it to increase the frequency and quality of the bids. Even from the beginning Sura had trained Elizabeth, and Virginia and Phyllis, before men, that they might, from the responses of males, hasten their progress in the arts of the slave girl. Once Elizabeth had told me that Sura had informed them that they would, after a time, be able to see faces from the block. That was apparently important, being able to see the eyes of men, the attitude of their bodies, the movements of their shoulders.

There was the sudden crack of a whip, loud and sharp, and the crowd leaped to its feet, for the sale had begun.

A girl, wild, clad only in a brief tunic of gray toweling, as though fleeing, ran to the surface of the block, weeping, circling it, her hands outstretched to the crowd; this was done to the music of the Musicians; she turned this way and that, acting the frantic role of the fleeing slave girl. In a moment or two, behind her, a powerful man in a short blue and yellow tunic, the auctioneer, carrying a slender slave goad, almost a wand, climbed to the surface of the block; seeing him the girl turned to flee, and having nowhere to go, fell to her knees weeping at the center of the block, where the bit of toweling was torn from her and she leaped to her feet laughing, her hands wide to the crowd, to their shouts of amusement and encouragement.

Then the auctioneer briefly and expertly displayed the girl, with deft touches of the wandlike slave goad, and began, simultaneously, to raise the first block calls. "Verbina, she is," called he, "who so fears a man that she would flee him, at the risk of death and torture, White Silk and never before owned, yet certified ready for the chain of a master who would use her as she so richly deserves!" The crowd roared with amusement, enjoying the sport of the auctioneer. The first bid was some four gold pieces, which was good, and suggested that the night might go well. Prices of girls vary considerably with her caste, the supply of her general type and the trends of the market. A girl in the Curulean is seldom sold for less than two gold pieces. This is largely, doubtless, because the Curulean refuses to accept women for sale who are not genuinely attractive. In a rather brief amount of time Verbina was auctioned to a young Warrior for seven gold pieces. An extremely good price, under relatively normal market conditions, for a truly beautiful woman of High Caste tends to be about thirty pieces of gold, though some go as high as forty, and fifty is not unknown; these prices, for women of low caste, may be approximately halved.

The next lot was an interesting one, consisting of two slave girls, clad in the skins of forest panthers, from the northern forests of Gor, and chained together by the throat. They were driven up the steps by a whip slave and forced to kneel at the center of the block. The northern forests, the haunts of bandits and unusual beasts, far to the north and east of Ko-ro-ba, my city, are magnificent, deep forests, covering hundreds of thousands of square pasangs. Slave girls who escape masters or some free women, who will not accept the matches arranged by their parents, or reject the culture of Gor, occasionally flee to these forests and live together in bands, building shelters, hunting their food, and hating men; there are occasional clashes between these bands of women, who are often skilled archers, and bands of male outlaws inhabiting the same forests; hardy Slavers sometimes go into the forests hunting these girls, but often they do not return; sometimes Slavers simply meet outlaws at the edges of the forests, at designated locations, and buy captured girls from them; interestingly, at other locations, on the eastern edges of the forests, Slavers from Port Kar meet the female groups and purchase men they have captured; it is not too uncommon that a Slaver Warrior has entered the forest only to be captured by his prey, enslaved, and eventually, when the girls tire of him, be sold, commonly for arrow points and adornments, to Port Kar Slavers, whence he will find himself chained to the oar of a cargo galley.

To the amusement of the crowd it took the whip slave, and two others, to strip the biting, scratching forest beauties. The pair was eventually sold to a collector for ten gold pieces; I trust the security of his Pleasure Gardens is superb, else he might waken to a knife at his throat and the demand for a tarn, and, perhaps eventually, in the rags of a slave, a seat on the bench of a cargo galley.

The third lot was a High Caste girl of Cos who stood before us clad in the complete robes of Concealment, which, piece by piece, were removed from her. She was beautiful, and had been free; she was not trained; she was of the Scribes, and had been picked up by pirates from Port Kar. She did nothing to move the buyers but stood, head down, numb on the block until she was completely revealed. Her movements were wooden. The crowd was not pleased. There was only a two gold piece bid. Then taking the whip from the whip slave the auctioneer stepped to the disconsolate girl; suddenly, without warning, he administered to her the Slaver's caress, the whip caress, and her response was utterly, and uncontrollably, wild, helpless. She regarded him with horror. The crowd howled with delight. Suddenly she threw herself, screaming hysterically, on the auctioneer, but he cuffed her to one side and she fell to her knees weeping. She was sold for twenty-five gold pieces.

"The sales go well," said Cernus to me.

Again I refused to respond to him.

Some of the girls, as the sales progressed, I recognized as from the House of Cernus. Lana, I recognized, who was sold for four gold pieces. Lot followed lot, and the bidding, on the whole, tended to increase. Usually the better merchandise is saved for later in the evening, and many of the buyers were waiting. Particularly, I suspected, were they waiting for the more than one hundred barbarians that Cernus had promised them, girls kidnapped from Earth to be Gorean pleasure slaves.

Occasionally, during the evening, the auctioneer had dropped certain disparaging remarks about barbarians, comparing some of the beauties on the block to such. The crowd had growled at these remarks, and Cernus had smiled. I supposed the auctioneer had received his instructions from the House of Cernus. The auctioneer was to appear skeptical, cynical.

I myself, in spite of my predicament, found myself being awestruck, again and again, by the beauty, the performances, the dances of the girls who were, lot by lot, brought before us; how beautiful are women, how fantastic, how tormenting, how superb, how marvelous, how excruciatingly maddening, and beautiful and marvelous they are!

At last, late in the evening, the auctioneer remarked, with something of a sneer, that the first barbarian would be presented, and to remember that he had warned them to expect nothing.

The crowd cried out angrily, "The barbarian! The barbarian!"

I was startled when I saw the girl brought forth. It was perhaps the plainest of all the barbarians who had been brought on the black ships; though I knew the girl to be among the most intelligent, and also, I had heard, among the most responsive. She was an extremely quick-witted, lively girl, though perhaps somewhat plain. Now, however, as I saw her shuffled across the boards, stiff, wrapped in a worn, dark blanket, she looked dull, stupid. Her eyes didn't seem to focus, and her tongue occasionally protruded at the side of her mouth. She scratched herself, and looked about herself, seemingly obtuse and surly. The crowd was taken aback, for such a wench would scarcely be presented on the meanest block of the smallest market in the city. I myself was startled, for I had seen the girl before and knew her somewhat; this was not her real person; the crowd, of course, would not know that. The auctioneer, as though desperately, tried to do his best for the girl, but soon jeers were forthcoming from the crowd, hissings and shoutings; when her blanket was removed from her, gracefully by the auctioneer, as though removing an expensive wrap from a lady of pearls and sophistication, she slouched so that one might have thought her back had been built in pieces, haphazardly; the crowd cried out in fury. The auctioneer, apparently losing his temper, responded angrily to some critics in the first tiers, and was himself hooted and decried. The girl seemed to understand nothing. Then, when poked with the slave goad, she called out in a nasal tone, not her own, in painfully, apparently memorized Gorean, "Buy me, Masters." The crowd howled with disgust and laughter. The auctioneer seemed beside himself. The auctioneer, subtly, or apparently so, then administered the Slaver's caress to her, but she scarcely noted the touch. Then I understood what was going on, perhaps belatedly, for I knew the girl, Red Silk before the black ships, was extremely responsive, and had even been used in the hall of Cernus for the amusement of his Warriors and guards; she had known the caress would be given; she had been ready; she had perhaps, in fact probably, been anesthetized. The crowd hooted and screamed for her to be taken away, while she looked at them in puzzlement, like a bosk cow, scarcely comprehending or concerned. I angrily admired the skill of Cernus. Doubtless, after this, the next lot would be his finest, and the comparison with this girl would be so startling as to cause men to forget the beauties who had preceded her; after this girl, a magnificent actress, the plainest of presentable women would have seemed brilliantly attractive; and a truly beautiful woman or women would be stunning beyond comparison.

"What am I offered for this slave?" called the auctioneer.

There were jeers and cries.

Yet when he persisted, there were some token offers, perhaps by men who wished to obtain a kettle girl for next to nothing; I was not surprised to note that each time a legitimate offer was made, though small, it was topped slightly by a fellow in the robes of the Metal Workers, whom I knew to be a guard in the house of Cernus; at last, this agent of Cernus had purchased her back for the House for only seventeen copper tarn disks. I knew later, perhaps in another city, she would be well presented and would bring a good price.

277

The auctioneer, as though in the throes of misery, almost threw the poor girl back down the stairs of the block, kicking her bit of dark blanket angrily after her.

He glared up at the crowd. "I told you!" he cried. "Barbarians are nothing!"

The auctioneer conferred with a market official, who kept lists of lot numbers and confirmed the bids and final sale with the buyers or their agents at the side of the block. The auctioneer looked dejected when he returned to the center of the block.

"Forgive me, Brothers and Sisters of my City, Glorious Ar," he begged, "for I must bring yet more barbarians before you."

The crowd, or much of it, stormed to its feet. I even heard some angry pounding on the wooden screens surrounding the box of Cernus. But Cernus only smiled. They screamed imprecations on the auctioneer, on the Curulean, even some of the braver ones, anonymous in the pressing throng, on the House of Cernus itself.

"Observe closely," said Cernus to me.

Again I did not deign to respond to the Slaver, now Ubar of Ar.

Suddenly the lights of the amphitheater went out, plunging that great, crowded room into darkness. There were shouts of surprise from the crowd, some screams of startled women. Then, after a moment, the great block, and that alone, was again illuminated with a blaze of light. The crowd shouted its pleasure.

It was as though the sales were beginning again, and now truly for the first time.

The auctioneer sprang to the block and, from the darkness at the foot of the steps, was hurled a chain leash, and then two more. He held them for a moment and then, keeping them taut, stepped back. He met resistance. Below, in the darkness, there came the sudden, startling, savage report of a slave whip, snapped three times.

Then, regally, in black cloaks, with hoods, three women, two girls and their leader, climbed the stairs to the block, backs straight, heads high, their features concealed in the folds of the hood. Each of them had her wrists braceleted before her body, and each slave chain led to the slave bracelets of one of the girls; the lead girl, probably Elizabeth, was on a somewhat shorter chain than the two behind her, one on each side, doubtless Virginia and Phyllis. Their black cloaks were rather like ponchos with hoods, save that there were slits through which their arms emerged. The length of the cloak, which was full and flowing, fell to their ankles. Their feet, of course, were bare. They stood near the center of the block, their leashes in the hands of the auctioneer.

"These are three barbarians, two White Silk, one Red Silk," called the auctioneer, "all from the House of Cernus, whom it is our hope you will find pleasing."

"Are they trained?" called a voice.

"They are so certified," responded the auctioneer. He then summoned three whip slaves to the block, and each held the chain of one of the girls.

At the auctioneer's command the slaves led the girls about the block, and then brought them again to its shining, shallowly concave center.

"What am I offered?" called the auctioneer.

There was silence.

"Come now, brothers and sisters of Glorious Ar, citizens and gentle buyers of Glorious Ar, and friends of Ar and hers, what am I offered for these three barbarians?"

There was a bid of three gold pieces from the auditorium, probably intended to do little more than initiate the bidding.

"I hear three," called the auctioneer, "do I hear four?" As he said this, he moved to one of the girls and threw back her hood. It was Virginia. Her head was back, and she looked disdainful. She wore the cosmetics of a Pleasure Slave, applied exquisitely. Her hair, glistening, fell to her shoulders. Her lips were red with slave rouge.

"Eight gold pieces!" I heard cry from the crowd.

"What of ten?" asked the auctioneer.

"Ten!" I heard cry.

The auctioneer then threw back the hood of the second girl, Phyllis.

She seemed coldly furious. The crowd gasped. The cosmetics enhanced and heightened the drama of her great natural beauty, but with an insolent and deliberate coarseness that was a gauntlet thrown before the blood of men.

"Twenty gold pieces!" I heard cry. "Twenty-five!" I heard from another area.

Phyllis tossed her head and looked away, over the heads of the crowd, nothing but contempt on her face.

"What of thirty?" called the auctioneer.

"Forty!" I heard cry.

The auctioneer laughed and approached the third girl.

Cernus leaned over the arm of his chair, toward me. "I wonder," he said, "how she will feel when she learns she has been truly sold?"

"Put a sword in my hand," said I, "and face me!"

Cernus laughed and turned his attention again to the block.

As the auctioneer reached for the hood of the third girl, she turned away and suddenly, though chained by the wrists, darted toward the stairs; the slack in the chain was taken up in her flight and, on the second or third stair down, she was spun about and thrown to the steps, half on them, half on the block. The whip slave who held her chain then hauled her cruelly, on her stomach, and then on her back, to the center of the block. There the whip slave stepped on the chain fastened to her slave bracelets about six inches from the bracelets, pinning her wrists to the block. The auctioneer, with his foot on her belly, held her in place.

"Shall we have a look at this one?" the auctioneer inquired of the crowd.

There were eager shouts.

I was angry. I knew that, in effect, this was a performance, each detail planned expertly, choreographed and rehearsed in the House of Cernus.

Cernus chuckled.

The crowd shouted eagerly to see the rebellious girl.

The auctioneer thrust his hand beneath the hood and, with his fist in her hair, drew her to her knees before the buyers. Then he brushed back her hood.

The light over the block took the glint of the tiny, fine nose ring in the nose of Elizabeth Cardwell.

The crowd gasped.

How startling, and incredibly beautiful she was!

She seemed fine and savage, as vital and dangerous and beautiful as the she-larl. She was a woman who could well have stood among the most marvelous of Gor.

She wore the cosmetics of the slave girl.

There was silence.

It was a tribute in its way, the honoring by way of awe this magnificent captive female, to be sold.

The silence was broken by a bid. "One hundred gold pieces," spoken by a Slaver who wore the insignia of Tor, some feet from the box of Cernus.

"A hundred and twenty," said another, soberly, matter-of-factly, this man, too, a professional Slaver, he wearing on his left shoulder the sign of Tyros.

The three girls then stood rather together, Elizabeth somewhat forward, the other two a bit behind and flanking her; then they were led on their chains again about the block.

The bids increased to a hundred and forty gold pieces. Then the girls were spaced on the block, Elizabeth toward the front and middle, and Virginia and Phyllis on alternate sides. The chains were then removed from their slave bracelets and the three whip slaves retired. The auctioneer then, with his key, removed the left slave bracelet from the wrist of each, permitting it to dangle from the right wrist.

He then removed the black cloak from Virginia, who stood before us in the brief, sleeveless yellow livery, slashed to the belt, of a slave girl.

There were cries of approval.

He then drew the cloak from Phyllis, who was attired as was Virginia.

The crowd cried out with enthusiasm.

He then went to Elizabeth and removed her cloak also.

The crowd roared with pleasure.

Elizabeth had been clad in the brief leather of a Tuchuk wagon girl, simple, rough, sleeveless, the short skirt on the left side slit to the belt, so that the saddle of the kaiila, mount of the Wagon Peoples, would be permitted her.

"Two hundred gold pieces," said a merchant from Cos.

"Two hundred and fifteen," called out a high officer in the cavalry of Ar.

Again the girls were commanded to walk about the block, and they did so, proudly, irritably, as though wishing to express only contempt for what they seemed to regard as the rabble about them. When they had finished, Virginia now stood toward the center, with Phyllis behind her and to her left, and Elizabeth behind her and to her right.

The three whip slaves then again climbed to the block. By this time the bids had increased to two hundred and forty. There were some cries of protest, perhaps from less-affluent bidders, that the girls were not of High Caste.

The auctioneer then motioned to the whip slave who stood behind Virginia. He drew her left wrist behind her back and snapped it into the open slave bracelet, thus confining both wrists behind her. Then he, pulling at the shoulders of her livery, jerked it down to her waist. This pleased the crowd. There was a bid of two hundred and fifty then for the lot. The auctioneer then signaled the whip slaves and the girls rotated their position, bringing Phyllis to the front of the block. There, she, like Virginia, was similarly secured and revealed. The bids then increased to two hundred and seventy-five gold pieces. Then the girls rotated again and this time Elizabeth stood at the center of the block.

"It appears," said the auctioneer, "that this was once a wench of Tuchuks."

The crowd grunted its approval. The Tuchuks, one of the distant Wagon Peoples, tend to be, to those of northern Gor, a people of mystery and intrigue; to those of the southern plains, of course, they tend to be little more than efficient, fierce and dreaded foes.

"Can you guess," asked the auctioneer, "which of the three slaves is Red Silk?"

The crowd roared with amusement.

"Doubtless," called the auctioneer, "her Tuchuk master used her well."

The crowd laughed.

At this point, savagely, Elizabeth spat into the face of the auctioneer.

The crowd screamed with amusement, but the auctioneer did not seem much pleased. Angrily he motioned back the whip slave, who stood behind the girl, and then he himself threw her hands cruelly behind her back and snapped shut the slave bracelets, thus himself confining her.

"You have pleased ignorant herders," he said. "Now we shall see if you can please the men of Ar."

So saying, he himself stripped her to the waist before the crowd.

Elizabeth was beautiful. The placement of her wrists, of course, like that of the other girls was no accident. It is done so that there be no impediment to the vision of the buyers.

I found I wanted to take her in my arms and kiss the slave rouge from her mouth. I suppose my responses were not much different from those of other men in the crowd.

"Three hundred gold pieces!" called a rich man of Ar.

The crowd shouted its approval of the bid.

"Three hundred and five," said the professional Slaver from Tor.

"Three hundred and ten!" announced the Slaver who wore upon his shoulder the sign of Tyros.

The auctioneer looked into the crowd. "Is not Samos," he asked, "First Slaver of Port Kar with us this evening?"

All eyes turned to one of the boxes near the front of the block.

There, slumped in a marble chair, was an indolent figure, yet indolent as is the satisfied beast of prey. About his left shoulder he wore the knotted ropes of Port Kar; his garment was simple, dark, closely woven; the hood was thrown back revealing a broad, wide head, close-cropped white hair; the face was red from windburn and salt; it was wrinkled and lined, cracked like leather; in his ears there were two small golden rings; in him I sensed power, experience, intelligence, cruelty; I felt in him the presence of the carnivore, at the moment not inclined to hunt, or kill.

"He is," said the man.

This Slaver had not yet made a bid.

"Surely Samos of Port Kar, First Slaver of Gor's Tatrix of the Sea, noble Port Kar, cares to express interest in these unworthy wenches?"

There was silence.

"Show me the women," said Samos.

The crowd shouted with pleasure.

The auctioneer bowed low to Samos, First Slaver of Port Kar.

Almost instantly, by the whip slaves, the three barbarian beauties from the House of Cernus were revealed to the buyers of Ar.

The crowd rose to its feet shouting and stamping, drowning out what bids might have been made.

How beautiful were the three women, the slaves.

When the tumult subsided, the voice of Samos was heard again.

"Remove the bracelets."

This was done and the three whip slaves retired, taking with them the bracelets which had confined the lovely commodities that now graced the block of Ar.

The crowd shouted and roared, and stamped its feet.

The girls stood in the light, lifting their heads to the crowd, nude and proud on the block, in the wild shouting and stamping and crying out, and knew themselves beautiful and prized. How marvelous and female they seemed, the three slaves, in that moment.

There were perhaps dozens of bids that were shouted forth and lost in the acclaim of the crowd. I managed to hear one bid for four hundred pieces of gold. At last, once again the crowd subsided.

Again the auctioneer looked to the box of Samos, First Slaver of Port Kar.

"Does noble Samos now care to express interest?" inquired the auctioneer.

"Let them perform," said Samos.

Again the auctioneer bowed to Samos. The crowd shouted with delight.

"Shall Pleasure Silks be brought?" inquired the auctioneer.

"No," said Samos.

Again the crowd roared its pleasure.

The Musicians took up their instruments and, together, as three slaves, women who would be owned by men, the girls danced.

In the crowd men cried out with pleasure; I heard even gasps from women, perhaps amazingly, startled that their sex was capable of such beauty; the eyes of some of the women shone with ill-concealed admiration and excitement; I could mark the quickness of their breath in their veils; the eyes of others seemed terrified, and, shrinking, they looked from the block about themselves, suddenly fearing the men with whom they shared the tiers; I heard the tearing of a veil and heard a girl scream and turned to see her lips being raped by the kiss of a Warrior, and then she was yielding to him; the crowd went wild; here and there there was the cry of a woman in the throng who was seized by those near her; one girl tried to flee and was dragged screaming by the ankle to the foot of a tier; another woman, with her own hands, tore away her veil and seized in her hands the head of a man near her, pressing her lips to his, and in a moment she lay, robes torn, in his arms, weeping, crying with pleasure.

Four dances the girls danced while the crowd screamed and roared, and then, at an instant, their dances ended, they stood suddenly motionless, splendid, animal, magnificent, inciting.

Then they, breathing deeply, stained with sweat, stepped back on the block, and the auctioneer stepped forward.

He did not even call for a bid.

"Five hundred gold pieces!" called the rich man of Ar.

"Five hundred and twenty!" called the Slaver of Tor.

"Five hundred and thirty!" called another man.

"Five hundred and thirty-five!" called the Slaver from Tyros.

The auctioneer turned then to the box of Samos, First Slaver of Port Kar.

"Does noble Samos, First Slaver of Port Kar, jewel and mistress of the sea, not care to express interest in these unworthy wenches? Would they not cheer the heart of a seaman returned from long at sea?"

There was laughter from the crowd.

"Would such not be pleased to be served his paga by such as these? Would he not care to see them dance for him? Would the sight of them, eager, lips lifted, in the shadows of a tavern's alcoves, not soothe his weary eyes aching from the sun and salt of gleaming Thassa?"

The crowd roared with laughter. But Samos did not speak. His eyes revealed no expression.

"Would they not be a fitting gift for the palace of the very Ubar of Port Kar, beautiful jewel and mistress of gleaming Thassa?"

The crowd was silent.

Inwardly I raged, but too I was overcome with horror, for I could not allow even in my imagination that the girls might be sold to one of Port Kar. Never has a slave girl escaped from canaled Port Kar, protected on one side by the interminable, rush-grown delta of the Vosk, on the other by the broad tides of the Tamber Gulf, and beyond it, the vast, blue, gleaming, perilous Thassa. It is said that the chains of a slave girl are heaviest in Port Kar. Perhaps nowhere on Gor would the slavery of a girl be so complete, so abject, as in squalid, malignant Port Kar. I would not admit to myself, even in speculation, that such a fate might befall the helpless prizes now upon the block of Ar, years of miserable, unrelieved servitude, to live at the beck and call of masters among the most cruel of Gor, existing only to give pleasure to one to whom they would be always nothing, only slave.

"I do not choose now to bid," said Samos, First Slaver of Port Kar.

The auctioneer smiled and bowed low.

"Five hundred and forty gold pieces!" cried the rich man of Ar, and the crowd cheered its approval of the bid.

Then there was silence.

"I am offered five hundred and forty gold pieces for these hot-blooded barbarian beauties," called the auctioneer, "only five hundred and forty gold pieces for this exquisite set of animals, in prime condition and superbly trained to tantalize you, to torment you, to drive you wild with pleasure! Do I hear more? Come now, gentle brothers and sisters of Ar, when again will such superb creatures be yours to ensteel for only a paltry sum of golden coin!"

There was laughter from the crowd.

"Five hundred and forty-five," growled the Slaver from Tyros.

The crowd greeted the bid with pleasure, but then it seemed quiet.

The auctioneer looked from face to face, and there were no more bids forthcoming.

He lifted his hand, palm up, open, to the crowd. If he closed his fist it meant he had accepted the bid.

There was silence.

Suddenly, to my horror, Elizabeth strode forth to the front of the block.

She stood there with her hands on her hips, her head back.

"The men of Ar are cheap!" she announced.

Laughter greeted her, and she, too, laughed. "Yes, cheap they are!" she laughed. She turned about and went to Virginia. "Here," said she, tauntingly, "is a slim beauty, lithe and swift, White Silk, intelligent, curious for the touch of a man, who for the right man would be the most abject and servile wench a beast could wish. Imagine her, noble men of Ar, chained to your slave ring! She alone is worth five hundred pieces of gold!"

The crowd roared its approval and the auctioneer dropped his hand and stepped back, perhaps as surprised as any in that room.

"And this wench!" said Elizabeth, striding to Phyllis, "What of her?"

Phyllis looked at her, startled.

"Place your hands behind the back of your head, Slave," ordered Elizabeth. "Put your head back, no, farther back, farther! Are you stupid? Now turn, slowly, unworthy slave, for the noble buyers of Ar!"

Startled, Phyllis did precisely as she was told, beautifully.

"Oh, Masters," taunted Elizabeth, "would you not like this one to wear your collar?"

There were shouts of agreement.

"But I warn you," said Elizabeth, "she hates men!"

There was laughter.

Phyllis looked at her in anger.

"Do not lower your arms, Slave," barked Elizabeth.

Phyllis remained as she was, her head back, her back arched. There were tears in her eyes.

"She does not think the man lives who can master her," said Elizabeth. "She does not think the man lives who can make her truly a slave girl!"

There were cries of derision, much laughter.

"She is perhaps right!" cried Elizabeth. "Surely none of Ar could make such a wench cry with pleasure!"

There were some angry shouts from the crowd, but mostly roars of laughter.

"Would it not be worth five hundred gold pieces," asked Elizabeth, "to put your leash on this one and lead her home, to teach her the worth of a man of Ar, if worth they have, and then send her weeping and aching to the kettles of the kitchen until she begs to sleep beneath your slave ring?"

There was a roar of pleasure, of amusement from the crowd.

Phyllis' eyes were filled with tears.

"Lower your arms, Slave," commanded Elizabeth, and Phyllis did so, stepping back, and went to stand beside Virginia.

Then Elizabeth herself strode to the front of the block. "And me!" she laughed. "Which of you would like to put me in steel?"

The crowd roared and stamped, and its men rose to their feet, shouting, pounding their right fists on their left shoulder, in Gorean acclaim.

"I am, I think," cried Elizabeth, laughing, "a not unworthy wench."

There were shouts of agreement.

She pointed her finger at a fine-looking fellow, grinning in the audience, a Saddlemaker. "Would you not like to own me?" she asked.

He slapped his knees with his hands and laughed. "That I would!" he cried.

"You!" cried Elizabeth, pointing to a merchant in rich robes in the fifth tier. "Would you not be pleased to have me submit to you?"

"Indeed, Wench," he laughed.

"Is there a man here," asked Elizabeth, "who would not wish to take me in his arms?"

The deafening response, "No!" shouted from thousands of voices, shook the amphitheater.

"Who wants me?" she cried.

"I!" came the thousands of responses, making the very walls ring with their pleasure.

"But," wailed Elizabeth, "I am only a miserable girl without a master." She held her wrists together and out to the crowd, as though they had been braceleted. "Who will buy me?" she wailed.

The thunder of bids was deafening.

Elizabeth backed to the other girls and took each by an arm, and together they came to the front of the block.

"Who will buy us?" called Elizabeth.

"Eight hundred gold pieces!" came one cry.

"Eight hundred and fifty," came another. Then we heard nine hundred and fifty bid, and then, incredibly, a thousand, and then a bid for the astounding sum of fourteen hundred pieces of gold.

The auctioneer signaled to the Musicians again and once more, to the shouts of the crowd, while he held open his hand, not yet closing it, taking bids, the girls performed the last moments of Ar's dance of the newly collared slave girl, who dances her joy at the thought that she will soon be in the arms of a strong master. When the dance ended the three girls, slaves, knelt in the position of submission, arms extended, heads lowered, wrists crossed as though for binding; Elizabeth knelt facing the crowd and, perpendicular to her, on her left and right, knelt Virginia and Phyllis, a vulnerable, submitted flower of slave girls.

The auctioneer waited for some minutes for the acclaim of the crowd to subside. The last bid he had received had been an astounding fifteen hundred pieces of gold. To my knowledge never in the

Curulean had a set of three girls brought such a price. The investment of Cernus had been, it seemed, a good one.

The auctioneer called out to the crowd, now silent. "I will close my fist!"

"Do not close your fist," said Samos, First Slaver of Port Kar.

Deferentially the auctioneer regarded the Slaver of squalid, malignant Port Kar, mistress and scourge of gleaming Thassa.

"Does Samos, First Slaver of Port Kar, mistress and jewel of gleaming Thassa, now care to express interest?"

"He does," said Samos, dispassionately.

"What is the Curulean bid?" inquired the auctioneer.

"It is bid," said the man, "by Samos, First Slaver of Port Kar, for the wenches now on the block three thousand pieces of gold."

There was an audible gasp throughout the audience in the swirling amphitheater.

The auctioneer stepped back, astonished. Even the girls lifted their heads, startled, breaking the discipline of the submitted flower. Then, smiling, Elizabeth lowered her head again, and so, too, did Virginia and Phyllis. I felt sick. Doubtless Elizabeth thought Samos the agent of Priest-Kings, sent to purchase them and carry them to safety and freedom.

Cernus was chuckling.

The fist of the auctioneer closed, as though grasping a handful of golden coins. "The women are sold!" he cried. The crowd shouted its pleasure, its delight.

The girls were now on their feet and whip slaves were braceleting their wrists before their bodies and attaching the lead chains to the bracelets, preparing to conduct the purchased merchandise from the block.

"More barbarians!" cried the crowd. "Let us see more barbarians!"

"You shall!" cried the auctioneer. "You shall! We have many sets of barbarians to present for your consideration and pleasure! Do not be disappointed! There are more! There are many more barbarians to be sold, beautiful and splendid lots, superbly trained!"

The crowd trembled with excitement.

Elizabeth and the other two girls had now been secured, braceleted and on their leashes. The ordeal of the sale over, Virginia and Phyllis were weeping. Elizabeth, by remarkable contrast, seemed exceedingly well pleased. When they had turned and were being led from the block by the whip slaves who held their leashes, Cernus spoke to two of the guards behind me. "Throw the fool on his feet," said he. "Let her see him!"

I struggled but could not resist the men who hauled me to my feet.

"Behold an enemy of Cernus!" cried Philemon to the block.

The girls turned and then Elizabeth, peering out into the crowd, for the first time, saw me, in the rag of a slave, my wrists bound behind my back in steel, the helpless captive of Cernus, Slaver, Ubar of Ar.

Her eyes were wide. She stood as though stunned. She put her braceleted hands before her mouth. She shook her head disbelievingly. Then, by the chain and bracelets, she was rudely turned about. She looked back over her shoulder, her eyes wide with horror. Then, fighting the chain and bracelets, she was dragged stumbling down the steps. It was then she understood herself sold. She cried out wildly, helplessly, a long screaming wail of misery and understanding. I heard the sound of a slave whip below the block, the hysterical, wild sobbing and screaming of a slave girl. Then, as she was dragged away, the sound of the whip and of her cries grew more distant, and then I could hear them no more.

"Before she is delivered to Samos," Cernus was saying, "I think I will have her returned to the house and use her. She intrigued me this evening. Since she is Red Silk Samos will not object."

I said nothing.

"Take him away," said Cernus.

In a moment, manacled, a guard holding each arm, I was being conducted from the amphitheater.

The lights of the amphitheater briefly went out, and then flashed on again.

I heard the crowd cry out.

I heard the auctioneer making his call for the first bid. I knew that behind me, on the block, there would be a new lot for sale, more to please the buyers of Ar.

Twenty

A Game is Played

"This," cried Cernus, lifting his cup aloft, is a night for rejoicing and amusement!"

Never had I seen the customarily impassive Slaver so elated as on this night, following the sales in the Curulean. The feast was set late in the hall of Cernus and the wine and paga flowed freely. The girls chained at the wall for the amusement of his guards clutched drunkenly, ecstatically, at those who used them. Guards stumbled about with goblets in their hands. The Warriors of Cernus sang at the tables. Roasted tarsks on long spits were borne to the tables on the shoulders of nude slave girls. Girls still in training, unclothed as well, served wine this night of feasting. Musicians wildly, drunkenly, picked and pounded at their instruments.

Hooded, stripped to the waist, chained, I had been beaten from one end of the room to the other with sticks.

Now, unhooded, but chained, I knelt bloody before the dais of Cernus.

A few feet from me, wretched, dazed, chained like I before the dais of Ar's Ubar, knelt Elizabeth Cardwell, her only garment the chain of Cernus, with its medallion of the tarn and slave chains, about her throat.

To one side, to my dismay, I saw Relius and Ho-Sorl chained. Near them, kneeling, her wrists and ankles bound with slender, silken ropes, knelt Sura, head forward, her hair touching the floor.

The doll which she had so loved, which she had had from her mother, which she had so jealously protected in her compartment that she had attacked me with the slave goad at the Kill Point, lay on the tiles before her, torn asunder, destroyed.

291

"What is their crime?" I had asked Cernus.

"They would have freed you," laughed Cernus. "The men we apprehended after severe fighting, trying to cut their way to you when you lay in the dungeon. The woman tried, with paga and jewels, to bribe your guards."

I shook my head. I could not understand why Relius and Ho-Sorl would make my cause theirs, nor why Sura, though I knew she cared for me, would so risk her life, now doubtless lost. I had done little to deserve such friends, such loyalty. I felt now in my plight that I had betrayed not only Elizabeth, and the other girls, and the Priest-Kings, but perhaps allies even unknown to me, among them perhaps Relius, Ho-Sorl, Sura, others. How overcome I felt, with fury, with rage, with helplessness. I looked across to Elizabeth, the chain of Cernus looped about her neck, staring numbly, woodenly, down at the tiles of the hall, half in shock.

I had failed them all.

"Bring Portus!" called Cernus.

The Slaver who had been chief competitor to the House of Cernus was brought forward, doubtless from the dungeons of the Central Cylinder of Ar, on order of its Ubar, Cernus, once of the Merchants, now of the Caste of the Warriors.

Portus, half wasted now, his skin hanging about his frame, was brought, manacled, stripped to the waist, to the square of sand.

His manacles were removed and a naked hook knife was thrust in his trembling hand.

"Please oh mighty Cernus!" he whined. "Show mercy!"

The slave whom I had originally seen victorious in the sport of hook knife sprang to the sand and began to stalk Portus.

"Please, Cernus!" cried Portus as a long line of blood burst open across his chest. "Please! Please! Caste Brother!" he cried, as the slave, swift, eager, laughing, struck him again and again, with impunity. Then Portus tried to fight but, weakened, unskilled, clumsy, he stumbled about, being again and again streaked with blood, no cut mortal. At last he fell into the sand covered with blood at the feet of the laughing slave, quivering, whining, unable to move.

"Feed him to the beast," said Cernus.

Whimpering, Portus was dragged from the sand, leaving blood across the tiles, and was taken from the hall.

"Bring the Hinrabian!" called Cernus.

I was startled. The entire Hinrabian family, in caravan, had been ambushed, months ago, shortly after leaving the vicinity of Ar enroute to the desert city of Tor. It was assumed the entire family had been destroyed. The only body not recovered had been that of Claudia Tentia Hinrabia, who had been originally the unfortunate victim of the intrigues of Cernus, the means whereby was brought about the downfall of the house of Portus.

I heard, far off, a weird scream, that of Portus, and a wild, savage cry, almost a roar.

Those in the hall trembled.

"The beast has been fed," said Cernus, chuckling, drinking wine, spilling some of it down his face.

A slave girl was brought, a slim girl, in yellow Pleasure Silk, with short black hair, dark eyes, high cheekbones.

She ran timidly and knelt before the dais.

I gasped, for it was Claudia Tentia Hinrabia, once the spoiled daughter of a Ubar of Ar, now a rightless wench in bondage, not unlike thousands of others in Glorious Ar.

She looked about herself, with wonder. I doubted that she had been before in that room.

"You are the slave girl Claudia?" asked Cernus.

"Yes, Master," said the girl.

"Do you know what city you are in?" asked Cernus.

"No, Master," whispered the girl. "I was brought hooded to your house."

"By what men?" inquired Cernus.

"I do not know, Master," whispered the girl.

"It is said you claim to be Claudia Tentia Hinrabia," said Cernus.

The girl lifted her head wildly. "It is true!" she cried. "It is true, Master!"

"I know," said Cernus.

She looked at him in horror.

"What city is this?" she asked.

"Ar," said Cernus.

"Ar?" she gasped.

"Yes," said Cernus, "Glorious Ar."

Hope sprang in her eyes. She almost rose to her feet. There were tears in her eyes. "Ar!" she cried. "Oh free me! Free me!" She lifted her hands to Cernus. "I am of Ar! I am of Ar! I am Claudia Tentia Hinrabia of Ar! Free me, Master!"

"Do you know me?" asked Cernus.

"No, Master," said the girl.

"I am Cernus," said he, "Ubar of Ar."

She gazed upon him, thunderstruck. "Noble Cernus," she whispered, "if you be my Master, free me, free me!"

"Why?" asked Cernus.

"I am Claudia Tentia Hinrabia," she said, "of Ar!"

"You are a slave girl," said Cernus.

She looked at him in horror. "Please, Ubar," she wept. "Please noble Cernus, Ubar of my city, free me!"

"Your father owed me moneys," said Cernus. "You will remain my slave."

"Please!" she wept.

"You are alone," said Cernus. "Your family is gone. There is no one to protect you. You will remain my slave."

She buried her head in her hands, weeping. "I have been in misery," she wept, "since I was stolen by the men of the house of Portus and enslaved."

Cernus laughed.

The girl looked at him, not understanding.

"How could the men of Portus enter the Central Cylinder and carry you away?" he inquired.

"I do not know," she admitted.

"You were hooded and abducted by Taurentians," said Cernus, "the palace guard itself."

She gasped.

"Saphronicus, their Captain," said Cernus, "is in my hire."

She shook her head numbly.

"But the House of Portus—" she said. "I saw the collar on a slave girl—"

Cernus laughed.

He strode from the dais to stand over her.

"Stand, Slave," said he.

The Hinrabian did so.

She regarded him with horror. He parted the Pleasure Silk and threw it from her.

He then took the heavy chain with its medallion from the neck of Elizabeth Cardwell and placed it about the throat of the Hinrabian girl.

"No! No!" she cried, throwing her hands to the side of her head, and fell screaming and weeping to her knees at the feet of Cernus.

He laughed.

She raised her horror-stricken eyes to him. "It was you!" she whispered. "You!"

"Of course," said Cernus. He then took back from her his medallion and chain, and placed it about his own neck. He then returned to his place on the dais.

The room roared with laughter.

"Bind her arms and wrists tightly," said Cernus to a guard.

This was done to the Hinrabian girl, who, stricken with horror, seemed scarcely able to move.

"We have another surprise for you, my dear Claudia," said Cernus.

She looked at him blankly.

"Bring the pot wench," said Cernus to a subordinate and the man, grinning, sped from the room.

"Claudia Tentia Hinrabia," said Cernus to those assembled, while he quaffed yet another goblet of Ka-la-na, "is well known throughout Ar as a most strict and demanding mistress. It is said that once, when a slave dropped a mirror, she had the poor girl's ears and nose cut off, and then sold the then worthless wench."

There were shouts of commendation from the men at the tables.

Claudia was held on her knees by two guards, her arms and wrists tied tightly behind her. Her face began to turn white.

"I searched long in the kitchens of Ar until I found that wench," said Cernus.

I recalled that in his kitchen, seemingly months ago, though only a handful of days past, I had seen a mutilated girl.

"And purchased her," said Cernus.

There was a shout of pleasure from the tables.

Claudia Tentia Hinrabia, in her bonds, seemed frozen, horror-stricken, unable to move.

A girl came in from the kitchens, followed by the man who had gone to fetch her. It was the girl to whom I had, some days ago, on the evening of my capture, tossed a bottle of paga. Her ears had been cut from her, and her nose. She might otherwise have been beautiful.

When the girl entered the room Claudia was turned by her guards, still on her knees, bound, to face her.

The girl stopped stunned. Claudia's eyes regarded her, wide with horror.

"What is your name?" asked Cernus of the girl kindly.

"Melanie," said she, not taking her eyes from the Hinrabian, startled, astonished that she should so find her former mistress.

"Melanie," said Cernus, "do you know this slave?"

"She is Claudia Tentia Hinrabia," whispered the girl.

"Do you remember her?" asked Cernus.

"Yes," said the girl. "She was my mistress."

"Give her a hook knife," said Cernus to one of the men near him.

A hook knife was pressed into the hands of the mutilated girl.

She looked at the knife, and then at the bound Hinrabian, who shook her head slightly, tears in her eyes.

"Please, Melanie," whispered the Hinrabian, "do not hurt me."

The girl said nothing to her, but only looked again from the hook knife to the bound Hinrabian.

"You may," said Cernus, "remove the ears and nose of the slave."

"Please, Melanie!" cried the Hinrabian. "Do not hurt me! Do not hurt me!"

The girl approached her with the knife.

"You loved me," whispered the Hinrabian. "You loved me!"

"I hate you," said the girl.

She took Claudia's hair in her left hand and held the razor-sharp hook knife at her face. The Hinrabian burst into tears, hysterically weeping, begging for mercy.

But the pot girl did not touch the knife to the Hinrabian's face. Rather, to the wonderment of all, she let her hand drop.

"Cut off her ears and nose," ordered Cernus.

The girl looked on the helpless Hinrabian. "Do not fear," she said, "I would not injure a poor slave."

The girl threw the hook knife from her and it slid across the tiles.

Claudia Tentia Hinrabia collapsed weeping at the feet of the guards.

Cernus rose behind the table on the dais.

I heard someone ask, "Was she of High Caste?"

"I was the daughter of a Cloth Worker," said Melanie.

Cernus was furious. "Take them both away," he said. "In ten days, bloody them and bind them back to back, and feed them to the beast."

Slave bracelets were snapped on the wrists of Melanie and she and her weeping, stumbling former mistress, the helpless, bound Claudia Tentia Hinrabia, were conducted from the hall.

Cernus sat down, angry. "Do not be disappointed," he cried. "There is more sport!"

There were some tentative grunts about the table, some attempt to muster enthusiasm.

"Noble girl!" I called after Melanie, as she left the room.

She turned and smiled, and then, with Claudia Tentia Hinrabia, and their guard, left the room.

A Warrior in the hire of Cernus struck me across the mouth.

I laughed.

"Since I am Ubar of Ar," said Cernus to me, "and of the Caste of Warriors—"

There was mirth at the tables, but a look from Cernus silenced it in a moment.

"I am concerned," continued Cernus, "to be fair in all matters and thus propose that we wager for your freedom."

I looked up in surprise.

"Bring the board and pieces," said Cernus. Philemon left the room. Cernus looked down at me and grinned. "As I recall, you said that you did not play."

I nodded.

"On the other hand," said Cernus, "I of course do not believe you."

"I play," I admitted.

Cernus chuckled. "Would you like to play for your freedom?"

"Of course," I said.

"I am quite skillful, you know," said Cernus.

I said nothing. I had gathered in the months in the house, from what I had seen and heard, that Cernus was indeed a fine player. He would not be easy to beat.

"But," said Cernus, smiling, "since you are scarcely likely to be as skilled as I, I feel that it is only just that you be represented by a champion, who can play for you and give you some opportunity for victory."

"I will play for myself," I said.

"I do not think that would be just," said Cernus.

"I see," I said. I then understood that Cernus would appoint my champion. The game would be a meaningless charade.

"Perhaps a slave who scarcely knows the moves of the pieces," I suggested, "might play for me—if such would not be too potent an adversary for you?"

Cernus looked at me with surprise. Then he grinned. "Perhaps," he said.

Sura, bound, lifted her head.

"Would you dare to contend with a mere slave girl," I asked, "one who has learned the game but a day or two ago, who has played but an Ahn or so?"

"Whom do you mean?" inquired Cernus.

"He means me, Master," said Sura, humbly, and then dropped her head.

I held my breath.

"Women do not play the game," said Cernus irritably. "Slaves do not play!"

Sura said nothing.

Cernus rose from the table and went to stand before Sura. He picked up the remains of the small cloth doll which lay torn before her and tore them more. The old cloth broke apart. He ground the bits of the doll into the tile with the heel of his sandal.

I saw tears from the eyes of Sura fall to the tiles. Her shoulders shook.

"Have you dared to learn the game, Slave?" inquired Cernus, angrily.

"Forgive me, Master," said Sura, not raising her head.

Cernus turned to me. "Pick a more worthy champion, fool," said he.

I shrugged. "I choose Sura," I said. Cernus would surely have no way of knowing that Sura possessed perhaps one of the most astounding native aptitudes for the game that I had ever encountered. Almost from the beginning she had begun to play at the very level of Players themselves. Her capacity, raw and brilliant, was simply a phenomenon, one of those rare and happy gifts one sometimes discovers, to one's delight or dismay, and she had caused me much of both. "I choose Sura," I said.

The men about the tables laughed.

Cernus then, for no reason I understood clearly, struck Sura with the back of his hand, hurling her to the tiles.

I heard one of the men near me whisper to another. "Where is Ho-Tu?"

I myself had been curious about that.

The other whispered in return. "Ho-Tu has been sent to Tor to buy slaves."

The first laughed.

I myself thought it was perhaps well that Cernus, doubtless by design, had sent Ho-Tu from the house. Surely I would not have expected the powerful Ho-Tu to stand by while Sura, whom he loved, was so treated, even by the Master of the House of Cernus. With hook knife in hand, against a dozen blades, Ho-Tu would probably have rushed upon Cernus. I was, as I suggested, just as well satisfied that Ho-Tu was not now in the house. It would be one less to die. I wondered if Cernus would have him slain on his return. If Sura were permitted to live I supposed Ho-Tu, too, would live, if only to be with her, to try to protect her as he could.

"I will not play with a woman!" snarled Cernus and turned away from Sura. She looked at me, helpless, stricken. I smiled at her. But my heart had sunk. My last hope seemed now dashed.

Cernus was now again at the table. In the meantime Philemon had brought the board and arranged the pieces. "It does not matter," said Cernus to me, "for I have already arranged your champion."

"I see," I said, "and who is to be my champion?"

Cernus roared with laughter. "Hup the Fool!" he cried.

The tables roared with laughter, and the men pounded with their fists on the wood so pleased were they.

At this point, from the main entryway to the hall, there entered two men, shoved by guards. One retained a certain dignity, though he held his hands before him. He wore the robes of a Player. The other rolled and somersaulted onto the tiles and bounded skipping to his feet, to the amusement of those at table. Even the slave girls clapped their hands with amusement, crying out with pleasure.

Hup was now backing around ogling the slave girls, and then he fell over on his back, tripped by a Warrior. He sprang to his feet and began to leap up and down making noises like a scolding urt. The girls laughed, and so, too, did the men.

The other man who had entered with Hup was, to my astonishment, the blind Player whom I had encountered so long ago in the street outside the paga tavern near the great gate of Ar, who had beaten so brilliantly the Vintner in what had been apparently, until then, an uneven and fraudulent game, one the Player had clearly intended to deliver to his opponent, he who had, upon learning that I wore the black of the Assassins, refused, though poor, to accept the piece of gold he had so fairly and marvelously won. I thought it strange that that man should have been found with Hup, only a fool, Hup whose bulbous misshapen head reached scarcely to the belt of a true man, Hup of the bandy legs and swollen body, the broken, knobby hands, Hup the Fool.

I saw Sura regarding Hup with a kind of horror, looking on him with loathing. She seemed to tremble with revulsion. I wondered at her response.

"Qualius the Player," called Cernus, "you are once again in the House of Cernus, who is now Ubar of Ar."

"I am honored," said the blind Player, whose name I had just learned.

"Would you care to play me once more?" asked Cernus.

"No," said the blind Player dryly. "I beat you once."

"It was a mistake, was it not?" asked Cernus humorously.

"Indeed," said Qualius. "For having bested you I was blinded in your torture rooms and branded."

"Thus, in the end," said Cernus, amused, "it was I who bested you."

"Indeed it was," said Qualius, "Ubar."

Cernus laughed.

"How is it," inquired Cernus, "that my men, sent for Hup the Fool, find you with him?"

"I share the fool's lodging," said Qualius. "There are few doors open to a destitute Player."

Cernus laughed. "Players and fools," said he, "have much in common."

"It is true," said Qualius.

We turned to look at Hup. He was now sneaking about the tables. He took a sip from one of the goblets and narrowly missed an amused, swinging blow aimed at him by the man whose goblet it was. Hup ran scampering away and crouched down making faces at the man, who laughed at him. Then Hup, with great apparent stealth, returned to the table and darted under it. On the other side his head suddenly appeared, then disappeared. Again he came under the table, and this time his hand darted out and back, and he began to chew on his prize, a peel of larma fruit snatched from a plate, discarded as garbage. He was grinning and cooing to himself while chewing on the peel.

"Behold your champion," said Cernus.

I would not reply to him.

"Why not slay me and be done with it?" I asked.

"Have you no faith in your champion?" asked Cernus. Then he threw back his head and laughed. The others, too, in the room laughed. Even Hup, his eyes watering, sat on his rump on the tiles and pounded his knees, seeing others laugh. When the others ceased to laugh, so, too, did he, and looked about, whimpering, giggling.

"Since you have a champion," said Cernus, "I thought it only fair that I, too have a champion."

I looked at him, puzzled.

"Behold my champion," said Cernus, "who will play for me." He expansively lifted his hand toward the entryway. All turned to look.

There were cries of astonishment.

Through the entryway, rather angrily, strode a young man, perhaps no more than eighteen or nineteen years of age, with piercing eyes and incredibly striking features; he wore the garb of the Player, but his garb was rich and the squares of the finest red and yellow silk; the game bag over his left shoulder was of superb verrskin; his sandals were tied with strings of gold; startlingly, this young man, seeming like a god in the splendor of his boyhood, was lame, and as he strode angrily forward, his right leg dragged across the tiles; seldom had I seen a face more handsome, more striking, yet rich with irritation, with contempt, a face more betokening the brilliance of a mind like a Gorean blade.

He stood before the table of Cernus and though Cernus was Ubar of his city he merely lifted his hand in common Gorean greeting, palm inward. "Tal," said he.

"Tal," responded Cernus, seeming somehow in awe before this mere boy.

"Why have I been brought here?" asked the young man.

I studied the face of the young man. There was something subtly familiar about it. I felt almost as though I must have seen him before. I felt it was a face I somehow knew, and yet could not know.

I happened to glance at Sura and was startled to see her. She could not take her eyes from the boy. It was as though she, like myself, somehow recognized him.

"You have been brought here to play a game," said Cernus.

"I do not understand," said the boy.

"You will play as my champion," said Cernus.

The boy looked at him curiously.

"If you win," said Cernus, "you will be given a hundred gold pieces."

"I will win," said the boy.

There had been nothing bold in his tone of voice, only perhaps impatience.

He looked about himself, and saw Qualius, the blind Player. "The game will be an interesting one," said the boy.

"Qualius of Ar," said Cernus, "is not to be your opponent."

"Oh?" inquired the boy.

Hup was rolling in a corner of the room, rolling to the wall, then back, then rolling to it again.

The boy looked at him in revulsion.

"Your opponent," said Cernus, pointing to the small fool rolling in the corner, "is he."

Fury contorted the features of the boy. "I will not play," he said. He turned with a swirl of his cloak but found his way barred by two guards with spears. "Ubar!" cried the boy.

"You will play Hup the Fool," laughed Cernus.

"It is an insult to me," said the boy, "and to the game. I will not play!"

Hup began to croon to himself in the corner, now rocking back and forth on his haunches.

"If you do not play," Cernus said, not pleasantly, "you will not leave this house alive."

The young man shook with fury.

"What is the meaning of this?" he inquired.

"I am giving this prisoner an opportunity to live," said Cernus, indicating me. "If his champion wins, he will live; if his champion loses, he will die."

"I have never played to lose," said the young man, "never."

"I know," said Cernus.

The young man looked at me. "His blood," he said to Cernus, "is on your hands, not mine."

Cernus laughed. "Then you will play?"

"I will play," said the young man.

Cernus leaned back and grinned.

"But let Qualius play for him," said the young man.

Qualius, who apparently knew the voice of the young man, said, "You need have no fear, Ubar, I am not his equal."

I wondered who the young man might be if Qualius, whom I knew to be a superb player, did not even speak as though he might force a draw with him.

Again I glanced at Sura, and was again startled at the intentness, almost the wonder, with which she regarded the incredibly handsome, lame boy who stood before us. I racked my brain, trying to understand something which seemed somehow but a moment from comprehension, something elusive, hauntingly near and yet undisclosed.

"No," said Cernus. "The Fool is your opponent."

"Let us be done with this farce," said the boy. "Further, let no word of this shame be spoken outside this house."

Cernus grinned.

Philemon indicated the board, and the young man went to it and took a chair, Cernus' own, surrendered eagerly by him, at the table. The boy turned the board irritably about, taking red. Philemon turned the board back, that he might have yellow, and the first move, permitting him to choose his opening.

The young man looked about him with disgust, but did not protest.

"To the table, Fool," cried Cernus to Hup.

Hup, as though shocked, leaped to his feet, turned a somersault, and bounded unevenly to the table, where he put his chin on the boards, trying to nibble at a piece of bread lying there.

Those in the room laughed, with the exception of Relius, Ho-Sorl, the young boy, and myself, and Sura. Sura was still looking at the boy. There were tears in her eyes. I tried to place the boy, his features.

"Would you not care," asked Cernus of the boy, "to inform the prisoner of your name?"

The handsome boy looked down from the chair of Cernus on me. His lips parted irritably. "I am Scormus of Ar," he said.

I closed my eyes and began to shake with laughter, seeing the joke on myself. And the others, too, those with Cernus, laughed, until the room roared with their mirth.

My champion was Hup, a Fool, that of Cernus was the brilliant, fiery, competitive Scormus of Ar, the young, phenomenal Scormus, who played first board of the city of Ar and held the highest bridge in the city as the province of his game, the master not only of the Players of Ar but doubtless of Gor as well; four times he had won the cap of gold at the Sardar Fairs; never had he entered a tournament he had not won; there was no Player on Gor who did not acknowledge him his master; the records of his games were hungered for throughout all the cities of Gor; his strategy was marked with a native and powerful subtlety, a profundity and brilliance that had made him, even in his youth, a legend in the harsh cities of Gor; it was little wonder that even Cernus himself stood in awe of this imperious youth.

Suddenly Sura cried out. "It is he!"

And in that instant the recognition came to me so suddenly and powerfully that the room seemed black for a moment and I could not breathe.

Scormus looked irritably from the board at Sura, kneeling bound on the tiles.

"Is your slave mad?" he asked of Cernus.

"Of course he is Scormus of Ar, Foolish Slave," cried Cernus to Sura. "Now be silent!"

Her eyes were glistening with tears. She put down her head and was weeping, shaking with emotion.

I, too, trembled.

And then it seemed to me that Cernus might have miscalculated.

I saw Hup waddle over to Sura and put his bulbous head to hers. Some of those at the table laughed. Sura did not draw back from that fearful, grotesque countenance that faced her. Then, to the wonder of all, Hup, the misshapen, misformed dwarf and fool, gently, ever so gently, kissed Sura on the forehead. Her eyes were wet with tears. Her shoulders were shaking. She smiled, crying, and put down her head.

"What is going on?" demanded Cernus.

Then Hup gave a wild yip and turned a backward somersault and bounded suddenly, squealing like an urt, after a naked slave girl, one of those who had served the tables. She screamed and fled and Hup stopped and turned around several times rapidly in the center of the room until, dizzy, he fell down on his seat and wept.

Scormus of Ar spoke. "Let us play."

"Play, Fool!" cried Cernus to Hup.

The little fool bounded to the table. "Play! Play! Play!" he whimpered. "Hup plays!"

The dwarf seized a piece and shoved it.

"It is not your move!" cried Cernus. "Yellow moves first."

Irritably, with genuine disdain and fury, Scormus thrust out a Tarnsman.

Hup picked up a red piece and studied it with great care. "Pretty, pretty wood," he giggled.

"Does the fool know the moves of the pieces?" inquired Scormus acidly.

Some of those at the table laughed, but Cernus did not laugh.

"Pretty, pretty," crooned Hup. Then he put the piece down on the intersection of four squares, upside down.

"No," said Philemon, irritably, "on the color, like this!"

Hup's attention was now drawn to the side of the table where there was a sugared pastry, which he began to eye hungrily.

Scormus of Ar, I was pleased to note, regarding the board, suddenly eyed Hup warily. Then the boy shrugged and shook his head, and moved another piece.

"Your move," prompted Philemon.

Without looking at the board Hup poked a piece, I think a Ubar's Scribe, with one of his swollen fingers. "Hup hungry," he whined.

One of Cernus' guards threw Hup the pastry he had been eyeing and Hup squealed with pleasure and sat on the dais, putting his chin on his knees, shoving the pastry in his mouth.

I looked at Sura. Her eyes were radiant. She saw me and through her tears, smiled. I smiled back at her. She looked down at the remains of the doll on the tiles before her and threw back her head and laughed. In her bonds she threw back her head and laughed.

She had a son. His name, of course, was Scormus of Ar, her son by the dwarf Hup, conceived years ago in the revels of Kajuralia. I now, clearly, recognized the boy, though I had not seen him before. His features were those of Sura, though with the heaviness of the masculine countenance, the bred slave lines of the House of Cernus. Cernus himself had not recognized them; perhaps none in the room had; the lame foot was perhaps the legacy of his misshapen father; but the boy was fine, and he was brilliant; he was the marvelous Scormus, youthful master Player of Ar.

I looked at Sura and there were tears in my eyes, with my happiness for her.

Hup had kissed her. He had known. Could he then be the fool he pretended? And Scormus of Ar, the brilliant, the natively brilliant master Player was the offspring of these two. I had sensed the marvelous raw power of Sura, her amazing, almost intuitive grasp of the game; and I wondered of Hup, who could be the father of so brilliant a boy as Scormus of Ar; perhaps Hup, the Fool, was no stranger to the game; I looked to one side and saw Qualius of Ar, the blind Player; unnoticed, he was smiling.

After Hup's second move Scormus of Ar had looked for a long time at the board, and then at Hup, who was devouring his pastry.

Cernus seemed impatient. Philemon suggested three or four counters to the position now on the board.

"It is impossible," said Scormus, more to himself than another. Then he shrugged and pushed his third piece.

Hup was still eating his pastry.

"Move!" cried Cernus.

Hup leaped dutifully up and, crumbs on his mouth, seized a yellow piece and shoved it sideways.

"No," said Cernus, intensely, "you move red pieces."

Hup obediently started shoving the red pieces about the board.

"One at a time!" screamed Cernus.

Hup cringed and, lifting his head timidly over the board, pushed a piece and darted away.

"His moves are random moves," said Philemon to Scormus.

Scormus was looking at the board. "Perhaps," he said.

Philemon snorted with amusement.

Scormus then made his fourth move.

Hup, who was waddling about the walls, was then summoned again to the board and he hastily picked up a piece and dropped it tottering to a square, and went back to the walls.

"His moves are random," said Philemon. "Develop your Tarnsmen. When he places his Home Stone you will be able to seize it in five moves."

Scormus of Ar regarded Philemon. His look was withering. "Do you tell Scormus of Ar how to play the game?" he inquired.

"No," said Philemon.

"Then be silent," said Scormus.

Philemon looked as though he might choose to reply, but thought the better of it, and glared angrily at the board.

"Observe," said Scormus to Cernus, as he moved another piece.

Hup, singing some mad little song of his own devising, bounded back to the table, turned a somersault, and crawled up on the dais, whence he seized another piece in his small, knobby fist and pushed it one square ahead.

"I will give you two hundred pieces of gold if you can finish the game in ten moves," said Cernus.

"My Ubar jests," said Scormus of Ar, studying the board.

"I do not understand," said Cernus.

"I should have known my Ubar would not have perpetrated the farce he pretended," said Scormus, not raising his eyes from the board. He smiled. "It is seldom that Scormus of Ar is so fooled. You are to be congratulated, Ubar. This joke will bear telling in Ar for a thousand years."

"I do not understand," said Cernus.

"Surely you recognize," asked Scormus, curiously, looking up at him, "the Two Spearman variation of the Ubar's Scribe's Defense, developed by Miles of Cos and first used in the tournament at Tor held during the Second Passage Hand of the third year of the Administrator Heraklites?"

Neither Cernus nor Philemon said anything. The tables were silent.

"The man I am playing," said Scormus of Ar, "is obviously a master."

I cried out with joy, as did Sura, and Relius and Ho-Sorl. We, the four of us, cheered.

"It is impossible!" cried Cernus.

Hup, the Fool, blinked, sitting on the tiles before the dais.

Scormus of Ar was studying the board intently.

"Hup, my friend," said the blind player Qualius, "can play with Priest-Kings."

"Beat him!" cried Cernus.

"Be quiet," said Scormus. "I am playing."

There was little sound in the room save the occasional noises of Hup. The game continued. Scormus would study the board and move a piece. Hup would come from somewhere in the hall, rolling, skipping or bounding, sniffing, gurgling, glance at the board, cry out, and poke a piece about. And then Scormus would again, head in hands, face not moving, study the board once more.

At last, after perhaps no more than half an Ahn, Scormus stood up. His face was hard to read. There was something in it of irritation, but also of bafflement, and of respect. He stood stiffly, and, to the wonder of all, extended his hand to Hup.

"What are you doing?" cried Cernus.

"I am grateful to you for the game," said Scormus.

The two men, the young, fiery Scormus of Ar, and the tiny, misshapen dwarf, shook hands.

"I do not understand," said Cernus.

"Your departure from the Two Spearman Variation on the sixteenth move was acute," said Scormus to Hup, paying the Ubar of Ar no attention. "Only too late did I realize its position in your plan, the feint of the four-piece combination covering your transposition into the Hogar Variation of the Centian, striking down the file of the Ubara's Scribe. It was brilliant."

Hup inclined his head.

"I do not understand," said Cernus.

"I have lost," said Scormus.

Cernus looked at the board. He was sweating. His hand trembled. "Impossible!" he cried. "You have a winning position!"

Scormus' hand tipped his Ubar, resigning the game.

Cernus seized the piece and righted it. "The game is not done!" he cried. He seized Scormus by the cloak. "Are you a traitor to your Ubar?" he screamed.

"No, Ubar," said Scormus, puzzled.

Cernus released Scormus. The Ubar trembled with fury. He studied the board. Philemon did, too. Hup was looking away from the table, scratching his nose.

"Play!" cried Cernus to Scormus. "Your position is a winning one!"

Scormus looked at him, puzzled. "It is capture of Home Stone," said he, "in twenty-two."

"Impossible," whispered Cernus, trembling, staring at the small pieces of wood, the intricate pattern, the field of red and yellow squares.

"With your permission, Ubar," said Scormus of Ar, "I shall withdraw."

"Begone!" cried Cernus, regarding the board.

"Perhaps we shall play again," said Scormus to Hup, inclining his head to the dwarf.

Hup began to dance on one foot, turning about.

Scormus then went to Qualius, the blind player. "I leave," he said. "I wish you well, Qualius of Ar."

"I wish you well, Scormus of Ar," said Qualius, the blind, branded face radiant.

Scormus turned and regarded Hup. The little fellow was sitting on the edge of the dais, swinging his feet. When he saw Scormus regarding him, however, he stood up, as straight as he could with his crooked back and one short leg; he struggled to stand straight, and it must have caused him pain.

"I wish you well, Small Master," said Scormus.

Hup could not reply but he stood there before the dais, as straight as he could, with tears in his eyes.

"I shall play out your position and win!" screamed Cernus.

"What will you do?" asked Scormus, puzzled.

Cernus angrily moved a piece. "Ubar's Tarnsman to Ubara's Scribe Four!"

Scormus smiled. "That is capture of Home Stone in eleven," he said.

As Scormus, his path uncontested, took his way from the room, he stopped before Sura, who lowered her head, shamed that she should be so seen before him. He regarded her for a moment, as though puzzled, and then turned and faced Cernus once again. "A lovely slave," he commented.

Cernus, studying the board, did not respond to him.

Scormus turned and, limping, left the room.

I saw that Hup now stood close to Sura, and once again, gently, he kissed her on the forehead.

"Little Fool!" cried Cernus. "I have moved Ubar's Tarnsman to Ubara's Scribe Four! What will you do now?"

Hup returned to the table and, scarcely glancing at the board, picked up a piece and dropped it on a square.

"Ubar's Tarnsman to Ubara's Tarnsman Six," said Cernus, puzzled.

"What is the point of that?" asked Philemon.

"There is no point," said Cernus. "He is a fool, only a fool."

I counted the moves, eleven of them, and, on the eleventh, Cernus cried out with rage and dashed the board and its pieces from the table. Hup, as though puzzled, was waddling about the room scratching his nose, singing a silly little ditty to himself. In one small hand he held clutched a tiny piece of yellow wood, the Home Stone of Cernus.

I gave a cry of joy as did Relius and Ho-Sorl. Sura, too, was radiant.

"I am now free," I informed Cernus.

He looked at me in rage.

"You will be free tomorrow," he screamed, "to die in the Stadium of Blades!"

I threw back my head and laughed. Die now I might, but the vengeance of the moment was sweet. I had known, of course, that Cernus would never free me, but it had given me great pleasure to see his charade of honor unmasked, to have seen him humiliated and publicly exposed as a traitor to his word.

Relius and Ho-Sorl were laughing as, chained, they were taken from the room.

Cernus looked down on Elizabeth, chained at the foot of the dais. He was in fury. "Deliver this wench to the compound of Samos of Port Kar!" he screamed.

Guards leaped to do his bidding.

I could not stop myself laughing, though I was much beaten, and laughing I still was when, chained, I was conducted stumbling from the hall of Cernus, the noble Ubar of Ar.

Twenty One

The Stadium of Blades

Outside, as though from a distance, I could hear the roar of the crowd packed into the tiers of the Stadium of Blades.

"Murmillius is apparently victorious again," said Vancius of the House of Cernus, lifting a blind helmet and fitting it over my head.

Vancius, of the guards, turned the key in the helmet lock that fastened the helmet on my head.

Within the heavy metal casque I could see nothing.

"It will be amusing," said he, "to see you stumbling about on the sand, sword in hand, thrashing here and there, trying to find your foes. The crowd will love it. It provides comic relief between the serious bouts and the animal fights to follow. It is also a time for patrons to stretch, buy their pastries, relieve themselves and such."

I did not respond.

"Surely the famed Tarl Cabot, master swordsman of Gor," said Vancius, "prefers to die with blade in hand."

"Remove my manacles," said I, "and blade or no, let me give response as might a Warrior."

"Your manacles will be removed," Vancius assured me, "when you are in the arena."

"If I do not choose to fight?" I asked.

"Whips and hot irons will encourage you," he said.

"Perhaps not," I said.

"Then be encouraged by this news," he laughed. "Your opponents will be the finest swordsmen in the Taurentians."

"In blind helmets?" I queried.

He laughed. "It will appear so," said he, "for the sake of the crowd. Actually their helmets will be perforated. They will be able to see you but you will not be able to see them."

"It will indeed be amusing," I said.

"Indeed," laughed Vancius.

"Doubtless Cernus will be in the stands to enjoy the spectacle," I said.

"No," he said.

"Why is that?" I asked.

"He sits this day in the box of the Ubar at the races," said Vancius. "Races in Ar being more popular than the games, it is only appropriate that Cernus preside."

"Of course," I admitted. Within the closed steel locked on my head I smiled. "Cernus," said I, "though a prominent patron of the Greens, must be disturbed that the Yellows have this year stood above them."

"It is only thought," said Vancius, "that Cernus favors the Greens."

"I do not understand," I said.

"Actually," said Vancius, "Cernus favors the Yellows."

"How can this be?" I asked.

"Dense one," laughed Vancius. "The very fact that Cernus appears to be of the faction of the Greens influences thousands of our citizens; it itself, with the frequent victories of the Greens, is enough to make the Greens generally favored in the betting. But when over the long run you have examined victors, you will discover the Yellows have won not only more races, but generally those on which more was wagered."

Involuntarily my wrists fought the steel that shackled them.

Vancius laughed. "By betting secretly on the Yellows, whom he controls," said Vancius, "Cernus has accumulated, through agents, vast fortunes in the races." Vancius laughed again. "Menicius of Port Kar, of the Yellows, greatest rider in the races, rides for Cernus."

"Cernus is a clever man," said I. "But what if the fans of the races should learn of his true allegiance, that his true faction is that of the Yellows?"

"They will not learn," said Vancius.

"The Steels," I said, "threaten the Yellows."

"They will not win the great race," said Vancius, "the Ubar's Race."

The Ubar's Race is the final and climactic race of the Love Feast.

"Why not?" I asked.

"Menicius of Port Kar rides for the Yellows," said Vancius.

"You have great respect for him," I said.

Vancius laughed. "As I have great respect for the banded ost," said he.

I smiled. The banded ost is a variety of ost, a small, customarily brilliantly orange Gorean reptile. It is exceedingly poisonous. The banded ost is yellowish orange and is marked with black rings.

"Menicius has been instructed to win the great race," said Vancius. "And he will do so, even should it be necessary to kill."

I said nothing for a time. Then, curious, I asked, "What of Gladius of Cos?"

"He will be warned not to ride," said Vancius.

"And if he does?" I asked.

"He will die," said Vancius.

"Who is Gladius of Cos?" I asked.

"I do not know," said Vancius.

Within the helmet I smiled. That secret, at least, had been well kept.

"We have let it be known in the taverns of Ar," said Vancius, "that Gladius of Cos, should he dare to ride, will die. I do not think he will appear at the Stadium of Tarns."

This angered me. Should I not take my saddle this afternoon there would be few in Ar but would suppose that I had succumbed to fear.

"What is wrong?" asked Vancius.

"Nothing," I said.

There was a distant roar again from the crowd in the tiers far above.

"Murmillius again!" cried Vancius. "What a man! That is his fifth opponent downed this afternoon!"

"What of the girls sold at the Curulean?" I asked. "Those who brought top price?"

"By now," said Vancius, "they are doubtless well-thonged in tarn baskets and on their way to the pleasures of Port Kar."

I heard a distant trumpet, the warning trumpet.

"It will soon be time," said Vancius.

There was a bit of scuffle some feet away, the sound of a girl, and then another.

"You can't enter here," called a guard.

"I must see Vancius!" cried the voice of a girl.

"Who is it?" queried Vancius, puzzled, irritated.

The voice struck me as familiar, as being one I had heard somewhere before.

"Beloved Vancius!" I heard.

"Who are you?" Vancius was asking.

Inside the blind helmet I could see nothing. I pulled at the manacles.

I heard light, bare feet run into the room. "Vancius!" I heard a girl cry. I could not place the voice.

Then, unmistakably, I heard her run to Vancius and, apparently to his surprise, and consternation, but not displeasure, she flung herself into his arms. I heard their words not plainly, his question, her asseverations of passion, mixed in the meetings of their mouths. I gathered it was a slave girl, many of whom are extraordinarily passionate, who had seen him, followed him, and was now desperately importuning him for his touch.

"Vancius, I am yours!" I heard.

"Yes, yes!" I heard him say.

I then heard a heavy sound, as though someone had been struck heavily from behind.

"Now, Vancius," I heard, "you are mine!"

I tried to tear the steel helmet from my head with my manacled wrists. I fought the heavy chain that bound me to the stone table on which I sat. "Who is there?" I whispered.

I heard the girl's voice again. "Take dear Vancius," she was saying, "bind his wrists and ankles, and put him in a slave hood, one with a gag. I may use him for my pleasure later."

"Who is there!" I demanded.

"What of the other guard?" asked a girl's voice.

"Bind him as well," said the first girl.

"May I have him?" asked the second girl.

"Yes," said the first girl. "Tie him with Vancius."

I felt a man's hands then fumbling with the steel hood I wore.

"Who is there!" I demanded.

I heard the key move in the lock, and felt air as the helmet was lifted.

"Ho-Tu!" I cried.

"Be quiet," said Ho-Tu. "There are other men of Cernus about."

"It was said you had gone to Tor to buy slaves!" I said.

"This is scarcely the time to go to Tor and buy slaves," smiled Ho-Tu.

"You did not go?" I asked.

"Of course not," said Ho-Tu.

"What are you doing here?" I asked.

Ho-Tu grinned.

"Your life is in danger," I told him.

"We are all in danger," said Ho-Tu. "Great danger."

I looked beyond him, to see a long-legged, black-haired girl, her hands on her hips, regarding me.

"It is you!" she laughed.

"And it is you!" I said.

It was the leader of the girls of the Street of Pots. I saw two of her girls behind her.

"What are you all doing here?" I demanded.

"It is on this day," said she, "that Ar will be free or slave."

"I do not understand," I stammered.

There was the sound of another trumpet, the second.

"There is no time!" said Ho-Tu. "Bring the other helmet!"

One of the girls presented Ho-Tu with another helmet. It seemed identical to the one I had worn. Then I saw that it was perforated.

"It is such a helmet," said Ho-Tu, "that your opponents, the finest swordsmen in the Taurentians, will wear."

He fitted it over my head.

"I like it better," I said grimly, "than the former one."

One of the girls had found the key to the chain that bound me by the waist to the stone table. She sprang open the lock. Another girl, from the body of the unconscious, now hooded and bound Vancius, found the key to my manacles. She handed it to Ho-Tu. Ho-Tu wore the garb of one of the guards of the House of Cernus. He now took up the discarded helmet of Vancius and drew it on. He unbuckled his own sword belt and buckled it about me. He drew the sword. I smiled. It was my own, carried even at the siege of Ar, so many long years ago.

"Thank you," said I, "Ho-Tu."

He resheathed the blade in my scabbard.

He was now buckling about his waist the sword and belt of Vancius.

Within the helmet I saw him grin.

We heard then the third trumpet, signaling the beginning of the sport.

"They are waiting for you," said Ho-Tu, grinning, "Warrior."

"Do not yet lock the helmet," said the leader of the girls of the Street of Pots.

"They are waiting for him," protested Ho-Tu.

"Let them wait," said she.

She then lifted the helmet from my head and kissed me.

"Hurry!" said Ho-Tu.

I returned her kiss.

"What is your name?" I asked.

"Phais," she said.

"It is a beautiful name," I said.

She smiled.

"Truly beautiful," I said.

"If you wish," she said, "come again to the Street of Pots."

"If I do," I said, "I think that I shall bring an army with me."

She smiled. "We would like that," she said.

"Hurry! Hurry!" cried Ho-Tu.

He set the helmet over my head, and Phais locked it, putting the key in my belt.

I heard the crowd crying far off.

I heard the snapping of a whip. It was Ho-Tu. "Hurry! Hurry!" he said.

Then, pretending to grope with my manacled hands, deliberately stumbling and scraping, smiling, I left the room. Ho-Tu came behind me, fiercely cracking the whip, crying out, "Hurry, Lazy Slave! Hurry!"

I heard men in the tunnel laugh.

At the entrance to the Stadium of Blades the blaze of the sun off the white sand momentarily blinded me. I felt Ho-Tu remove the manacles with the key stolen from Vancius.

"Hurry!" I heard a stadium attendant call. I did not look directly at the man, fearing that perhaps he might note the nature of the helmet I wore. The man was one of those slaves who, garbed in black, armed with iron hooks, drag the dead, human or beast, from the sand.

The trumpet of beginning blared again, frantically.

The crowd was hooting and howling.

Ho-Tu shoved me with the whip, cracking it occasionally. I permitted myself to be apparently driven to a place before the box of the Ubar. The Ubar, of course, was not in the box, but an agent of his was, Philemon, of the Caste of Scribes. I noted other men, apparently miserable wretches in blind helmets, being driven to a place before the box. I did not look at them closely. I knew them to be Taurentians. I knew they wore helmets through which they could see.

One or two of them, acting their roles, were whining piteously. Another had fallen to his knees and was begging mercy from the crowd, which jeered him.

At last we were lined up, facing one another, before the box.

"Raise your swords!" called a man.

Obediently we unsheathed our blades.

There was great laughter from the crowd.

"Salute!" ordered the man.

There was another roar of laughter from the crowd. It was done much as though we were actually trained arena fighters, instead of, supposedly, poor fools and criminals brought in for the sport of the patrons of Ar's cruelest games.

The salute was an ancient one, and I have little doubt it was brought to Gor centuries earlier, perhaps by men who had been familiar with arena sports and had initiated them in luxurious Ar, men doubtless from other places and times. I recalled the antiquity of the Voyages of Acquisition, once conducted by Priest-Kings.

Hail Cernus, Ubar of Ar!

We who are about to die salute you!

I did not join in this salute.

Four trumpets blared and we squared off against one another.

I observed my opponent swinging about as though he could not see me, stumbling here and there, being poked in my direction by an attendant with a whip. Another with a hot iron stood nearby, shouting at the other pairs. I knew they would not injure one another though they would appear to fight. Men in these games, in actual blind helmets, often, not really knowing, exchanged opponents; sometimes several would join in a slashing melee.

"He is straight ahead of you," cried out an attendant to the man moving toward me. He seemed to thrash about wildly with his sword. For sport I, too, took a few wild swings, to the delight of the crowd. I noted however, that, my opponent was moving subtly but obviously intently toward me. He was crying out as though in rage and fear. I rather admired his performance. I did not think it would last longer than I cared. I have little to commend me. There are others more learned than I, others doubtless shrewder and more subtle, others before whom, for their many talents, I stand in awe. I, Tarl Cabot, am a simple man, poor in many qualities, one who is doubtless much excelled. There is little, I suspect, that I could do better than many others. I am a man who is surely next to nothing, one unworthy of note. Yet I think there is one talent I have, though it is unimportant and unworthy, a gift toward which I have mixed feelings, a gift which is both boon and curse, one which has caused me feelings of horror and guilt, and yet to which I have owed my life and that of those I have loved. It is a gift I have sought not to exercise, a gift I have feared, and sometimes would put aside, but cannot do so. He who is a Singer must sing; he who weaves the beautiful rugs of Ar or Tor must weave; the Physician must heal; the Builder build; the Merchant buy and sell; and the Warrior must fight.

The steel struck my own and I parried the blow, moving the blade aside easily.

I saw the Taurentian step back, could sense his surprise.

I felt the sword in my hand, brought to me by Ho-Tu, the sword I had carried in the siege of Ar, years before, which I had taken to Tharna, which I had carried to the very nest of Priest-Kings, which had been with me on the vast, southern prairies of Gor, and which I had brought once more to the gates of Glorious Ar months before.

Then the Taurentian struck again and again I moved his steel to one side.

He then stood back, stunned, and withdrew a step, and put himself at the ready.

The crowd cried out, confused, not understanding, then angry.

I laughed, the keen ring of the fine steel still burning in my ear.

My entire body suffused with pleasure. Elation, like Ka-la-na, suddenly flooded every muscle and vessel in my being. I laughed again. Gone was the guilt. I had heard the ring of steel. The Physician must heal; the Builder build; the Merchant buy and sell.

"I am Tarl Cabot," I laughed. "Know that. Know too that I understand that you can see. Know as well that I can see you. Leave the arena now or I will kill you."

With a cry of rage he threw himself at me and the cry died in his throat, he sprawling in his astonishment, his death and his blood, crosswise in the sand.

I went to the next man and spun him about.

"I do not play games," I told him. "You are a Taurentian. I am Tarl Cabot. I am your enemy. Leave the sand or die upon it."

The man turned and attacked and I laughed suddenly with the thrill of the steel, the flashing ring of work upon the Warrior's anvil.

He cried out and fell before me, twisting in the sand, clawing at it.

"He can see!" cried one of the Taurentians.

The crowd, struck, was silent. Then, sensing the intended execution, some of them began to scream angrily.

The other men in the helmets, and the attendants as well, one for each original pair, turned to face me. One or two of the attendants ran from the arena. I gathered they had no wish to stand between Warriors.

"Leave the arena," I told the Taurentians. "Men die in this place."

"Together!" cried their leader. "Attack!"

He died first, being the first to reach me.

In a moment I fought surrounded by Taurentians, said to be among the finest in the guard.

The crowd now began to scream angrily as the many rushed upon and swirled about the one. The fans of the games of Ar had been fooled. They did not relish being witness to the private joke of some high person, doubtless the Ubar himself. As fans they shouted their anger at the deceit which had been practiced; as men they roared their fury at the unfair odds now designate upon the sand.

320

My world now was small, bright, alive, consisting of little other than swift, flashing, ringing patterns before me, then to the side, and once more before me. I moved swiftly drawing one Warrior or another after me, and he who was swiftest died first; I turned and spun, accepting or not accepting an attack, always to isolate a man; vaguely, as though far off, I heard the screaming of Philemon in the Ubar's box, the shouting of Taurentians; in a moment's respite I saw a Taurentian slay a citizen who would have leaped into the arena to aid me; other Taurentians, with their spears, were forcing back the crowd, which seemed enraged.

"Kill him! Kill him!" I heard Philemon screaming.

Another Taurentian fell from my sword.

One of the attendants with a whip struck me as I fought and I spun on him. He threw the whip to the sand and ran howling from the arena. Another approached me warily with his hot iron.

"Begone," I told him.

He looked about himself and dropped the iron and fled. The other attendants followed him.

I now stood and faced some six Taurentians, who stood in the defensive picket formation, three men forward in this case, and, in the interstices, three men back. This permits the men in reserve to move into the forward line to form a solid line, or, if the first line withdraws, to have space to take its place. It allows a great deal of mobility and, on the level of squad tactics, has its affinity to the Torian Squares; the space allows the swordsmen, of course, room in which to handle their weapons, room in which to properly attack or defend themselves; in this case I expected the center man to engage me, defending himself on the whole, while the flanking men would strike; should one of these three fall, of course, his place would be taken by one of the men in the reserve line.

Slowly, swords ready, the picket advanced on me. I stepped back, over fallen bodies. It is hard to break or attack the picket. I pretended to stumble and the center man rushed forward to press his putative advantage.

"Wait!" cried the leader, in the rear rank.

The man who had been the center man was at that time dead.

I pretended my blade had been wedged between the ribs of the center man.

Another Taurentian, by instinct, but not trained instinct, hurled himself forward, and so died.

The four remaining men attempted to retain the picket. Moving back warily I remained as close as I could to the picket, but out of reach, hoping to draw yet another Warrior prematurely into attack. They remained together. As a Warrior, though it was not to my advantage, I found this satisfying.

A close-formed military formation is difficult to maintain over rough terrain. Indeed, the Torian Squares, which I have mentioned, common among Gorean infantries, with their superior mobility and regrouping capacities, had, long ago, made the phalanxes of such cities as Ar and, in the south, Turia, obsolete. The Gorean phalanx, like its predecessors of Earth, consisted of lines of massed spearmen, carrying spears of different lengths, forming a wall of points; it attacked on the run, preferably on a downgrade, a military avalanche, on its own terrain and under optimum conditions, invincible; the Torian Squares had bested the phalanx by choosing ground for battle in which such a formation would break itself in its advance. The invention and perfecting of the Torian Squares and the consequent attempts to refine and improve the phalanx, failures, were developments which had preceded the use of tharlarion and tarn cavalries, which radically changed the face of Gorean warfare. Yet, in the day of the tharlarion and tarn, one still finds, among infantries, the Torian Square; the phalanx, though its impact could be exceeded only by the tharlarion wedge or line, is now unknown, except for a defensive relic known as the Wall, in which massed infantry remains stationary, heroically bracing itself, when flight is impossible, for the devastating charge of tharlarion. It seemed to me obvious that the men who faced me intended to do so as a group; already two had been lured from the picket and had died; I did not expect that another of the four would singly rush upon me. I backed among the bodies of the fallen Taurentians. Unevenly, with difficulty, the picket followed, their eyes on me. Then the picket charged but, as I had intended, across the field of their own fallen. I leaped to one side. The end man stumbled in an attempt to turn to me and I passed the side of the blade beneath the helmet and was behind them. Attempting to remain together they wheeled, each in place. One man lunged for me, but stumbled across another fallen Taurentian and his fellow, moving forward, fell across him; rather than attack the men who had fallen, on whom the attack would be expected, I struck the remaining man, he standing, the leader, engaging him singly in the moment and felling him. The remaining two Taurentians who had stumbled scrambled to their feet, scraping awkwardly back through the sand.

He of the two who was senior told the other, "Withdraw." No longer did they wish to press the battle. No longer could they be as confident of the odds as they had been but a moment before.

The two men withdrew.

The crowd was howling with pleasure, well pleased at what spectacle they had witnessed.

Then they began to scream with anger. Taurentians, perhaps two hundred of them, were filing rapidly to the sand, weapons ready.

So it is thus I die, I said to myself.

I heard the leader of the men I had attacked laugh.

"How does it feel," he asked, "you who are about to die?"

The laugh died in his throat for through his breast there suddenly flew a heavy Gorean arena spear.

I spun and saw, standing beside me, on my right, sword drawn, in the heavy helmet of the arena fighter, with the small round shield, the sheathed right arm and shoulder, Murmillius.

My heart leaped.

"Charge!" cried the leader of the new Taurentians, those who had rushed down to the arena.

The crowd began to press against the spears of the Taurentians in the tiers, who, at the edge of the tiers, at the top of the wall overtopping the sand, resolutely held them back.

The Taurentians rushed upon us and, side by side, with the marvelous and gigantic Murmillius, I fought.

Steel rang on steel and then we stood back to back, cutting and jabbing. Foe upon foe fell from those two fierce blades.

And then there stood another with us, in the garb of an arena fighter.

"Ho-Sorl!" I cried.

"You were long in coming," commented Murmillius, meeting steel upon steel, dropping a foe.

Ho-Sorl laughed, lunging here and there, kicking back a Taurentian. "Cernus had planned that I, too, wear the blind helmet," said he. "But Ho-Tu, of his house, did not care for the plan."

Another stood beside us, and we four fought.

"Relius!" I exclaimed.

"I, too," said he, blade flashing, "was destined for the sport of the blind helmet. Fortunately I too encountered Ho-Tu."

"And," grunted Murmillius, laughing, turning back an attack, "I wager the girls of the Street of Pots."

"If it must be known," granted Relius, driving his blade between the ribs of a Taurentian.

Murmillius, with a marvelous thrust, as though weary of sustaining the attack of his man, dropped him. "A likely lot of wenches they are," said he.

"Perhaps," said Ho-Sorl, "any Taurentians that are left over we can give to the girls of the Street of Pots."

I turned a blade from my breast, as another four or five Taurentians pressed in upon me.

"Excellent idea," said Murmillius.

"If," qualified Ho-Sorl, "any are left over."

Another dozen Taurentians pressed forward.

I noted that one Taurentian after another, in a line, approaching, slipped to the sand.

Ho-Tu, his hook knife dripping, a buckler on his left arm, now stood beside us.

I parried a blade from his heart.

"I think you will find," said Murmillius, "a sword is more useful here than your small knife."

Ho-Tu drew his blade and acquitted himself sturdily.

"Kill them!" I heard Philemon scream.

More Taurentians, perhaps a hundred, leaped over the wall into the arena and rushed forward.

We moved through those weary, bloody, reeling bodies about us, to their amazement cutting our way to our new foes.

I heard Relius cry to Ho-Sorl. "I have slain seventeen!"

"I lost count long ago," responded Ho-Sorl.

Relius laughed with exasperation and added another to his list.

"It must be some two or three hundred by now," surmised Ho-Sorl, breathing heavily.

Fortunately only a few Taurentians could approach us at one time.

"Boastful sleen!" cried Relius. Then he shouted, "Nineteen!"

Ho-Sorl dropped a man. "Four hundred and six!" he cried, lunging at another.

"Silence!" roared Murmillius and, obediently, we fought in silence, save for the crying of men, our breathing, the sparkling ring of blades tempered by wine and fire.

"There are too many!" I cried.

Murmillius did not respond. But he fought.

I turned in an instant's respite from the attack. I could not see the features of the magnificent fighter who stood beside me.

"Who are you?" I asked.

"I am Murmillius," he laughed.

"Why does Murmillius fight at the side of Tarl Cabot?" I asked.

"Let it be said as truly," said he, "that Tarl Cabot fights at the side of Murmillius."

"I do not understand," I said.

"Murmillius," said he, proudly, "is at war."

"I, too," said I, "am at war." Again Taurentians pressed inward and again we met them. "But," said I, "my war is not that of Murmillius."

"You fight in wars," said Murmillius, "you know nothing of."

"In what war do you fight?" I demanded.

"In my own," said Murmillius, meeting an attacker and insolently felling him.

Then to my surprise I saw, with us, fighting, a common Warrior, not a Taurentian, one whose helmet was not laced with gold nor his shield bound with silver, nor his shoulders covered with the purple of the Ubar's guard.

I did not question him, but accepted gratefully his presence at our side.

More Taurentians, perhaps two hundred more, leaped down from the wall.

I now saw fights in the audience in the tiers, some between Taurentians and citizens, others between citizens themselves. In some places armed Warriors, of common rank, stood against the purple-clad Taurentians.

Now those Taurentians left in the stands suddenly failed to restrain the crowds and thousands of citizens were leaping into the arena and others were swarming across the tiers toward the box of the Ubar. I saw Hup bounding and skipping on the tiers, crying out, and saw men throwing off cloaks, revealing blades, and rushing to meet Taurentians.

I saw Philemon, his face white, his eyes wide, turn and flee through the private passage that gives access to the box of the Ubar. He was followed by some seven or eight Taurentians.

"The people rise!" cried Ho-Sorl.

"Now," laughed Murmillius, looking to me, "I think you will find there are not too many."

I saw the Taurentians who had been facing us, perhaps three or four hundred, begin to disperse, fleeing toward the exits leading beneath the stands. The crowds, in their thousands, began to swarm over the walls, dropping to the sand screaming. Among them, shouting orders, were dozens of men, apparently of all castes, each with a scarf of silk of imperial purple wrapped about his left arm.

Murmillius and I stepped back and, among the bodies, Relius, Ho-Sorl and Ho-Tu, standing to one side, regarded one another.

He made no move.

I gave Ho-Tu the key to the helmet I wore, which Phais had thrust in my belt. Ho-Tu removed the helmet.

The air felt good. The crowd pressed about. I could make nothing of what they were saying.

"May I not now look upon the face of Murmillius?" asked I.

"It is not time," said Murmillius, regarding me.

"In this war of yours," said I, "what is the next step?"

"It is your step," said he, "Tarl Cabot, Warrior of Ko-ro-ba."

I looked at him.

He pointed to the top of the tiers. There I saw a man with a brown tarn, holding its reins.

"Surely," said he, "Gladius of Cos races this afternoon in the Stadium of Tarns?"

"You know of him?" I stammered.

"Hurry!" commanded Murmillius. "The Steels must have victory!"

"What of you?" I asked.

Murmillius spread his hand over the crowds on the sand and in the tiers.

"Through the streets," said he, "we march to the Stadium of Tarns."

I raced from the sand to the wall and, seizing a cloak lowered by one who wore the armband of imperial purple, scrambled upward. In an instant I was racing up the long tiers. When I reached the top there stood there a man with a purple scarf of silk, that armband indicating the imperial party. He held the reins of a common saddle tarn. I looked back down the long valley of stone tiers to the sands far below, seeing there in the circle of the arena, seeming small, Murmillius, Ho-Sorl, Relius, Ho-Tu, the milling, stirring crowd. Murmillius lifted his blade to me. It was the salute of a Warrior. A Warrior, I thought to myself, he is of the Warriors. I returned the salute.

"Hurry!" said the man who held the reins of the tarn.

I seized the reins of the tarn and leaped to the saddle. I hauled upon the one-strap and took the bird from the heights of the Stadium of Blades, streaking in a moment through the cylinders of Ar, leaving behind me men with whom I had fought, stained sand, and whatever we had together begun there.

Twenty Two

The Stadium of Tarns

I brought the tarn down behind the tiers in the Stadium of Tarns, in the Readying Compound of the Steels.

I heard the warning bar for a race about to begin.

As my bird, with a flash of wings, struck the sand of the compound, four men armed with crossbows rushed forward.

"Hold!" I cried. "I am of the Steels!"

Each of those who charged wore upon his shoulder the grayish patch that betokened the faction.

I found myself covered by their weapons.

"Who are you!" cried one.

"Gladius of Cos," I told them.

"It may be," said one, "for he is of the size and build."

The crossbows were not lowered.

"The tarn will know me," I said.

I leaped from the back of the tarn I rode and ran through the compound toward the perch of the black tarn.

Midway I stopped. Near one perch there lay a dead tarn, a small racing tarn, its throat cut. Near it, being tended for wounds, lay its intended rider, groaning. I knew the man. His name was Callius.

"What is this?" I cried.

"We enjoyed a visit by the Yellows," said one of the men grimly. "This tarn was slain and the rider direly wounded. We beat them off."

Another of the men gestured with his crossbow menacingly. "If you be not Gladius of Cos," said he, "you will die."

"Do not fear," I said and grimly strode toward the perch of the great black tarn, the majestic tarn of Ko-ro-ba, my Ubar of the Skies.

Approaching him we heard a wild tarn scream, of hate and challenge, and we stopped.

I beheld, in its compound, strewn about its perch, more than five men, or the remains of such.

"Yellows," said one of the men with the crossbow, "who tried to slay the bird."

"It is a War Tarn," said another.

I saw blood on the beak of the bird, its round black eyes, gleaming, wild.

"Beware," said one of the men, "even if you be Gladius of Cos, for the tarn has tasted blood."

I saw that even the steel-shod talons of the bird were bloodied.

Watching us warily it stood with one set of talons hooked over the body of a yellow. Then, not taking its eyes from us, it put down its beak and tore an arm from the thing beneath its talons.

"Do not approach," said one of the men.

I stood back. It is not wise to interfere with the feeding of a tarn.

I heard the judge's bar ringing three times signaling tarns to the starting perches. I heard the crowd roar.

"Which race is it?" I asked, suddenly afraid that I might be too late.

"The eighth," said one of the men, "that before the Ubar's Race."

"Callius was to have ridden this race," I said.

But Callius lay wounded. His tarn was dead.

"We stand one race behind at the beginning of the eighth," said one of the men.

My heart sank. With Callius wounded and tarns at, or near, their perches, the Steels would have no rider. My own tarn, if it could be readied at all, could not be brought to the starting perches before the ninth race, that of the Ubar. The Steels could not, thus, even did they win the Ubar's race, carry the day.

"The Steels are done," said I.

"But one rides for the Steels," said one of the crossbowmen.

I looked at him suddenly.

"Mip," said he.

"The little Tarn Keeper?" I asked skeptically.

"He," said the man.

"But what mount?" I queried.

"His own," said the man. "Green Ubar."

I was stunned. "The bird is old," I said. "It has not raced for years." I looked at them. "And Mip," I said, "though he knows much of racing is but a Tarn Keeper."

One of the men looked at me and smiled.

Another lifted his crossbow, leveling the weapon at my breast. "He is perhaps a spy of the Yellows," said he.

"Perhaps," agreed the leader of the crossbowmen.

"How do we know you be Gladius of Cos?" asked another.

I smiled. "The tarn will know me," I said.

"The tarn has tasted blood," said the leader. "It has killed. It feeds. Do not approach the tarn now or it will mean your death."

"We have little time to waste," I said.

"Wait!" cried the leader of the crossbowmen.

I stepped toward the great black tarn. It was at the foot of its perch. It was chained by one foot. The run of the chain was perhaps twenty-five feet. I approached slowly, holding my hands open, saying nothing. It eyed me.

"The bird does not know him," said one of the men, he who had suggested I might be a spy of the Yellows.

"Be still," whispered the leader of the group.

"He is a fool," whispered another.

"That," agreed the leader, "or Gladius of Cos."

The tarn, the great, fierce saddlebird of Gor, is a savage beast, a monster predator of the high, blue skies of this harsh world; at best it is scarce half domesticated; even tarnsmen seldom approach them without weapons and tarn goad; it is regarded madness to approach one that is feeding; the instincts of the tarn, like those of many predators, are to protect and defend a kill, to the death; Tarn Keepers, with their goads and training wires, have lost their lives with even young birds, trying to alter or correct this covetousness of its quarry; the winged majestic carnivores of Gor, her tarns, do not care to share their kills, until perhaps they have gorged their fill and carry then remnants of their repast to the encliffed nests of the Thentis or Voltai Ranges, there to drop meat into the gaping beaks of white tarnlings, the size of ponies.

"Stand back!" warned the leader of the men.

I stepped forward, until I stood within the ambit of the tarn's chain.

I spoke softly. "My Ubar of the Skies," I said, "you know me." I approached more closely, holding my hands open, not hurrying.

The bird regarded me. In its beak there hung the body of a Yellow.

"Come back!" cried one of the crossbowmen, and I was pleased that it was he who had thought I might be a spy for the Yellows. Even he did not care for what might now occur.

"We must ride, Ubar of the Skies," said I, approaching the bird.

I took the body of the man from its beak and laid it to one side.

The bird did not attempt to strike me.

I heard the men behind me gasp with wonder.

"You fought well," said I to the bird. I caressed its bloodied, scimitarlike beak. "And I am pleased to see you live."

The bird gently touched me with its beak.

"Ready the platform," said I, "for the next race."

"Yes," said the leader of the men, "Gladius of Cos!" His three companions, putting aside their bows, rushed to prepare the wheeled platform.

I turned to face the man and he tossed me a leather mask, that which Gladius of Cos wore, that which had, for so many races this fantastic summer, concealed his features. "Mip," said the man, "told me this was for you."

"My gratitude," I said, drawing the mask over my head.

I heard the judge's bar, a bristling fire of wings, and the sudden, wild roar of the crowd. "The eighth race has begun," said the leader of the crossbowmen.

I slapped the beak of the bird affectionately. "I shall see you shortly," said I, "Ubar of the Skies."

I strode from the bird's side and made my way through the readying compound of the Steels until I climbed the stairs inside the low wall separating it from the area leading out onto the broad path leading to the starting perches; I dropped over the wall and made my way across the sand until I came to the dividing wall separating the two sides of the track. I ascended stairs there until I stood, with many others, on the dividing wall, and from there could watch the race. The leader of the crossbowmen in the compound of the Steels followed me.

I heard cries of astonishment from those I passed. "It is Gladius of Cos!" I heard. "It is he!" "I thought he feared to appear." "No, Fool, not Gladius of Cos!" "Assassins lurk!" "Flee, Rider, flee!" "Flee, Gladius of Cos!"

"Be silent," said the man with me, he who had given me the mask, the leader of the crossbowmen, quieting with his command the cries and admonitions of those about us.

The birds, some nine of them, only a few feet overhead and to one side, flashed past, wings cracking like whips, beaks extended, the riders hunched low in the saddles. Those on the dividing wall staggered back.

I caught a glimpse of Green Ubar, Mip in the saddle, lost in the flurry of whipping wings.

I saw six wooden tarn heads mounted on poles at each end of the dividing wall, indicating the laps remaining.

Some seventy or eighty yards away I saw the box of the Ubar and, upon the throne of the Ubar, Cernus, of the House of Cernus, in the imperial purple of the Ubar.

For the moment his attention was distracted from the race, as a messenger, a fellow I had seen but a moment before on the dividing wall, hastened to his side, whispering something in his ear.

I suddenly saw him look to the dividing wall.

Masked, I stood there, facing him.

Angrily he turned to the man and gave him a command.

Again the furious passage of the tarns overhead was marked in the beating of wings, the cries of the riders, now the flash of tarn goads, the turbulence of the air slashed from their path driving against us.

This time, on the center side ring, a nonfaction tarn was forced into the padded bar by a sudden swerve of Menicius of Port Kar, riding for the Yellows. I had seen him use this several times before. I noted that Mip had been following Menicius, and when Menicius had swerved Mip had taken advantage of the opening thus presented and, like a knife, had plunged for the heart of the ring. The bird that had struck the ring was tumbling stunned into the net. The great heavy ring was swinging on its chains. Menicius, I saw, savagely dragged his bird back to the center of the flight path, cursing, realizing how Mip had waited to take advantage of his momentary surrender of the center.

The crowd, regardless of which patch they wore, cried out with admiration.

A tarn of the Reds, a large-winged bird, goaded almost to madness by a small, bearded rider, wearing a bone talisman about his neck, held the lead. He was followed by two brown racing tarns, their riders wearing the silk of the Blues and the Silvers. Then followed Green Ubar, Mip one with the winged beast, high stirrups, his small body hunched down, not giving the bird its head. I wondered at the bird. I knew its age, the diminishment of its strength, that it had not raced in many years. Its feathers lacked the fiery sheen of the young tarn; its beak was not the gleaming yellow of the other birds, but a whitish yellow; its breathing was not that of the other birds; but its eyes were those of the unconquerable tarn, wild, black, fierce; gleaming with pride and fury; determined that no other bird nor beast shall stand before it.

I feared for the strain on that old heart, redoubtable and valiant.

"Beware!" cried my fellow, he with the crossbow, and I spun to catch the wrist of a man striking toward my back with a dagger.

I broke his neck and threw him to the sand at the foot of the dividing wall.

He was the man who had reported my presence to Cernus, he to whom Cernus had issued an order.

I turned and regarded the box of the Ubar. Saphronicus, of the Taurentians, stood beside him.

The hand of Saphronicus was on the hilt of his sword. The fists of Cernus were white, clenched on the arms of the Ubar's throne.

I returned my attention to the race.

My fellow, now, instead of watching the race, stood, armed, with his back to mine, his crossbow ready.

The tarns, like a torrent of beating wings and talons, swept by again.

The large-winged tarn had fallen back now, the lead being taken by the rider of the Blue, a small, shrewd man, a veteran rider but one too precipitate. I knew his bird. He had moved too soon.

I smiled.

Mip, on Green Ubar, swept past the large-winged tarn. Second in the race was now the rider who wore the silk of the Silvers. Already he permitted his bird freedom of the reins. I saw there were two tarn heads left on the poles. I did not know the strength of the bird. With a clear strike at the first of the end rings, however, the bird, headstrong, resenting the sudden pressure on the control straps, went wide.

Mip took advantage of this cutting in closely, following now the rider in blue silk.

Menicius of Port Kar, riding for the Yellows, tearing at the control straps of his bird, tarn goad showering sparks to the sand below, tarn screaming, fought his way, birds buffeting, past the Silver trying to regain the center of the rings.

The Blue, leading now, expertly blocked Mip at ring after ring. I noted that the bird ridden by the rider in blue silk was tiring. But yet the race could be won on blocking. Menicius of Port Kar had been slowed by the Silver's attempt to stop him.

Again and again Mip tried to pass above the bird of the Blues, ring after ring, and then, lifting the bird again, he suddenly cut low and to the left, executing the dangerous talon pass. The bird of the Blues raked downward, with talons that could have torn Mip from the saddle, but Mip had judged the distance superbly. I heard the rider of the Blues curse and those who favored the Steels leaped roaring to their feet.

"Look," said the crossbowman, who stood near me. He pointed to a spot about a hundred yards away, on a small wall, built itself on the dividing wall, near the pole of the wooden tarn heads.

I cried out with rage.

There I saw a Taurentian, armed with a crossbow, lifting it, preparing to fire as Mip passed through the third of the far end rings. The Taurentian had the stock of the crossbow to his shoulder, waiting.

The crossbowman with me said, "Do not fear." He raised his weapon to his shoulder. Mip was clearing the center ring of the end rings when the heavy leather-wrapped cable of the crossbow sprang forward and the quarrel hissed from the guide.

I watched the dark, swift flight of the quarrel, like a black needle, and saw it drop into the back of the Taurentian, who suddenly stiffened, seeming inches taller, the metal fins of the bolt like a tiny dark triangle in the purple of the cloak, and pitched lifeless from the wall.

Mip cleared the third of the end rings and streaked on.

"An excellent shot," I said.

The crossbowman shrugged, drawing back the heavy cable on the bow.

There was now but one tarn head left on the pole.

The crossbowman fitted another quarrel to his bow and stood as before, examining the crowd.

The crowd roared.

Mip held the lead.

Then the Yellows sprang to their feet in the stands.

Menicius of Port Kar, his tarn young, swift, competitive, was making his move, gaining rapidly.

Mip released the reins. He did not strike Green Ubar with the tarn goad. He shouted to him, crying encouragement. "Old Warrior, fly!" he cried.

I saw Green Ubar begin then to hold his lead, his wings striking with the accelerating, timed frenzy of the racing tarn, each stroke seeming to carry him swifter and farther than the last. Then, to my horror, I saw the wings miss their beat and the bird screamed in pain, and began to turn in the air, Mip spinning with the bird, trying to control it.

Menicius of Port Kar streaked past and as he did so his right hand flew forward and I saw Mip suddenly lose the reins of the tarn and clutch spasmodically at his back, as though trying to reach something. Mip was thrown back in the two thin safety straps of the racing saddle and then sagged in the saddle, leaning to one side.

I clutched the arm of the crossbowman.

The tarn of the Blues, and then of the Silvers, and then of the Reds flashed past the reeling tarn and its rider.

The crossbowman raised his weapon. "Menicius will not live to finish the race," he said.

"He is mine," I said.

Suddenly Green Ubar, in the flash of the wings and the cries of the riders passing him, righted himself and with a cry of rage and pain burst toward the rings, Mip sagging in the saddle.

Then the bird, which had in its time won a thousand races and more, addressed itself again to that fierce and familiar path in the Stadium of Tarns.

"Look!" I cried. "Mip lives!"

Mip now hung on the neck of Green Ubar, his body parallel to the saddle, clinging to the bird, his face pressed against it, his lips moving, speaking to it.

And it is hard to say what I then saw.

The crowd roared, the tarns screamed, and Green Ubar, his rider Mip, flew, eyes blazing, for those final moments marvelous and incandescent in his youth, like a bird and rider come from the dreams of old men, as they knew them once, when they too were young. Green Ubar flew. He flew. And what I saw seemed to be a young bird, in the fullness of his strength, at the pitch of his prime and pride, his cunning and swiftness, his fury and power. It was Green Ubar as I had heard speak of him, Green Ubar of the legends, Green Ubar as he had been in the stories told by men who had seen him years before, Green Ubar, greatest of the racing tarns, holder of awards, victorious, triumphant.

When the bird came first to the perches of victory there was no sound from the crowd, that vast multitude totally silent.

Second was the startled Menicius of Port Kar, the palm of victory snatched from his grip.

Then all, save perhaps those closest to the noble Ubar of the city, began to cry out and cheer, and pound their fists on their left shoulder.

The bird stood there on the perch, and Mip straightened himself painfully in the saddle.

The bird lifted its head, resplendent, fantastic, and uttered the victory scream of the tarn.

Then it tumbled from the perch into the sand.

I, the crossbowman, and others, raced to the perch.

With my sword I cut Mip free of the safety straps and drew him from the tarn.

I jerked the small knife from his back. It was a killing knife, a legend carved about its handle. "I have sought him. I have found him."

I lifted Mip in my arms. He opened his eyes. "The tarn?" he asked.

"Green Ubar is dead," I told him.

Mip closed his eyes and between the pressed eyelids there were tears.

He stretched out his hand toward the bird and I lifted him, carrying him to the side of the inert, winged beast. He put his arms about the neck of the dead bird, laying his cheek against that fierce, whitish-yellow beak, and he wept. We stood back.

After a time the crossbowman, who stood beside me, spoke to Mip. "It was victory," he said.

Mip only wept. "Green Ubar," he said. "Green Ubar."

"Fetch one of the Caste of Physicians," cried an onlooker. The crossbowman shook his head negatively.

Mip lay dead across the neck of the bird he had ridden to victory.

"He rode well," I said. "One might have thought him more than a simple Tarn Keeper."

"Long ago," said the crossbowman, "there was a rider of racing tarns. In a given race, attempting the head pass, he misjudged the distance and was struck bodily from the saddle by the high bar of the first of the center side rings. He was dropped broken into the path of following tarns, torn, and fell again to the lower bar of the ring and then to the net. He raced once or twice after that, and then no more. His timing, his judgment were no longer sure. He feared then the rings, the birds. His confidence, his skill, his nerve were gone. He was afraid, deathly afraid, and understandably so. He did not race more."

"Mip?" I asked.

"Yes," said the crossbowman. "It would be well," he said, "if you understand the courage of what he did here today."

"He raced well," I said.

"I watched," said one of the men of the Steels standing nearby. "He did not fear. There was no fear in his handling of the tarn. There was only sureness, and skill, and nerve."

"And pride," added another man.

"Yes, that, too," said the first man.

"I remember him," said another man, "from years ago. It was the Mip of old. He rode as he had ridden years before. Never did he ride a finer race."

There were murmurs of assent from those gathered about.

"He was then," I asked, "well known as a rider."

The men about looked at me.

"He was the greatest of the riders," said the crossbowman, looking down at the small, still figure of Mip, his arms still about the neck of the tarn, "the greatest of the riders."

"Did you not know him?" asked one of the men of me.

"He was Mip," I said. "I knew him only as Mip."

"Then know him now," said the crossbowman, "by his true name."

I looked at the crossbowman.

"He was Melipolus of Cos," said the crossbowman.

I stood stunned, for Melipolus of Cos was indeed a legend in Ar and in the hundred cities in which races were held.

"Melipolus of Cos," repeated the crossbowman.

"He and Green Ubar died in victory," said one of the men present.

The crossbowman looked at him sharply. "I remember only," said he, "the victory perch, Mip lifting his hands, the tarn's scream of victory."

"I, too," said the man.

The judge's bar rang twice, signaling the preparation for the ninth race, that of the Ubar.

I picked up the small knife which had slain Mip, that hurled by Menicius of Port Kar. I thrust it in my belt.

The platforms, bearing the tarns for the ninth race, were being wheeled onto the track area, approaching the starting perches.

Attendants rushed forward.

I picked up Mip in my arms and handed him to one of the Steels. The body of Green Ubar was placed on a platform and taken from the area.

The crowd was stirring in the stands. The caste colors of Gor seemed turbulent in the high tiers. Men rushed here and there securing the clay disks confirming their bets. Hawkers cried their wares. Here and there children ran about. The sky was a clear blue, dotted by clouds. The sun was shining. It was a good day for the races.

On a large board, against the dividing wall, on which the day's results were tallied, and lists and odds kept of the coming races, I saw them place as the winner of the eighth race Green Ubar, and his rider Melipolus of Cos. I supposed it had been years since the board had been so posted.

Menicius of Port Kar would, of course, ride in the Ubar's Race for the Yellows. His mount was the finest in their tarncots, Quarrel, named for the missile of the crossbow, a strong bird, very fast, reddish in color, with a discoloration on the right wing where, as talk had it, protagonists of the Silvers, long ago, had hurled a bottle of acid. I thought it a good bird. I respected it. But I had little doubt Ubar of the Skies, whose name I saw posted now for the Steels, was his master.

The races now stood even between the Steels and the Yellows. The Ubar's Race would decide the honors of the day, and of the Love Feast and, for most practical purposes, the season.

I looked to the box of the Ubar, and to that of the High Initiate, Complicius Serenus. Both boxes were draped with the colors of the Greens. I wondered if Cernus had yet received word of the events at the Stadium of Blades. Even now, through the streets, men were marching.

I walked to the board, where men were entering the information. There was no name following Ubar of the Skies for the Steels.

"Put there," I told the men, "the name Gladius of Cos."

"He is here!" cried one of them.

The other hastened to put up the name, letter by letter. The crowd roared with pleasure. I saw men from the betting tables conferring, some of them then approaching the board. Odds began to shift on the great board.

I heard the judge's bar ring three times, signaling the birds to their perches.

I strode in the sunlight across the sand toward the starting perches.

I saw Menicius of Port Kar standing on the platform, on which, hooded, trembling with anticipation, stood Quarrel, that marvelous reddish tarn, prince of the tarncots of the Yellows.

Before Menicius of Port Kar, and surrounding the platform as well, I saw a guard of Taurentians.

I approached them but did not attempt to penetrate their line. Menicius of Port Kar, his face white, climbed to the saddle of his bird.

I called to him. "Gladius of Cos," I said, "following the race would confer with Menicius of Port Kar."

He said nothing.

"Stand away!" ordered the leader of the Taurentians.

"Menicius of Port Kar," I said, "was in the city of Ko-ro-ba during En'Var of last year."

Menicius' fists went white on the reins of the tarn.

I took the killing knife from my belt, poising it in my fingers.

"He recalls a Warrior of Thentis," I remarked.

"I know nothing of what he says," growled Menicius.

"Or perhaps he does not recall him," I conjectured, "for I expect he saw little other than his back."

"Drive him away!" cried Menicius.

"A green patch might easily have been placed on the bridge a day before, an hour before. Menicius of Port Kar is skilled with the killing knife. The strike was made doubtless from the back of a racing tarn, a small swift tarn, maneuverable, darting among the bridges."

"You are mad!" cried Menicius of Port Kar. "Slay him!"

"The first man who moves," said the voice of the crossbowman behind me, "will swallow the bolt of a crossbow."

None of the Taurentians moved against me.

An attendant unhooded Quarrel, tarn of the Yellows. Its reddish crest sprang erect and it shook its head, rippling the feathers. It lifted its head and screamed at the sun.

When the attendant had unhobbled the bird it sprang to its starting perch, the first, or inside perch. It stood there, its head extended, snapping its wings.

It seemed to me a fine bird.

My own tarn, on its platform before the fourth perch, was unhooded.

The crowd cried out, as it always did, at the sight of that monstrous head, the wicked beak, that sable, crackling crest, the round, black gleaming eyes. An attendant for the Steels unlocked the hobble from the right leg of the bird and leaped aside. The steel-shod talons of the war tarn tore for a moment at the heavy beams of the platform on which it stood, furrowing it. Then the bird threw back its head and opened its wings, and, eyes gleaming, as though among the crags of the Thentis Range or the Voltai, uttered the challenge scream of the Mountain Tarn, shrill, wild, defiant, piercing. I think there were none in that vast stadium who did not for the moment, even in the sun of summer, feel a swift chill, suddenly fearing themselves endangered, suddenly feeling themselves unwitting intruders, trespassers, wandered by accident, unwilling, into the domain of that majestic carnivore, the black tarn, my Ubar of the Skies.

"Mount!" cried the crossbowman, and I did so. I would miss Mip at my stirrup, his grin, his advice, the counsel, his cheery words, the last slap at my stirrup. But I remembered him only now as he had held the saddle of Green Ubar, dying, but his hands lifted, in victory.

I looked across to Menicius of Port Kar. His eyes darted from mine. He bent over the neck of Quarrel.

I saw that he had been given another knife, a tarn knife, of the sort carried by riders. In his right hand, ready, there was a tarn goad. To my surprise I noted, coiled at the side of his saddle, in four loops, was a whip knife, of the sort common in Port Kar, a whip, but set into its final eighteen inches, arranged in sets of four, twenty thin, narrow blades; the tips of whip knives differ; some have a double-edged blade of about seven or eight inches at the tip; others have a stunning lead, which fells the victim and permits him, half-conscious, to be cut to pieces at the attacker's leisure; the whip knife of Menicius, however, held at its tip the double-edged blade, capable of cutting a throat at twelve feet.

I noted Taurentians going to the other contestants in the race, conveying messages to them. Some of these men were protesting, shaking their fists.

"It would be well," said the crossbowman, standing by my stirrup, "not to fall behind in this race."

I saw a Taurentian bring Menicius of Port Kar a container, wrapped in silk, which he thrust in his belt.

"Look," I said to the crossbowman, indicating Taurentians, carrying crossbows, slipping into the crowd.

"Race," said he to me. "There are those of ours among the tiers."

I took the great tarn up with a snap of his wings to my starting perch, the fourth.

Menicius of Port Kar no longer seemed white, no longer afraid. His lean face was now calm; there was a cruel smile about his lips, his eyes. He looked to me, and laughed.

I readied myself for the sound of the judge's bar. The starting rope was strung before the tarns.

I noted, to my surprise, that the padding on the rings had been removed by attendants, and replaced with bladelike edges, used not in races but in exhibitions of daring riding, stunts in effect, in which riders appear to court death at the rings.

The crowd, all factions, cried out in protest at this.

The riders, with the exception of myself and Menicius of Port Kar, looked from one to the other warily, puzzled.

"Bring me," I said, to the crossbowman, standing at the foot of the perch, "from the belongings of Gladius of Cos, kept in the compound of the Steels, the bola of the Tuchuks, the kaiila rope, the southern quiva."

He laughed. "I wondered," he said, "when you would understand that you ride to war."

I smiled at him, under my mask.

An attendant of the Steels threw a package up to my saddle.

I laughed.

"We had them ready," said the crossbowman.

Another man, one of the Steels, who had ridden to victory earlier in the day, ran to the foot of the perch. "There are tarnsmen," said he, "Taurentians, but in plain garb, gathering outside the stadium."

I had expected as much. Such men doubtless had been used in the attack on the caravan of the Hinrabians. "Bring me," I said, "the small horn bow of the Tuchuks, the barbed war arrows of the Wagon Peoples."

"These, too," said the crossbowman, "are at hand."

"How is it," I asked, "that these things are ready?"

"Mip," said the crossbowman, by way of explanation. "He well knew the race you would ride."

An attendant, from beneath his cloak, threw to the saddle the tiny, swift bow of Tuchuks, the narrow, rectangular quiver, with its forty arrows.

Not hurrying I strung the bow. It is small, double-curved, about four feet in length, built up of layers of bosk horn, bound and reinforced with metal and leather; it is banded with metal at seven points, including the grip, metal obtained from Turia in half-inch rolled strips; the leather is applied diagonally, in two-inch strips, except that, horizontally, it covers the entire grip; the bow lacks the range of both the longbow and the crossbow, but, at close range, firing rapidly, it can be a devastating weapon; its small size, like the crossbow, permits it to clear the saddle, shifting from the left to the right, or to the rear, with equal ease, this providing an advantage lacked by the more powerful but larger longbow; but, like the longbow, and unlike the crossbow, which requires strength and time to reset, it is capable of a considerable volume of fire; a Tuchuk warrior can, in swirling combat, from the saddle of the running kaiila, accurately fire twenty arrows, drawn to the point, in half an Ehn.

The small bow, interestingly, has never been used among tarnsmen; perhaps this is because the kaiila is almost unknown above the equator, and the lesson of kaiilaback fighting has not been much available to them; perhaps it is because of tradition, which weighs heavily in Gorean life, and even in military affairs; for example, the phalanx was abandoned only after more than a century of attempts to preserve and improve it; or perhaps the reason is that range is commonly more important to tarnsmen in flight than maneuverability of the bow. I suspect, however, that the truest reason is that tarnsmen, never having learned respect for the small bow, tend to despise such a weapon, regarding it as unworthy a Warrior's hand, as being too puny and ineffective to win the approval of a true Gorean fighting man. Some of the riders of the Steels, I recalled, seeing it among the belongings of Gladius of Cos, had jested with me about it, asking if it were a toy, or perhaps a training bow for a child; these men, of course, had never, on kaiilaback, and it is just as well for them, met Tuchuks. It seemed to me that combat on kaiilaback, and combat on tarnback, had much in common; I suspected that the small bow, though it had never been proven in battle on tarnback, might prove that it had worth in the Gorean skies as well as on the dusty, southern plains; I had further, in many nights of training with my tarn, taught it to respond to a variety of voice commands, thus freeing my hands for the use of weapons. Commonly, the tarn responds only to one voice command, that of "Tabuk," which tends, roughly, to mean "Hunt and feed"; further, I would have liked to use the Tuchuk temwood thrusting lance from the saddle of a tarn. The tarnsman commonly carries, strapped to the saddle, a Gorean spear, a fearsome weapon, but primarily a missile weapon, and one more adapted to infantry. The tarnsmen, of course, centuries before, had been developed from land forces; it had always seemed to me that the tarn cavalries of Gor might be considerably improved by a judicious alteration of weapons and training practices; however, I had never had a command of tarnsmen of my own, and my ideas were of little interest, even to the tarnsmen of Ko-ro-ba, my city.

The Tuchuk horn bow was now strung, the quiver attached to the saddle, with the rope and bola. I wore my sword; I carried the killing knife I had taken from the back of Mip; lastly, thrust in my belt, was the double-edged quiva, the Tuchuk saddle knife.

There was a sudden clang of the judge's bar and the rope stretched before the tarns was jerked away.

The tarns, with the exception of my own, hurled themselves screaming, wings snapping, from the perches and streaked for the first of the side rings.

"Hold!" I had cried, and the great beast I rode, though it trembled, eyes blazing, did not leave the perch.

There was a cry of dismay from those near my perch. There was a roar of surprise, and of consternation, from the stands.

I looked across to the box of Cernus, Ubar of Ar, and lifted my hand to him, in mock salute.

Clutching the arms of his throne, he was staring at me, dumbfounded.

"Ride!" cried the crossbowman.

"Ride!" cried the others of the Steels.

Already the other birds in the race, nine of them, were approaching the first turn.

I looked at the poles bearing the twenty wooden tarn heads, signaling the circuits of the track to be made. The Ubar's Race is the longest, the most grueling of the tarn races. Its prize is the greatest, a thousand double-tarns of gold.

"Ride!" cried those of the tiers.

I laughed and then bent down to the neck of the black tarn.

"Let us fly," said I, "Ubar of the Skies."

With a sudden scream and a snap of the wide black wings the War Tarn of Ko-ro-ba was aloft. I bent over the neck of the bird, the wind tearing at the mask on my face, my clothes. The tiers, like startled horizontal lines, flashes of blurring color, fled behind me. I was exultant.

I wanted the tarns before me to space themselves, so that I might pass them singly if possible. I was certain their riders had had orders from the box of Cernus to see that I did not win; it would be difficult for a single tarn to block a ring, but two together might well manage; further, in not taking the lead immediately, which I believe I could have done, I hoped to postpone the entry into the matter of the race of enemy tarnsmen, who surely would not interfere unless it seemed the victory of Menicius might be threatened; lastly I wished to remain behind Menicius of Port Kar as long as possible; I did not wish him, with his tarn knife, behind me.

Shortly before the first circuit of the track had been made I swept past the last bird, a nonfaction bird, whose rider, caught unaware, threw a wild glance over his shoulder as I, a shadow upon a flying shadow, hurtled by over his head and to the left.

There was a roar from the crowd.

This warned the rider of the eighth bird, a Gold, and he, bent low in the saddle, looked behind him to see, piercing the rings, eyes blazing, wings snapping, the great black tarn.

To the crowd's astonishment, but not to mine, he wheeled his tarn, a rare, gloriously plumaged jungle tarn from the tropical reaches of the Cartius, to block the first of the right center rings. The bird, beautiful, fierce, talons lifted, wings beating, hanging almost motionless before the ring, faced us.

My tarn struck him like a screaming saber of black lightning flashing through the ring.

I did not look back.

The crowd seemed stunned.

The seventh rider was a nonfaction rider, but a veteran rider, who, upon orders from the Ubar or not, did not intend to wheel his tarn to face me, thus surrendering his opportunity of victory.

Ring after ring he blocked us well.

I admired his skill and fought, in the circuits remaining, to seize upon his pattern, as he, doubtless, sought mine. My bird was the swifter. Both of us passed a startled rider for Silver, and then another nonfaction bird. He was now the fifth rider and I the sixth. Ahead of us there was Blue, Red, Green and, as Yellow, Menicius of Port Kar. I heard a scream of horror from behind us as one rider, pressing another, forced him against the side of the edged ring. The wind racing against me, I shuddered, for striking such a ring edge, at the speed of the racing tarn, might well cut a man or bird in two.

I glanced at the tarn heads remaining on the poles and saw, to my dismay, only eleven remained.

I could have forced my way past the nonfaction rider ahead of me but, with the edged rings, it would be at great risk to both of us, and to our tarns. He, no more than I, I am sure, cared to kill his bird or slay the opposing rider. It is one thing to force a bird or rider into the padded bars, and another against the great, swinging knives that were now the rings.

As I coursed behind him I realized that he, doubtless, like many others, had studied the races of Gladius of Cos, as Gladius of Cos had studied theirs. Yet, unfortunately, though the man ahead of me was a veteran rider he had ridden little at the Stadium of Tarns, being from distant Tor. I had never seen him race before, and Mip had told me nothing of him. If he had studied the races of Gladius of Cos, probably his blocking pattern was based on his supposition as to my inclinations in passing. Accordingly, though it ran against the grain of my instincts, though I found it actually painful to me, the next time I felt that my strike should be the upper right I took the tarn to the lower left. To my chagrin he met the move and again I passed through a ring following him. I doubt that he was consciously reasoning these matters, but his apprehension, almost instinctual, based on watching me race, and on his years of experience, had led him to suspect even my pattern alterations. I knew Mip had had something of this rare gift and did not suppose that others, skilled, veteran riders, would be completely without it. I began to regret that I had so willingly surrendered the lead at the beginning of the race. Menicius, on Quarrel, was moving farther ahead each circuit.

I then recalled a conversation with Mip about such matters, the memory rushing through my consciousness like the flash of a metal bolt.

"What if your opponent, through luck or skill, senses your pattern, your every variation?" I had asked, more for amusement than anything else.

At the tavern of the Greens, he had put down his goblet of paga, and had laughed, spreading out his hands, "Then," had said he, "you must have no pattern."

I had laughed at his jest.

But he had looked at me, seriously. "It is true," he had said. And then he had smiled again.

There are four poles on the dividing wall at one end, and another four at the other end. These poles both keep the laps. At the beginning there had been, on each set of poles, twenty wooden tarn head, five to each pole. Now two poles of each set were empty. One of each set bore five tarn heads, and the other bore four. There were nine laps remaining. I decided at the next attempt in passing I would, regardless of what I felt like, pass at the position of the numeral nine on Gorean chronometers.

I heard a curse as I shot past the startled rider, who seemed suddenly confused, looking about. His tarn lost its rhythm. I heard another bird, one following it, strike it, screams of rage, those of tarns and men.

By the time there were seven tarn heads remaining on the poles I had caught up to the rider for the Blues, who held a poor fourth.

He was on a swifter bird than the rider from Tor but he was not the rider that was the other. I passed him on the lower left after a feint to the upper right. Trying to block in the wrong position he nearly hit the top of the edged ring and the startled bird was carried far out of the ring track and had to wheel to reenter the track.

The screams of the crowd were now deafening, though one could make out no words; the effect of the sound, as I flew through it, was, as I had often found it, a fascinating phenomenon, its pitch varying considerably, as one would expect, with my speed and position, particularly as I made the turns.

I heard a sudden hiss in the air and bent lower in the saddle. I had not seen it, but I knew the sound of the passage of a bolt from a crossbow. There were two more hisses. "On!" I cried. "On, Ubar of the Skies!"

The bird, oblivious of the missiles, smote his way forward.

Out of the corner of my eye I saw perhaps fifty tarnsmen on the wall over the high tier on my right, perched there, waiting.

"On!" I cried. "On!" The bird sped on. "On, Ubar of the Skies!" I shouted.

Then, to my horror, I saw that both the rider for the Reds and he for the Greens had wheeled their tarns and stood ready at the left center ring to block my passage.

The crowd was screaming in anger. It did not occur to me at the moment but the fact that one of these men was the rider for Green had made the allegiance of the Ubar clear to all. He, supposedly favoring the Greens, had apparently given orders to them as well that I should not win. Menicius on Quarrel streaked forward.

My tarn struck the other two and in a moment, tarn goads flashing, talons clutching, birds screaming and biting, we found ourselves as in a clenched, winged fist of fury, beating and turning before the left center ring. Then we were struck by another bird, the Blue I think, and then by the bird ridden by the Torian, and then one of the others.

The Green, rider cursing, tumbled back out of the fist, bleeding at the side of the throat, out of control, screaming. The Red rider broke free and returned to the race. He had also, like Menicius of Port Kar, and two of the other riders, raced in the eighth. He was a small bearded man, stripped to the waist; about his neck he wore a bone talisman for good luck.

The Silver bird flashed past.

My tarn was locked, talon to talon, with a nonfaction bird; each was tearing at the other; the tarn goad of the rider struck me, almost blinding me with pain; for an instant my consciousness seemed nothing but a blinding shower of yellow, fiery needles; his tarn struck for me and I beat its beak away with my own tarn goad, cursing wildly; we turned and, held in the saddles by safety straps, spinning, we struck at one another, tarn goads like swords, splashing light about; and then we were past the ring and broke apart; my bird would have stayed to kill; but I drew it away. "On, Ubar of the Skies!" I cried. "On!"

There were now three birds beyond us, the Red, the Silver, and the Yellow.

I saw the brightly plumaged bird, who had first contested a ring with us, in the net below, alive but trembling.

Somewhere behind I heard a scream and the judge's bar signaling that a ring had been missed. I sped on.

Another bolt from a crossbow hissed past.

"On!" I cried. "On!"

Ubar of the Skies, like black fire, burned past one ring and another.

There were still five tarn heads on the poles when he overtook, between rings, and passed the Silver. In another turn he passed the Red. The man was beating his tarn unmercifully with the tarn goad, the bone talisman on its string flying behind his neck. As I drew near, and then abreast of him, I saw madness and fury in his eyes. He attempted, in moving through the rings, to force us to the left, into the heavy edge, but before he could do so, we had passed him.

I cried out exultantly. Ahead there was but one tarn, that of Menicius of Port Kar.

"Now," said I, "let us fly, Ubar of the Skies."

The bird gave a great scream and the wings began to strike the air with the fury of victory.

Low on the bird's neck I saw, ahead, the bent figure of Menicius of Port Kar, astride Quarrel, growing larger and larger.

I saw four tarn heads left on the poles.

I laughed.

The great black tarn hurtled on. "Victory will be ours!" I cried to him.

Even faster did he fly.

Suddenly, to my dismay, I heard about us shouts and the thunder of wings and, closing in upon us, and following us, and rushing to meet us, were tarnsmen.

The crowd's protest of fury must have torn its way to the very clouds in the calm, blue sky.

I whipped out the Tuchuk bow and, in the instant, found myself wheeling and fighting in the midst of more than a dozen tarnsmen, while many others, wheeling about, attempted to press in upon me. Ubar of the Skies suddenly uttered a scream that terrified even me, raising the hair on my neck and arms; it was not simply the challenge scream of his kind; it was a scream of pleasure, of horrifying eagerness, of the tarn's lust for blood and war; steel-shod talons grasping, screaming, beak tearing, Ubar of the Skies, his black eyes blazing with delight, hurled himself on odds that pleased him, odds which even he, that majestic carnivore, could accept as worthy.

Again and again the small bow, swift and vicious, fired, twenty barbed arrows in half an Ehn, tarnsmen struggling to reach me with their swords, thrusting with their heavy spears, and all the time Ubar of the Skies tearing and ripping, his beak and steel-shod talons engines of fierce carnage; I felt blood along the side of my neck as a bronze-headed spear seemed to flash in my face and then I saw, to my horror, the arm that had thrust the spear seized in the beak of my tarn and wrenched from the hideous body torn screaming from the saddle of its tarn, the safety strap parting like twine.

The tarnsmen, packed together, impeding one another's movements, were fodder for the slaughter of the Tuchuk bow, and then, crying out with fear, they turned aside their mounts and broke before us.

"The race!" I cried. "The race!"

The tarn, to my amazement, turned from the fray in an instant and smote his way from the environing, reeling tarns and struck out again for the rings.

Menicius of Port Kar was now far in the advance but my tarn, silent, save for the crack of his great wings, eyes bright, blood on its beak and steel-shod talons, again took up the pursuit.

In the time we had fought four tarns had passed us, though the rest were still behind, either fallen from the race or unable to pass the rings where tarnsmen still wheeled in disarray. I heard the judge's bar ring twice, indicating two had failed to clear one ring or another.

Swiftly we passed one tarn, a nonfaction bird.

The Silver, the Red and the Blue were still ahead of me, as well as the Yellow, that of my foe Menicius, he of Port Kar.

Two wooden tarn heads now surmounted the high poles.

Another crossbow bolt feathered its swift way, a line of blurred light, soft, past me.

When I came to the right center rings I again encountered tarnsmen, now regrouped. Again and again the Tuchuk bow fired and again and again unwilling tarnsmen felt the lightninglike kiss of the barbed steel. Then the arrows, of which there had been forty, were gone.

I heard an exultant shout from behind me and saw the leader of the tarnsmen signal his men across the dividing wall again, to meet me at the left center rings.

We passed the Silver, and then the Blue, between the rings.

I noted that the Red was gaining rapidly on Menicius, who was blocking him at the side rings. I could see the talisman of bone flying behind the neck of the bearded rider on Red. I had seen the maddened eyes of the rider on Red, his frenzy with the tarn goad; he was clearly, Ubar or no Ubar, intent upon the race. I smiled.

Then, suddenly before me, at the left side rings, closing the rings to us, hovered some ten tarnsmen, weapons ready. Ubar of the Skies did not hesitate but hurtled into their midst, beak rending, and then was clear; they turned in pursuit but four of them, caught in the wide loop of the Tuchuk rope, were cursing, cutting at it, while the tarns, suddenly startled, finding their movements inhibited, broke formation;

the tarns, the men, struggling in the wide boskhide loop, wrenched this way and that, and tumbled to the net; the others cut across the dividing wall to head me off once more.

Now there was but one tarn head on the poles when I came again to the right center rings.

Already the Tuchuk bola was whirling, a blur of leather and lead.

Again the tarn cut through and two of the tarnsmen were screaming, trying to shield themselves from the weighted straps, flying about them; the weights in the Tuchuk bola can crush a skull, the leather can strangle.

A tarnsman pressed in with sword upon us and I met the sword with tarn goad, with a bright yellow flash; his tarn veered away and I hurled the tarn goad savagely at another bird dropping toward me, talons opened; the goad struck him with a blinding flash and he, too, veered away; I then drew my sword, parried twice and thrust home with a fifth man; the sixth man, the leader of the tarnsmen, drew his bird away from our path, cursing.

The last tarn head loomed on the pole.

"Ubar of the Skies," cried I, "fly! Fly now as you have never flown before!"

We flashed through the end rings and, on the straight-away, saw, ahead, the Yellow and the Red approaching the left side rings. Like an arrow, a black torrent, Ubar of the Skies flashed toward the side rings. I think that there could be on Gor no tarn his equal. "Har-ta!" I cried. "Faster! Har-ta! Faster! Faster!"

Then, approaching the last of the left side rings, Ubar of the Skies, striking for the heart of the ring, burst between the startled Red and Menicius, who led him by perhaps four yards. I saw a look of wild hatred transform the features of Menicius and he jerked at something in his belt. The Red, cursing, tried to force us up, where we might strike the unpadded bar; at our speed we might be cut in two; my tarn struggled to avoid the bar, not turning to do battle, but persisting in his race; I was suddenly aware of the arm of Menicius flying forward and I instinctively threw myself forward even lower on the tarn's neck; there was the crash of a vial and I heard a hideous scream from the bearded man who was suddenly tearing at his body and face with his fingernails; his tarn, startled, veered up and to the right, out of control, and the man's shoulder struck the bar and he was cut from the safety straps and thrown rolling and screaming, bloody, whimpering, to the net yards below.

I heard a frightful crack and my left arm broke open bloody in two lines; my sword leaped up and the next time the whip knife struck I severed it; Menicius, with a curse, threw the coil of whip at me and it passed overhead; we shot through the first of the final rings, the end rings; his tarn knife was in his hand but suddenly, eyes wide, he saw my arm back, the Tuchuk quiva poised; "No!" he cried, wheeling the tarn to shield himself; my tarn struck his and together, passing through the second of the final three end rings, saddle to saddle, hand to hand, we grappled, I holding his wrist, he mine; he cried out with pain and dropped the knife; we heard the judge's bar; both of us had missed the final ring; I thrust the quiva in my belt; "Does Menicius of Port Kar care to race?" I asked, wheeling my tarn back to negotiate the final ring. With a curse he jerked savagely at the control straps of Quarrel and that fine bird instantaneously responded and together Quarrel and Ubar of the Skies passed through the final ring; with a snap of his great wings Ubar of the Skies struck the winner's perch, seized it in his steel-shod talons and threw back his head with a scream of victory. I lifted my arms.

Quarrel, automatically, had struck the second perch only an instant behind us.

The cries of the crowd were deafening.

Menicius, fumbling, unstrapped himself from the tarn saddle and leaped to the sand, running toward the box of the Ubar, his hands outstretched.

I saw four crossbowmen at the box of the Ubar, on a signal from Saphronicus, who stood there, fire. Menicius, hit four times with iron bolts, spun and fell into the sand. I saw one of the four crossbowmen fall, an arrow from the stands transfixing him. I saw Cernus, in the swirling robe of the Ubar, leap to his feet, summon Taurentians about him. In the distance I heard singing, a song of Ar's glory; in the stands the song was picked up. Men began to stand in the tiers, singing.

"Stop!" cried Cernus. "Stop!"

But the song became louder and louder.

There was an anger in the song, and a triumph, a defiance and a pride, a pride of men in their city, Glorious Ar. One citizen tore down the banners of green which draped the box of the Ubar and of the

High Initiate. Complicius Serenus, unsteadily, withdrew from his box. Another citizen, rushing forward, oblivious of the crossbows of Taurentians, hurled a banner of yellow across the box of the Ubar; another such banner was thrown over the railing of the box which had been occupied by Complicius Serenus, High Initiate of Ar.

Cernus did not dare have his men fire on those citizens who so acted.

He stood raging in the box of the Ubar. "Stop!" he cried. "Stop singing!"

But the song continued, growing stronger as more and more men took it up, and soon the tiers themselves rang with the sound.

One after another of the tarns of the race, those who could complete the race, struck the finishing perches but no one paid them heed.

There was only the song, and more and more voices, and more men standing in the tiers.

Then gates leading onto the sand burst open and thousands of citizens, come from the Stadium of Blades, marching and singing, entered the Stadium of Tarns, at their head, helmeted and mighty, sword in hand, the magnificent Murmillius, hero of the Stadium of Blades.

Though I was not of Ar I, too, still in the saddle of the black tarn, joined in that song, that song of Glorious Ar.

Cernus regarded me with fury.

I drew from my features the leather mask.

He cried out in horror, staggering backwards. Even Saphronicus, Captain of the Taurentians, stood stunned, disbelieving, shaken.

And then, followed by his thousands, singing, across the sand, strode Murmillius.

He stopped before the box of the Ubar. The crossbowmen there set their bows against him.

He removed his helmet, the arena helmet which had for so many months concealed his features.

Cernus threw his hands before his face. With a cry of horror he threw off the robe of the Ubar and, turning, fled from the box.

The crossbowmen threw their weapons into the sand.

Saphronicus, Captain of the Taurentians, removed his purple cloak and his helmet, and walked down the steps from the box to the sand. There he knelt before the man who stood there, and placed his sword at his feet, in the sand.

The man then ascended to the box of the Ubar, where he set his helmet on the arm of the throne. The robe of the Ubar was placed about his shoulders. His sword across his knees, he took his seat on the throne.

There were tears in the eyes of those about me, and my own eyes were not dry as well.

I heard a child ask his father, "Father, who is that man?"

"He is Marlenus," said the father. "He has come home. He is Ubar of Ar."

Once again the thousands in that place began to sing. I dismounted and went to the body of Menicius, pierced by four bolts. I took his killing knife from my belt and threw it, blade down, into the sand beside the body. The scroll on the knife read, "I have sought him. I have found him."

Then I retraced my steps to the tarn. My sword was in my sheath, the quiva in my belt.

I remounted.

I had business remaining in the house of Cernus, once Ubar of Ar.

Twenty Three

I Finish My Business
in the House of Cernus

I waited in the hall of Cernus, on his own great chair. Before me, on the wooden table, there lay my sword.

I had had little difficulty in arriving at his House before him. I had ridden the black tarn. My eyes had not permitted any to dispute my passage, and, indeed, the halls of his house were now largely empty. Word had apparently reached the House of the doings at the Stadium of Blades before it had come to the Stadium of Tarns, much farther away.

I had walked through the largely deserted halls, empty save for a scurrying slave or a furtive man-at-arms, gathering his belongings, preparing to make away. I passed numerous prisoners, slaves, male and female, some chained to walls, many locked behind bars.

In her chamber I had found Sura.

She was lying on the straw of a slave, but she had wrapped about her body the garment of a free woman. The collar, of course, was still at her throat. Her eyes were closed; she was extremely pale.

I rushed to her side, took her in my arms.

She opened her eyes weakly, and did not seem to recognize me.

I cried out in anger.

"He was a beautiful boy," she said. "He is a beautiful boy."

I put her down and tore rags to wrap about her wrists.

"I will call one of the Caste of Physicians," I whispered to her. Surely Flaminius, drunk, might still be in the house.

"No," she said, reaching for my hand.

"Why have you done this?" I cried in anger.

She looked at me in mild surprise. "Kuurus," she said, calling me by the name by which she had known me in the house. "It is you, Kuurus."

"Yes," I said. "Yes."

"I did not wish to live longer as a slave," she said.

I wept.

"Tell Ho-Tu," she said, "that I love him."

I sprang to my feet and ran to the door. "Flaminius!" I cried. "Flaminius!"

A slave running past stopped on my command. "Fetch Flaminius!" I cried. "He must bring blood! Sura must live!"

The slave hurtled down the hall.

I returned to the side of Sura. Her eyes were closed again. She was pale. The heartbeat was all but inaudible.

About the room I saw some of the things with which we had played, the silk marked with the squares of the game, the small bottles, the vials.

Sura opened her eyes one last time and regarded me, and smiled. "He is a beautiful boy, is he not, Kuurus?" she asked.

"Yes," I said, "he is a fine boy."

"He is a beautiful boy," she said, a smile of reproach in her eyes.

"Yes," I said. "Yes."

Then Sura closed her eyes. She smiled.

Flaminius came in but a few moments. With him he carried the apparatus of his craft, and a canister of fluid. There was paga on his breath but his eyes were sober. At the door, suddenly, agonized, he stopped.

"Hurry!" I cried.

He put aside the things he had brought with him.

"Hurry!" I cried.

"Can't you see?" he asked. "She is dead."

Flaminius, tears in his eyes, came and knelt with me beside Sura. He choked and put his head in his hands.

I had risen to my feet.

I waited now in the Hall of Cernus. It was empty. I looked about me at the tables, at the tiled floors; at the slave rings by the wall; at the square pit of sand between the tables. I had taken my seat on the chair of Cernus; I had drawn my sword, and laid it across the wood before me.

I could hear shouting outside in the streets but, because of the thick walls of the House of Cernus, it seemed distant. Here and there I heard snatches of the song of Ar's glory.

It was dark and cool in the hall. It was quiet. I waited. I was patient. He would come.

The door burst open and five men entered, Cernus, wild-eyed, suddenly haggard, and behind him Philemon, of the Caste of Scribes, the man who had commanded the fifty tarnsmen who had ridden against me in the Stadium of Tarns, and two Taurentian guardsmen.

As the men burst into the room I stood behind the table, in the half-darkness, setting the point of my sword in the wood, holding the hilt with both hands, surveying them.

"I have come for you, Cernus," said I.

"Kill him!" cried Cernus to the man who had ridden against me, a Taurentian, and to the other two Taurentians, guardsmen.

The man who had ridden against me threw me a look of hatred and drew his sword, but, angrily, he threw it to the tiles.

Cernus cried out in rage.

The other two Taurentians, one after the other, drew their swords and threw them to the tiles.

"Sleen!" cursed Cernus. "Sleen!"

The three Taurentians turned and ran from the room.

"Come back!" screamed Cernus.

Philemon, of the Caste of Scribes, his eyes wide with fear, threw a look after the guards, and then he, too, turned and fled.

"Come back!" screamed Cernus. "Come back!" Then he spun and faced me.

I regarded him, not speaking. My face must have been terrible to look upon.

"Who are you?" stammered Cernus.

In that moment I believe perhaps I did not appear Tarl Cabot, whom Cernus surely knew me to be, but some other. It was as though he had never looked upon the face that now, dispassionately, regarded him.

"I am Kuurus," I said.

I had, in my passage from Sura's chamber to the Hall of Cernus, stopped in the chambers where I had resided. There I had once more donned the black of the Assassin. There, once more, I had affixed on my forehead the mark of the dagger.

"The killer?" said Cernus, his voice breaking.

I said nothing.

"You are Tarl Cabot!" he cried. "Tarl Cabot of Ko-ro-ba!"

"I am Kuurus," I told him.

"You wear upon your forehead the mark of the black dagger," whispered Cernus.

"It is for you," I told him.

"No!" he cried.

"Yes, Cernus," said I, "it is for you I wear the black dagger."

"I am innocent!" he cried.

I would not speak.

"Menicius!" he cried. "It was he who slew the Warrior of Thentis! Not I!"

"I have taken gold," I told him. I would not yet speak to him of Sura.

"It was Menicius!" he wept.

"It was you who gave the order," I said.

"I will give you gold!" he cried.

"You have nothing," said I, "Cernus." I regarded him evenly. "You have lost all."

"Do not strike me," he begged. "Do not strike me!"

"But," I laughed, "you are first sword of the House of Cernus. You are even, I hear, of the Caste of Warriors."

"Do not strike me!" he whimpered.

"Defend yourself," I said.

"No," he said. "No. No."

"Noble, proud Cernus," I scoffed.

"No," he said. "No. No. No."

"Very well," I said. "Disarm yourself and surrender. I will see that you are conveyed safe to the courts of the Ubar, where I trust justice will be dealt."

"Yes," whimpered Cernus, "yes." He reached humbly, brokenly, into his robe, drawing forth a dagger. I eyed him narrowly. Suddenly he cried, "Die!" and hurled it at me. I had expected the move and had turned. The knife struck the back of the chair before which I stood, striking through the wood, stopping only with the hilt.

"Excellent," I commented.

He stood now with his sword in hand, eyes bright.

I cried out with a shout of exultation and leaped over the table towards him.

In an instant our blades had met in the swift discourse of flashing steel.

He was an excellent swordsman, very fast, cunning, strong.

"Excellent," I told him.

We moved about the room, over the tables and behind them, across the square of sand.

Once Cernus, moving backward, defending himself, fell over the dais, and my sword was at his throat.

"Well," I said, "will it be my steel or the impaling spear of Ar's justice?"

"Let it be your steel," he said.

I stepped back and permitted him to regain his feet. Again we fought.

Then I drew blood, from the left shoulder. I stepped back. He tore his robe from his body and wore only the belted house tunic; the left shoulder was soaked with blood.

"Yield," I told him.

"Die!" he screamed, rushing again towards me.

It was a superb attack but I met it and drew blood twice more, once from the left side, once from the chest.

Cernus reeled back, his eyes glazed. He coughed and spit blood.

I did not follow him.

He regarded me, breathing hard. He wiped a bloody forearm across his face.

"Sura is dead," I told him.

He looked startled. "I did not kill her," he said.

"You killed her," I said.

"No!" he cried.

"There are many ways in which a man can kill," I said.

He looked at me, haggard, bloody.

I moved my position. He looked over his shoulder, saw the door from the hall which led to the stairs and passage leading to the chambers of the beast. I saw a sudden, wild elation cross his features. He set himself as though to receive my attack. Then, suddenly, he spun and ran for the door.

I let him reach the door, jerk it open, take his stumbling flight up the stairs, into the passage.

At the head of the stairs, I at the foot, he turned. "It will protect me!" he cried. "You are a fool, Tarl Cabot!" He hurled his sword down the stairs at me. I stepped aside and it clattered past. Then he turned and fled down the passage.

I climbed the stairs slowly.

At the head of the stairs I saw that the room at the end of the passage was open. As I had expected there were now no guards posted.

I saw the trail of blood on the boards of the hall, marking the flight of Cernus.

"You would never make a Player, Cernus," said I to myself.

I heard the horrid scream from the room at the end of the hall, and a frightening roar, and strange noises, human, and snarling and feeding.

When I had come to the room, sword ready, the beast was gone.

I ran through the room. It opened into a larger room. One with a vast portal open to the air, sheer on all sides. In the larger room I smelled the odor of a tarn, mixed with another odor I could not place, but animal. Outside the room, mounted in the wall of the cylinder of Cernus, was a tarn perch. I saw, in the distance, something large on the back of a great tarn, humped, shaggy.

I turned back and looked into the room. In it I saw the rifle which had been brought from Earth. About the walls of the room there was much delicate apparatus, reminding me somewhat of instrumentation I had seen in the Nest long ago; complex paneling, wires, disks; the dials, I noted, were adopted for a visually oriented organism, needles quivering against a metric of spaces; a cone was flashing on and off in the instrumentation; I lifted a matching cone from its placement on a horizontal panel; putting the cone to my ear I heard a splattering of signals of varying pitch; they came more and more frequently, and at greater and greater intensity; then, to my amazement, the signals stopped; there was a pause; then there came a strange sound, which could have been uttered by no human throat, but articulate, repeated again and again.

I put the cone down. The sound continued.

Ho-Tu, his hook knife in his hand, entered the room. "Cernus?" he asked.

I pointed to the rags and the part of a body that was thrown into a corner of the room, mixed with litter and bones.

"What more could you have done?" I asked.

Ho-Tu looked at me.

"Sura," I said, "told me to tell you that she loved you."

Ho-Tu nodded. There were tears in his eyes. "I am happy," he said. Then he turned and left the room.

I saw on the part of a body lying among the bones the chain and medallion of Cernus, now stained with blood, the tarn, gold, slave chains in its talons.

I pulled it through the body and threw it onto the horizontal panel, next to the flashing cone, to the other cone from which unusual sounds, inhuman sounds, continued to emanate.

I looked about. Throughout the room there was the heavy animal odor. I saw the webbing on which the thing had apparently slept, judged its strength, noted its width. I saw the small boxes which had been brought from the black ships. I saw cases of metallic disks, perhaps mnemonic disks or record disks. Priest-Kings could make use, I supposed, of the contents of this room. I expected they could learn much.

I went to the horizontal panel and picked up the cone through which the sounds were being transmitted; I noted a switch in the cone and pushed it; immediately the voice stopped.

I spoke into the cone. I spoke in Gorean. I did not know to whom I spoke. I was certain that my transmission, like others, would be taped or recorded in some fashion. It would, now, or later, be understood.

"Cernus is dead," I said. "The beast is gone. There will be no answer."

I clicked the switch again. This time it was silent.

I turned and left the room, barring it on the outside, that others might not enter it.

In passing again through the hall of Cernus I encountered Flaminius. "Ho-Tu," he said.

I followed him to the chamber of Sura.

There Ho-Tu, with his hook knife, had cut his own throat, falling across the body of Sura. I saw that he had first removed from her throat the collar of Cernus.

Flaminius seemed shaken. He looked to me, and I to him.

Flaminius looked down.

"You must live," I said to him.

"No," he said.

"You have work to do," I told him. "There is a new Ubar in Ar. You must return to your work, your research."

"Life is little," he said.

"What is death?" I asked him.

He looked at me. "It is nothing," he said.

"If death is nothing," I said, "then the little that life is must be much indeed."

He looked away. "You are a Warrior," he said. "You have your wars, your battles."

"So, too, do you," said I, "Physician."

Our eyes met.

"Dar-Kosis," I said, "is not yet dead."

He looked away.

"You must return to your work," I said. "Men need you."

He laughed bitterly.

"The little that men have," I said, "is worth your love."

"Who am I to care for others?" he asked.

"You are Flaminius," I told him, "he who long ago loved men and chose to wear the green robes of the Caste of Physicians."

"Long ago," he said, looking down, "I knew Flaminius."

"I," I said, "know him now."

He looked into my eyes. There were tears in his eyes, and in mine.

"I loved Sura," said Flaminius.

"So, too, did Ho-Tu," I said. "And so, too, in my way, did I."

"I will not die," said Flaminius. "I will work."

I returned to my own chambers in the House of Cernus. Outside I could hear the song of Ar's glory. I washed from my forehead the mark of the black dagger.

Twenty Four

The Court of the Ubar

In the Central Cylinder of Ar, that in which the Ubar has his palace and holds his court, in a room assigned to me, I drew upon my body the tunic of a Warrior.

It was fresh and clean, bright scarlet, pressed with hot, round irons warmed over fires. I buckled about my waist the belt and scabbard. They were of new leather, black and shining, with embossings of brass. But it was my old sword, the fine, familiar steel, remembered even from the siege of Ar, many years before, that I dropped into the scabbard. Sitting on the edge of the stone couch I bent down to tie my sandals. Hup was sitting cross-legged on a chest across the room, his chin in his hands. There was much sun in the room.

"I am the agent of Priest-Kings in Ar," said Hup. "From the beginning I have followed your movements in the city."

"You are also of the party of Marlenus," I said.

"He is my Ubar," said Hup. "I have been honored to participate in his return to power."

"I wonder if the Priest-Kings are much pleased by that turn of events?"

"They are realists," said Hup.

"With Marlenus on the throne," I said, "Ar will be dangerous."

Hup smiled. "Ar is always dangerous." He scratched one ear. "Better Marlenus than Cernus, surely," said he.

"True," I laughed.

"It has taken years for Marlenus to return," said Hup. "Many things were essential. In the time of Kazrak there was little that could be done. Kazrak, though uninspiring as a Ubar, and worse, not of Ar, was nonetheless an estimable ruler, an honest man, an intelligent, brave man, who sought the good of the city."

"And Marlenus?" I asked.

"With all his faults," said Hup, "he is Ar itself."

I thought of the magnificent Marlenus, swift, brilliant, decisive, stubborn, vain, proud, a master swordsman, a tarnsman, a leader like a larl among men, always to those of Ar the Ubar of Ubars. I knew that men would, and had, deserted the Home Stone of their own city to follow him into disgrace and exile, preferring outlawry and the mountains to the securities of citizenship and their city, asking only that they be permitted to ride beside him, to lift their swords in his name. Marlenus was like a god and a beast among men, inspiring the most fanatic loyalties, the most intense of enmities. There are few men such that other men would fight for the right to die for them, but Marlenus, arrogant soldier, laughing Warrior, was such a man. Marlenus, I knew, could never be second in a city. He had now returned to Ar.

"With the departure of Kazrak and the appointment of Minus Tentius Hinrabius as Administrator of the City," Hup continued, "the return of Marlenus became practical." He rubbed his nose and looked at me. The left eye was the larger one, and green. The right eye was normal, save that it, unlike its fellow, was blue. "By this time we already had a network of agents in the city, both free and slave. Some of these you perhaps know."

"The slave Phais," I said, "and the girls of the Street of Pots were of your party."

"Yes," said Hup, "and most useful. Slave girls, as is not the case with free women, may go almost anywhere in the city, gathering information, carrying messages. Few suspect that a collared wench may be on important business. Even if apprehended they seldom suffer more than a lashing while serving the pleasure of those who have apprehended them. Phais once so suffered at the hands of Vancius, of the guards of Cernus. I think that Marlenus will give him to her."

"Poor Vancius," I said.

"Doubtless the girls of the Street of Pots will be given some male slaves," said Hup.

I did not envy them.

"Our most important single source of information," said Hup, "was the girls of the baths, particularly the Capacian. There is little in Ar that is not known in the baths. These girls were invaluable, both in the acquisition of information and in the arrangement of contacts. It was through the girls of the baths that the plans for the uprising were transmitted to those who would follow Marlenus."

"Was a girl named Nela," I asked, "of the Pool of Blue Flowers, among the agents of Marlenus?"

"She was chief among them," said Hup.

"I am pleased," I said.

"She, with the others of the baths who worked for Marlenus, has already been freed," said Hup.

"Good," I said. "I am much pleased." I looked at him. "But what of those girls who did not work for Marlenus?" I asked.

Hup looked puzzled. "They still wear their chain collars," said Hup, "and serve in the baths as slave girls."

"In the guise of Murmillius," I said, "Marlenus of Ar, as things went from bad to worse in the city, in the midst of corruption and crime, gathered about himself a following."

"He gave the men of Ar," said Hup, "something to identify with, a hero, mysterious and overwhelming, a hero to sway their imaginations. He won the love of the city."

"And the Steels," I said, "the new faction, had their role to play in bringing about the downfall of the influence of Cernus, and later, his downfall as Ubar."

"Of course," said Hup. "Through the Steels we wished to have a faction that would, like Murmillius, in the Stadium of Blades, sway the imagination of men, and win the allegiance of thousands of those of Ar. It would be an independent faction, a new faction, cutting through and across the loyalties and politics of the older factions. Further, it would be the means of defeating the Yellows. As we thought, when it became clear that the Steels truly threatened the Yellows, Cernus' secret faction, his interest and allegiance would become clear. His betrayal of the Greens and his secret endorsement of the Yellows, which could only be for purposes of mercenary gain, was made clear in the events of the race of the Ubar. This secret interest and allegiance, regarded as treachery, as perfidious, by the racing crowds of Ar, alone would have served to turn men against him. His true faction interests were revealed, infuriating all those in the Stadium, and perhaps mostly those of the Greens and the Steels. Then Marlenus, as Murmillius, entered the Stadium of Tarns, followed by his hundreds, followed by their thousands. Men had been turned against Cernus in both the Stadium of Blades and in that of Tarns, and in both by the cruelty and treachery of the man they had honored as Ubar. These things, together with the dissatisfaction of men with the governance of the city and the safety of their homes, coupled with the memories of Ar's greatness when Marlenus had worn the medallion of supreme office, of Ar's splendor when she had stood in his day feared, foremost, magnificent and glorious among all the cities of Gor, all these things turned the tides of power to our ends."

"To those of Marlenus," I said.

"His ends are our ends," said Hup. "The ends of Marlenus are the ends of Ar." Hup looked at me. "Marlenus," he said, "is the city. He is Ar itself."

I said nothing.

I remembered the daughter of Marlenus, Talena, from long ago.

Nothing more was known of her in Ar than had been known in Koro-ba, or in the very Nest of Priest-Kings itself.

Hup leaped from the chest.

"Come," said he, "let us go to the court of the Ubar."

I looked at him. "The Ubar," I said, "may hold his court without me. I must soon be on my way from Ar."

I had little wish to share now the glories of Marlenus, or whatever rewards he might, in his generosity, choose to shower upon me.

I was sad.

Marlenus had been kind to me. Yesterday evening, a guard had presented himself in my room.

"I bring you a girl," had said the man, "who would tie your sandals, who would serve you wine."

I had sent him away, not even looking upon the girl. The bright sunlight in the room, the scarlet of my tunic, the new leather, the metal embossings, seemed nothing to me. I wanted to be alone.

The cause of Priest-Kings had been advanced; the restoration of Marlenus to the throne of Ar had been accomplished. But beyond this there was little in which I could rejoice.

"Please," said Hup. "Accompany me to the court of my Ubar."

I looked down at him and smiled. "Very well, Small Friend," said I.

We began the long journey through the halls of Ar's great Central Cylinder, almost a city in itself. At times we walked up swirling gradients, at times stairs, swirling and broad, leading higher and higher into the cylinder; sometimes we walked through marble-floored passageways, in which, through narrow windows, designed to be too small for a body to pass, but large enough for use as crossbow ports, I could see the blue sky of Ar's bright morning; through the ports I could hear, ringing here and there in the city, signal bars proclaiming the gladness of the people; then we would be walking deeper within the cylinder, down broad, carpeted, tapestried halls, set with energy lamps, seldom found in the homes of private citizens, emitting a soft, glowing light; many of the doors had locks on them, the vast ornate locks in the center of the door, so common in the northern cities; some others were secured only by signature knots, presumably the doors to the compartments of unimportant retainers or members of the staff, in many cases perhaps the doors to the compartments of mere slaves.

In the halls we passed many individuals, who would normally, in Gorean fashion, lift the right hand, palm inward, saying "Tal," which greeting, in turn, we returned.

There were now no Taurentians in the Central Cylinder. The Taurentians had been disbanded, disgraced and exiled from the city. Only the day before their purple cloaks and helmets had been taken from them before the great gate; their swords had been broken and they had been conducted by common Warriors, to the music of flute girls, a pasang beyond the walls of Ar, and ordered from her environs. Saphronicus, their Captain, with other high officers, including Seremides of Tyros, who had replaced Maximus Hegesius Quintilius as leader of the forces of Ar, now lay chained in the dungeons of the Central Cylinder. The palace guard was now made up of Warriors who had been of the party of Marlenus. Their helmets and cloaks were no different from those of the armed forces of Ar generally. The palace guard, I had learned from Hup, would be, on a staggered basis, rotated, in order that the honor of serving the Ubar would be more broadly distributed, and, further, presumably, that no given faction of men could come, in time, to dominate the guards; the pay of the guards, incidentally, was substantially reduced, perhaps in order that, in virtue of this sacrifice, the honor of the post might be more clear, and that fewer invidious distinctions might grow up between the palace guard and the military generally, from which it was now composed.

Most of the individuals in the Central Cylinder were men of lower caste, attending to their duties, with the exception of numerous Scribes. I saw two Physicians. From time to time I saw a slave girl in the halls. The female state slave of Ar wears a brief, gray slave livery, with matching gray collar. Save for the color it is identical with most common slave livery. About her left ankle is normally locked a gray steel band, to which five simple bells of gray metal are attached. Many years ago, in Ar and Ko-ro-ba, and several of the other northern cities, the common slave livery had been white but diagonally striped, in one color or another; gradually over the years this style had changed; the standard livery was also, now, commonly, slashed to the waist; as before, it remained sleeveless; these matters, as generally in the cut of robes and style of tunics, undergo the transitions of fashion. I smiled. One of the decrees of Marlenus, uttered at his victory feast, yesterday evening, to rounds of drunken cheers and applause, had been to decree a two-hort, approximately two and one-half inch, heightening of the hemline in the already rather briefly skirted livery of female state slaves; this morning I supposed this decree would be adopted by the private slave owners of Ar as well; indeed, I noted that already the effects of the decree were evident in the livery of the girls I passed in the halls. The hair of the female state slave of Ar, incidentally, is normally cut rather short and brushed back around the head; the common slave girl, on the other hand, normally has rather long hair, which is unbound.

"Was Philemon captured?" I asked Hup, as we walked through the halls.

Hup laughed. "Yes," he said. "He tried to take refuge in the private compartments of Cernus."

"He told me," I said, "that he used to have access to them to copy documents."

Hup laughed again. "Apparently he was not as familiar with the apartments of Cernus as he led you to believe."

I looked down at Hup as we walked.

He grinned up at me. "In attempting to enter the compartments of Cernus he triggered a pit-lock device, and plunged twenty feet into a smooth-sided capture pit. We drew him out at our convenience."

I laughed.

"He is now, chained, on his way to the Sardar, along with the materials taken from the room of the beast and what had been brought in from the black ships. He, under the interrogation of Priest-Kings, will doubtless reveal whatever he knows. I expect they will learn much from the other materials, probably more than from Philemon."

"Was the strange crossbow taken to the Sardar?" I asked, referring to the rifle in that fashion.

"Yes," said Hup.

"What will be done with Philemon in the Nest, when they have learned what they wish from him?"

"I do not know," said Hup. "Perhaps he will be kept as a slave."

We were now passing along a carpeted corridor, rather more plain than many. I noted the doors here were secured only with signature knots. They were perhaps the doors to the compartments of slaves, housing little more doubtless than a straw mat, a washing bowl, and a small box in which might be kept some slave livery and perhaps simple utensils, a plate and a cup.

I glanced at the knots on the doors, as we passed them.

Soon we had emerged in the great domed chamber set with lights and stones in which, on a high, stepped dais, sits the marble throne of the Ubar of Ar. Warriors saluted as I entered, lifting their swords from their sheaths. I lifted my hand, returning the salute. The room was filled with men in the robes of many castes, both high and low. On the throne itself, in the purple robes of the Ubar, regal, magnificent, sat Marlenus, Ubar of Ar, Ubar of Ubars. At his side and about the steps, in rough garb, stood Warriors who had been with him as long ago as his exile in 10,110, who had fled with him to the Voltai and shared his outlawry, and now shared the glory of his restoration. There were, I noted, no Initiates in the room. I gathered their influence in Ar was at an end, at least in the court of the Ubar. Marlenus lifted his hand to me. "Tal," said he.

"Tal," said I, "Marlenus of Ar."

I then stood to one side, Hup at my side, to behold the doings of the Ubar's court.

Many were the honors and awards bestowed by Marlenus on faithful retainers. Many were the new appointments to posts of importance in the city.

I recall certain matters more clearly than others. Saphronicus, former Captain of the Taurentians, and his high officers, and Seremides of Tyros, who had replaced Maximus Hegesius Quintilius as leader of the forces of Ar, were at one point brought forward, chained. Kneeling on the tiles before their Ubar, they pleaded no mercy nor were they given any. They were ordered to Port Kar, in chains, to be sold to the galleys.

I saw Flaminius, at one point, standing before the throne of the Ubar. The Ubar gave him pardon for his actions on behalf of the House of Cernus, and he requested permission to remain within the city. He would return to his research.

At one point, to the shouts and delight of the men of the Ubar some two or three hundred girls were ushered quickly into the room of the court. They wore the brief gray livery of the state slave of Ar, slashed to the waist, knotted with a gray cord; about their throats was locked the gray metal collar of Ar's state slave; they were barefoot; on the left ankle of each was the gray metal band, with its five gray bells, worn by the female state slave. Their hair, in state fashion, had been cut short, shaped, and combed back around the head. The wrists of each were confined behind her back with gray slave bracelets. They were chained in long lines by the collars, five-foot lengths of chain being used, with a snap at each end, each end fastening to a given collar, each collar, save for those terminating a line, being fastened on two sides.

"Here are the most choice of the female slaves of the House of Cernus," said Marlenus, expansively gesturing to the two or three hundred girls.

There was a cheer from the many partisans of Marlenus in the room.

"Pick your slave," said he.

With great cheers the men hurried to the girls, to pick one that pleased them.

There were shouts of pleasure, and screams, and protests, and cries and laughter, as the men clapped their hands on wenches who struck their fancy. When the men had taken their pick the girls were released from the common chain and the key, that which served to unlock collar, bracelets and anklet, was given to he who had chosen his prize. Scribes at nearby tables endorsed and updated papers of registration, that the ownership of the girls be legally transferred from the state to individual citizens.

There was silence in the room when one girl, alone, was brought forth. She was attired as were the others, in the brief livery of the state slave of Ar. Her wrists, like theirs had been, were confined behind her back. The belled anklet was the only sound in the room as she came forward, trembling. She walked between two Warriors. Each held a five-foot chain leash that was snapped on her gray collar. When she had reached the tiles before the throne of the Ubar, she knelt, head down. The Warriors, holding their leashes, stood on each side of her.

"Slave," said Marlenus.

The girl lifted her head. "Master?" she said.

"What is your name?" asked he.

"Claudia Tentia Hinrabia," she whispered.

"You are the last of the Hinrabians?" asked Marlenus.

"Yes, Master," she said, her head down, not daring to lift it, to gaze into the terrible countenance of Marlenus, her Ubar.

"Many times," said Marlenus, "your father, when Administrator of Ar, by stealth and openly, sought my destruction. Many times did he send Assassins and spies, and tarnsmen, to the Voltai, to find me and my men, and destroy us."

The girl trembled, saying nothing.

"He was my enemy," said Marlenus.

"Yes, Master," she whispered.

"And you are his daughter," he said.

"Yes, Master," whispered the girl. She trembled in the chains of the state slave. The Warriors seemed very tall and powerful beside her. She suddenly put her head down to the tiles.

"Shall it be torture and public impalement for you?" asked Marlenus.

She trembled.

"Well?" asked Marlenus.

"Whatever Master wishes," she whispered.

"Or perhaps," said Marlenus, "it might be more amusing to keep you as a Pleasure Slave in my Pleasure Gardens."

The girl dared not lift her head. "Whatever Master wishes," she whispered.

"Or should I free you?" asked Marlenus.

She looked up, startled.

"That you may be kept locked in a compartment of the Central Cylinder, not as slave but prisoner, a high-born woman, to be mated in the future as best accords with the politics of Ar, as I see fit?"

There were tears in her eyes.

"That way," said he, "a Hinrabian might at last well serve the interests of Ar."

"That way," whispered the girl, "I would be more a slave than a slave."

"I free you," said Marlenus, "but I free you that you may be at liberty to go where you will, and do what you wish."

She looked at him, suddenly, her eyes wide, startled.

"You will receive a pension from the state," said Marlenus, "ample to the needs of a woman of High Caste."

"Ubar!" she cried. "Ubar!"

He now spoke to the guards with her. "See that she is in all things treated as the daughter of a former Administrator of Ar."

Claudia, weeping, was conducted from the hall.

Following this more business was conducted. I remember among this business arose the matter of more than one hundred exotic slaves from the House of Cernus, the white-robed girls who had been raised without the knowledge of the existence of men.

"They know nothing of slavery," said Marlenus. "Let them not learn now."

The girls would be treated gently, and brought well into the world of Gor with as much tenderness as so harsh a society permitted, being freed and domiciled individually with Gorean families, whose households did not contain slaves.

I had been given the thousand double tarns of gold for the victory in the Ubar's race. I saw Flaminius briefly in the room of the court. Eight hundred double tarns I gave to him that he might begin well his research once more.

"Press your own battles," said I, "Physician."

"My gratitude," said he, "Warrior."

"Will there be many who will work with you?" I asked, remembering the dangers of his research, the enmity of the Initiates.

"Some," said Flaminius. "Already some eight, of skill and repute, have pledged themselves my aids in this undertaking." He looked at me. "And the first, who gave courage to them all," said he, "was a woman of the Caste of Physicians, once of Treve."

"A woman named Vika?" I asked.

"Yes," said he, "do you know her?"

"Once," said I.

"She stands high among the Physicians of the city," he said.

"You will find her, I think," I said, "brilliantly worthy as a colleague in your work."

We clasped hands.

Of the two hundred remaining double tarns from the victory in the Ubar's race I gave all but one to free Melanie, who had served in the kitchens of Cernus, and arrange a livelihood for her. With the money remaining over from her purchase price, which was negligible, she, who had been of the Cloth Workers, could open a shop in Ar, purchase materials, and hire men of her caste to aid her in the work.

The one double tarn remaining from the victory gold I pressed into the hands of blind Qualius, the Player, who stood at the court of the Ubar, having been, like Hup, of the party of Marlenus.

"You are Tarl Cabot?" he asked.

"Yes," I said, "he who was Kuurus, and the double tarn I give you now I give for your victory over the Vintner long ago near the great gate of Ar. You would not then accept my gold, thinking it black gold."

Qualius smiled and took the piece of gold. "I know the gold of Tarl Cabot," he said, "is not black gold. I accept your gold, and am honored in so doing."

"You earned it," I assured him.

In the room of the Ubar's court, I briefly saw Nela, who had been of the baths, and several of the other girls. I kissed her, she joyful in her freedom. I also saw Phais and several of the girls of the Street of Pots. They, like others of the Ubar's party, had been freed. Further, at their request, they had been given several of the guards of the House of Cernus, including Vancius. I did not envy them. After the girls tired of them they would be at liberty to sell them for whatever they might bring.

I was now ready to leave the room of the Ubar's court.

"Do not go yet," said Hup.

"Nonsense, Small Friend," said I.

I turned and left the room, to return to my compartment. Perhaps within the hour I and the black tarn would depart the walls of Ar. My work in this city was done.

There was a darkness in my heart as I walked alone in the halls of the Central Cylinder of Ar.

In so much I had failed.

Through corridor after corridor I walked, retracing the steps which had taken me from my compartment to the court of the Ubar.

Door after door I passed, most with the heavy ornate locks, some secured merely with the signature knots of lowly men, or even slaves.

Within the hour I would leave the city.

I stopped suddenly, regarding one of the small, narrow wooden doors, giving entry surely only to the quarters of a slave.

I stood, stunned, shaken. I trembled.

My eyes regarded the signature knot securing the humble portal.

I fell to my knees at the door. My fingers scarcely seeming mine, scarcely able to move, touched the knot.

It was an intricate knot, feminine, complex, with playful turnings here and there, small loops.

I could not breathe. For the instant it seemed the world shook beneath me.

It was a beautiful knot.

I touched it, and, trembling, scarcely breathing, carefully, began to untie the knot, counting each bend and turn, each delicate twist and motion of the cords. I had untied only a bit of the knot when I leaped to my feet with a cry and turned, running as though demented, crying out, down the corridors once more to the court of the Ubar. Slave girls regarded me as though I might have lost my senses. Men stood aside. There were shouts. But I ran, and ran, and did not stop until I burst again into the court of the Ubar.

There, before the throne of the Ubar, stood, in the brief livery of the state slave of Ar, two girls.

I stopped.

Hup seized my hand and held me where I stood.

The girls were being unshackled, to be given to Warriors.

They were both beautiful, in the gray livery, with their hair brushed back about their heads, with the gray collars, with the matching gray bands with their five simple bells locked about their left ankles.

One was slender, a fragile girl, with deep gray eyes; the other had dark eyes and hair, a body that might have been that of a bred passion slave.

The two Warriors who stepped forward to claim the girls were Relius and Ho-Sorl.

I looked down at Hup, stunned.

Hup smiled up at me. "Of course," said Hup. "Priest-Kings, and their men, are not such fools as others would think."

"But Samos of Port Kar," I stammered, "he purchased the girls."

"Naturally," said Hup. "Samos of Port Kar is an agent of Priest-Kings, their agent in Port Kar."

I could not speak.

"It was clear months ago that Cernus would attempt to market the girls, among other barbarians, on the Love Feast in the Curulean." Hup grinned. "Therefore, that Vella, and the others, because with her, not fall into the wrong hands, it was resolved to purchase them."

"Philemon," I said, "told us that Vella was to be purchased by an agent of Priest-Kings."

"He did not know how truly he spoke," smiled Hup.

"Where is Elizabeth?" I asked.

"Elizabeth?" asked Hup.

"Vella," I said.

"She is not here," said Hup.

I would have pressed the small fellow on this but, at that moment, I saw Relius standing before Virginia. Her head was down and he, with his hand, lifted her head. Her eyes, deep and fine, met his; her lips were slightly parted.

Gently he lowered his head and kissed her. She cried out, pressing her head to his shoulder.

He removed from her throat the slave collar.

"No," she said. "Please, no!" She looked at him, suddenly afraid. "No!" she cried. "Keep me! Keep me!"

"Would you consent," asked Relius, "to be the companion of a Warrior?"

"Companion?" she asked.

Relius nodded his head. He held her very gently. She looked at him, unable to comprehend his words.

"It is the hope of Relius," said he, "that the free woman, Virginia, might care for a simple Warrior, one who much loves her, and accept him as her companion."

She could not speak. There were tears bright in her eyes. She began to cry, to laugh.

"Drink with me the cup of the Free Companionship," said Relius, rather sternly.

"Yes, Master," said Virginia, "yes!"

"Relius," said he.

"I love you!" she cried. "I love you, Relius!"

"Bring the wine of Free Companionship!" decreed Marlenus.

The wine was brought and Relius and Virginia, lost in one another's eyes, arms interlocked, drank together.

He carried her from the court of the Ubar, she lying against him, weeping with happiness.

There were cheers in the court of the Ubar.

Phyllis, her eyes bright with tears of happiness for Virginia, turned her back to Ho-Sorl, that he might similarly remove from her throat the degrading band of steel that marked her as only slave.

"I love you, Ho-Sorl," she said. "And I will accept you as my companion!"

Her face was radiant as she waited for him to unlock the steel that encircled her throat.

"Companion?" asked Ho-Sorl.

"Of course, Companion," said she, "you beast!" She spun to face him.

Ho-Sorl looked puzzled.

"Surely," she cried, "you have no intention of keeping me as a slave!"

"That was my intention," admitted Ho-Sorl.

"Beast!" she cried. "Beast!"

"Do you wish this slave?" asked Marlenus, from the throne.

"Let her submit to whomsoever she chooses," yawned Ho-Sorl.

"Very well, Wench," said Marlenus, "choose your master—"

"Ubar!" she cried.

"Or be returned to the pens of state slaves."

Phyllis looked at him.

"Choose!" ordered Marlenus.

Phyllis looked about herself in rage. Then, in fury, she knelt before Ho-Sorl, head down, arms extended and crossed at the wrists, as though for binding.

Seldom had I seen a woman so enraged.

"Well?" asked Ho-Sorl.

"The slave Phyllis submits to the Warrior Ho-Sorl," she shouted.

"Of Ar," added Ho-Sorl.

"The slave Phyllis submits to the Warrior Ho-Sorl of Ar!" shouted Phyllis.

Ho-Sorl said nothing.

Phyllis looked up, angrily.

"Do you beg to be my slave girl?" asked Ho-Sorl.

Her eyes filled with tears. "Yes," she said, "I beg to be your slave girl!"

"I have waited long," said Ho-Sorl, "for this moment."

She smiled through her tears. "So, too, have I," said she. "Since first I saw you I have wanted to kneel before you and beg to be your slave girl."

There was a great cheer in the court of the Ubar.

Phyllis, radiant, opened her wrists, extending her hands to Ho-Sorl that he might now lift her to her feet as a free woman, to be his sworn and beloved companion.

"I love you, Ho-Sorl," said she.

"Naturally," said Ho-Sorl.

"What!" she cried.

He clapped slave bracelets on her wrists.

She drew back her wrists, seeing them closely confined in steel. She looked on them disbelievingly. Then she looked up at Ho-Sorl. "Beast!" she cried. She leaped to her feet, swinging her manacled wrists at him but he ducked neatly and scooped her up, throwing her over one shoulder. She was wriggling madly on his shoulder, pounding him on his back with her chained fists.

"I hate you," she was screaming, pounding him. "I hate you, you beast, you big beast!"

Amidst the laughter of the court of the Ubar Ho-Sorl carried his prize from the chamber, the lovely, squirming slave girl, Miss Phyllis

Robertson. I expected that Ho-Sorl, who was difficult to please, would be a most exacting master. Already Marlenus had ordered wines and slave chains, and dancing silks, of diaphanous scarlet, sent to the Warrior's compartment.

I strode forward to the place before the throne. And Marlenus, Ubar of Ar, looked down upon me.

"You come forward," asked he, "to claim your honors, your glories and awards?"

I said nothing, but stood before him.

"Ar owes you much," said he. "I, Marlenus, her Ubar, owe you much as well."

I nodded my head, acknowledging his statement.

"It is hard to know what would be fitting payment for the great services rendered by Gladius of Cos, in my cause."

I said nothing.

"Or for the great services rendered by Tarl of Ko-ro-ba, in the songs called Tarl of Bristol."

It was true. Marlenus, and Ar, owed me much, though I wished little.

"Therefore," said Marlenus, "prepare to receive your dues."

I stood before him, and looked into the eyes of Marlenus, that larl among men, Ubar of Ar, he, Ubar of Ubars.

Those fierce eyes in that mighty face regarded me.

To my astonishment bread, and salt, and a small, flaming brand were brought to him.

There were shouts of dismay from those assembled.

I could not believe my eyes.

Marlenus took the bread and broke it apart in his large hands. "You are refused bread," said Marlenus, placing the bread back on the tray.

There were shouts of astonishment in the court.

Marlenus had taken the salt, lifted it from the tray, and replaced it. "You are refused salt," he said.

"No!" came the shouts from hundreds of voices. "No!"

Marlenus then, looking at me, took the small brand of fire in his hand. There was a leaf of fire, bright yellow, at its tip. He thrust the brand into the salt, extinguishing it. "You are refused fire," he said.

There was silence in the court of the Ubar.

"You are herewith, by edict of the Ubar," said Marlenus, "commanded from the city of Ar, to depart before sundown of this day, not to return on pain of penalty of torture and impalement."

Those assembled could not believe their ears or eyes.

"Where is the girl, Vella?" I asked.

"Depart from my presence," decreed Marlenus.

My hand was at the hilt of my sword. I did not draw my weapon, but my mere gesture had caused a hundred swords to leap from the sheath.

I turned, the room seeming to swirl about me, black and startling, and, scarcely feeling the tiles beneath my feet, departed from the court of the Ubar.

Enraged, I wandered the corridors, black hatred consuming me, my heart pounding with fury.

Why had this been done to me? Was this the reward for my services? And what of Elizabeth? Was it that Marlenus had looked upon her and so pleasing did he find her that he had decreed that she be reserved for the very Pleasure Gardens of the Ubar of Ar himself, to serve him as a silken wench, one of perhaps hundreds waiting perhaps a year for his casual notice or his touch? Men such as Marlenus are wont to take what pleases them, and to hold it, should they wish, at the point of a blade. Had it been that his eye had glanced upon her and he had, by the prerogative of the Ubar, commanded her to his slave ring? But was this honor? My hatred for the Ubar of Ar, whom I had helped restore to his throne, welled up within me, volcanic, molten and black. My hand was clutched on the hilt of my sword.

I threw open the door to my compartment.

The girl turned and faced me suddenly. She wore the briefly skirted gray slave livery of the state slave of Ar, the gray collar, the slender band of gray metal with its five simple bells locked about her left ankle. I heard the bells as she moved toward me. In her eyes there were tears.

I took Elizabeth Cardwell into my arms. I felt that never would I let her go. We wept, our tears meeting in her hair and on our cheeks as we kissed and touched. The tiny, fine golden ring of the Tuchuk woman was in her nose.

"I love you, Tarl," she said.

"I love you," I cried. "I love you, my Elizabeth!"

Unnoticed Hup, the small Fool, had entered the room. He carried with him some papers. There were tears in his eyes.

After a time, he spoke. "There is only an hour," said he, "until sundown."

Holding Elizabeth I looked at him.

"Thank Marlenus, Ubar of Ar, for me," said I.

Hup nodded. "Yesterday evening," said he, "Marlenus sent her to you, to tie your sandals, to serve you wine, but you refused even to look upon her."

Elizabeth laughed and pressed her cheek to my left shoulder.

"I have been refused bread, and fire and salt," I said to Elizabeth.

She nodded. "Yes," she said. She looked at me, bewildered. "Hup told me yesterday it would be so."

I looked at Hup.

"But why has this been done to me?" I asked. "It seems unworthy of the hand of a Ubar."

"Have you forgotten," asked he, "the law of the Home Stone?"

I gasped.

"Better surely banishment than torture and impalement."

"I do not understand," said Elizabeth.

"In the year 10,110, more than eight years ago, a tarnsman of Ko-ro-ba purloined the Home Stone of the city."

"It was I," I told Elizabeth.

She shuddered, for she knew the penalties that might attach to such a deed.

"As Ubar," said Hup, "it would ill become Marlenus to betray the law of the Home Stone of Ar."

"But he gave no explanation," I protested.

"An Ubar gives no accounting," said Hup.

"We fought together," said I, "back to back. I helped him to regain his throne. I was once the companion of his daughter."

"I say because I know him," said Hup, "though I might die from the saying of it, Marlenus is grieved. He is much grieved. But he is Ubar. He is Ubar. More than man, more than Marlenus, he is Ubar of my city, of Ar itself."

I looked at him.

"Would you," asked Hup, "betray the Home Stone of Ko-ro-ba?"

My hand leaped to the hilt of my sword.

Hup smiled. "Then," said he, "do not think Marlenus, whatever the price or cost, his grief, his dream, would betray that of Ar."

"I understand," I said.

"If a Ubar does not respect the law of the Home Stone, what man shall?"

"None," said I. "It is hard to be Ubar."

"It is less than an hour to sundown," said Hup.

I held Elizabeth to me.

"I have brought papers," said Hup. "They have been endorsed to you. The slave is yours."

Elizabeth looked at Hup. He was Gorean. To him she was that, simply, a slave.

To me she seemed the world.

"Write on the papers," said I, "that on this first day of the restoration of Marlenus of Ar, the slave Vella was by her master, Tarl of Ko-ro-ba, granted her freedom."

Hup shrugged, and so endorsed the papers. I signed them, my name in Gorean script, followed by the sign of the city of Ko-ro-ba.

Hup gave me the key to Elizabeth's collar and anklet and I freed her of the steel that marked her slave.

"I will file the papers in the Cylinder of Documents," said Hup.

I took the free woman, Vella of Gor, Elizabeth Cardwell of Earth, in my arms.

Together we ascended the stairs to the roof of Ar's Central Cylinder and looked across the many towers of the city, at the bright clouds, the blue sky, the ridges of the scarlet Voltai in the distance.

The saddle packs of the tarn had been provisioned. But only I could saddle the sable monster.

I lifted Elizabeth to the saddle and, with binding fiber, tied her to its high pommel.

Hup stood there on the roof of the cylinder, the wind blowing his hair, his eyes, of uneven size and color, looking up at us.

Then we saw Relius and Virginia and, to my surprise, Ho-Sorl, followed by Phyllis, emerging to the roof.

Virginia was clad in garments cut from the beautiful, many colored robes of concealment of the free woman. But, proud of her beauty and glorious in her joy, she had boldly shortened the garments almost to the length of slave livery, and a light, diaphanous orange veil loosely held her hair and lay about her throat. She wore the robes of concealment in such a way as not to conceal but enhance her great loveliness. She had discovered herself and her beauty on this harsh world, and was as proud of her body as the most brazen of slave girls, and would not permit its being shut away from the wind and the sunlight. The garments suggested the slave girl and yet insisted, almost demurely, on the reserve, the pride and dignity of the free woman. The combination was devastating, tormentingly attractive, an achievement so tantalizing and astoundingly exciting that I would not be surprised if it were adopted throughout Ar by the city's free women, rebellious, proud of their bodies, at last determined to throw off centuries of restriction, of confinement and sequestration, at last determined to stand forth as individuals, female individuals, sensuous as slave girls but yet rich in their own persons, intelligent, bold, beautiful, free. I mused to myself that slave raids on Ar might grow more frequent.

Elizabeth and I wished Relius and his Companion, Virginia Kent, well.

Phyllis, standing a bit behind Ho-Sorl and to his left, looked at us, tears in her eyes.

"Greetings, Slave," said Elizabeth.

Phyllis smiled. "Greetings, Mistress," she said.

Ho-Sorl permitted Phyllis to hold his left arm, and she did so, standing close to him, her cheek against his left sleeve.

She wore dancing silk. It was scarlet.

I looked boldly upon her, for a Warrior does not avert his eyes from the beauty of a woman, particularly that of a mere slave.

"Your slave is beautiful," said I, "Ho-Sorl."

"She will do," said Ho-Sorl.

"Your master is a beast, Slave," Virginia informed Phyllis.

"I know," smiled Phyllis, "Mistress." She took the cloth of Ho-Sorl's sleeve between her teeth, delicately, pulling at it.

"I wish you well," said Ho-Sorl.

"We, too," said Elizabeth, "wish you all well."

"I wish you well," said Hup, raising his hand.

"I wish you well, Small Friend," said I. I raised my hand to the others. "I wish you all well."

I drew on the one-strap and the tarn, wings beating, lifted itself beautifully from the cylinder. We circled the cylinder once.

"Look!" cried Elizabeth.

I looked down and saw now that another figure stood on the roof of the Central Cylinder of Ar, a giant figure, one who wore the purple of the Ubar.

Marlenus lifted his hand in farewell.

I, too, lifted my hand, saluting him, and turned the tarn from Ar.

The sun was sinking behind the great gate of Ar as the tarn streaked over the walls, departing from the city.

Printed in the United States
120290LV00003B/49-51/A